Like Dandelion Dust

Like Dandelion Dust

KAREN KINGSBURY

CENTER
STREET®

NEW YORK   BOSTON   NASHVILLE

This book is a work of fiction. Names, characters, places, and incidents are the product of the author's imagination or are used fictitiously. Any resemblance to actual events, locales, or persons, living or dead, is coincidental.

Cover design by Claire Brown
Cover photo of boy by J Grooss/roberstock.com
Cover photo of dandelion by Terry Why/Index Stock

Grand Central Publishing
Hachette Book Group USA
237 Park Avenue
New York, NY 10017
Visit our Web site at www.HachetteBookGroupUSA.com.

Printed in the United States of America

Originally published in trade paperback by Center Street.
First Mass Market Edition: January 2008

10 9 8 7 6 5 4 3 2 1

Dedicated to

Donald, my prince charming. In this season of life, with you working as full-time teacher here at home for our boys, I am maybe more proud of you than ever. I am amazed at the way you blend love and laughter, tenderness and tough standards to bring out the best in our boys. Don't for a minute think that your role in all this is somehow small. You have the greatest responsibility of all. Not only with our children, but also in praying for me as I write and speak and go about this crazy fun job God has given me. I couldn't do it without you. Thanks for loving me, for being my best friend, and for finding "date moments" amidst even the most maniacal or mundane times.

Kelsey, my precious daughter. You are sixteen, pushing seventeen, and sometimes I find myself barely able to exhale. The ride is so fast at this point that I try not to blink so I won't miss a minute of it. Like the most beautiful springtime flower, I see you growing and unfolding, becoming interested in current events and formulating godly viewpoints that are yours alone. The same is true in dance, where you are simply breathtaking on stage. I believe in you, honey. Keep your eyes on Jesus and the path will be easy to follow. Don't ever stop dancing. I love you.

Tyler, my beautiful song. Can it be that you are thirteen and almost taller than me? Just yesterday people would call and confuse you with Kelsey. Now they confuse you with your dad—in more ways than one. You are on the bridge, dear son, making the transition between being a kid and becoming a strong, godly young man. Keep giving Jesus your very best, and always remember that you're in a battle. In today's world, Ty, you need His armor every day, every minute. Don't forget . . . when you're up there on stage, no matter how bright the lights, I'll be watching and cheering you on. I love you.

Sean, my wonder boy. Your sweet nature continues to be a bright light in our home. Those tender days when we first brought you home from Haiti seem like a lifetime ago. It's been my great joy to watch you grow and develop this past year, learning more about reading and writing and, of course, animals. You're a walking encyclopedia of animal facts, and that, too, brings a smile to my face. Your hugs are something I look forward to, Sean. Keep close to Jesus. I love you.

Josh, my tender tough guy. You continue to excel at everything you do. I love that moment late at night when

I poke my head into your room and see that—once again—your nose is buried in your Bible. You really get it, Josh—that by being strong in Christ, first and foremost, you'll be strong at everything else. Keep winning for Him, dear son. You make me so proud. I love you.

EJ, my chosen one. You amaze me, Emmanuel Jean! You have become a different little boy while attending your daddy's home school. In every possible area you have improved. I see you standing straighter and taller, articulating more, making eye contact, and feeling confident and proud. I know that Jesus is leading the way, and that you are excited to find out the plans He has for you. This year will always stand out as a turning point to me. Congratulations, honey! I love you.

Austin, my miracle child. Can my little boy be eight years old? I love that you still wake up every now and then and scurry your way down the hall to our room so you can sleep in the middle. But most of all I love your tender heart. Just last week you looked at me and said, "Mommy, you're so pretty." Talk about making my day! Then you were at a basketball game with us and you sat on Daddy's knee and hooked your arms around his neck and said, "You're my best friend, Daddy. Thanks for loving me." Wow. It's so wonderful to see a reflection of my own heart in you, my littlest son. I thank God for your health, precious boy. I love you.

And to God Almighty, the Author of life, who has—for now—blessed me with these.

Acknowledgments

This book couldn't have come together without the help of many people. First, a special thanks to my friends at Time Warner Book Group, who were patient with me during this sad season in my life. My only brother, David, 39, died in his sleep on October 1, 2005, during the writing of this book.

My friends at Time Warner Book Group sent flowers and even an entire ham dinner while my family congregated at my house and somehow survived the funeral week. We spent a lot of time together, my brother and I, and in the final weeks of his life he seemed to be doing better than ever. Closer to God, closer to all of us, and excited about the future. In all ways possible, he seemed like someone on the brink of living life to the fullest.

And he was. Just not in the way we imagined.

I am comforted by the truth that Dave now has all he ever dreamed of—perfect health, perfect love, and forever to enjoy it. But that comfort was made complete in part because of the prayers and support and grace given me by my publishing friends at Warner.

Also a big thank-you to my agent, Rick Christian, president of Alive Communications. I am amazed more as every day passes at your great integrity, your talent, and your commitment to getting my Life-Changing Fiction™ out to all the world. You are a strong man of God, Rick. You care for my career as if you were personally responsible for the souls God touches through these books. Thank you for looking out for my personal time—the hours I have with my husband and kids most of all. I couldn't do this without you.

As always, this book wouldn't be possible without the help of my husband and kids, who are so good about eating tuna sandwiches and quesadillas, and bringing me plates of baked chicken and vegetables when I need the brain power to write past midnight. Thanks for understanding the sometimes crazy life I lead, and for always being my greatest support.

Also, thanks to my mother and assistant, Anne Kingsbury, for her great sensitivity and love for my readers. And to Katie Johnson, who runs a large part of my business life. The personal touch you both bring to my ministry is precious to me, priceless to me. . . . Thank you with all my heart.

And thanks to my friends and family who continue to surround me with love and prayer and support—especially in this time of loss. Of course, the greatest thanks goes to God Almighty, the most wonderful Author of all—the Author of life. The gift is Yours. I pray I might have the incredible opportunity and responsibility to use it for You all the days of my life.

Forever in Fiction™

A special thanks to my **Forever in Fiction**™ winners whose character names appear in this book. I created **Forever in Fiction**™ as a live-auction item for charities. Every penny of the winning bid for **Forever in Fiction**™ goes to the charity that holds the auction. So far, more than $100,000 has been raised for charities across the country from people winning **Forever in Fiction**™. If you or your group is interested in the donation of a **Forever in Fiction**™ package, visit my Web site at www.KarenKingsbury.com. I donate approximately six of these packages per year.

As much as possible, I try to give my characters identifying features that correlate with the person for whom that character is named. Still, the **Forever in Fiction**™ characters in this novel are entirely fictional.

And so thanks go to the two **Forever in Fiction**™ winners whose names appear in *Like Dandelion Dust*. The first package was won by a group of friends at the Summit View Church auction. Anne Fraser, Jaymi Sutton, Vicky Dillon, Joan Smith, Barbara Seifert, and

Michael Petty combined for the winning bid and presented **Forever in Fiction**™ to Beth Petty for her fortieth birthday. Beth is a wonderful wife, mother, and friend. She and her husband, Michael, have four children: Cammie, 14; Blain, 10; Braden, 7; and Jonah, 5. They have a female golden retriever named George Brett and a life that is full of love, laughter, and devotion to the Lord. Beth, your friends and family love you very much. They pray that this gift will remain as living proof of their feelings for you.

Also thanks to Kym Merrill, who won **Forever in Fiction**™ at the Discovery Church Women's Christmas Brunch auction. Kym chose to honor her sister, Allyson Page Bower, by having a character named after her. Allyson, 45, is mother to Tavia, 21; Travis, 15; and Taylor, 7. She is also grandmother to Harley, 4. A hard worker whose sole focus is caring for and loving her children, Allyson loves digging in the garden and sitting on the beach, and is known for baking the best banana pudding in the state. Allyson, your sister loves you very much. She prays that you will catch a glimpse of that love in the honor of finding your name **Forever in Fiction**™.

Like Dandelion Dust

Chapter One

Once in a while Molly Campbell wondered if other people saw it. When strangers passed by her and Jack and little Joey, maybe they could actually see a golden hue, pixie dust on the tops of their heads or a light emanating from the air around them, telling all the world what the three of them inherently knew.

That life couldn't possibly be more perfect.

Sometimes when Molly walked through the Palm Beach Mall, hand in hand with four-year-old Joey, her purse holding a couple hundred dollars cash, two debit cards, and a Visa with five figures open to buy, she'd see a tired-looking, disheveled man or an aging woman with worn-out shoes—hollow-eyed and slack-jawed—and she'd wonder what had happened. How had life placed these people in their separate worlds, and how had she and Jack and Joey found their way to the right side?

The good side.

Molly felt that way now, sitting at the Cricket Preschool parents' conference, listening to Joey's teacher rave about his progress in math and spelling. She held the hand of her quick-witted, rugged husband and smiled at Joey. "That's what we like to hear, buddy."

"Thanks." Joey grinned. His first loose tooth—the one in the middle, upper left—hung at a crazy angle. He swung his feet beneath the table as his eyes wandered around the room to the dinosaur poster and the T. rex. Joey loved the T. rex.

The teacher continued, "Your son is charming, a delight to everyone." Mrs. Erickson was in her sixties, silver-haired with a gentle hand, a teacher who preferred to use colored marbles or M&Ms rather than a stern voice and repetition to teach the alphabet. "He's reading at a first-grade level, and he won't be five until fall. Amazing." She raised her brow. "He's computing beyond his years, as well. And he's extremely social."

Then the teacher shared an anecdote.

One day the week before, Joey came to class a few minutes early, and there sat Mark Allen, a child with learning disabilities. Mark Allen was staring at his empty lunch box, tears streaming down his face. Somehow his mother had sent him to school without any food for snack time.

"I was in the supply closet," the teacher explained. "I didn't see what was happening until I returned."

By then, Joey had taken the seat next to Mark Allen, pulled his Batman lunch box from his backpack, and spread the contents out on the desk. As the teacher walked in, Joey was handing the boy his peanut butter crackers and banana, saying, "Don't cry. You can have my snack."

"I can only tell you," the teacher concluded, her eyes

shining at the memory, "Joey is the kindest, most well-adjusted four-year-old I've taught in a long time."

Molly basked in the glow of the teacher's praise. She let the story play over in her mind, and when the conference was over and they left the classroom, she grinned at her husband. "He gets it from me, you know." She lifted her chin, all silliness and mock pride. "Sharing his snack with that little boy."

"Right." Jack's eyes danced. "And the social part." He gave her a look. "He gets that from you, no doubt."

"Definitely."

"But the smarts"—he tapped his temple, his voice full of laughter—"that's my doing."

"Wait a minute . . ." She gave him a shove, even if she couldn't keep the smile from her face. "I'm definitely the brains in this—"

"Let's go, sport!" Jack took hold of Joey's hand and the two of them skipped ahead as they reached the parking lot. It was a beautiful South Florida May afternoon, cooler than usual, all sunshine and endless blue skies and swaying palm trees. The kind of day that made a person forget the humidity and unbearable temperatures just a few weeks away. Molly could hear Jack and Joey giggling about recess and playground rules and tetherball. As they reached their blue Acura SUV, Jack gave Joey a few light pokes in his ribs. "So, sport . . . got a girl-friend?"

"No way." Joey shook his head. "Us boys have a club. The Boys Are Best Club." He put his hands on his waist. "No yucky girls."

"Oh . . . good. Boys Are Best." Jack gave a few thoughtful nods. He opened the driver's door as he pulled

Joey close and gently rubbed his knuckles against Joey's pale blond hair. "You boys are right." He winked at Molly. "Girls are yucky."

Joey looked at her and his expression softened. " 'Cept for Mommy."

"Really?" They climbed into the car. From the driver's seat, Jack looped his arm around Molly's shoulders and kissed her cheek. "Well . . ." He grinned at her. "I guess Mommy's not so bad. As long as she stays out of the kitchen."

"Hey!" Molly laughed. "It's been a month since I burned anything."

Jack raised his eyebrow at Joey. "Today made up for it. Flaming cinnamon rolls—that'll go down in the family record book."

"They shouldn't put 'broil' and 'bake' so close together on the dial."

Jack chuckled. "We shouldn't put you in the kitchen. Period."

"You might be right." Molly didn't mind her reputation for foul-ups at mealtime. Cooking bored her. As long as they ate healthy food, she had no interest in creating elaborate recipes. Simple meals worked just fine.

When they were buckled in, Joey bounced a few times on the seat. "Can we get pizza, huh? Please?"

"Great idea. That'll keep Mom out of the kitchen. Besides"—Jack gave a pronounced tap on the steering wheel—"anyone who gets a perfect report in preschool should be allowed pizza."

"Pineapple pizza?"

"Definitely pineapple pizza."

As they drove to Nemo's Deli a few blocks east of the

school, a comfortable silence settled over the car. In the backseat, Joey found his library book, a pictorial on the Great White Shark. He hummed "Here We Go 'Round the Mulberry Bush" as he turned the pages. Molly reached over and wove her fingers between Jack's. "So . . . isn't it amazing?" She kept her voice low, the conversation meant for just the two of them.

Jack grinned, keeping his eyes on the road. "Our little genius, you mean?"

"Not that." Sunshine streamed through the windshield, sending warmth and well-being throughout her body. She smiled. "The kindness part. I mean . . ." There was laughter in her voice. "I know he's a prodigy in the classroom and a natural on the playground. But how great that the teacher would call him 'kind.' "

"The kindest boy she's seen in a long time."

"And well-adjusted." Molly sat a little straighter.

"Very well-adjusted."

They were half teasing, bragging about Joey the way they could do only when no one else was around. Then the smile faded from Jack's face. "Didn't you think it'd be harder than this?"

"Harder?" Molly angled herself so she could see him better. "Preschool?"

"No." Jack gripped the steering wheel with his left hand, more pensive than he'd been all afternoon. He glanced at the rearview mirror and the fine lines at the corners of his eyes deepened. "Adopting. Didn't you think it'd be harder? School trouble or social trouble? Something?"

Molly stared out the window. They were passing Fuller Park on their right, a place they'd taken Joey since he came into their lives. Home was only a block away. She squinted against the sunlight. "Maybe. It seems like a lifetime ago."

"When we brought him home?" Jack kept his eyes on the road.

"No." She drew a slow breath through her nose. "When we first talked about adoption, I guess." She shot a quick look at Joey in the backseat, his blond hair and blue eyes, the intent way he sat there looking at shark pictures and humming. She met Jack's gaze again. "As soon as they put him in my arms, every fear I ever had dissolved." A smile started in her heart. "I knew he was special."

Jack nodded slowly. "He is, isn't he?"

"Yes." She gave his hand a gentle squeeze. "As my sister would say, he's a gift from God. Nothing less than a miracle."

"Your sister . . ." Jack chuckled. "She and Bill are about as dry as they come."

"Hey." Molly felt her defenses come to life. "Give them time. They just moved here a week ago."

"I know." Jack frowned. "But can't they talk about something besides God? 'God's will this' and 'God's will that'?"

"Jack . . . come on." Molly bristled. Beth was her best friend. The two were eighteen months apart, inseparable as kids: Beth, the younger but somehow more responsible sister, and Molly, the flighty one, always in need of Beth's ability to keep her grounded. For the past three years Molly had worked on Beth, trying to get her and Bill and their four kids to move to West Palm Beach. "Be fair." She was careful with her tone. "Give them a chance."

The lines around Jack's eyes relaxed. "I'm just saying . . ." He raised his brow at her. "They're uptight, Molly. If that's what church does to you"—he released her hand and brushed at the air—"count me out."

"The move's been hard on them."

"I guess."

"Hey, Daddy, know what?" Joey tapped both their shoulders and bounced in his booster seat. "The Great White is as long as four daddies. That's what the picture shows."

The sparkle instantly returned to Jack's expression. "Four daddies! Wow . . . how many little boys would that be?"

"Probly a million-jillion."

They turned in to the restaurant parking lot. "Here we are!" Jack took the first space available. "Pineapple pizza coming up."

"Jack . . ." Molly wasn't finished. She winced a little. "I forgot to mention—" She already knew the answer, but her sister made her promise to ask. "Beth and Bill want us to come to church with them Sunday. They're trying out the one down the street from the school."

Jack leaned over and kissed her cheek. He kept his face a few inches from hers. "When Bill says yes to one of my poker parties, I'll say yes to church."

"Okay." She hid her disappointment. "So that's a no?"

"That's a no." He patted the side of her face. The teasing left his eyes for a moment. "Unless you want me to. If it matters to you, I'll go."

Molly loved that about Jack. He had his opinions, but

he was willing to do things her way, always ready to compromise. "No." She gave him a quick kiss. "We're going out on the boat this Sunday. That'll put us closer to God than a church service ever could."

Joey was already out of the car and up on the sidewalk, waiting for them. Jack opened his car door and chuckled. "Well said, my dear. Well said."

Not until they were inside the restaurant ordering their pizza did a strange ribbon of fear wrap itself around Molly's throat. Their attitude toward church was okay, wasn't it? They'd never been church people, even though Beth talked to her about it often.

"You need to take Joey," Beth would say. "All children need to be in church."

Molly looked at Joey now, golden-haired, his eyes adoringly on Jack as they considered the options at the pop machine. What they had was fine, wasn't it? They believed in God, in a distant sort of way. What harm was there in finding Him at a lake instead of in a pew? Besides, they already had everything they needed.

Jack's recent promotion had placed him in a dream job as vice president of sales for Reylco, one of the top three pharmaceutical companies in the world. He was making a healthy six-figure salary, overseeing top international accounts, and traveling half as often as before. They lived on a corner lot in Ashley Heights, one of West Palm Beach's finer upscale neighborhoods. The three of them took trips to Disney World and Sanibel Island and the Bahamas, and they fished at Lake Okeechobee once a month.

Every now and then they spent a Saturday afternoon serving lunch at a homeless mission in Miami, and then they'd take in a play in the city's art district. On week-days, after dinner, they walked to Fuller Park with Joey and Gus, their friendly lab. There Jack and Molly stole kisses and laughter, watching sunsets while Gus ran cir-cles around the playground and Joey raced to the top of the slide over and over and over again.

They kept an Air Nautique ski boat at Westmont Pier, and on most Sundays they drove to the white sandy seashore and cruised to the bay, where water was smooth and deep blue and warm. They'd take turns skiing, and Joey would sit in the back, watching, pumping his fists in the air when one of them cleared the wake. This spring, for the first time, they'd bought a pair of training skis for Joey. More sunshine and laughter, day after day, year after year.

These thoughts chased away Molly's strange fear, and she found a window table where she could wait for her men. The uneasy feeling lifted. Why worry? The golden hue, the shining light, the pixie dust—all of it must be real. They were happy and healthy and they had every-thing they'd ever wanted. Most of all, they had Joey.

What more could God possibly give them?

Chapter Two

Wendy Porter stared out the windshield and tried to slow her breathing. A cigarette. That's what she needed— a strong, no-filter cigarette. She reached over and rummaged through her purse, past the Wal-Mart receipts and old tubes of lipstick and the pink cracked mirror. Beneath her wallet and the smashed breakfast bar she'd kept there for the past month. Through the crumbs and loose change that had gathered at the bottom. *Where were they?* She took her eyes off the road and gave a quick look into the purse. She still had a few Camels, right? The good kind?

Then she remembered, and she put her hand back on the wheel.

The smoke would cling to her pretty pink blouse and black dress slacks. It would linger in her freshly washed hair and ruin her minty breath. Five years had passed since her husband, Rip, had been a free man. She didn't want to put him in a bad mood.

The news she had to tell him would take care of that.

Wendy tapped one slim fingernail on the steering wheel. So maybe it didn't matter if she had a cigarette. She tapped some more. No, better not.

"Dirty habit," Rip used to tell her before his arrest. Sometimes he'd snatch a cigarette from her lips and break it in half. "I hate when you smoke. It isn't sexy."

Not that Rip had ever been the picture of sex appeal. Last time they were together, he'd slugged her in the jaw while the two of them yelled at each other in the Kroger parking lot. The reason he was angry? She'd forgotten to clip the fifty-cent coupon for ground round. A police officer a dozen yards away saw everything and hauled Rip in for battery. With a list of priors, Rip was lucky to get six to eight in the Ohio State Penitentiary, out in just five for good behavior.

Wendy turned onto the interstate and pressed her high-heeled shoe hard against the gas pedal. It was four o'clock—almost rush hour. She had to make time while she could. A quick check in her rearview mirror and she switched to the fast lane. With any luck she'd reach the prison in half an hour. She and Rip had a lot to talk about. The last thing she wanted was to get things off to a bad start by being late.

She cracked her window and a burst of fresh air filled the car. Her mama had told her to leave Rip years ago. Way before the Kroger incident. And truth was, there'd been other guys in the past five years. A girl couldn't sit home year after year waiting for her man to get out of jail. Even a man she was crazy about. She hadn't been sure he'd even want to see her when he was released. Not until last week. The phone call came as she walked through the back door after church.

"Baby . . ." His voice was more gravelly than before. "It's me."

The call made her breath catch in her throat. She set

down her Bible and the church bulletin and pressed the
receiver hard against her ear. "Rip?"

"Yeah, baby." There was a tenderness in his voice, the
tenderness that had attracted her so long ago. "Did you
miss me?"

"It's . . . been a long time, Rip."

He rarely called, hated having a long-distance relationship. At Wendy's last visit, fourteen months earlier, he'd
told her not to come again until he was released. Seeing
her made the time pass too slowly, he said. So how was
she supposed to take that? She was not for a minute
expecting a call from Rip.

Of course, she'd drop everything if he was interested
again. She'd given her heart to Rip a long time ago. He
would own it until the day she died. She gathered herself.
"You mean . . . you wanna see me?"

"See you? I'm crazy about you, baby. And get this . . .
I'm out in a week. The thing I want more than anything
in life is to walk out these doors and see you there.
Waiting for me." He hesitated, and she could hear the
voices of other prisoners in the background. "Be there,
baby . . . please?"

"Oh, Rip." When she could breathe normally, she
grabbed a piece of junk mail and a pen. "When are you
getting out?"

He gave her the details, and then he exhaled, slow and
tired. "I'm sorry, Wendy." His tone was broken. Maybe
that's why his voice sounded strange at first. He sniffed
hard. "What I did . . . it was wrong. You don't have to
worry. It ain't gonna happen again."

Wendy felt a bubble of anxiety rise within her. He'd
been sorry before, right? Why would this be different?

Every time Rip Porter walked back into her life, breathing apologies and lies, he left her with a broken heart and a few broken bones. Her mama said she'd be crazy if she took him back again, but that was just it. She was crazy. Crazy for Rip, in a way that didn't make sense. She loved him, that's all she knew. No matter his history, no matter the times when she was the target of what felt like a lifetime of rage, she loved him. There would never be anyone for her but Rip.

"I missed you, baby." His voice grew huskier as he breathed across the line. "I hope you kept my side of the bed open."

Fear poured into Wendy's veins. What if Rip found out about the other men? There hadn't been many, really. Four or five, maybe, and not for the past six months. That's why she was back at church. Trying to make a new go of things. Still, Rip hated other men. Hated when they looked at her, and hated it more when she looked back. If anyone from the pool hall ever told him about the other men, he'd . . . well . . . Wendy was sure whatever happened would make the incident at the Kroger look like horseplay.

But before she could think it all through, trying to imagine what life would be like with Rip back at home, she gave him the answer he wanted. "I'll be there."

"Okay, baby." His relief was tangible over the phone line. "I'll be counting the days."

Wendy settled back against the driver's seat and stared at the road ahead.

Since that phone call, her emotions had been all over the map. Excitement and the thrill of imagining herself in his arms gave way to a very real, very consuming fear.

She hadn't told him about the boy. Now that he was getting out, she had no choice. He'd find out one way or another, and the longer she waited, the angrier he'd be. Rip couldn't really blame her for not telling him sooner. The two of them barely saw each other over the past five years, and as for her little boy—she tried not to think about him. Only on his birthday in September and a few other times each month when her heart raced ahead of her.

She reached over and rifled through her purse again. A piece of gum, that's what she needed. When she knew Rip was coming home, she'd hidden her smokes in a box in the garage. But now she was going crazy without them. Her fingers brushed against a sticky ballpoint pen and a wad of tissue paper, and then finally what she was looking for. A broken stick of peppermint Eclipse. She brushed off a layer of lint and popped the gum between her lips.

She hadn't planned to ever tell Rip about the boy. It wasn't any of his business. She'd had the baby at the beginning of his prison sentence, after all—a sentence that kept Rip in the slammer for five years. There were reasons why she gave the boy up, why she found a nice family and turned him over. But part of it was a matter of being practical. She had to work two jobs to pay the bills, right? How would she do all that and raise a baby by herself?

She found out about the baby the week after Rip was locked up. Rotten luck, nothing but rotten luck. She didn't visit Rip after her fifth month of pregnancy, not until she had her shape back and the baby was safe in his new home. Rip never suspected a thing. But the baby was his, that much she was sure about. The other men didn't come into the picture until the second year of his term.

The traffic grew heavier. She switched lanes again. The truth was, she'd almost done it, almost kept the boy. She didn't sign the paperwork until after she had him and held him and—

She blinked and the memory stopped short. There was no going back, no such thing as what might've been. What she did that day, she did for her baby, her son. He deserved more than round-the-clock day care and a father in prison for domestic violence. She picked the family, after all. They were perfect for her baby, willing to give him the life he could never have had with her and Rip.

But more than that, her decision was ultimately based on one simple fact. She couldn't tolerate seeing her little boy hurt. And if Rip got out and fell into one of his rages . . . Wendy shuddered and took tighter hold of the wheel. A man with a temper like Rip's had a heap of changing to do before he could be any kind of father. It didn't matter now. She'd signed both their names on the adoption papers and never looked back.

Almost never.

Tears stung her eyes and she cursed herself for being weak. The boy was better off, no question. What she'd done by giving him up made her the best mother in the world. Period. She drew a quick breath and dabbed her fingers along her upper cheeks. "Enough."

Her focus had to be on Rip now, and whether the two of them had anything left after five years of being apart. Had he gotten help for his temper, or maybe found Jesus? Or had the guys he ran with made him meaner? This was his second time in prison. Last time he came back showering apologies and sweet nothings, and he was hitting her again by the end of the week. Still, she loved him. Loved him and pined for him and wanted him back in the worst way.

So maybe this time would be different. Wendy worked her gum, demanding what was left of the peppermint. Rip had sounded nice enough on the phone. Maybe he really had changed, and this time things would be better between them. He'd come home and give up the anger and shouting and hitting, and turn into the kind gentleman she had always known was buried somewhere inside him. It would happen one day, she knew it. Deep inside he had a heart of gold, Rip Porter. She would give him another chance, same as always, and maybe this time love would win out over all the anger.

She eased her car back into the fast lane and picked up speed again. Yes, maybe everything would work out. Then when Rip's temper was under control and he had a steady job, they could have another child, maybe two or three. A light rain began to pepper the windshield, and traffic slowed. Great. Rip hated when she was late.

She flipped on the radio, gave each station three seconds to prove itself, and flipped it off again. Silence was better anyway. How was she going to bring up the subject, the idea that, hey, by the way, there was a baby and now he's living with another family? Before they could move ahead, she had to give him the truth about the boy. No way around it; she had to.

Brent and Bubba down at the pool hall both knew about her pregnancy. Brent lived a few blocks over. He and Bubba were on their way out one afternoon when she was at the curb getting the mail. She was days from delivering, and big as a house.

Brent stopped and rolled down his window. He gestured at her belly. "That Rip's kid in there?"

Wendy glared at the man and gave no thought to her answer. "Of course it's Rip's."

"Well, I'll be . . ." Brent cussed and chuckled all at the same time. "Poor kid. Future's already written with Rip as a daddy. Him sittin' in the pen and all."

In the seat next to him, Bubba slapped his knee and laughed out loud. "Got that right!"

Wendy waved them off, angry. "Aw, go off and get drunk," she shouted. "And mind your own business!"

Months could go by without seeing the rusty backside of Brent's beat-up Ford. Wendy didn't see Brent or Bubba again for almost a year. But just yesterday she was mowing the yard—getting things in order for Rip—when Brent drove up and once more rolled down his window. "Heard Rip was gettin' out." He stretched his head through the window, shouting to be heard over the roar of the mower.

"Yeah." Wendy killed the engine. Sweat dripped down the side of her face, and she dragged her hand across her forehead. "Good news travels fast."

Brent craned his neck, peering into her side yard. "What happened to the kid?"

Wendy was glad she was holding onto the lawn mower. Otherwise she would've fainted dead away, right there on the freshly cut grass. She had no family, no friends other than the people she'd met at church here and there. The baby was her deal, her decision. Not until that moment did it ever occur to her that just maybe the news might get back to Rip.

Brent was waiting for an answer.

"He, uh . . . we gave him up . . . to a family in Florida." She tried to sound matter-of-fact, as if giving the baby up for adoption was common knowledge. "Rip and I didn't want a baby while he was in prison. You know?"

"Hmmm." Brent hesitated. "Doesn't sound like my main man, Rip Porter. Guy always wanted a son." He shrugged. "Not that it's any of my business." After a minute of small talk, he flashed her a grin that showed his silver tooth. "Tell Rip I got first game when he chalks up his cue stick."

"Yeah." Wendy rolled her eyes and gave the mower cord a jerk. "Sure thing."

The man drove away in a cloud of exhaust fumes, but the conversation stuck. Now, twenty-four hours later, she had a knot in her stomach, thinking about the task that lay ahead. She had to tell Rip the truth. Tonight. When she picked him up. If she told him right up front, he wouldn't have to hear the news from anyone else. That had to be better, right?

The Ohio State Penitentiary was outside the city limits. Over the last few miles she picked up the time she'd lost. She wheeled the car into the parking lot and hurried herself toward the visitor area. The heel of her right shoe got stuck in a warm patch of asphalt. "Come on," she whispered. Her heart beat so hard she wondered if it would break through her chest and race her to the front door. Once she was inside, her steps clicked out a nervous rhythm. She checked in, found a chair across the room from the prison door, and waited.

At two minutes after five, Rip walked through the door holding a brown paper bag. It took him a few seconds to find her, but when he did, he lit up like a bar sign at sundown. "Wendy!"

Here we go. She stood and smoothed the wrinkles out of her dress slacks. Her knees felt weak at the sight of him. *What have I gotten myself into?* She found her smile. "Rip!" She mouthed his name. With a roomful of tired-looking visitors watching, this wasn't the place for dramatic reunions. But she didn't care. She had missed him more than she knew.

Rip looked at the guard who had accompanied him to the waiting room. The guard nodded. Rip was free; he could do as he pleased. Without another moment's hesitation, Rip took long strides toward Wendy. His grin took up his whole face. He wore a tight white T-shirt and jeans, his blond hair trimmed neatly to his head. He had filled out, probably from hours spent in the prison weight room.

She held her arms out toward him, and her heart fluttered as he came near. Something was different about Rip—his eyes, maybe. Whatever it was, Wendy felt herself drawn to him, taken by him. "You look great."

"Hey." He took gentle hold of her shoulders, drank her in like a man too long in the desert. Then he planted a long kiss smack on her lips. When he pulled back, he searched her eyes. "That's my line." His eyes drifted down the length of her and back up again. "You look like a million bucks, baby." He kissed her again. "I mean it."

Wendy could feel the eyes on them. She cleared her

throat and took a step to the side. She could hardly wait to be alone with him. "Let's go, okay?"

Rip looked around the room at the dozen people watching them. "That's right!" he shouted, his tone full of laughter. "Eat your heart out. I'm going home!"

Wendy hung her head, her cheeks hot. Okay, so maybe he hadn't changed. Rip was always loud this way, the center of attention. He thought he was funny, and when his behavior made people pull away or caused someone to ask him to be quiet, Rip would flip them the bird or snarl at them. "No one tells me what to do," he'd say. Then he'd go on being loud and obnoxious as ever.

Sometimes Wendy didn't mind when Rip acted up. He was just having fun, right? But once in a while Rip's public behavior had caused a private fight between the two of them, the kind that led to blows. That's why she wasn't saying anything tonight. Rip could stand on the roof of the car and sing the national anthem off key and she'd go along with it. Anything so she wouldn't make him mad. Not with the news she still had to tell him.

Rip raised his paper bag to the roomful of visitors, put his arm around Wendy's shoulders, and led her outside. The moment they were free of the building, he handed her the bag, took a few running steps, stopped, and raised both fists in the air. He let out the loudest whooping victory cry she'd ever heard. "I'm free!" A few more hoots, then he hurried to her and took her hands in his. The bag fell to the ground. "I'm a changed man, Wendy Porter. All my life's been leading up to this one single minute."

His excitement was contagious. She felt herself getting lost in his eyes. "Really?" She uttered a soft laugh and eased closer to him. Okay, maybe she was wrong.

Something about him was different, definitely different. She was suddenly breathless, and she chided herself for worrying about his behavior. This was Rip Porter, the man she'd fallen for in high school. She was as in love with him now as she'd been the first time she saw him. "What happened to you in there, Rip?"

He spun her in a small circle before stopping and searching her face. "I got help, that's what." He caught his breath, and his smile faded. "I'm sorry, Wendy. It was all my fault."

Her heart was beating hard again. Was he serious? Wasn't this what she'd always wanted? Her hunky Rip, kind and gentlemanly? A ripple of nervous laughter slipped from her throat. "Really, you mean that?"

"Yes!" He raised one fist in the air and hooted so loud the sound filled the parking lot. "I love you, Wendy." He took her hand and began running toward the rows of cars. "Let's go home and celebrate."

The celebration started in the car and lasted long into the night. At two in the morning, still smiling, Rip finally fell asleep. Wendy hadn't dared ruin his joy and exhilaration in the hours after his release, but come morning she would have to tell him about the boy. Then she'd know whether Rip Porter had truly changed. Or whether the rage would find him again.

The way it had every other time.

Chapter Three

The barbecue was Beth's idea.

Most of their boxes were unpacked, and though they'd been in town only three weeks, Beth knew where to find the can opener, and the ceramic serving platter with the watermelon slices painted around the edge, and the dehydrated onions. That and some hamburger meat and buns, and they were ready for company.

Not that Molly and Jack and Joey were company.

Beth took a handful of ground beef and pressed it between her palms. *God . . . let tonight work out. . . . Let it be the beginning. . . .* After all, this sort of thing—coming together for a Sunday evening barbecue—was what she and her older sister had dreamed about since they'd left home for college: the idea that one day they'd have families, and live a block from each other, and share meals on the weekend while they raised a passel of kids.

She and Bill had four: Cammie, twelve; Blain, ten; Braden, eight; and Jonah, five.

There had been speed bumps along the way, but here they were. Bill had taken a stable job at Pratt and Whitney, supervising the creative-design division of commercial jet-engine development. The position had more security than the one he left in Seattle, and best of all, she and Molly could be together. The whole move felt like an answer from God, a miracle in the making.

Bill came into the kitchen, dirt smudges on his cheek. "The garage isn't half done." He turned on the water, took a pumpful of soap, and rubbed his hands together. "When'll they be here?"

The clock on the microwave said 3:17 p.m. "Two hours." Beth rounded the edges of the meat patty and set it on a stack with four others. "They went boating this morning, remember?"

"Right. While we were at church."

Beth sucked the inside of her cheek. "They invited us."

"Knowing we wouldn't say yes because of church." He gave a sad chuckle. "You can see through that, right?" He leaned his hip against the kitchen counter and picked a piece of masking tape from the bottom of his shoe. "Besides, I'm not sure I'd do well out on the ocean."

"Bill . . ." Beth didn't want trouble—not now. "They'll invite us again." She rushed on. "You can keep working in the garage if you want."

"I wanted to work through the night." He gave her a wry smile. "Monday morning comes early."

"I know." Beth's tone was sheepish. "I guess I figured the garage could wait." She hesitated. "Right?"

Bill released a slow breath. The corners of his lips lifted, and the light in his eyes was genuine. "Right." He kissed the top of her head. "I'm glad they're coming."

"Even Jack?"

The smile faded. "Jack doesn't know me." He dried his

hands on a paper towel. "I guess the more we see each other, that could change."

Beth bit her lip. "Sorry. About Jack . . . about the garage."

"Don't worry about it." He kissed her cheek and looked out at the backyard. "I'll wipe down the patio furniture."

She watched him go. This was one of the speed bumps.

She and Molly hadn't attended church as kids. Their parents were nice people, good people. The sort of people who always had an extra plate at dinner, an extra pillow and blanket and spot on the sofa for someone who needed a place to stay. They believed in God, but they didn't pay Him much heed.

It was Bill who changed all that for Beth.

The two of them met at a jazz club a few blocks from Pike's Place in downtown Seattle. They snapped their fingers to the same songs and joined up at the coffee bar for espresso shots twice in the first hour. When the second hour started, Bill moved his coffee to her table. "Alone?"

She smiled at him over the edge of her cup. "I can think here."

"Me, too."

And that was that. They talked the rest of the evening. She loved bluesy jazz (especially in A-minor), fresh Alaskan salmon, hiking the shoreline at Depoe Bay, and jeans. She was a sophomore at the University of Washington studying nutrition, thousands of miles from her Central Florida home. Bill was a junior engineering major with a minor in accounting, a walk-on for the Husky swim team, and a Christian who was fascinated with the Bible.

On their first date, he showed up fifteen minutes early so they could read together from the New Testament. Bill read aloud from Philippians while Beth rolled her eyes and checked her watch. Once he put away his Bible, Bill was a fascinating date. But after three months of discussing Scripture, their discussions came to a head.

God wasn't a must-have, was He? She could live a good life without guidance from the Bible, couldn't she? Never mind that Bill was loyal and funny and that he had a standard of character that Beth hadn't seen in other guys. She was tired of talking about God. One afternoon when they were standing near Bill's car, Beth grabbed his leather-bound Bible and threw it on the ground, breaking the binding and scattering sections of the book across the road.

Bill didn't say anything. He just picked up the pieces, got into his car, and drove away without a fight.

That would've been the end of things, but there was a problem. Beth couldn't sleep. She couldn't eat or study or think, either. Not when every waking moment she kept replaying the scene in her head. How could she defend a life that was good and right by breaking a Bible? With her world spinning out of control, she went to the local bookstore and bought a Bible and an exhaustive concordance.

Between the reference tool and Scripture, days later Beth was convinced of two things. First, the Bible was full of sound wisdom, and second, the message might amount to more than head smarts. It might hold the difference between life and death.

She apologized to Bill and they never looked back, except when it came to Beth's family. Her parents were mildly tolerant of her newfound faith, but Molly thought her sister had been swallowed whole. A year went by before the two of them got together for lunch and laughed about the changes in Beth.

"I thought I'd lost you." Molly wrinkled her nose from across the table. "My little sister, Miss Bohemian Seattle, gobbled up by religion."

Beth downplayed the issue and the subject easily shifted to Molly and her own social life, mainly the relationship she'd found with Jack Campbell at Florida State University.

After that Molly never brought up Bill and Beth's faith except in passing—"Be careful what you say; Beth's in the room." Other than that kind of comment—usually born out of an attempt at sensitivity—the deep friendship and closeness between the two sisters remained.

The strain came because the men they'd married were so different. Jack was hip, with a winning personality, business savvy, and a light tan no matter what time of year. Jack smiled a lot. He was a walking picture of success and he'd done it all without God. If he were a movie star, Jack would be Brad Pitt. His self-sufficiency pervaded everything about him. Bill was more like Dustin Hoffman, serious and compassionate but with an underdeveloped fun gene. He was better in reports than in person. When the families got together once or twice a year at the home of Molly and Beth's parents, Jack kept his distance.

Both men were crazy about championship golf and Wimbledon tennis, and NASCAR. They liked Bill Murray comedies and scouring the business page for changes in their stocks. But none of that mattered. If Bill was in the TV room, Jack stayed in the kitchen. When

Bill came in for a handful of Doritos or a cheeseburger off the grill, Jack would find his way outside to whatever relatives were smoking on the front porch. The distance between the two never translated to overt tension or trouble. But it was distance all the same.

"Jack can't get past the religion thing," Molly would say. Her tone always held the apology that never came. "Don't take it wrong, Beth. If they saw each other more often, it'd be different."

This was their chance. Now that their families lived so close they would finally find out if the guys could learn to be friends. Beth took another handful of raw hamburger. Yes, they were about to see. In this next season of their lives, they would certainly spend more time together, enjoy more barbecues like this one. It was the life they'd dreamed about.

She pressed the soft meat with her thumb until the edges were round; then she placed the patty on the platter with the others. Her candle set was still packed; otherwise this would be the time to light them—anything to add to the ambiance, the sense that she and Bill were warm and friendly and unthreatening.

Her cupboards were already full and fairly organized. Beth put her hands on her hips and surveyed her kitchen. Cinnamon sticks. That's what she needed. She found the spice cupboard, grabbed the cinnamon and filled a pan with water. It was a trick their mother had taught them. Boil cinnamon sticks in a pan of water and the house would smell good for days. When the water came to a boil, she turned down the heat, finished working with the hamburger, and moved on to the vegetable tray.

Everything would work out with their two families.

Molly was her best friend, after all. They knew things about each other no one else would ever know. Not ever. And on days when Beth didn't feel she had a friend in the world, there was Molly. It had been that way since they were little girls.

If only they shared their faith.

Bill was lighting the barbecue and Beth was giving the kitchen counter a final wipe-down when the doorbell rang. A surge of excitement bubbled up inside her. It was really happening. She and Molly, together again. Neighbors, even. As she reached the entryway, she had no doubt. Of course Bill and Jack would find a way around their differences.

Beth opened the door, held out her hands and squealed. "Can you believe it?"

"No." Molly rushed into her arms and the two of them hugged for a long time. When Molly drew back, they looked at each other. "I feel like our suitcases should be waiting out in the car."

Beth laughed. "Me, too."

Jack and Joey sidestepped them and Jack gave Beth a quick smile. "Hey." He held a tray of fruit with a can of whipped cream balanced on top. "I'll take this to the kitchen."

"Hi, Aunt Beth." Joey looked up at her and grinned. He was tanned, his blond hair lighter than usual. "We brought yummy fruit."

"I see that." Beth released her sister and put her hands on Joey's shoulders. "Mister Joey's been in the Florida sunshine."

He giggled. "Mommy bought me a swimming pool." He did a little jump and raised his fist in the air. "Me and

Gus play there every day. Sometimes his tail hits me in the face and it tickles." His eyes caught Molly's. "I'm gonna help Daddy."

Molly smiled as he skipped off. "That child loves his father."

"Yes." Beth leaned against the wall and looked at her sister. "You let Joey *swim* with the dog?"

Molly shut the front door and let loose an exaggerated sigh. "It's a wading pool, Beth." She conjured up a mock look of concern. "Don't tell me! You read something online about dog germs and how they can spread through water." She raised her brow. "Right?"

Beth chided herself. She hated sounding like their mother, always finding something to correct about Molly. But she couldn't seem to stop herself. She shrugged one shoulder and led the way to the kitchen. "It's possible." Her tone was lighter than before. "All that hair and dirt in the same water as Joey. Yuck!"

"Lighten up." Molly set her purse down on the counter and rolled her eyes in a silly sort of way. "A little dog hair never hurt a growing boy."

"I guess." Beth took a plastic pitcher from a lower cupboard and filled it with water. "It's just . . . I wouldn't let George Brett swim with the kids."

"You might." Molly took one of the kitchen stools and leaned her forearms on the counter. "Wait 'til summer hits. Even George Brett will need a way to cool off." She grinned. "I still can't believe you named a female golden retriever George Brett."

Beth smiled. She felt her tension ease. "Not like I had a choice."

When Jonah was born, she and Bill disagreed over his

name. Beth wanted Jonah; Bill wanted George Brett, after his favorite Major League baseball player. They compromised. Beth got to name Jonah, and Bill got naming rights for their next dog. When the dog turned out to be a female golden retriever, Bill didn't waver. "George Brett is a fine name for any dog," he still said. "Even a girl." The name stuck.

Across from Beth and Molly, Jack had Joey in his arms, and for a minute Beth was struck by the picture they made. Nose to nose, lost in a conversation all their own. Molly was right. Jack and Joey shared something very special. And whatever germs Gus carried, they didn't seem to be slowing Joey down. She reached into the freezer, took out a tray of ice cubes, and popped them into the water pitcher. "The kitchen's almost unpacked."

"I see that." Molly sat up straighter. "You're amazing, Beth. I'd be living out of boxes for the first month."

They heard the sound of the patio slider and immediately the shouting voices of Beth's kids. "Mom!" Cammie raced around the corner with a hula hoop in her hand. Blain and Braden were quick on her heels, with Jonah bringing up the rear. Cammie stomped her foot. "Tell Jonah it's mine."

"No!" Jonah caught up to her, his face a twist of anger. "It's my turn. Daddy said she has to share the hoop-a-hoop."

"Hula hoop." Beth caught both kids by the shoulders and stooped down to their level. She looked at Cammie. "And yes, you do have to share. That's what Jesus wants us to do, and it's the right thing." Beth thought she saw Jack shoot a look to Molly. It didn't matter. She wouldn't change the way she raised her kids just because Molly and Jack would be around more often. She leveled a smile at Cammie again and then at Jonah. "Besides, look who's here!"

The kids lifted their eyes and Jonah's face lit up. "Joey!"

"Why don't the three of you go out front and play? George Brett's out there and I think a few kick balls, too. You can take turns." She glanced at Molly. "I love the fence out front. Makes it so safe."

Before Beth could add that now would be a good time for Jack to join Bill out back at the barbecue, Jack eased Joey to the floor and took his hand. "I'll go, too." He gave the women a lopsided grin. "I was hula-hoop champ in fourth grade." He pointed at Molly. "Bet you didn't know that."

"Wow." Molly flashed flirty eyes at her husband. "Such a talented man I married."

"That's right." His look back at her was just short of suggestive. "Don't forget it."

Beth watched, amazed. Molly and Jack had been married almost ten years. Shouldn't the teasing and flirting have worn off by now? Maybe that's what she and Bill needed. More of whatever it was that came so easily to Molly and Jack.

Silence filled the kitchen as the group tromped off, Cammie still clinging to her prized toy. Molly stood, found a plastic tumbler, and poured herself some water. "It's a hot one out there." She looked out the window at the sky overhead. "Looks like summer's here."

"I know." Beth pulled the vegetable tray from the refrigerator and peeled back the plastic wrap. "It's okay for the kids to be outside, right? I mean, it's not too humid?"

Molly laughed and the sound lightened Beth's mood. "This is nothing. Wait 'til August and we'll talk about whether it's safe to play outside."

"Right." Beth laughed, too, but it sounded forced. Why was it so hard for her to find that natural sister rhythm with Molly? *Come on,* she told herself. *Molly's right. Lighten up.* She popped a cucumber slice into her mouth and looked out the window. Bill was flipping burgers, not even aware that Molly and Jack and Joey had arrived. She turned back to Molly and crossed her arms. "Bill's adjusting at work."

"I figured." Molly took a baby carrot and dipped it into the ranch dressing at the center of the tray. "The guy's a brainiac." She finished the carrot. "Everything else falling into place?"

"Yep." Beth took another cucumber slice. "Took care of updating our driver's licenses and applied for new voter's registration cards."

Molly shook her head. A thoughtful smile played at the corners of her lips. "You never quit, do you?"

"Meaning what?"

"Meaning the licenses and the voter cards." She waved her hand in the air. "The unpacking thing, the organizing thing." A chuckle filled her throat. "Aren't there days you just want to go to the clubhouse and sit by the pool?"

"Well"—Beth poured herself a cup of water and looked at her sister—"I guess I figure there'll be time for that." The clubhouse was five doors down, one of the benefits of buying in Ashley Heights. Other than a quick look around, Beth and Bill and the kids hadn't spent any real time there.

Molly took her place on the barstool again and let her shoulders slump a little. "Sorry we couldn't make church."

Beth worked to keep her tone even. "Maybe in a few weeks." She lifted her chin and met her sister's eyes, unblinking. "Sorry we couldn't make boating."

Molly smiled. "It was nice. This is my favorite time on the water. Maybe you can join us next Saturday."

"We'd like that." Beth felt it. Molly was trying. "Bill's never spent much time on the ocean." She giggled. "Might be fun to see him get a little green around the edges."

"Beth . . ." Molly snickered. "Be nice."

"I am." She ran her fingers through her bangs. "I guess we both need to lighten up a little."

"Right. Maybe." Molly angled her head. "Hey, what church is it again? Where you went this morning?"

"Bethel Bible. A mile from here." She hesitated, not sure how much to say. "We tried the Wednesday night group and—"

"Loved it." Molly reached for another carrot. "Right?"

Beth lowered her chin. "Why do I sense sarcasm?"

"Beth . . ." Molly was on her feet, her tone apologetic. She came close and slipped her arms around Beth's neck. "I'm sorry." She wrinkled her nose in the cutesy way she'd done since she was five. "I could never be you; that's all." Her mouth curved up into a sweet smile. "Come on, don't be mad."

"I'm not." Beth removed Molly's arms from around her neck. "I have to get dinner going." Even now when things didn't feel quite right between them, Molly was lighthearted. Like she'd spent the previous four hours at a spa and nothing could possibly ruffle her. It didn't make sense. Molly was the one who needed God. If anyone should've been at ease, it was Beth and Bill and their kids.

Instead, even George Brett was uptight.

Molly returned to the barstool. She sipped her water and peered at Beth over the edge of her cup. After a long drink she set the cup down. "Well? Am I right?"

"About what?"

"The Wednesday night meeting—the church?" She rested her elbows on the counter. "You loved it, right?"

"Fine." Beth tried to hold it in, but she couldn't. A quick burst of giggles came from her lips and she blew at a wisp of her bangs. She could never stay mad at Molly. Never. "Yes. It was perfect. All of it." She exhaled and felt the tension between them lift. "Maybe this Wednesday you and Jack and Joey could—"

Molly held up her hand, though her smile remained. "Stop."

Beth hung her head for a moment. "I'm sorry." Her eyes found Molly's. "It's just . . . the Wednesday program is so good for kids and . . ."

"I have friends there." Molly took another carrot. "It's a good church, Beth. I'm just not ready to go." She popped the carrot into her mouth as if to punctuate her statement. As she chewed, she grinned and when she swallowed she held out both hands, palms up. "I love you. Can't we agree to disagree on that one area?"

The dream—the one Beth had always nurtured—had the two sisters living in the same city and the same neighborhood, but also taking their kids to the same church, sharing in the same Sunday afternoon potluck suppers. Sharing the same faith, the same purpose for getting up in the morning. If Molly wasn't ready for that, well then at least they were neighbors, close enough for days like this.

Beth grinned. She parted her lips and pretended to bite her tongue—the sign the two sisters had always used to signal that, whatever the discussion, it wasn't worth fighting over. They both laughed, and Beth looked past the silliness to the deep layers of Molly's heart. "Yes. We can agree to disagree."

They heard the patio door again and Bill came in, both hands covered with oversized oven mitts. He grinned at Molly. "Barely off the moving van and already Beth has me at the barbecue grill."

"I see that." Molly slipped off the stool, walked to Bill and gave him a quick hug. "The oven mitts and everything." She patted Beth on the shoulder. "When I moved here, it was two months before I found my oven mitts."

Beth opened the refrigerator and pulled out the tray of meat patties. "Okay, so I mark the boxes." She handed the tray to Bill. "How hard is that?"

"That's my Beth." Bill gave her a kiss on the cheek. "Don't let your sister tease you, honey. I wouldn't change a thing." He stopped and looked around the kitchen. "Where's Jack and Joey?"

Beth jumped in. "Out front." She kept the concern from her voice. "Jack's keeping an eye on the kids."

"Oh." Bill raised the tray of meat a few inches and gave the two of them a quick shrug. "Guess I'm on my own, then."

The women watched him go, and Beth let her gaze fall

to the floor. When she looked up, Molly was watching her. "Bill sees through it."

"I know. I'm sorry." Molly frowned. Her expression held no excuses. "We have to give the guys time."

It was a thought that hung over the entire evening. Jack kept himself busy with the kids, even leaving the dinner table early to get refills of strawberry Kool-Aid. When it was just Molly and Beth and Bill at the table, Molly tried to cover up for her husband, gushing about how he was such a hands-on dad, and how he rarely took time to sit and listen to anyone, even her.

"He loves that boy, I tell you." She found a bit of laughter. Then she looked at Bill and folded her hands beneath her chin. "Hey, Beth tells me the two of you like your new church."

Bill set his burger down and dabbed a blob of ketchup off the corner of his mouth. "Yeah. We do."

"It's active, that's for sure." Beth didn't want to push, but since Molly asked . . .

Bill lifted his hamburger bun and slipped a few potato chips on top of the cooked meat. "I was on their Web site last night. They have a summer adventure program, family activities almost every day for three weeks straight, mission trips and work trips. . . ." He took another bite of his burger and raised his brow.

"Really?" Beth glanced at Molly. She was picking the sesame seeds from the top of her bun. "I'm not so sure about those trips. So much can go wrong."

"Like what?" Bill was ready to take a bite of his burger, but he froze. "I thought it sounded like fun."

"Fun? Parasites and malaria and terrorists and violent street gangs?" There was enough to worry about right here in West Palm Beach. Beth shook her head. "No mission trips."

"Well . . . maybe you could think about it." Bill worked his napkin over his mouth again. "They're taking a work trip to Haiti at the end of summer. It's for families—even young kids." Bill set his burger down. "That sort of thing could be life-changing."

"In more ways than one." Beth stirred her fork through her fruit salad.

The conversation fell flat for a few seconds. Bill leaned back in his seat and looked at Molly. "Did Jack get enough to eat?"

"I think so. You know Jack." She gave another nervous laugh. "Can't sit still for fifteen minutes. Last time we went somewhere with Joey he was up pitching balls before . . ."

She ran on about Joey and baseball for another minute, but Beth stopped listening. Molly's excuses for Jack were limitless. No matter how much she tried to explain the situation, the truth was painfully obvious. Jack was uncomfortable around them, uneasy with their faith. Maybe worried that Beth and Bill would try to convert him. Whatever it was, it left a tension denser than the pound cake she served for dessert.

That night before they turned in, Beth had to wonder. The last thing she wanted was a strained relationship with her sister. When Molly lived across the country, the two sisters shared weekly phone calls and got along great. Maybe it wasn't such a good idea that they spend every weekend getting their families together.

The smell of cinnamon floated up to their bedroom, but any ambiance it might've created was lost. Bill was already snoring. Beth closed her eyes. *God, what about my sister? She needs You, but I don't know. Maybe I'm not the one to help her. Show me, God . . . please.* Even as her quick prayer came to an end, she had the sinking feeling they were headed for trouble. With the tension that had plagued her sister's visit that afternoon, not only were weekly visits likely to be a bad idea.

But maybe it would've been better if she and her family had never moved to Florida at all.

Chapter Four

Wendy Porter was stirring the scrambled eggs when Rip came up behind her and wrapped his hands around her waist. She squirmed and clicked off the heat beneath the frying pan. "Rip . . ." The frozen sausages were already heated in the microwave, the orange juice poured, toast buttered and on the table. She turned and faced him. "Mmmm." He was fresh from the shower, clean shaven. "You smell nice."

"Right back at ya." He nuzzled her neck. "Last night was amazing." He left a trail of kisses along her collarbone and then straightened to his full height. He wasn't a tall man—five-ten on a good day. But she was just over five feet in her slippers, and he towered over her. The look in his eyes made her knees tremble. "Talk about your welcome-home parties."

"Rip . . . you're getting me flustered." She smiled and sidestepped him. The heat in her face was from more than the stove. No matter how charming he was, no matter how much he wanted the celebration to continue, they needed to talk. If he heard about the boy from Brent or Bubba, Rip would never forgive her. She took the glasses of juice to the table. "Thought you'd like a real breakfast on your first morning out."

"That's my baby. The perfect homemaker." He grabbed the frying pan and scraped the eggs into an empty serving dish. "Can't believe I still know my way around the place."

Wendy looked back at the frying pan. Images of other men she'd entertained in this very kitchen flashed in her mind. If Rip found out about them, there'd be no reasoning with him. She already planned to deny any talk of cheating. But the boy . . .

Rip was saying something, and she tried to focus. ". . . when I woke up, and sure enough—I checked the classifieds first thing, and there it was! Manager Wanted, Cleveland Regal Cinemas!" He slid his chair up to the table and raised his hands. "Everything's falling into place."

Manager of a movie house? Rip had never held any manager jobs before, and him just out of prison? Wendy tried not to let her doubt show. It was possible, right? With Rip's charm and all? She smiled. "That's wonderful, Rip." She took a sip of orange juice. "You can call about it after breakfast."

"That wasn't the only one." He took a large scoop of eggs and slapped it on his plate. "They got a whole list of jobs in auto work. Right up my alley, and . . ."

Wendy stopped paying attention. She took some eggs, but after one bite she lost her appetite. In half a day she'd learned much about her husband's transformation. He'd found religion, or so he said, gotten himself into some sort of counseling, and taken classes for something the prison people called "rage management."

The training was about to be tested.

"Rip . . ." She looked up and met his eyes. His mouth hung open and he looked surprised. He was probably still talking. "Oh . . . sorry." She set her fork down. Her hand was shaking. "Go ahead."

Rip hesitated. "That's okay, baby." He flashed a quick grin. "Must be important." He set down his piece of toast. "What's on your mind?"

"Well—" She remembered to smile, but she could feel it stop far short of her eyes. She breathed out. Her stomach hurt. It felt like someone was turning a wrench on her insides, making them tighter with every tick of the clock. "There's something you need to know." Her voice grew soft, timid. "Something I wanted to tell you first thing when you got out."

Rip grew stone-still. His smile was still stuck on his face, but his eyes changed. Fear and curiosity, the hint of anger, and then a deliberate patience. Each emotion took turns with him. Even so, the only obvious sign that something wasn't right was the way he held his glass of juice. He was squeezing it so tight his knuckles were white. Same way they were whenever Rip was about to hurl something across the room. "You, uh"—he gave a short laugh and set his juice glass down—"you cheatin' on me, Wendy?"

"No! Rip, it's nothing like that, nothing at all." She stumbled over her words. "There's no one else, I promise." Not for six months, anyway. She swallowed. He hadn't asked her to go on, but she had no choice. "That's not it." She picked up her fork and poked her sausage. Her eyes stayed on his. "Remember back when you first got sent away?"

"Yeah. Worst day of my life." Rip looked more relaxed. She wasn't seeing someone else, so what was there to worry about, right? He took another swig of juice. "What about it?"

"Okay, well—" She set her fork down again. Why was the room so stuffy? She stood, crossed the kitchen and slid open the window over the sink. "There. That's better." A few steps and she was back at the table.

Rip was taking another piece of toast from the serving plate. He took a bite and started to chew. "So what about it?" He chuckled. "Used to be I couldn't shut ya up. Now what—cat got your tongue?"

Wendy pressed her fists against her middle. Anything to ease the tightness there. "A few weeks after you left, I was late." She looked at him, waiting for him to understand.

"Late?" Rip slapped a forkful of eggs onto his toast, folded it over, and shoved half of it into his mouth. "Late for what?"

"Rip . . ." Her tone sounded painful now. He wasn't making this any easier. "My period was late."

Rip kept chewing, but his motions grew slower. "Meaning what?"

"Well . . ." She exhaled hard and covered her face with her hands. When she looked up, she shook her head. How could she have waited this long to tell him? "I took a test. . . . I was pregnant."

For a moment, time seemed to stop. Rip stared at her, unblinking. "What?"

"I was pregnant, Rip." She lifted her hands and let them fall to the table. "You got me pregnant right before you left. I had a baby boy." Her voice fell off. "Eight months later."

"A boy?" Again Rip released a sound that was part laugh, part confusion. "You're keeping a kid from me?" He glanced around the kitchen and peered beneath the table. "So where is he?"

Wendy moaned. Her head fell back a few inches. *You can do this. . . . Finish, already.* She looked at Rip. "I gave him up. To a family in Florida."

Rip dropped his piece of toast. The eggs that had balanced there splattered to the floor. "You *what*?"

The linoleum felt like liquid beneath her feet. "I . . . I gave him up, Rip." She raised her voice without meaning to. "What was I supposed to do?"

"Wait . . ." He pushed his chair back. For a moment he didn't move or breathe or speak. "You gave away . . ." His tone fell to a whisper, "You gave away my . . . *son*?"

"Rip!" Like a lead blanket, fear draped itself over Wendy and made it almost impossible to breathe. The rage was coming, she was sure of it. Like a barrage of bullets, like an air raid, he was about to unleash his anger, and this time maybe she wouldn't survive. She stood and took small steps backward. "I had no choice! You were in prison and I—"

"Stop." He held up a single hand. This was the moment when he would normally explode, only instead of rage, his eyes held a strange mix of shock and anger and fear. He stared at his plate of half-eaten eggs and toast as if he were trying to put together pieces of a puzzle that wouldn't quite take shape. After a long time, he looked up, his eyes narrow. "Shouldn't I have signed something?" His words were quick and clipped, like the ticking of a time bomb. "Don't both parents have to sign when you give a kid away?"

Wendy took another few steps back until she hit the wall. She opened her mouth but no words came. This was the hardest part, the worst of it. She had to tell the truth, or Rip would find out for himself and then . . . then she'd never come out alive. She twisted her fingers together and looked down somewhere near her feet. *Why did I ever think I could pull this off?* She lifted her eyes to his. "I . . . I signed both our names."

The statement was like a lit fuse, and all at once Rip was on his feet. "You can't be serious." He took quick, menacing steps toward her, his eyes dark and flinty. He was a foot from her now. She could see the greasy toast crumbs on his lip. When he spoke again, his words came through clenched teeth. "You signed my name? So you could give my son to some family . . . in *Florida*?"

She nodded fast. "Yes, Rip." With every sentence he sounded angrier, more incredulous. Coffee percolated in the background, but the smell was too strong. It made her sick to her stomach. "I had no choice."

"That's it . . ." He raised his fist and she could feel it, feel his knuckles crashing down on her skull, feel herself being knocked to the floor. Except the blow never came. Instead he turned just enough and his fist smashed clean through the wall beside her, inches from her face.

She slid sideways, away from the damage, away from her husband. She was next, absolutely. She squinted, afraid to look. Her hands came up in front of her, shielding herself, creating a layer of defense between the two of them. But again the blow didn't come. After a few seconds she opened her eyes and looked at him.

He worked his hand free of the crumbling drywall, shook off the dust and debris. Almost in slow motion his shoulders hunched forward and his arms fell slack to his sides. He hung his head and his voice slipped to a monotone. "What am I doing?" The question was geared to himself, not her.

She moved a few more feet away from him.

"Wendy"—he twisted his brow and stared at her, deep at her—"I was never going to do that again. Never."

"I'm sorry." A good three feet separated them now. "I . . . you were in prison, Rip." She was shaking so hard her teeth chattered. "I didn't know what to do, and I couldn't handle raising a baby by myself, and I looked into adoption, and—"

Again he held up one hand. "I get it." The knuckles on his right hand were bloodied. He pulled his fist close and cradled it against his waist. She heard him exhale. He was trembling, the rage trying to find a peaceable way to leave his body. His face was pale and little drops of sweat dotted his forehead. His eyes found hers. "I'm so sorry. . . ." He held up his bloodied hand. "I didn't mean it." He hid his face with his good hand and groaned. "I shouldn't have . . . I'm sorry."

Wendy felt herself relax. Maybe he wasn't going to hit her or knock her to the floor. She straightened some. Truth was *she'd* done wrong by Rip. She should've taken the paperwork to the prison and convinced him fair and square to give up the boy. But then . . . "I never should've signed your name."

"Wait . . ." Slowly, hope seemed to grab Rip by the shoulders and his expression changed. "You know what?" This time his eyes flashed with new life, new excitement. "Maybe it's not too late."

Not too late? Was he crazy? The child would be four now. Five in the fall. He'd been with the nice couple from Florida since he was a few days old. She and Rip couldn't just call up and say, "Hey, we changed our minds. We're back together and we want our boy."

She thought hard. *Could they?*

No, they couldn't. Of course not. She had to tell her husband before he got his hopes up. "Rip, they don't just give 'em back. The boy thinks *they're* his family now."

Rip pierced the air in front of himself with one finger. The rage was gone, but the intensity of his tone, his words, was still enough to take her breath away. "I never signed the paper." He walked to the phone and picked up the receiver. "You went through child welfare, right?" He looked at the keypad. "If I call information, who do I ask for?"

"Rip!" Suddenly it dawned on her what he was doing. "You can't call and tell them I forged your name. They'll have police down here in ten minutes, and then it'll be my turn in the slammer!"

He didn't say it would serve her right, but his eyes spoke loud and clear. He put the receiver back on the base and stroked his chin. "There has to be a way." He took a few steps toward her and then turned and walked to the phone again. "We need a plan . . . a story. Something they'll believe."

In all her years knowing Rip, Wendy had seen only two sides of the man: loving kindness and blazing rage. But now he was almost frenzied with determination, looking for a way to bring home his son. Like a person driven, the way a drowning man is driven to get his next breath. She moved a little closer. "You're serious about this." She gripped the counter.

Just for an instant, the rage flashed again. Then it was gone, his tone almost matter-of-fact. "Yes. I'm serious." He brought his face closer to hers. "My only son is somewhere out there." He pointed sharply at the kitchen window. "You gave him away without asking me, so yes . . . I'm serious about this."

He eased back and pulled out a tired smile. "I'm willing to forgive you." He strained his neck forward some, as if the task of forgiving was as easy as swallowing a turkey leg. He pointed at the telephone. "But I'm making the call, and yes, I want him back." He slumped against the kitchen counter, their elbows touching. "The sooner the better."

Rip raked his fingers through his hair, something he did when he was frustrated. What he'd never done, though, was back down from a fight—the way he'd just done with her. He looked at her, half grinned, and patted her arm. "I'm going for a walk." He winked. "Anger management."

Wendy watched him go. Her knees stopped knocking even before he shut the door. Tigger the cat brushed up against her ankles, but she barely noticed. Her eyes were still on the door, her mouth still open, unsure of what to do or say. Was he serious? Had he really just gotten what must've been the worst news of his life, smiled at her, and made the decision to take a walk?

A walk, of all things?

Rip Porter had made promises to her since she was a seventeen-year-old high school junior. Never once had he made good on his word, never stayed away from the easy girls, never quit thc bottle for more than a few months, and never—never once—had he been able to keep his hands off her when he was mad.

Until now.

Sure, he'd punched the wall. But a lifetime of rage was bound to take some time to fix. Theirs wasn't a house with patched-up walls. She'd taken every one of the blows in the past. She blinked and her eyes found the hole, the one he'd just made. Yes, there it was. So, maybe Rip was right, maybe the prison classes had worked and now he could handle getting angry without hurting her.

His words played again—*I want him back . . . the sooner the better.*

For the first time, Wendy considered the possibility. Rip had a point. Since his name was forged, the paperwork was a lie. Fraudulent, right? Wasn't that the word? She gripped the countertop behind her. Could they really do it? Could they think up a story, a reason why Rip's name was forged, and keep her from getting handcuffed in the process?

She thought of the baby, the way he'd looked and felt and smelled in her arms all those years ago. And suddenly, in a rush of loss and regret and a love deeper than the ocean, it all came back. Every moment, every memory. She was no longer standing in the kitchen of their small two-bedroom ranch, smelling the mix of cooked sausage and thick coffee. She was in the hospital, doing the one thing the social worker had advised her not to do.

She was holding her newborn son.

Chapter Five

With Rip gone for a walk, the memories swirled in Wendy's head, drawing her back with a power she couldn't fight. In as many seconds, four and a half years disappeared and she was lying in a hospital bed, the day she delivered her baby.

He had the palest peach-fuzz hair and a perfectly round face. But it was his eyes she remembered most, the eyes she would never forget. They were light blue, almost transparent. And as she held him, as she snuggled his warm little body against her chest and stared at him, his eyes seemed to see straight into her heart.

If he could talk he would've said, *Mommy, don't give me away. I don't care if it's just me and you.*

She held her finger out to her son and he grabbed it, held tight as if he would do everything in his power to stay with her. But she had to give him up, didn't she? What sort of life could she offer a little boy? She was working two jobs to make ends meet. She'd almost never see him. And Rip? He was rotting away in prison.

Still . . .

A wild and reckless love began to take root in her

heart, working its way deep, to the outer layers of her very soul. It was a love so strong it took her breath away and brought tears to her eyes. Maybe love would be enough. If he could stir up these sorts of feelings in just one day, then there was no limit to how much she might love him. She could love him more in the few hours a day she might have with him than other mothers could love in twenty-four straight, right?

For three crazy hours, her feelings waged war within her. Several times a nurse came in to see if she wanted a break, but each time she only held up her hand and shook her head. She was with her son. No one would disturb them until she was ready.

Finally, just as the third hour came to a close, she remembered what had driven her to the social services office in the first place. Rip Porter's fists. She could still feel his knuckles crashing down on her, breaking her collarbone one time and fracturing her eye socket another. Rip hadn't even served time for those beatings. "Bad spells," Rip called them.

So what if he got out of prison and had a *bad spell* with the precious baby in her arms? Newspapers were full of stories about guys like Rip and babies like this one. They were the sorts of stories that took up just a few inches in a news column on the fifth page: "Baby Dies after Beating." Nausea welled up in Wendy, and her tears came harder. If she kept Rip's baby, one day Rip would come home and she would take him back, because she always did. She didn't know how to not love Rip Porter. And then the baby would be just one more person to rage at. One more person at the wrong end of Rip's bad spells.

She clutched the baby more tightly and rocked him

close. His eyes told her how he felt. He was hers; he
wanted her to take him home and love him forever. But
she couldn't, wouldn't. Not with Rip in her life. Her tears
became sobs, deep and silent. "My little son, I'm sorry. I
have to . . . have to let you go."

Then, before she could change her mind, she rang for
the nurse. When the uniformed woman approached her,
she gave her son one last kiss and held him out. "Take
him. Please. The social worker is waiting down the hall."

The nurse hesitated, but Wendy waved her off.
"Please. I have to do this."

Later that afternoon the social worker stepped into her
hospital room with the paperwork. Allyson Bower was
her name, a woman with deep eyes and a story she hinted
at but never shared with Wendy. Like every other detail of
that time in her life, the social worker's name was never
more than a heartbeat away.

That day, after Wendy had said good-bye to her baby,
Allyson took the chair next to her. She looked at her for
a long moment. Then she sighed and spoke her question
at the same time. "Your husband's still in prison, is that
right?"

"Yes." Wendy felt dead, drained. Her arms ached to
hold her baby again. Something told her they would
always ache that way. "Outside Cleveland."

She pointed to a few marked places on the paperwork.
"I'll need his signature in order to sever your rights as
parents."

"Okay." Wendy squeezed her eyes shut. She crooked
her finger and pressed it to her lip to keep from crying.
"Thank you."

"Wendy . . ." The social worker hesitated. "Are you sure about this decision?"

"Yes." She looked straight at the woman and gritted her teeth. Should she tell her the truth, the real reason why she couldn't keep the beautiful baby in the other room? Then, before she could think it through, she pulled the top of her hospital gown down just enough to expose the bump on her collarbone, the place where she hadn't healed exactly right. "See this?"

When the social worker must've realized what she was seeing, her eyes hardened. "Your husband did that to you, didn't he?"

"Yes." She pulled her gown back into place. "The other scars have healed." Fresh tears clouded her eyes. "The ones you can see, anyway."

"Wendy . . ." Allyson took her hand, and for a moment she hung her head. When she looked up, new understanding filled her face. "Why didn't you tell me?"

Wendy lifted her hands as the tears splashed onto her cheeks. "He's in prison for domestic violence. What'd you think?"

"You said he pushed you in the Kroger parking lot." Allyson looked defeated. "Have you reported him?"

Wendy's voice cracked. "I can't." She bit her lip and shook her head. "I never could. I love him." In a distant room she could hear a baby crying and she wondered if it was hers. "But I can't . . . have my baby around that."

Concern added to the emotions on the social worker's face. "What about your husband?" She picked up her briefcase. "What if he won't sign?"

"He'll sign." Wendy's heart beat harder than before. *Rip would kill me if he knew what I was doing,* she thought. *He wouldn't sign the papers for a million dollars. He's always wanted a son, as long as I've known him.* She wiped the back of her hand across her cheeks. "He hates kids. I'll have the papers to you in a week."

Allyson filled her cheeks with air and released it slowly. She stood, righteous anger written in the lines on her forehead. "It's wrong, what he's done to you. I can get you counseling, someone to meet with every day. Whatever it takes to get him out of your life."

The ticks from the clock on the wall seemed to get louder. The right answer was obvious. Wendy would agree, of course. She would get help and she would put Rip Porter out of her mind forever. But as long as she'd known Rip, he'd always found his way back into her life.

"Well . . . ?" Allyson touched her shoulder. "Can I make the call?"

Wendy looked down at her hands, at the way they had clenched into fists. She shook her head without looking up. "It's no use. I'll never be rid of him."

The social worker tried for a while longer, but Wendy wouldn't budge. She couldn't expose her baby to Rip, and she couldn't get counseling for a problem she would keep going back to. Finally there was nothing else Allyson could say. "I'm sorry, Wendy." She gathered her briefcase and gave a nod to the paperwork. "Get it signed and back to me as soon as possible. The couple will be here at the end of the week. We'll keep the baby in short-term foster care until the papers are in order."

The couple. Her son's new parents.

Wendy had picked them from a nationwide data bank. Their bios were the only ones that grabbed her heart.

She still had them now, on the top shelf in the linen

closet. She crossed the kitchen to the front door and looked out the living-room window. Rip wasn't in sight. Still, she needed to find the file. Now, so she'd have it ready when he got home. The folder held everything— pictures, the information on the couple, details about her baby's birth.

Even a copy of the forged paperwork.

She went to the linen closet and opened the door. Every September 22—her son's birthday—she'd pull the file from the top shelf and remind herself that she'd made the right choice. Once in a while she'd take a look on a random day in March or June or just before Christmas. When she missed Rip or when she wondered whether her little boy was walking or running or reciting his alphabet.

Now she reached up and carefully pulled down the file. It smelled like cigarette smoke, proof that she usually couldn't get through the papers inside without chain smoking over every page. The top of the folder read "Porter Adoption File." Wendy read the words three times. Her mouth was dry, and her heart stuttered into an uncomfortable beat. She dropped to the floor cross-legged and opened the file.

And there they were. The faces of all three of them.

Clipped to the inside of the folder was a photo of her son, the only photo she had. Gently she slipped the picture from beneath the paper clip and held it closer. She could still hear his baby sounds, still feel the way he held tight to her finger. "What did they name you, little boy?" Softly, with great care, she brought the photo to her lips and kissed it. "Have they told you about me?"

At times like this, the ache was so great she could hardly stand it. She eased the picture back beneath the clip and forced herself to look at the first pages in the file, the couple's bios. Back then he was thirty and she was twenty-eight. The woman was a dark-haired version of Kate Hudson, with laughing eyes and a carefree face. The man looked a little like Rip. Same rounded shoulders and dark blond hair.

They were successful, no question. He was an international businessman making more money a year than Wendy would ever see in ten. His smile had Rip's charm, but this man had obviously found a way to turn the charm into more than cheap one-night stands. Their house was a three-story on the edge of a lake in southwest Florida. They had a boat and nice cars and all the stuff rich people like to own. But it wasn't their looks or their success or even their stuff that sold Wendy on them. It was what they'd written about themselves. She moved her eyes halfway down the page and began to read.

Hi. This is Jack. I work for Reylco, Inc., as manager of international corporate accounts, overseeing sales of pharmaceuticals. Reylco is the world's largest supplier of cancer drugs. Okay, that's the boring stuff. Here's the rest. My work schedule's flexible. Sure, I travel a lot, but I take my wife with me half the time, and when we have children I'll take them, too.

Travel's great, but home's better. I love Saturday bike rides and Sunday afternoon football games and the smell of my wife's spaghetti sometime midweek. Yes, she makes a lot of spaghetti and sometimes she burns the French bread, but I love her anyway. If I wanted gourmet dinners I wouldn't have married her.

Everyone thinks I'm safe and conservative, and I guess I am. I'm a stickler for seatbelts and helmets and life jackets. But here's a secret. Sometimes at night Molly and I take our speedboat out and open up the engine. Just open it up all the way, blazing through the darkness, wind in our hair, stars in our eyes. I know, I know. It's a little dangerous. But out there the corporate world falls away and it's just us, loving life, loving each other, living in the moment.

The guys at work know the other me. The boating thing would surprise them.

Anyway, I guess I should tell you I'm a romantic. I write music and play the guitar, and if I'm sure no one else is in the house, I sing at the top of my lungs. Sometimes I dream about walking away from the whole corporate game, the long hours and heavy demands, and taking my family far, far away. We'd set up on some deserted beach on an island out in the middle of the ocean and I'd drink raspberry iced tea and write songs all day.

But I'll probably save that for our vacations.

See? That's the romantic in me. One time I tricked my wife into coming out onto the porch when she thought I was in Berlin on business. I had a CD player ready, and when she walked out the door I held up a sign that read, "Wanna dance?" We laughed and looked into each other's eyes and waltzed on the porch that night. Fifteen minutes

*later I handed her the CD, gave her a kiss, and
caught a late flight out to Germany.*

That's how I like to live.

*We stay fit, because it feels better to be healthy.
But I have a confession. I hate exercise. I used the
stair-step machine at the gym for a while, but now
my wife and I wake up early and jog together, six
days out of seven. I still hate it, but with her there,
I laugh a lot. They say laughing burns calories and
it's good for your liver. So I guess we'll keep jogging.*

*I almost forgot. We have a yellow Labrador
retriever named Gus. He's part of the family, but
he's willing to give up the crib when the baby
comes.*

*That's about it. Oh, one more thing. I want chil-
dren more than I want my next breath. And somewhere out there, I believe with everything I am, that
you'll find this and know—absolutely know—that
we're the couple you're looking for. Life is short
and time is a thief. We would make every day something magical and marvelous for your baby. The
place in our hearts and homes has been ready
for years. I already wrote a song for our firstborn.
Maybe I'll sing it for your baby one day.*

Thanks for your time.

Wendy had goose bumps on her arms the first time she
read the man's letter. She felt dreamy when he talked
about taking his wife on their boat late at night and flying
like the wind across the water, and she got tears in her
eyes when she pictured him dancing with his wife on the

front porch and catching a later flight for his business trip.

She giggled when he talked about hating exercise and she burst out laughing when he mentioned that Gus, the dog, would be willing to give up the crib when the baby came. The couple had the sort of marriage everyone wanted. Between their laughter and loving, they would give her son a dream life—the sort he could never have with her.

Guilt washed over Wendy as she finished reading it now. How could she even consider taking the boy away from a couple like that? But then . . . they'd been fine before adopting. They'd be fine if things didn't work out, wouldn't they? They'd still have the nice house and the fast boat, the laughter and love, right? They'd still have Gus.

Wendy sat back against the hallway wall and read the woman's bio. It was shorter, but it had been the icing on the cake.

I'm Molly, Jack's wife. I love theater and law and sunsets over the lake behind our house. I have a degree in political science and once, a long time ago, I wanted to spend my life putting away bad guys. That or work as a Broadway actress. Being a lawyer would've been a little of both, I guess.

Jack and I met at Florida State University the fall of my sophomore year. We were both cast in "You're a Good Man, Charlie Brown." He was Charlie and I was The Little Red-Haired Girl —the one Charlie has a crush on. I guess the rest was history. Well, not really. But after a few bends in the road and broken hearts, it was history. He's always been the only man for me.

Our social worker told us to write about things that were important to us. Top of the list is high morals and strong character. Both our families believe in God, and even though we're not big churchgoers, we believe in living right—doing unto others as you would have them do to you. That sort of thing.

Jack and I always wanted a bunch of kids, but things didn't work out that way. We're hoping for a baby through adoption, the child we will love and raise and cherish all the days of our lives. We look forward to hearing from you.

Wendy pulled her legs up and rested the file on her knees. Again Rip's words shouted at her. *I want him back . . . the sooner the better.* If that was true, she couldn't spend another minute thinking about the nice couple in Florida.

She flipped the page, and there it was. The place at the bottom where she'd signed Rip's name. How could she and Rip explain the forgeries any other way? A handwriting expert could tell, right? They could check and figure out that her signature and his were written by the same person. But if they had the right story, maybe no one would ever check.

She stared at the signatures. What had the social worker asked her to do? Take the papers to the prison and have Rip sign them, right? Her mind began to turn, creating lies, sorting through possibilities. What if she'd taken the paperwork to the prison and left it with a guard? And what if the guard gave it to the wrong prisoner? Maybe someone who didn't really care for Rip? Then that prisoner might've read the documents and thought, why not? Why not sign someone's papers?

By the time the paperwork was returned to the guard, the damage would've been done, right? And she would've dropped by the prison, picked up the documents, and never looked back. She hadn't talked to Rip much the whole time he was in, so it was possible the issue of the boy might never have come up.

The longer she played the story over in her mind, the more sure she became. The lie might just work. All they had to do was convince the social worker Rip was a victim, that he had no idea he was a father until he was released from prison, and that someone else—another inmate—had signed his papers.

She was perfecting the story when she heard the door open.

"Wendy . . . baby, I'm sorry." There was the sound of his footsteps, and then he found her, sitting in the hallway, the file on her lap. His face was dark with sorrow and remorse. He dropped to his knees beside her and framed her face with his hands. "I'm sorry. I'm not mad at you." He had never sounded more genuine, more loving. "I just want our boy back." He hesitated. "Help me find him, okay?"

And with that, the only real reason she'd given her son up faded entirely from the picture. Rip was a changed man, completely changed. He was kind and compassionate, and even when he was angry he wouldn't hit her. The hole in the wall was proof. The Florida couple would be all right one day. They could adopt another kid. What mattered was the boy, and the fact that he belonged with his real parents.

Suddenly she could almost see their lives laid out before her. Their son would come home, and whatever loss he felt, she and Rip would make up for it. He would be happy and well-cared-for, playing ball with his daddy on spring days and fishing all summer long. With Rip back to work at the movie theater or the local garage, they might move into a bigger house, in a nicer neighborhood. Their son would have other siblings one day, and the Porter family would live happily ever after.

She searched Rip's eyes. "I'll help you." The first bit of a smile lifted her lips. She handed him the file. "You need to read this."

He took it, his movements slower, gentler than before. After he looked at the cover he lowered himself the rest of the way to the floor and sat beside her. "The adoption file."

"Yes. And, Rip . . ." She drew a slow breath. "I think I have a story that'll work."

With that they set their plans in motion. Now it was only a matter of carrying them out and waiting for the day Wendy never thought she'd see.

The day her son would come home to stay.

Chapter Six

By the time Molly picked Joey up at Cricket Preschool that Wednesday, she'd finished half her to-do list: an early workout with Jack in the weight room upstairs, an hour of unofficial secretarial duties—typing a letter and organizing his files on the Birmingham Remming account, the one that always drove him crazy. He had a secretary at the office, but Jack was ambitious. With his pace, he needed extra help, and she was happy to give it. Besides the work for Jack, she had her monthly phone meeting with their property manager to make sure all was well with their rental houses.

She still needed groceries and a phone call with Beth. Just to clear the air after their barbecue. The few times they'd talked since the weekend, Beth had seemed short, the way she always acted when her feelings were hurt.

Molly lined up with the other mothers outside Room 4, Mrs. Erickson's room. When Joey spotted her, his face came alive. He held up a small white teddy bear. "I won, Mommy. I did my best and I won!"

"Thatta boy!" She stooped down and held out her

hands the way she always did when she picked him up from school.

He was only fifteen feet away, but he ran with all his might and jumped into her arms. He was getting bigger, and the lift up was harder all the time. But she was still able to swing him up into her arms. He wrapped his little legs around her waist, and they touched foreheads.

"Eskimo noses first, okay?" He hid his stuffed bear behind his back and waited for her response.

"Eskimo noses it is!" She brushed the tip of her nose against his.

"Butterfly kisses, too." He brushed his eyelashes against hers.

"Butterfly kisses." Her heart melted. She loved everything about being Joey's mother. "Okay." She drew back and grinned at him. "How'd you win the bear?"

"I knew my ABCs." He pulled out the stuffed toy and held it inches from her face. "He's the bestest bear ever, Mommy. Softy and furry and growly on the inside." Joey's brow lowered and he tried to make himself look mean. "I named him Mr. Growls. 'Cause bears aren't really that friendly with little boys and girls. That's what teacher said." He cocked his head. "But he'll get along with Mr. Monkey, right? 'Cause Mr. Monkey is my bestest animal friend."

"Right. They'll be pals, I'm sure." She hid her laugh and eased him back to the ground beside her. They walked outside and stopped on the sidewalk. "Okay, let's see this softy, furry, growly bear." She held out her hand.

Joey giggled and plopped the bear into her fingers. "See? Isn't he perfect?"

"Oh, my." Molly studied the toy, turning him sideways

and upside down. She jumped back and held him out to Joey again. "He is growly. He scares me."

"Mommy!" He drew out her name the way he did when he thought she was being silly. Again Joey laughed, and the sound bathed the cloudy morning in warmth and sunshine. She took hold of his hand and they crossed the parking lot toward their SUV. "I have a surprise!" She looked down at him, at his bouncy way of tagging along beside her. She could feel her eyes dancing.

"What?" He stopped and faced her. He had Mr. Growls by the ear as he did a few jumps.

"Costco!" She raised her fists in the air as if this were the best possible surprise a mother could give her son.

He lowered his chin and gave her a pointed look that was all Jack's. "Aw, Mommy. You still have errands, you mean? I want to play give-and-go today. Me and you and Gus."

She wrinkled her nose. "Yeah." She clicked the locks open on the door and helped him into the back. He hopped up into his booster seat, and she buckled him in. "We'll play when we get home, okay, buddy?"

"Okay." He wasn't disappointed. His eyes shone with the same sweetness they'd had when he walked through the classroom door a few moments earlier.

"One more thing . . ." She kissed his cheek. "Don't forget about the samples."

A smile brought his dimples to life again. "Oh, yeah. They have the bestest samples, Mommy. Remember?"

"I know." She closed the door and climbed into the front seat. "That's why I saved that errand 'til you were with me."

"Okay." In the rearview mirror she could see him

studying Mr. Growls again. He scrunched up his face as mean as he could and growled at the bear. The scowl faded when he saw her eyes in the mirror. "I love samples."

Costco took longer than she wanted. Joey sampled enough teriyaki chicken and buttered bread to make up for lunch, so they decided to pass on the sandwiches. When they got home, Joey helped her carry in the groceries, managing the super-sized paper towels on one trip and the giant package of paper plates on another.

"That's almost bigger than you, buddy." Molly was trailing him. She wasn't sure he could see over the top of the package. "Want some help?"

"Nope." He heaved the plates a little higher, stumbled, and caught his balance. "Daddy says real men help out."

She sucked her cheeks so she wouldn't laugh out loud. He wasn't *trying* to be cute, after all. When she had her composure, she steadied the box in her own arms and leaned over him to open the garage door. "Well, no question about it. You're a real man, Joey. Definitely."

He puffed his chest out and carried the plates the rest of the way to the kitchen without any further stumbling. When the groceries were put away, they went out to the basketball hoop in the driveway. The clouds had parted and the afternoon promised to be nothing but blue skies and warmth.

"I love give-and-go, Mommy." Joey put one foot forward.

She bent over and tied his shoelaces. "I love it, too."

Give-and-go was something Joey had picked up watching basketball with Jack. During warm-ups, a player would pass the ball to a teammate at the free throw line. That player would then pop the ball right back to the first player as he cut to the basket, just in time for him to make an easy layup.

Molly finished tying his shoes and took up her position. She still needed to call Beth, though something about the pending conversation made her feel unsettled. She held out her hands. "Okay, I'm ready."

Joey dribbled the ball—a miniature replica of the kind used in the NBA—and pretended to pass it to a couple of invisible teammates. Then he did a sharp bounce pass to her and took off toward the basket.

In a single motion, she caught the ball and passed it back to him nice and easy. Jack had lowered the hoop so it was only nine feet high. Joey stopped as he reached it, and with impressive form, he sent the ball up and into the net. He pumped his fists into the air. "Yes! LeBron James scores again!"

"LeBron James?" Molly brushed a piece of hair back from her forehead. "I thought you were Shaq."

He shook his head. "Shaq's old, Mommy. Daddy says I shoot like LeBron James. He's the most amazing player ever. Maybe more amazing than Michael Jordan!"

"Oh . . . I see." She held out her hands. "Okay, LeBron. I'm ready for the next pass."

His giggles filled the air and soothed her soul. They played for an hour before Joey started yawning. At four years old he still took a nap. He made a few more shots, and they went inside. She read him *Yertle the Turtle*, his favorite Dr. Seuss book. Then she bent down and kissed the tip of his nose. "Have a nice nap."

The navy curtains were drawn, the baseballs and basketballs and footballs that decorated his wallpaper, cool and shadowy. She gave him Mr. Monkey, the well-loved stuffed animal he'd had since his first birthday, and then Mr. Growls. Joey tucked them in next to him. He looked at her longer than usual, straight to her heart. "Know what, Mommy?"

"What?" She studied him, her precious son.

"You're pretty." He grinned, his loose tooth hanging a little more crookedly.

Molly felt her heart light up. "Well, thank you, kind sir."

"Know what else?"

She smiled. These were the fractions of minutes—before he fell asleep—when he said the things that mattered most. When all talk of growly bears and basketball players faded and the deeper places in his soul came to life. She messed her fingers through his hair and smiled. "What?"

"You're my best friend." He thought for a second. "You and Daddy, o' course."

"Thanks, buddy." She felt a tug on her heart, the one that reminded her that he was her everything. "How come?"

He put his hand over hers and smiled. "'Cause you play with me. And that's what best friends do."

"Well." Molly kissed him on the cheek this time. "I guess that makes you my best friend, too." She tickled his stuffed bear. "And that leaves Mr. Growls with Mr. Monkey."

Joey laughed. "That's okay. Bears like monkeys."

She stood and waved good-bye. "See you in an hour."

He yawned and nodded. "'Kay, Mommy. Love you."

"Love you, too."

It was two-thirty when she walked down the hall and into the family room. Beth would be home, making sure Jonah was down for a nap. The older kids wouldn't be back from school yet. No time like now for a phone call. Molly clicked a button on the keypad at the corner of the room. The Steve Wingfield Band came to life, filling their home with the melodious background sounds of "I'll Be Seeing You." She smiled. Nothing like big-band slow songs.

She reached for the phone, but her eye caught something on the bottom shelf of the bookcase. It was an old photo album, the one Beth had made for her as a high school graduation present. She'd pulled it out the other day so she could take it to the barbecue at Beth's house, but she must've gotten distracted and forgotten it.

"Photographs and Memories," the cover read. Molly picked it up and took a seat on the sofa next to the phone. She picked up the receiver and dialed Beth's number. A busy signal sounded in her ear. Beth didn't believe in call-waiting. She said every caller deserved her full attention. Molly put the phone on the base again and turned back to the photo album.

She opened the cover. How long had it been since she'd taken a walk through their high school days? Beth had made the album for her. Beth, who was always doing thoughtful things, always so proud to be her little sister. On the inside cover she'd written something in neat, perfect handwriting. It was faded some, but she could still make it out. *Molly . . . I can't believe you're graduating. What will I do next year without you? I made you this album so you won't ever forget the fun we've had these last three years. I love you so much. Beth.*

They grew up in Orlando, Molly and Beth, the two of them one year apart in school. They ran in different circles—Beth in the social crowd, Molly with the dancers and theater types. But they found common ground on the cheer squad. The first picture was of the two of them the year Beth entered West Ridge High. They had their arms around each other's necks, silly grins plastered on their faces.

What the photo didn't show was the reason they were hugging.

Molly squinted at the photo and the years fell away. The picture was taken after homecoming game that fall, hours after one of her worst moments in high school. It was halftime, and the squad had shared a cheer with the opposing team. They were heading back to their locker room to freshen up when all ten of the West Ridge High cheerleaders stopped in their tracks.

There was Molly's boyfriend of the past year, Connor Aiken, star wide receiver, fully making out with one of the seniors from the dance team. The two were so lost in the moment, neither of them looked up or even noticed the cheerleaders passing by. All of the girls knew Connor belonged to Molly. They whispered and stared and cast pitiful looks in her direction.

Right away Beth was at her side, looping her arm through Molly's. "The guy's a jerk. I knew he was a jerk."

When they had rounded the corner, Molly couldn't take the humiliation another minute. She was stunned, unable to speak or cry or scream. She dropped her pom-poms and ran around another corner to the bike racks outside the athletic building, the darkest place she could find.

Molly looked at herself, the way she'd been back then. Even now she remembered the pain of that moment. She had loved Connor—at least she thought she did. She figured she'd stay there in the dark, crying her eyes out until the game was over. But she was alone in the darkness for only half a minute.

By the time the tears hit, Beth was by her side. "Molly . . . Oh, Molly, I'm so sorry." She put her arms around Molly's neck. "But he *is* a jerk. I always thought so."

Molly sniffed and peered at her in the darkness. "You did?"

"Yes." She made a sound that showed her level of disgust. Then she gave Molly a list of Connor's shortcomings. Ten minutes later she was still talking.

Tenderly, Molly put her hand over Beth's mouth. "Okay, little sister." She released a long sigh. "I'm going to be all right—is that what you're saying?"

"I'm saying you're the best girl in all the world, Molly." She pointed an angry finger toward the place where they'd witnessed the kissing scene. "You deserve better than that. And right now I think your life's just about to get very exciting." Beth handed Molly her pompoms. "Come on. Hold your head high. We have a game to finish."

Something about Beth, about the way she believed in her even when Molly felt ugly and worthless, gave her strength to pick up and go back onto the field. Whenever she found herself looking for Connor's number among the players, she would catch Beth's eye. Beth would shake her head and force a smile, reminding her to do the same.

After the game, Connor came looking for her. By then he'd heard the news that the entire cheer squad had caught him kissing another girl. He was panicked when he found Molly in the school parking lot. Beth was with her, but she walked a few yards ahead so the two of them could talk. Connor's apology was only just underway when Molly held up her hand. "We're done, Connor." She caught up with Beth and grinned back at him. "My life's about to get very exciting."

Before she and Beth met up with their ride that night, one of the other cheerleaders snapped their picture. Beth and Molly. Sisters and best friends.

Molly turned the page. There were several layouts of Disney pictures. The cheerleaders competed at a sports complex outside Disney World and afterward they spent two days at the parks. Even though they were locals.

She and Beth walked through the gift store on the second day, taking pictures of all the things they couldn't buy. There was a photo of the two of them wearing pointed princess hats, and another with Beth dressed as a pirate, and Molly as Tinkerbell.

A few more pages and there was the beach trip they'd taken to Sanibel Island the summer before Molly's senior year. Their parents had invited another couple, so that left Molly and Beth by themselves much of the time. One of the pictures was of the two girls standing between two guys—locals they met the second day of the trip.

Again the photo didn't tell the whole story.

That night, the boys invited them to a bonfire half a mile down the beach. Beth hadn't liked the idea from the beginning, but Molly—always the sillier, more spontaneous one—had pushed until Beth agreed. Their parents were playing bridge that night with their friends, and gave their approval without asking many questions.

Molly and Beth and the boys walked to the party, and at first their behavior seemed harmless. But then one of the boys brought them glasses of punch. Beth took a sip and spit it out on the sand. "Don't drink it, Molly. It's spiked."

The guys laughed. "Looks like your little sister's never had island punch."

"Island punch?" Molly sniffed it. "Is she right? Is there alcohol in it?"

"Of course not." One of the guys put his arm around her. "Your sister's just a worrier."

"Molly, don't!" Beth took hold of her free hand. "Let's go. We shouldn't be here."

But Molly didn't want her younger sister telling her what to do. She grinned at the boys and drank the cup of punch in a series of quick gulps. Fifteen minutes later she knew the truth. Beth was right. The drink had to have been mostly alcohol. Molly was so drunk she couldn't talk or walk straight.

There wasn't much she remembered about that night, but she found out later what happened. The guys tried to talk Molly into taking a walk with them down to the water, but Beth wouldn't let them. She took hold of Molly's arm and half carried her all the way back to the hotel. When their parents wanted to know what had happened, Beth covered for her.

The pages of the photo album hinted at stories Molly had almost forgotten about. Near the end of the book came the saddest photo of all. Molly had a guy friend, Art Goldberg, someone she'd been close to since fifth grade.

Though the two of them never dated, she could always call Art when she needed advice from a guy or just a fresh set of ears to tell her stories to.

Art hung out at the house, and Beth and her parents often teased Molly that the guy had a crush on her. Molly never saw it. She and Art were buddies, nothing more. But on the last day of Christmas break her senior year, Art's mother called with tragic news. Art and a few of his guy friends had gone up to Michigan for a snowmobile trip. Two days before his eighteenth birthday, a few of them took an afternoon run on a well-marked trail. Art was leading the way, but he took a turn too fast, flew off the machine, and hit a tree.

He died at the scene. His mother was crying on the other end of the phone. "I . . . thought you should know."

Molly remembered her reaction. She was unable to tell Art's mother how sorry she was, unable to ask for details or even hang up the phone. The pain was so great, it was like someone had cut off her right arm. She collapsed to the floor in slow motion and from somewhere in the depths of her heart she let out a deep, gut-wrenching wail that rang in her heart to this day. Their parents were at work, but Beth was reading in the other room. She came running, and when Molly could finally explain what had happened, Beth held her and rocked her for almost an hour.

In the months that followed, when Molly wanted only to go to the room they shared, crawl under the covers, and sleep away the afternoon, Beth wouldn't let her. The two of them started taking runs after school, and holding long conversations about Molly's memories of Art and how much she missed him.

Beth's perfect 4.0 grade point average slipped that semester, and she had little time for after-school activities. She devoted that much of herself to Molly, making sure Molly survived. No doubt, that's what happened. Molly had survived because Beth willed her to survive. Those were the days before Beth found God, so it wasn't about praying and reading Scripture. It was just one sister devoting herself to another so that healing could happen.

Tears filled Molly's eyes as she studied the pictures on that page. Throughout the album, there'd been shots of Art Goldberg and Molly. But this page was sort of a tribute, a collection of last moments. The first was of Art and Molly, sitting next to each other on her family's sofa, watching television. It was dated fall, her senior year—one of the last times they shared an afternoon that way. The next showed Art and her sitting in a single lounge chair near the pool in her family's backyard. This time the date was November—still plenty warm enough for parties around the pool, and probably the last time the two of them swam together.

There was a copy of Art's senior picture, and next to it Beth had written, "Art will live on, always, in the memories the two of you made together."

The last picture was taken at his memorial service. It showed Molly, dressed in her church clothes, standing at the podium, tears streaming down her face. She could never have said good-bye to Art without Beth's help. Never. Molly ran her finger over Art's senior photo. "I still miss you, friend. Why did you have to drive so fast, you big dummy?"

She wasn't quite ready to turn the page when the

phone rang. It was Beth. She knew even before she glanced at Caller ID. She picked up the receiver and clicked the On button. "Hey, you."

"Hey." Beth let out an exaggerated breath. "I thought I'd get an hour to myself, but Jonah was bouncing off the walls."

"I tried to call you earlier. It was busy."

"I know." Beth laughed. "Jonah was practicing his phone manners—something they're working on in kindergarten, I guess. Only does he tell me he's got the phone off the hook? Of course not." She paused. "So what's happening at your house?"

"Well . . ." Molly could hear the sorrow in her voice. "I was looking at that old photo album, the one you made me when I graduated from high school."

Beth's laughter faded some from her voice. "Saddest day of my life." She made a sound that was more sigh than laugh. "I wasn't sure I'd ever forgive you."

"I was looking at the page about Art Goldberg."

Beth allowed a few seconds of silence. "He was a good guy, Art."

"I never would've gotten through losing him if it weren't for you." There were tears in her voice. "I guess I'd forgotten how much you were there that year."

"It made your leaving for college that much harder."

"Yes." Molly turned the page. Almost every photo was of the two of them, Molly and Beth, inseparable. "I left the last day of August. I cried all the way to my dorm room."

"I cried every night for a month." Beth groaned. "You weren't that far away, but all of a sudden everything was different. You might as well have been halfway around the world."

Molly sniffed, working hard to keep her tone light. "I was going to get there, turn right around and come home."

"I remember." Beth's voice was quieter, as if she, too, were reliving that day. "You called that night and said it was too much—you could attend community college, stay at home."

"And you told me not to dare think of such a thing." Molly smiled, even as her tears clouded her eyes. "You reminded me of every reason I'd chosen Florida State and you told me that besides, you were looking forward to having your own room." Molly laughed. "Something about your speech gave me the strength to stay. By Christmas I was in love with the place."

"I have a confession." Beth sounded sheepish. "I didn't want my own room. It took me most of that year to figure out how to fall asleep without those talks we had every night."

"I know, Beth. I think I knew it then." Molly leaned her head back and held the phone a little tighter. "Ever notice how we weren't like normal sisters? I mean, I was the oldest and you, the youngest." She sat up and looked at another picture of the two of them. "But every time I turned around, you were looking out for me. You never, ever let me fall apart."

Beth sniffed and Molly wondered if the memories had stirred tears for her, as well. "That's because you needed me. And I needed you."

"Yes." Molly turned to the last page. There were photos of her high school graduation and the going-away party her family threw her before she left for college. "We were something else."

The sound of children's voices made it hard to hear Beth's response. Instead Molly heard questions about snacks and homework being fired at Beth from Cammie and Blain and Braden.

"Hey," Beth had to yell to be heard. "The Indians are home."

"And they're restless."

"Exactly." The noise in the background grew. "Can I call you later?"

"Sure." Molly hesitated. "Hey, Beth. I love you."

"Yep." She could hear the smile in her sister's voice. "I love you, too."

They hung up, and Molly read the words Beth had written on the final page of the photo album: *Life will take us far from here. But one day when we're all grown up, when all our questions are answered, maybe we'll be neighbors and raise our kids together. For now, I'll miss you. I'll never forget sharing a room with you. And a whole lot more. I love you, Beth.*

Molly closed the book and held it to her chest. Beth was right. Life did take them far from their Orlando home. Beth got a scholarship to the University of Washington, and both girls married in their early twenties. Molly and Jack moved to West Palm Beach, and Beth and Bill settled in Seattle. They never went longer than a week without a conversation, but nothing had compared to those first growing-up years, the days when she and Beth were inseparable.

Never for a minute had either of them really believed that one day they'd be neighbors. But here they were, a lifetime spread out before them, endless seasons raising the children they loved and living with the men of their dreams.

And she and Beth, together again, right in the middle of it all.

Molly wiped at an errant tear and put the photo album away. Life couldn't possibly get better than this. In fact, it was so good it almost frightened her. As if by recognizing the idyllic lives they lived, she might somehow jinx them. Molly blinked and headed down the hall to check on Joey. Her fears were completely unfounded. Life was amazing and getting better all the time.

It was as simple as that.

Chapter Seven

The office was in a brick building in the heart of downtown Cleveland. "Department of Children's Welfare," the sign over the front door read. Wendy held tighter to Rip's hand. She hadn't slept at all the night before, replaying in her mind again and again details about the Florida couple. Were they wrong, coming here? What they were about to do *would* be for their son's best welfare, wouldn't it?

She stopped, her high heels unsteady on the wet sidewalk. Overhead another thunderstorm was rolling in. "We're doing the right thing, aren't we?"

"Of course." Rip smiled. He'd been mostly charming since their conversation on the hallway floor a week ago. He kissed her cheek. "Back then we weren't ready to be parents. Now we are."

"Right." She nodded, and he led her up the stairs and into the building. They had contacted the department the afternoon she showed Rip the file. Allyson Bower, the social worker, was still there.

They walked up to a window and Rip spoke into the small hole in the glass. "We have an appointment with

Allyson Bower. I'm Rip Porter." He touched Wendy's elbow. "This is my wife, Wendy."

The woman at the desk checked her computer. "It'll be a few minutes." She looked at Rip. "I'll tell her you're here."

Rip thanked the woman, and he led the two of them to a pair of open chairs. There were two other people in the waiting area: a sad-looking man in his thirties and a young girl, probably no more than eighteen. Wendy shivered and leaned into Rip's arm. "I'm nervous," she whispered near his ear. "What if they don't believe us?"

"They will." Rip's upbeat tone faded a little. "Remember what I told you? Act like it's true and this'll be a cinch."

"Okay."

Wendy didn't want to disappoint him. Not when this whole thing was her fault in the first place. In the past week, Rip had grown frustrated with her a few times when they'd rehearsed the story at the dining-room table. She would become flustered or miss a piece of the story and he'd snap at her. But right away he'd calm himself down and apologize. So far the anger management, or whatever they'd taught him in prison, was working.

Besides, there was no reason to be nervous. So far the social worker seemed to believe everything she'd said.

On their first phone call to her, the woman pulled her file and seemed to remember their case. "Your husband was in prison. You gave your baby up because you were concerned for his future." The social worker stopped short of saying whether she remembered the bump on Wendy's collarbone, or the fact that Wendy had feared for her son's life if Rip ever got out of prison.

"Yes." Wendy exhaled. Rip was watching her, desperate to know which way the conversation was going. She closed her eyes. "Anyway, there's a problem. My husband, Rip Porter, was released from prison this week." She forced herself to sound weak, victimized. "All this time I thought he had signed the paperwork, the release papers. But now he says he never knew about the baby at all." She hesitated. "He wants our son back, Allyson. We both do."

A long pause filled the telephone lines. There was the sound of shuffling papers and fingers tapping on a keyboard. Finally, Allyson sighed. "Let's arrange a meeting. This is the sort of thing we should discuss in person."

"Fine." She flashed the thumbs-up sign to Rip. "When can we meet?"

They scheduled the appointment, and every day for the past week, the idea became more exciting. Their son would've gotten a great start in life by now. Any healthy child would be able to make the adjustment from one home to another—especially if the move was handled right. They could tell him that his first family was sort of a foster family. Nice people who helped out for a few years. But now he was getting the chance to live with his real family.

Yes, that would take care of any issues the child might have. Wendy stared at her hands, folded in her lap. At least she hoped so. And if it took a little longer for their son to make the adjustment, then they'd all have to be patient. Because one day he'd understand. They were doing this because they loved him, because they truly thought he'd be better off with them.

His real parents.

A door opened and there was Allyson Bower. She looked the same as she had five years ago. The woman was in her mid-forties, tall and thin with hazel eyes. She wore a no-nonsense look, one that said she wasn't there to make friends. She did her job strictly on behalf of the children.

"Wendy?" Allyson gave her a wary look, and then shifted her attention to Rip and back again. Her tone fell somewhere between anger and impatience. "I'm ready to talk with you and your husband."

Rip took the lead. He met Allyson in the doorway and pumped her hand like a used-car salesman. "I'm Rip Porter." He grinned, pouring on all the charm he was capable of. "Thanks for meeting with us."

"Allyson Bower." She stood eye-to-eye with Rip. She didn't smile. "Follow me."

The knots in Wendy's stomach tightened. Allyson hadn't seemed so intimidating before. Wendy held onto Rip's arm and tried to remember her story. Dropping off the papers with the guards, getting them back signed, the long silence between her and Rip, figuring out that another prisoner must've done the deed, maybe as a trick.

Allyson opened the door to a small office and directed them to two chairs opposite a large wooden desk. A single folder sat neatly on top. Allyson sat in her chair, folded her hands, and rested them on the file. Once Rip and Wendy were seated, she looked at each of them for a long while. Then she drew a tired breath. "You realize what you're asking me to do?"

Across from Allyson, Rip didn't blink. "There's been a mistake, Mrs. Bower. We're asking you to get our son back for us."

"At this point"—she opened the file—"he's spent nearly five years as someone else's son." She looked at Wendy. "You picked the couple, remember?"

"I do." Wendy slid her chair closer to Rip's. "We never meant things to turn out this way."

Allyson studied the first page of the file for a while and shook her head. "Before we take this another step, I'm asking if you've considered the turmoil and devastation this could cause your son." She folded her hands again. Her eyes held a silent plea. "I've read the reports from the social worker in Florida. Your son is doing very well. Taking him from the only home he's known could cause him permanent damage."

Rip crossed his legs and leaned hard on the arm of his chair. He gave a brief, exaggerated laugh. "Making things right will be hard on everyone, Mrs. Bower." He lifted his hands and dropped them again. "But the boy's a child. A very young child." He looked at Wendy, nodded a few times, and turned his attention back to the social worker. "My wife and I think he'll be fine after he adjusts."

Allyson couldn't have looked more surprised if Rip had said he wanted to take their son to planet Mars. "The boy will not be fine, Mr. Porter. He is at an extremely impressionable age. He is excelling in every possible way." Her voice grew louder, and she brought it back down. "Removing him from his home is a decision I highly recommend against."

Rip must've seen that he had the edge. "You recommend against it." He pointed at her and then lowered his hand. "But it isn't up to you, isn't that right?" He nodded to the file on the desk. "If someone forged my name, then my rights were denied and the boy belongs to me."

A look of defeat washed over Allyson's face. She returned her attention to the file. Without looking up, she drew a slow breath. "So what you're saying is, if we can prove your name was forged on the paperwork, you want us to begin the process of having the boy removed from his adoptive home and placed into yours, with you and your wife." Her eyes lifted to Rip's. "Is that right?"

"Yes." Rip crossed his arms. "We're willing to deal with our son's adjustment."

The social worker tapped the file. "Fine. Let's look at the paperwork. Explain to me how your name might've been forged." She stared straight at Wendy. "Obviously if there is a forgery and we figure out who signed your name, this department will prosecute to the fullest extent of the law."

Wendy felt her palms get sweaty. She looked at Rip and back to Allyson. "That would be good. Prosecuting whoever did this." She gave a serious nod. "This is a terrible thing."

"Right." Allyson never broke eye contact. "So tell me how this happened. I have in my notes that I instructed you to take the documents to the prison and have your husband sign them."

"Yes." Wendy looked at Rip. "That's what I did."

Allyson raised her brow and pulled a notepad close. She picked up a pen and waited.

"Go ahead, honey." Rip motioned to Allyson. There was a warning in his eyes that only Wendy could read. *This is it. . . . Don't mess up.*

"Okay." She cleared her throat and leaned forward. Her eyes were entirely focused on Allyson. She clenched her fists and kept them tight against her body, out of sight.

"I did what you asked. I took the papers to the prison." She blinked. "My husband and I weren't exactly on speaking terms. I gave the guard at the desk the paperwork and a note explaining the situation. I was giving the baby up for adoption."

Across from her, Allyson scribbled something on the pad of paper. She glanced up. "Go ahead."

"I was very clear that the package was supposed to go to Rip Porter."

"See," Rip cut in. "It happened more than once where a guard would pass the mail to another guard and a few pieces would get delivered to the wrong inmate." He gave her a troubled smile. "We've talked about it, Wendy and me. That's all we can figure."

Allyson stopped writing. "So you think the guard gave the package to someone else."

Rip pointed at himself. "I know I didn't get it."

"And I know I gave it to the guard to give to Rip."

Allyson gave a long look, first to Wendy and then to Rip. "You're sure you never saw the paperwork."

"Never." Rip sounded convincing, because at least that part was the truth. He hadn't seen the papers.

Allyson studied her notepad and then wrote something else. "Okay, Wendy, what happened next?"

Wendy's palms grew even sweatier. She wiped at them with her fingertips. *This is it, make it sound good.* She steadied herself. "I went back a week later and the package was waiting for me at the guard desk. I checked the papers before I left." She shrugged one slim shoulder. "I didn't look real hard, but everything seemed right. How would I have known it wasn't Rip's signature I was looking at?"

"Most people recognize their spouse's signature." Allyson's answer was quick. "Wouldn't you agree?"

"Of course." She tried to sound indignant, as if she resented the social worker doubting her for any reason. "Rip's signature isn't real easy to read, and neither was this one. It looked close enough."

"So you turned in the paperwork." Allyson stared at her. "And until your husband was released from prison last week you believed that he'd signed off on the adoption."

"Yes." She felt her hands relax. *Was it that easy?* "That's what I believed."

They spent the next ten minutes helping Allyson understand that Rip and Wendy truly hadn't had more than a handful of awkward visits over the next four years, and that Wendy had been too disturbed by the adoption to bring up the baby when they were together.

"Out of sight, out of mind," Wendy finally said. "That's the way I figured it would always be. A mother would go crazy thinking all the time about a baby she gave up."

Rip reached over, took her hand and squeezed it. The hint of a smile on his lips told her she'd done well. He was pleased with her.

Finally Allyson had Rip sign several papers, swearing under penalty of law that he had known nothing about the adoption and that he hadn't signed the paperwork. There were other papers, and a sheet he had to sign several times so that a handwriting analyst could verify that the signature on the adoption documents truly wasn't his.

There was talk then about Rip's domestic violence charge and the counseling and rehabilitation he'd received in prison. "I'm a different man today, Mrs. Bower." He sat a little straighter. "I learned anger management. I'm ready to be a father."

"Yes." Allyson looked disgusted. "I'm sure."

When the meeting was over, Allyson stood and pointed them to the door. "As long as the handwriting analysis matches what you've told me, I'll have no choice. I'll conduct a home study with you and your wife at your house. Then I'll take the issue before a local judge, and most likely he will grant you custody, Mr. Porter." She sounded tired, defeated. "After that, I'll contact the social worker in Florida and we'll begin the process of removing the boy from his current home and placing him in yours."

"Hey, thanks for your time." Rip took hold of Wendy's hand and headed for the door. "We really appreciate your—"

"Don't." Allyson held up her hand. "I must say . . ." Her eyes were angrier than before. "I've never had a placement reversed because of a technicality. Almost always the system works on behalf of the child. But if you win custody of your son, Mr. Porter, I will be most certain that the system has failed." She clenched her teeth. "I wanted you to know that."

"Listen, that's none of your—" He stopped short.

Wendy held her breath. For a moment it looked like Rip might explode. "Honey . . ." She squeezed his hand, and suddenly he seemed to remember where he was and what was happening.

He frowned. "I'm sorry you feel that way, Mrs. Bower. Maybe when this is all over, you'll change your mind."

Allyson looked like she hadn't heard him. She picked

up the folder, turned, and filed it in the top drawer of a cabinet.

Rip didn't make another attempt. He nodded to Wendy and led the way through the door and into the hallway. When the door closed behind them, Rip eased his arms around his wife. "You were perfect." He swung her in a full circle. "He's as good as ours. They know where he is, and he's doing great."

"I'm so glad it's over." Wendy felt faint, anxious for the fresh air outside. They walked to the end of the hall, far from Allyson's office. She stopped and faced Rip. "She knew we were lying, don't you think? I mean, I kept waiting for her to tell us to go home and never come back."

"She couldn't do that." Rip's smile stretched the full width of his face. "I didn't sign those papers, and she can tell. No matter what she believes, it was wrong that I lost custody of my son."

"Yeah." Wendy pulled a piece of gum from her purse and popped it in her mouth. "I need a drink."

"Me, too." He wiped his brow and led her through the waiting room and outside onto the front steps. "Let's stop and get a twelve-pack." He kissed her hard on her mouth. "We have a lot to celebrate." He skipped down the steps, turned and took her hand, making sure her high heels didn't cause her to fall. A dreamy look filled his eyes. "I'll bet he's something else, that boy of ours." They linked arms as they walked to the car. "Everything's going to work out."

Wendy smiled. He was right. The meeting had gone better than they hoped. But somewhere inside her there was just the tiniest seed of concern. Maybe it was because of the social worker's warning early in the meeting. Allyson didn't think the move would be good for their son. She said he might never recover from it. And then there was the last thing she'd said—that if they got custody the system would've failed the boy. Whatever it was, it took the edge off the victory, and even that night when Wendy and Rip were halfway through the twelve-pack, the feeling most intense in her heart wasn't one of joy and excitement.

It was one of doubt.

Allyson Bower was tired.

She'd done everything she knew to get her mind off work. It was early summer—her favorite time of year—and the thunderstorms from earlier in the day had passed. As soon as she got home, she changed clothes and headed outside to her flower garden. Petunias and gardenias, roses and daffodils. All of them were thriving and would continue to thrive if she kept up on the weeds.

For the first hour after work, that's just what she did.

But with every weed, every flower, she could see the little boy's face, the pictures in his file. The ones she wouldn't show Rip and Wendy Porter until a judge ruled in their favor. Finally she tried something else to clear her mind. She went inside and checked her baking cupboard. Milk, cream, sugar, bananas. All the ingredients were there. Maybe if she made her famous banana pudding the boys would love it, and that would keep her too busy to think about the Porter case.

She pulled her recipe from the old box with the fading flowers. Each card was alphabetized, so she immediately found the one she was looking for. It took fifteen minutes to make the batter, and while the pudding was in the oven, she helped her boys with their homework. Travis, fifteen, had questions about lowest common denominators and factoring, and Taylor, seven, was trying to understand double-digit addition. More than enough to keep Allyson's mind distracted. Just before dinner, Tavia, her oldest, stopped by on her way home from work. She brought little Harley with her, Allyson's only grandchild. An hour of talk about Legos and dinosaurs and the chaos of fixing tortillas, beans, and rice with Harley underfoot, and Allyson wanted to think she'd put her work aside.

But it was impossible.

After the kids were in bed, she popped in a video of Alabama football highlights from the previous season, but even then she was distracted. Finally she clicked the Off button on the television, turned out the lights, and stared at the ceiling.

How could they do it?

The boy was absolutely perfect. He was ahead of his class in preschool, well-adjusted in every way possible. The latest report showed that relatives of the adoptive mother had recently moved to West Palm Beach. That meant the boy had an aunt and uncle and possibly cousins in the area.

She hadn't been lying to the Porters earlier that day. To tear him away from that environment truly would be devastating. She turned onto her side and stared through the sheer curtains to the streetlight outside. Something about their story didn't ring true. Even if a prison guard gave the packet of documents to the wrong prisoner, why would that prisoner forge Rip's name?

If it was a lie, it was a careful one. The way the story went, it didn't matter why someone would do such a thing. The culprit was nameless, faceless. Short of interviewing every inmate at the prison four years ago, there was no way to find out who might've received the package and forged Rip's name.

Allyson suspected it wasn't a prisoner at all, but Wendy Porter herself. She'd documented the conversation she'd had with the woman in the hospital four years ago. And she'd read it several times that day, both before and after the meeting with the Porters.

Wendy Porter had been afraid of Rip. She hadn't wanted him to come home from prison and release his rage on her baby son. That's the reason she gave him up. At the time Allyson had asked the woman whether Rip would have a problem signing the papers, and Wendy's answer had been quick. Definitely not.

But did that really make sense?

The branches in the trees outside her window swayed gently, casting moving shadows on her bedroom floor. If the man was abusive, and if he followed the profile of most domestic-violence perpetrators, he would never have signed away his rights to a son. Abusers tend to have a strong sense of ownership. It's at the root of why they are abusive in the first place. They see people as objects to be owned and manipulated. When a person doesn't respond correctly, the abuser unleashes on that person as a way of keeping his possession in line. Abusive people are very aware of their possessions.

Especially their wives and children.

Allyson breathed out long and slow. She could put the pressure on Wendy, make her take a lie-detector test or have her handwriting scrutinized to see if it might be possible that she—and not an erroneous prisoner—forged Rip Porter's name.

But what was the point?

If her theory was correct, they could prosecute Wendy, maybe even send her to prison for a few years. But the boy would still belong to Rip. And that was the one part of the story that did ring true—until he'd been released from prison, Rip Porter knew nothing about having a son. The name on the paperwork did, indeed, look different from the signature he'd supplied them that morning.

So how would it help having Wendy sent away?

If Rip was going to get custody, if the boy had to leave his home and start a new life in another state with people he didn't know, then Wendy should be part of the formula. The boy would need a mother, wouldn't he? Someone to watch out for him if Rip's rage ever returned?

No wonder sleep wouldn't come.

By tomorrow afternoon she'd have her answer about Rip's handwriting, whether the county expert thought his name had been forged. Then the judge would follow the established protocol for a situation like this. He'd grant custody to Rip and Wendy. And in a very short time, the boy's idyllic life would come to a screeching halt.

She closed her eyes and pictured her own children. Tavia with little Harley . . . Travis . . . Taylor. How would they respond if someone called and said that life as they knew it was over? That they would have to leave and go live with another family, never to look back again?

Allyson did not cry often. She had seen too much, gotten too hard to get emotional over every case that didn't turn out right. Usually it was the temporary custody, the times when a child was making progress with a foster parent only to be placed once more with a natural parent—a drug user or rehabilitated convict. Heartache was part of the job.

But now tears spilled from her eyes and onto her pillow.

Something about this case made her think of her own father, the man she'd loved and lost to cancer so many years ago. A series of sobs shook her. "Daddy . . . I still miss you. Tell me what to do." It wasn't right. Somewhere in Florida, a little boy who had known from birth a very special relationship with his parents was likely going to lose them both. Not because of cancer. But because the system was about to fail him utterly.

And that—more than anything that had come across her clean desk in the past decade—was enough to make her weep.

Chapter Eight

Beth sat next to Molly on the bench that faced the park swings. Joey and Jonah were racing, seeing who could swing the highest.

"I love this." Beth breathed in through her nose and smiled. "Those two boys are going to be best friends." She glanced at Molly. "Can't you just feel it?"

"Yes." Molly leaned forward and put her elbows on her knees. "Every time they're together."

The older kids were riding their bikes on the path that circled the park. School was out, and it was the middle of June. Humidity had hit—but not to the point of being unbearable. Blue skies, eighty degrees, and a light breeze made the South Florida afternoon feel perfect. The heat from earlier in the month had eased, and they all looked forward to their twice-weekly morning visits to the park. That morning Beth had called Molly, the way she'd done every Tuesday and Thursday since they unloaded the moving van. "Up for the park?"

Molly laughed. "Joey's been bugging me about it since he woke up. Let's bring a picnic."

Already the kids had been playing for almost an hour.

Beth leaned back. "Know what I was thinking?"

"Uh-oh." Molly looked over her shoulder at Beth and winced. "This isn't about church, is it?"

The question hurt. Beth hadn't brought up church since the barbecue; she'd made a promise to stay away from the topic. She felt her smile fade. "Thanks."

"What?" Molly was quick with an apologetic tone. She put her hand on Beth's shoulder. "Hey, don't get mad. I'm sorry." She giggled. "I'm just teasing. You've been very good about the whole church thing."

"Okay, then. Give me a little credit."

"I will." Molly angled herself so she was facing Beth. "What were you thinking?"

Beth took a minute to transition. When she spoke, some of her enthusiasm was gone. "I was thinking how the two of us were a lot like Joey and Jonah. When we were little, I mean."

Molly straightened and leaned back against the bench. She watched the boys, how Joey encouraged Jonah, spouting a series of pep talks and instructions. "Yeah. I can see that." She laughed. "Joey *is* sort of bossy."

"Not bossy." Beth angled her head, her eyes on the boys. "He cares about Jonah. Like he's personally responsible for Jonah's well-being."

Molly looked at her. "I was like that with you?"

"When we were little, yes." Beth crossed her ankles and stretched out her legs. "I can remember when we were learning to ride our bikes." She giggled, the hurt from Molly's earlier remark entirely gone. "Remember those burnt orange bikes with the white stripes on the sides?"

"And the white tassels flying from the handlebars?"

"Right." Beth looked up and watched a pair of blue jays land in a maple tree twenty yards away. "Anyway, you were seven and I was five, I think. You were learning to ride a bike, so I wanted to learn, too. It didn't matter if I was young."

"We had training wheels, right?"

"Right, but that summer Dad took them off." Beth could see them, scared to death about the prospect of riding two-wheelers. "Anyway, he worked with you first and then, I don't know, he must've gotten a phone call or something. He told you to keep practicing. He'd be out in a minute to teach me."

"Oh, yeah." Molly faced her again. "I remember now. As soon as he was in the house, I climbed off my bike and ran to you."

"Right. You said you didn't want to ride without me." Beth laughed and looked at the boys again. "Instead of practicing, you ran alongside me and after a few runs I was riding like a pro."

"But when I climbed back on my bike, I got about three wobbly feet and crashed to the ground."

Beth giggled. "Exactly." She watched the boys slow down, jump off the swings, and run for the merry-go-round. Joey was leading the way. "You weren't bossy. You were just looking out for me."

"The way you looked out for me when we were older."

"Yeah." Beth smiled at her. "Like that, I guess."

Just then the boys came running toward them, each shouting and pointing at the other. Jonah got his words out first. "He won't let me have a turn pushing the merry-go-round! He says I have to stay still and enjoy the ride."

"Joey . . . that's not very nice." Molly brushed her

knuckles against her son's face. "What have we taught you about sharing?"

"Yeah, but I'm taller than him, Mommy." Joey pointed back at the merry-go-round. "I can push 'cause I'm a big boy. Jonah's a little boy."

"Am not!" Jonah stuck his tongue out at Joey. "I'm older than you! So you're a little boy, Joey!"

"Mom . . ." Joey held out his hands, pleading with Molly. "It's better to ride, anyway. I'm just trying to be nice."

"Why don't you boys take turns?" Beth patted Jonah on the back. "You're both big enough to push. Let's see how that works out."

They looked hesitant, but they ran off anyway. Halfway there, Joey tapped Jonah on the shoulder and stuck his tongue out. "There," they could hear him say. "That's a payback."

Both women laughed. "Of course, there was plenty of that between us, too." Beth sorted through her lunch bag for an apple. "I remember the time when the dog ate the head off your Barbie. We were maybe ten and twelve. Remember that?"

"How could I forget? I stole your Barbie head to replace mine and tried to pretend like nothing was wrong."

"Only my Barbie had a headband that matched her dress." Beth took a bite of her apple and chuckled. "Must have been pretty easy for Mom to solve that one."

"I never was a very good liar."

"No."

The clouds were gathering faster, darkening the sky. They'd had thunderstorms nearly every day since their family landed in West Palm Beach, and today's forecast was for more of the same. "Looks like a storm."

"Better move this picnic to my house." Molly stood and collected her things—the lunch bag and the mesh net with Joey's sand toys. She motioned to the older kids. "Want me to tell them?"

"Thanks." Beth grabbed her bag and peered at the sky. Lightning pierced the closest clouds. "We better hurry. I'll go start the car. The kids can throw their bikes in the back." She cupped her hands around her mouth. "Come on, boys! Let's go—storm's coming."

Joey and Jonah hesitated, and for a moment it seemed they might complain about having to leave. But instead Joey jumped off the merry-go-round and tore across the sand for the grassy field adjacent to the play area. "Come on! Look at all the dandelions!"

"Just a minute." Molly jogged toward Beth's older kids and yelled for them to come to the car. Then she turned back to Joey. Just a month ago, the entire grassy field had been dotted with bright yellow dandelions. But now the ground looked like a million fuzz balls. When the boys raced across the field, they stirred up a cloud of seeds. Joey and Jonah giggled and ran back to Beth and Molly.

"There's a kabillion dandelions at this park, did you know that, Mommy?" Joey took Molly by the hand. "A super-kabillion."

"Yeah." Jonah skipped in alongside Beth. "They're fun to race through."

In the distance, another bolt of lightning flashed across the sky. "Okay, boys." Beth picked up her pace. "Time to run."

They piled into Beth's van just as the first raindrops hit the windshield. "Whew." Beth slid her key into the ignition. "That was close."

The older kids took the backseat. "I had the most laps." Cammie sounded proud of herself.

"Did not." Blain made a face at her. "I lapped you three times."

The debate continued. In the rearview mirror Beth could see Joey staring wide-eyed out the window. "I love storms."

"Except at night." Molly gave Beth a wry look. "He's in bed with us as soon as the first clap of thunder hits."

Joey leaned forward. "Yeah, Mommy, but that's because storms are 'posed to be shared."

"Right." Jonah nodded, his expression serious. "I like sharing storms with my mommy and daddy, too."

The conversation remained comical all the way to Molly's house, through her garage, and into the kitchen. While they spread out their lunches on the dining room table, Beth savored how good life felt. Her sister was once again her best friend. And their little boys were on their way to the same sort of friendship.

Still, there was something missing, something Beth didn't dare bring up. And as Molly went to check the phone messages, Beth said a silent prayer. *God . . . please give Molly a reason to need You. I won't bring it up . . . so give her a reason, God. Please.*

The kids were situated at the table, but the message light was flashing on the answering machine. Probably a salesperson. Jack would've called on her cell phone, and with school out there weren't many calls that needed her attention. Still . . . she wanted to check.

A burst of thunder rattled the windows, but Molly didn't mind. Lightning storms were a part of life in Florida. She'd grown up with them, and by now she rather liked them. They made her lakeside home feel safe and warm, like a cocoon against the elements.

She pressed the message button and waited.

"You have one new message," the automated voice announced. "First message, sent today at 10:31 a.m."

The message started. "Hello . . ." The caller hesitated. "This is Allyson Bower. I'm a social worker in Ohio, the one who handled the placement of your son."

Immediately Molly hit the volume button, bringing the sound down so that it was barely audible. Joey knew nothing about his adoption. Not yet. They were waiting until he started kindergarten to tell him something simple and straightforward.

Across the room, the message had caught Beth's attention. She stood and looked at Molly as if to say, "What's the problem?"

Molly waved her off and lowered her head so she could make out the rest of the woman's words. "I tried to contact the social worker in Florida who handled your case, but she's not with the department any longer." The woman released what sounded like a painful breath.

"Anyway," the message continued, "something's come up. I need to talk to you as soon as possible. I

leave the office at two o'clock, so if you or your husband could call back this afternoon or tomorrow morning, I can update you about what's going on." The
woman gave her name again and a number. Molly
stopped the machine and saved the message.

Her heart slammed about in her chest like a frenzied
pinball. What was the woman talking about? What
could possibly have come up? The adoption file had
been closed since Joey was six months old. The paperwork was signed, the courts had agreed, and that was all
there was to it.

So who was this Allyson Bower, and how had she
gotten their number?

Beth was at her side, her arm around Molly's shoulders. "Molly, you're white as a sheet." She led Molly to
a barstool. "What is it?"

"Joey . . ." Molly couldn't finish her sentence. She
pointed at the boys. "Joey."

"He's fine, Molly. I took out the sandwiches and got
them set up. Don't worry about him."

Molly blinked, and her trance suddenly lifted. Why
was she panicking? It was only a phone call, right? She
straightened and looked at Beth. "That was a social
worker . . . from Ohio. Something's come up. We have
to . . . have to call her back."

"Okay." Beth didn't look worried. "There's probably
some update they need for his file. Isn't that normal
with state adoptions?"

"An update?" Molly's heartbeat found a more normal
rhythm. "The social workers here in Florida do the
updates. Once a year until Joey's five. After that, it's up

to us to provide information for his file, for the . . . the birth parents."

"So maybe the social services in Ohio didn't get the update this time." Beth still didn't look worried. "Isn't that possible?"

Molly closed her eyes. Yes, that had to be it. Something missing from the file. What else could a social worker from Ohio want with her and Jack? The adoption was as neat as it could be. No loose ends, wasn't that what her Florida social worker had told her? But a call like this could mean . . .

She looked at Joey, blond hair and laughing eyes, taking the top slice of bread off his sandwich and licking the strawberry jam. She felt her shoulders relax a little. He was fine; he was theirs. She wouldn't let herself think about it. She'd known very little about Joey's birth mother. The woman wasn't on drugs, and she hadn't been a drinker. The biggest problem was her husband, a man in prison for domestic violence. According to her social worker, the woman had given Joey up for his safety. She had picked Molly and Jack after looking through profiles from a dozen different states.

There couldn't possibly be a problem.

Beth was saying something, but Molly couldn't focus. "You're right. A technicality, something missing in the file." She forced a quiet laugh. "I panicked for nothing." She looked at Beth. "We made sure everything was right. No loose ends. That's what they told us. No loose ends. Nothing to make this a problem down the road when Joey was—"

"Molly!" Beth took hold of her arm and gave her a

shake. "Shhh!" She looked behind her at the boys. "Joey'll hear you."

Molly held up her hands. "I'm fine." She lowered her voice. Had she been talking loud? She steadied herself against the back of a barstool. "Sorry. Everything's fine."

"Okay, then let it go." Beth's voice was urgent. "Come on."

She searched Beth's eyes, frantic for a reason to stave off the sudden, intense fear coming at her again. "Nobody would ever . . ." Her voice slipped to a whisper. "Ever try to take Joey from us." She faced her sister. "Would they?"

"No." Beth shook her head quickly. "Definitely not. The adoption was final years ago."

Yes, of course. Molly exhaled long and slow. All the reasons that had reassured her moments ago ran through her mind again. The adoption was final years ago. No one would question it after all this time. She ordered her heartbeat to slow down again.

"Mommy . . ." Suddenly Joey was at her side, tugging on her sleeve. "Are you sick?"

Molly let go of Beth and sat a little straighter. She looked down at Joey. "No, honey." She was still catching her breath. "Mommy's fine."

"How come you're not eating lunch with us?" He pointed back to the table. "It was a'posed to be a picnic for everyone. Even the moms."

"Right." Beth patted Joey's back and sent him in the direction of the table. "We'll be there in a minute."

"I'm on my second half, Mommy." Jonah held up his sandwich. "Hurry, okay?"

Another clap of thunder shook the house. Molly inhaled sharply and gave a quick shake of her head. "You're right." She stood and looked at Beth. "I won't worry about it."

"Good call." Beth spoke the words with certainty and confidence. "It's nothing—I'm sure."

"Right." She looked at the boys in the next room. Her body felt unsteady, but her breathing was normal now. "I guess I just have a phobia of social workers."

"Yeah." Beth gave her the cuckoo sign. "I can see that."

Molly held out her arms and Beth did the same. They came together in a hug that righted Molly's world. When she pulled back, she grinned at her sister. "What would I do without you?"

Beth smiled, and in that single smile Molly could see a lifetime of moments like this one. "The good news is, we won't have to find out."

"You're right."

"Okay then . . ." Beth took Molly by the hand and led her to the kitchen table. "I think we have a picnic to attend." She slid in next to Jonah.

"Yeah." Joey patted the seat next to him, and when Molly sat down, he put his arms around her neck and kissed the tip of her nose. "Before it's all finished."

Her appetite wasn't what it might've been, but Molly put on a good act. While the lightning and thunder continued outside, they ate their peanut butter sandwiches and carrot sticks and drank their juice packs.

Jonah was impressed with the way Beth could take tiny bites from the carrot, leaving a toothpick-thin center before popping it into her mouth. "I think you're a champion, Mommy."

"Yes." Beth raised her hands in the air and took a bow. "When it comes to carrots, no one can eat 'em like me."

Joey laughed when Molly tried and the carrot cracked in half. "You're not very good at it, Mommy."

"I guess not." She giggled. For the first time since getting the message, she felt her fears subside. Gus had been sleeping by the door, but now he stretched and came to sit between the two of them. Molly tossed her broken carrot pieces onto her plate. "I think Gus could do a better job than me."

"Hey, Gus-boy . . . I'm almost done with my picnic; then I can play." Joey cooed at the dog. "Can he have a carrot, Mommy? Please?"

Gus loved it when Joey fed him carrots. Either that, or he just loved Joey. "Okay. But don't let him lick your fingers. Not while you're still eating."

The picnic came to an end, and Beth and her kids went home. Before she left, she shook her finger at Molly and gave her a look that said, *Don't think about it.* Everything was going to be okay.

Molly nodded. But after Beth was gone, she sat in the living room, watching Joey and Gus. The boy would sit on the floor next to the dog for hours, his head resting on Gus's back. Every now and then Gus would release a sigh and cast a look at Joey as if to say, *Hey, best friend, don't ever grow up.* Gus was eight years old and not as spry as he once was. But when the storm let up, he'd match Joey step for step in a race across the backyard.

Joey ran his hand along the dog's neck. "We went on the merry-go-round today, Gus."

The dog lifted his head and cast a slow look at Joey.

"I know." Joey's sing-song voice filled the house. "I wish you were there, too." He thought for a minute. "You couldn't have pushed very good, but I bet you could hold on tight. Know why?"

The dog yawned.

"That's right." He patted Gus's front paws. "'Cause you've got good claws in your feet."

After a while, Gus put his head down and fell asleep. Joey lifted one furry ear. "You sleeping, Gus?"

When the dog didn't stir, Joey popped up and wandered toward Molly. Another clap of thunder made him hurry his steps. "Is it naptime?" He looked worried about the possibility.

"An hour ago." Molly lifted him into her lap and situated him so his legs stuck out to one side. "How 'bout we take a nap together on the couch today?"

"Yay! I like when we do that."

She stood him up, and stretched out on her side. There was still plenty of room for him, and he hopped up, cuddling against her as he closed his eyes. "Know why this is perfect, Mommy?"

"Why?" She kissed the side of his face. The social worker's message played in her mind again. It was nothing. A technicality. Something for his file. That's what Beth said.

"Because . . ." He opened his eyes so he could see her. He smelled like peanut butter and grass and Gus all at the same time. "Storms are 'posed to be shared."

"Yes, buddy." She held him a little closer. "They are."

This storm and any storm. As Joey fell asleep she hoped with all her heart that Beth was right. And that in the coming days the thunder and lightning outside would be the only type of storm they'd have to face.

Chapter Nine

Jack made the call early the next morning before work.

As soon as he'd gotten home from the office, Molly told him about the message from the social worker and he listened to it himself. He agreed with Beth. This Allyson Bower probably was missing a detail in Joey's file somewhere, a bit of information that was part of regularly updating the adoption files.

Still, the hour of wrestling on the floor with Joey and carrying him around on his shoulders like King Kong and reading him *Finding Nemo* before bed all took on extra significance. Joey's laughter filling the living room, the feel of his little-boy hands tucked safely in Jack's own, the smell of shampoo in his damp hair after bathtime. Jack was aware of every detail.

The boy was everything to them, the heartbeat of their home.

So even though he believed what Beth had told Molly, that the call wasn't important, that they'd laugh about it tomorrow, Jack had trouble sleeping. Couldn't the woman have left a more detailed message? Didn't she know how they'd take it if she told them something had come up?

By seven the next morning, Jack was ready to call the woman and be done with the situation. Joey was still asleep down the hall, and Molly sat on the bed beside him as he dialed the number. The radio played something soft and jazzy in the background. Molly gripped his knee with one hand and the bed with the other.

"It's nothing," he whispered to her as the ringing began on the other line. He checked his watch. Five minutes. That's all the call should take. Then they could wake up Joey, have cereal and bananas, and Jack would leave for work. Just like any other day.

On the second ring, a woman answered. "Allyson Bower, Child Welfare Department."

Jack's heart beat hard and then skipped a beat. "Hello." He used his business tone. "This is Jack Campbell, returning your call about our son, Joey." He paused. "You mentioned something had come up?"

On the other end, the woman hesitated. "Yes." She sounded tired or frustrated. He wasn't sure which. "Mr. Campbell, I'm afraid I have some bad news."

He didn't want to repeat what the woman said. Not with Molly sitting beside him, taking in every word. He pinched the bridge of his nose. "How's that?"

"Well, it's a long story. A few weeks ago I took a call from Joey's birth parents. Apparently his father was recently released from prison, and only then did he learn that his wife had given up their son for adoption. We had the paperwork examined, and the man's telling the truth. His name was forged on the release document.

Which"— she paused—"I'm sorry to say means Joey's adoption documents are fraudulent."

His heart tripped over itself. What had she said? *No! No, it isn't possible—this isn't happening.* He made a fist and pressed it to his brow.

"What?" Molly's eyes were wide, terrified. "What's she saying?"

He shook his head and motioned for her to wait a minute. The woman's words were swirling in his brain. He closed his eyes tight. Never was he at a loss for words. He made his living as a smooth-talking sales-man, after all. But here, now, even if he could think of something to say, he wouldn't be able to form the words. Nothing she was saying made sense. He reached over and hit the radio switch, killing the music. There. He needed silence.

The social worker was still trying to explain. "We're not sure who forged the birth father's signature, but I'm afraid it doesn't matter." She sounded beyond frustrated. "I'm so sorry, Mr. Campbell. I took the matter before a judge and the ruling was black and white." She paused. "Permanent custody of Joey has been reverted back to the boy's parents, with a shared custody arrangement that will play out over the next few months."

Jack clutched his throat, his eyes still shut. This time the words came despite his inability to think or reason. "Shared custody?" Next to him he could feel Molly los-ing control.

"There'll be a series of supervised visits, where Joey will spend part of a weekend with his birth parents and then return back to you and your wife." Every word sounded difficult for the woman. "This will happen every few weeks, and on the fourth visit custody of Joey will be turned over completely."

Jack was on his feet. He made a sound that was part anger, part disbelief. "Just like that? What about our attorney, our voice in the matter?"

Molly stood and began to pace. "No . . . no, this isn't happening." Her face was a pasty gray. She stopped and searched his eyes for answers, but he held his finger up and mouthed, "Wait!"

The social worker was going on. "Mr. Campbell, I'm sorry. In a case where adoption papers have been fraudulently signed, the law is clear-cut." She hesitated. "I was able to get just that one concession for you."

Concession? Concession about the custody of their son? Maybe this was the part where she'd tell him it was all a mistake and that the judge had changed his mind and tossed out the whole possibility of taking Joey away from them. Jack massaged his brow and tried to find a center of gravity. Everything was out of order, off balance. It was a nightmare, that was it. Joey had been theirs for almost five years. What judge in his right mind would grant custody of their son to someone else?

He forced himself to focus. "What . . . what concession?"

"The shared custody I told you about." She stopped, as if maybe he would express some sort of gratitude. He didn't, and she continued. "That's the best I could do."

Jack grabbed a deep breath and hung his head. Something inside him clicked, and he found center once again. "I'm sorry, what was your name?"

"Allyson Bower. I'm with the Child Welfare Department in Ohio."

"Yes, Mrs. Bower, well, I'm afraid your best isn't good enough in this case. I'll be contacting my attorney later this morning and we'll fight this as far and long as we have to fight it." He gathered his strength. Handling the social worker was nothing to the task that lay ahead—explaining the situation to Molly.

"Mr. Campbell, I'm afraid there's no further legal recourse in this matter, and that seeing your attorney would be a waste of—"

"Thank you, Mrs. Bower. My attorney will be in touch with you."

The minute he hung up, Molly grabbed his elbow, her eyes darting as she searched his face. "What is it? Tell me! Why do we have to call our attorney?" Her words came sharp and fast, saturated with a crazed fear. A fear he'd never heard in her voice before now.

Jack looked at the woman he loved more than life, and in that instant he would've given anything to make the entire situation go away. Somehow, by opening his mouth and answering her question, the sudden crisis they faced would be unquestionably real. But what choice did he have? He had to tell her; there was no way around it.

He faced her and put his hands on her shoulders. "Joey's birth father never signed the adoption papers." The words sounded like they belonged to someone else, as if any minute he should blink and apologize and none of what he was saying would be anything more than a bad joke.

"He never signed them?" Molly began to shake. Tears built up in her eyes. "So what does . . . what does that mean?"

"It means the adoption papers are fraudulent." He felt the tears welling in his own eyes, but at the same time a fierce anger began to build.

"Fraudulent?" The word was little more than a painful whisper. Her chest began working hard, her breaths coming twice as fast as before. "Meaning what, Jack? Just tell me!"

"Molly, calm down." His anger was taking the upper hand. This was all a mistake. He had access to some of the best attorneys in South Florida. Everything would work out fine in the end. He gritted his teeth. "A judge in Ohio has awarded permanent custody of Joey to his birth parents. The social worker said it was a black-and-white case. There's nothing more she can do."

"What?" Molly shrieked. She stood and stormed halfway to the door, and then back again. "Are they coming to get him? Right now?"

"No." He caught her arm and gently guided her back to the bed. "Don't panic." They sat down side by side, and he framed her cheek with his hand. "We'll hire an attorney." His reassurance was as much for him as for her. "Joey's not going anywhere."

She was shaking harder now. "W-w-when do they want him?"

"It won't happen." Jack didn't want to talk about the possibility.

"But if it does . . . how much time do we have?" Molly gripped his knee and leaned hard against him. She looked about to collapse.

"Molly, breathe. . . . We're going to fight this; I promise you."

She jerked away from him and stood. "I don't want to

breathe!" Her voice was loud, shrill, the voice of a crazy person. Her expression changed and she started to melt. Slowly, she collapsed against him. Frightening sobs came over her and she looked like she might be sick. She lifted her eyes to his. "Jack . . . help me!"

"Molly . . ." He held her up by her shoulders, his arm around her. "No one's going to take him. I won't let it happen."

"I can't do this, Jack, I can't . . . let him go." Her sobs grew softer. But they were gut-wrenching, coming from a place so deep inside her even he didn't know his way around it. She squeezed her eyes shut, rocking and weeping. "He's my baby, my only baby. Please . . . don't let him go."

"Shhh. . ." He covered her with his arms, protecting her the only way he knew. "Joey's not leaving us. It won't happen." He talked to her that way for ten minutes, saying only what he could, what little bit made sense, until finally she lifted herself halfway up.

"I can't lose him." Her words were weak, childlike.

He stroked her back. "You won't have to, honey. Come on, pull yourself together."

Another sob washed over her, and then she drew a deep breath and faced him. "When do they want him? I have to know."

Jack understood. Worst-case scenario, she had to hear the truth. He kept one arm around her shoulders. "She said something about a visit every few weeks." He could barely speak the words, as if doing so might somehow make them true. "On the fourth visit, Joey would move there permanently." Before she could respond, he rushed ahead. "But don't think about that. It won't happen. It won't."

She pushed herself to sit up the rest of the way, and after a few seconds she worked her way to her feet. "I need to wake Joey up. We're going to the pool with Beth and the kids today."

"That can wait. We have a lot to figure out."

"No." Her eyes were swollen, and she rubbed them with her palms, drying what was left of her tears. "He needs a normal life, Jack. A day at the pool will be good for him." She gave him a pointed look. "Like you said, they won't take him away. You won't let them, and I won't either." Her eyes grew so hard she barely looked like herself. "They'd have to kill me first."

And those were the words that stayed with Jack all day, as he called his lawyer and got a recommendation for a high-powered family attorney in downtown Miami, as he drove south into the city, the adoption paperwork at his side. This wasn't a simple custody battle he was trying to ward off.

It was a fight for the heart and soul and breath of their family.

The pool was wonderful.

Three hours of sunshine and splashing with Joey, and not for a minute did she allow her mind to venture to the unthinkable places of earlier that morning. Jack would take care of everything. She'd meant what she said. They'd have to kill her before she'd let her son go.

She and Beth were too busy at the pool to have more than a minute to talk, but afterward they went to Beth's house. Joey was asleep by the time they got there, and Molly cradled him in her arms and laid him on the sofa. Beth walked Jonah to his room and laid him down, and the older kids put a movie on in the family room.

Molly found a pitcher of iced tea in the refrigerator and poured glasses for her and Beth. This wasn't happening. The phone call was the one thing she had feared since she and Jack first considered adoption. She had to talk to Beth now, before she imploded. All those other times—days represented in the photo album—came to mind. Beth was there when Molly's boyfriend publicly humiliated her, she was the strong voice of comfort and reason when Art Goldberg died, and she was the only one Molly could turn to now.

Jack would take care of the details, but still she needed to talk, needed to share the fears she'd been running from all day. The moment Beth returned to the kitchen, Molly looked at her and opened her mouth. But no words would come. Where could she start? The entire situation was like a scene from someone else's movie. She hadn't had time to put the details into words.

"Hey . . . what's wrong?" Beth met her near the kitchen island. Her voice was gentle, tender, the way it was with her children when one of them was hurt. But this time fear had a place in her tone, too. "Molly, talk to me, sweetie. What is it?"

"The call . . ." She felt her face twist up. Sobs choked out the rest of her sentence.

Beth searched her eyes, and then her expression

changed. "The call? You mean the one from the social worker?"

"Yes." Molly took her tea and dropped to the nearest dining-room chair. Nothing made sense, not a bit of what she was about to say. "Joey's adoption paperwork was forged." She gripped the arms and stared at her sister. "His birth father never signed it."

"What?" Beth grabbed her glass and sat down beside her, facing her. Shock settled in the fine lines on her forehead. "Well, that's not your problem . . . is it?"

More tears, and Molly covered her face with her hands.

"Is it, Molly?" Beth put her arm around her shoulders. "I mean, that's something the social services people have to work out with the birth parents, right?"

"No." Molly dropped her hands and dabbed her fingertips beneath her eyes. She felt the fight rising up inside her. All morning at the pool, her feelings had warred within her. She'd be swimming next to Joey and she'd surface for air just as sharp terror made it impossible to draw a breath. Joey was everything to her—they wouldn't dare take him. Then she'd dive down to the floor of the pool and suddenly she'd be a mother bear, willing to do anything, all things, for the sake of her child.

Now she looked at Beth and grabbed a quick breath. "A judge in Ohio ruled earlier this week that custody will revert back to his birth parents in a few months. Because someone forged the father's name."

"It was probably the mother." Beth leaned her shoulder into the sofa. Her eyes never left Molly's. "Didn't you say the father was in prison for domestic violence when you adopted Joey?"

"Yes." She crossed her arms and pressed them to her waist. "He's out now."

"So if the mother forged his name, isn't that something the two of them have to work out?"

Molly narrowed her eyes, trying to remember. "The social worker said they didn't know who signed his name. So I guess they're ruling out his birth mother."

"That's crazy." Beth's voice rang with frustration. "What sort of protection does that give any adoptive parent?" She waved her hand in the air. "If birth parents can come back years later and complain about the paperwork, then no one's safe." She hurried on. "You're fighting it, of course."

"Jack's on his way to Miami right now. Our lawyer recommended some big shot in the city." Her shoulders had been tense, and she lowered them. *Relax, Molly. . . . Everything's going to be okay.* "Jack says not to worry; he'll take care of it."

"Good." Beth stood and put her hands on her hips. "The whole thing's insane. Imagine, taking a healthy child out of the only home he's known, the place where he's lived for nearly five years." She clenched her fists. "No one in their right mind would do that."

"Exactly." Molly savored the strength of Beth's words. Beth had always been more a fighter than a victim. "We should know something later today."

Beth's expression softened. "I know it's going to work out. It has to."

"It will." Molly repeated the words in her head for good measure. *It will work out; it will.* She drummed her fingers lightly on her knees. "Still, I wish there was something we could do today, this afternoon."

The fight left Beth. She sat down next to Molly. "There is." She held out her hands. "We can talk to God."

"I don't—" Molly started to bristle, but immediately she changed her mind. Beth had a Bible verse for every occasion. Suddenly, Molly wanted to know. "What would the Bible say about this? About a child's future . . . or losing a child, fighting for a child?"

Beth didn't hesitate. "Well, Scripture has a lot to say about children and the battles we fight in life." She held out her thumb. "First and most important, there's a verse in Jeremiah that says God knows the plans He has for us, plans to give us a hope and a future and not to harm us."

Molly thought that over. If it was true, then God had plans for Joey. Good plans. The news settled some of her anxiety. "What else?"

"I could get you a Bible promise book. That way you could look at Scripture by topics."

"Okay. I'd like that." Molly could hardly believe this was her talking. But with Joey's future on the line, she was willing to try anything. She looked at her watch. "As long as Joey's sleeping, maybe you could show me some of the verses now."

Beth did exactly that. Until Joey woke up from his nap they looked at Bible verses, and before she left, they even held hands and Beth prayed. All her life, Molly hadn't paid God any heed whatsoever. It seemed unfair that she should wait until now—her most dire hour—to consider whether He was really there, whether He could help her. For that reason, their conversation about God felt strange and even awkward. But when they finished talking, Molly had something she hadn't gotten from Jack or from the knowledge that he was at the attorney's office, or even from Beth.

She had peace.

Chapter Ten

Wendy was giddy with the way things were working out.

As long as she didn't think of her son's adoptive parents, as long as she didn't dwell on the loss they were about to experience, she went through each day happier than she'd ever been. Rip was home and handling himself carefully. He was looking for a job, and he'd already had two interviews at the movie theater. The manager position looked like a lock—which meant maybe in six months they could afford a bigger rental. But most of all, their son was coming home.

His name was Joey.

Allyson Bower had given them more information after the judge ruled in their favor. Now, in ten or fifteen minutes, Allyson would stop by to make sure their home was suitable for a child. After that, there'd be nothing left but the waiting. Joey would make his first visit to Ohio in two weeks.

Wendy grabbed a sponge and washed down the kitchen counter one more time. Tigger, the cat, knew better than to walk up near the dishes, but sometimes he forgot. Cat hair on the counter wouldn't look good to a social worker.

Tigger rubbed up against her ankles and mewed loudly.

"Later, kitty." It was almost noon, Tigger's favorite time to eat. "Mama's busy."

She worked the sponge over each section, careful to leave the counter cleaner than ever before. When she finished, she looked around the kitchen again. Everything was spotless. Rip had bought a jar of putty, and while he was out looking for work she'd patched up the hole in the wall. Yes, everything was in order.

But maybe Allyson would be hungry. The smell of something cooking in the oven was bound to make the place feel more like home. She opened the freezer, pulled out a can of pop-up cinnamon rolls, and read the directions. Five minutes later they were in the oven. She washed her hands and dried them on the worn-out kitchen towel folded by the sink. The nice one, the one with the blue stripes, was hanging neatly on the oven door. Wendy leaned back against the counter and caught her breath. Life had been one continuous blur since their meeting with the social worker.

The first good news was the report from the handwriting expert. No question, Rip hadn't signed the adoption documents. She had held her breath when Allyson gave her the news over the phone. If the department suspected her of signing the papers, the accusation would've come then.

It didn't.

Instead, a few days later, Allyson called again and told them to be at a hearing the following morning. Judge Rye

Evans would be looking at the case and making a decision. Rip and Wendy wore their best clothes, and Rip looked more handsome than he had when they got married.

The typing lady next to the judge couldn't keep her eyes off him.

Allyson did most of the talking. She told the judge that it had come to her attention that the adoption file involving the Porters contained a forged signature. She had no enthusiasm for the case; that much was obvious. At one point—after she presented the results from the handwriting expert—Allyson looked at the judge and said nothing for half a minute.

Finally she held up the file. "I have to say, Your Honor—this department does not believe it's in the best interest of the child to remove him from his adoptive home."

The judge nodded. He wore a scowl through most of the hearing, and he kept looking at a stack of papers on his desk. He asked about Rip's criminal background. Two assault convictions and a five-year sentence for domestic violence. Then he put Rip on the stand.

The questions were easy. Had Rip been through rehabilitation? Yes. Did he feel he'd learned his lesson? Of course. Was he a changed man? Definitely. Could he handle being a father? Yes, he was looking forward to it. Had he thought about how to discipline a child without resorting to rage? Yes, he would continue with counseling to make sure he was on the right track.

"Nothing more," the judge said. Rip stepped down. He smiled at the typing lady and took his place beside Wendy.

She was next. The judge asked even less of her. At one time she had wanted to give this child up for adoption, right? Yes, given the situation. But now she wanted to raise this boy with her husband? Right. She explained her motives. She hadn't thought he wanted the boy. Now she could only pray they'd have the chance they lost almost five years ago.

That was all.

Allyson sat at the front of the courtroom at a long table. Every now and then she looked at the file and shook her head. At one point she stood and asked the judge if he could postpone his decision until the adoptive parents had a chance to testify.

"Fraudulent paperwork is not of any consideration by the adoptive parents." The judge peered down from his elevated position. He looked almost sad. "If a birth parent's signature was forged, the adoption is no longer valid." He slumped a little. "You know that, Mrs. Bower."

She nodded and sat down.

The judge took half an hour to look over the paperwork and the information in the file. When he returned, his decision was quick. He used a lot of big words, lots that Wendy didn't understand. She held tightly to Rip's hand, waiting for the bottom line. Finally he said, "Therefore it is my duty under the laws of the state of Ohio to revert custody of this minor to his birth parents."

Allyson was on her feet again. She told the judge it wouldn't be fair to call the boy's adoptive parents and demand that they release him right away, with no warning. The judge agreed. He came up with a plan that Joey would have three visits over the next few months, and then he'd come to live with Rip and Wendy for good.

"Honey!" Rip's voice called from the bedroom, snapping her back to the present. "Where're my socks? I can't find a clean pair!"

"Oh, sorry." She jolted into action. How could she have forgotten? She'd done all the laundry, but the last load was still in the dryer. "Just a minute."

"Hurry up," he snapped. His temper had been a little short lately. Probably the stress of the meeting they were about to have.

She would've run across broken glass to keep Rip from being upset today. The social worker wouldn't just be assessing whether they had enough bedrooms. She would look for signs that Rip's anger was still a problem. Both of them knew it.

The dryer door was open, the clothes inside still damp. She must've forgotten to start it. Fear seized her. Rip would never stand for wet socks, never. She slammed the door shut, added twenty minutes to the cycle, and pushed the Start button. She looked around, frantic. What to do next? How could she get a pair of clean dry socks for Rip in the next half a minute?

Then it hit her. She raced around the corner, into their bedroom and past Rip.

"What're you doing?" He twisted his face, frustrated. "Where's my socks?"

"The dryer's acting up." She pulled a pair of athletic socks from her own drawer, and hurried to him. "Here. Wear these. You can change later."

He jerked them from her hand. "I hate wearing your socks."

"I know. I'm sorry." She gave him a weak smile. "The dryer's working now."

"Fine." He huffed at her. "Is the house clean?"

"Perfectly."

"Good." He sat on the edge of the bed and slipped the socks on. Then, as if it had just occurred to him that he wasn't acting very nice, he nodded at her. "Thanks for picking things up."

She felt herself light up inside. "You're welcome." She sat on the edge of the bed beside him. "I'd do anything to make this work."

"It will." Determination rang in his voice. "He's *our* little boy. I wish we were getting him back without all this visit garbage. As if we were some sort of strangers."

"Well . . ." She twisted her fingers together. She hated to go against him. "We sort of are strangers. For now, I mean." She uttered a nervous laugh. "He doesn't know us."

"He'll know us right off." Rip barked the words, but he kept his tone low. "Kids know their parents."

"Right." Wendy kept herself from saying that at this point Joey's parents were the nice couple in Florida. She understood what Rip meant. A child would know his birth parents simply because they were blood-related. She weighed the idea. Yeah, that might be true. Why not?

There was a knock on the door. "Get it." Rip gave her a quick shove. "I'll be right there."

"Okay." She hurried out of the room, straightening her beige slacks and patting her hair nice and neat. She opened the door and smiled at Allyson Bower. "Hello . . . come in."

"Hello." The social worker didn't look happy. "This shouldn't take long." She had a file in her hand and she stepped inside.

Only then did Wendy notice the curls of smoke coming from the oven. "Oh, no!" She gasped. "The cinnamon rolls!" She raced across the living room to the adjoining kitchen, grabbed a potholder, opened the oven door and yanked the tray out and onto the counter.

Allyson was a few steps behind. "Can I help?"

"No, it's okay." Wendy turned off the oven and shut the door. She'd let them cook four minutes longer than she was supposed to. Between the smoke and the blackened tops on every roll, the batch was a complete loss. She gave Allyson a quick smile over her shoulder. "My oven cooks a little hot lately."

At that moment, Rip came into the room. He smelled the smoke and frowned. "What happened?"

"I'm not sure." Another nervous laugh as she quickly dumped the burned rolls into the trash. "I guess the oven's cooking hotter than usual."

Allyson was getting situated at the kitchen table, so she didn't see the glare Rip gave Wendy. The minute the social worker looked up, Rip's expression changed to a smile. "Those electric ovens are touchy."

Wendy flipped on the exhaust fan over the stove and opened a window. She fanned at the smoke that still hung in the air. Then she pulled a few apples from the fridge, sliced them onto a plate, and brought them to the table. She took the seat between Rip and Allyson. "Okay." She smiled at her husband and then back at the social worker. "I guess we're ready."

The meeting didn't last long. There were questions about their daily schedules, and how available either of them would be for Joey. Wendy worked just one job now—a secretarial position at a local accounting firm.

She explained that she'd be gone nine to five, but that she had eighteen sick days built up in case Joey needed her for something.

"Otherwise, what's the plan for the child?"

"Day care." Rip made the word sound like a reward, like Disneyland. "We've got a great little place a few blocks away. Clean and friendly. Affordable."

"What about you, Mr. Porter? What will your work hours be?"

He stuck out his chest just enough for Wendy to notice. "I'm waiting to hear from the movie theater in town. They're considering me for the manager position. I'll work nights, of course. Otherwise I'll watch Joey, and most days we won't have to worry about day care."

The look on Allyson's face said she wasn't sure that was a good thing. She wrote something in her file. "Okay." She looked up. "I'll take a look around." She pointed toward the hallway. "Two bedrooms, right? One for you, one for the boy?"

"Right." Again Rip took the lead down the hall. Allyson followed, and Wendy was last. The rooms were small, but clean and neat. The social worker said nothing as she looked through each bedroom door and then at the bathroom at the end of the hall. "Full bath?"

"Yes." Rip sounded proud. "There's another one off the living room." He hesitated. "Of course, after I get the manager position at the theater, we'll have much more money. We'd like to rent a bigger house, something near the nicer schools. For when our son starts kindergarten."

Allyson looked at him, but again she said nothing. When they finished the tour, she wrote something else in her file. This time she led the way into the kitchen, where she motioned to the refrigerator. "May I?"

"If you can stand the smoke." Rip chuckled, but as soon as Allyson put her back to them, he scowled and shook his head.

The social worker gave the refrigerator a quick scan. Milk and eggs, cheese and vegetables. They'd gone shopping the night before and made sure the food was healthy and fresh. Allyson checked a few of the cupboards and asked about first aid. Wendy showed her a kit in one of the kitchen drawers.

After another few minutes she lowered the file to her side. "That's all I have." She nodded at them. "Thanks for opening up your house." She was heading out when she stopped and looked at the patched wall. Her brow lowered and she ran her finger over the patch. Then she turned and looked straight at Rip. "What's this?"

"My fault." Wendy took a step forward. She shrugged her shoulders and did a flustered laugh. "I was sweeping the other day, and pow! I poked the broom handle straight through the wall. Can you imagine?"

The look Allyson gave her said that no, she could not imagine any such thing causing a hole in the wall. She made a note in her file, nodded once more to the two of them, and told them she'd be in touch. Then she was gone.

As soon as the door closed behind her, Rip was in Wendy's face. "Burned rolls?" He forced the words through tight teeth. "Is that your idea of a good impression?" He groaned out loud and paced to the stove and back. The house was small, so his steps took only a few seconds.

"I thought they'd smell nice." She didn't want to fight with him. "Allyson didn't care. She even offered to help." Which was more than he had done. "Come on, Rip. Don't be mad."

"Mad?" His face was red now. His eyes bulged the way they did when he was about to lose it. "I'm beyond mad." He gave a sharp wave toward the laundry room. "First my socks." Another sharp wave toward the kitchen. "Then the rolls." He stormed over to the patched-up wall. He reared back and with a single ferocious blow he slammed his fist through the spot once more. He glared at her, plaster hanging from his knuckles the way it had before. "Then this." He took a few threatening steps toward her. "Your lousy repair job."

"Rip . . ." Was this it? The moment when it would be obvious to both of them that nothing had really changed, that they were crazy to be bringing a child into this environment? She held her breath. "Please . . ."

Suddenly, as if a switch had been flipped, he seemed to get a grip on his emotions. He exhaled hard and leaned against the back of the sofa. "I'm sorry." His anger faded, but he was a long way from happiness. He pointed to the hole in the wall. "Fix it right next time, will you?"

"Yes, Rip." Wendy took a few steps back. She would fix it right now, while he was watching. That way maybe he could offer a few hints so she wouldn't do such a bad job the second time around. "I'll get it right now so—"

He brushed his hand in the air over his head. "Never mind. It's my fault." He walked to the front door. "I'll fix it when I get back."

"Where are you going?"

"To cool down." He came to her and gave her a half-embrace. "I let the stress of that lady's visit get to me, that's all." His eyes met hers. "Forgive me?"

"Of course." She remembered to breathe. "Everything's going to be fine."

"Yes." His lips turned up just a little. "Thanks, Wendy. You're so good for me."

As soon as he was gone, the theater people called. "Have your husband contact us, please. He got the job."

Wendy kept her excitement down until she hung up. Then she ran out the door and down the sidewalk until she caught up with Rip. "You did it!" She took him by the shoulders. "You got the job!"

"I did?" His face lit up.

"Yes!" She squealed. Rip was right, things were all going their way.

Rip gave a victory shout. He picked her up and swung her around, the way he did when he was his happiest. And in that moment, Wendy knew she had nothing to worry about. Yes, it would be tough for the Florida couple to lose Joey, but they would be okay. The judge wouldn't have ruled for the change in custody if he was worried about them, right? And now that Rip had a job, he wouldn't be nearly so tense. They'd survived even the home study.

Now all they had to do was wait for Joey.

Chapter Eleven

Jack Campbell stayed in the slow lane all the way home from Miami. He was in no hurry to face Molly, to tell her that even the most high-powered attorney in all of Florida had nothing to offer them.

He wouldn't give up, of course. There had to be other attorneys, someone willing to take the case. But for now the news was horrible. It was shocking, the emergency conversation he'd had with the attorney completely hopeless.

"If the papers were forged, it's an open-and-shut case." The man was dressed to the nines, sitting behind an impressive desk in a corner office overlooking the city and the harbor beyond. At least he was kind. "Look, I cleared my calendar to meet with you. Your lawyer's a very good friend of mine." He slid his chair back and stretched out his legs. "If there was anything I could do to help you, I'd be on it."

Jack felt like a man slipping into quicksand. "Maybe I'm not making the facts clear." He sat on the edge of the chair, desperate to change the attorney's mind. "We were given signed and sealed adoption papers almost five years ago. The social worker promised us the birth parents could never come back looking for Joey." His voice had grown loud, and he lowered it again. "It was a closed adoption." He gripped the arms of the chair. "This was never supposed to happen."

The attorney stood and gazed out the window. "I realize that, Mr. Campbell." He turned around and faced Jack. "But those statements were made under the assumption that the documents were accurate, that the signatures truly belonged to the people who were supposed to sign them."

"Okay, so how often does something like this happen? What protection do adoptive parents really have?"

"Most departments are requiring notarized signatures now." He frowned. "That wasn't the case when your adoption was being handled."

Jack was stunned. "So you're saying that would've averted the problem? If we would've insisted on a notarized signature, even though the department didn't require it?"

Sunlight streamed in through the windows, but a shadow fell over the attorney's face. "The way I understand it, the birth father in this case wouldn't have signed the papers, Mr. Campbell. He had no idea his wife had given birth. So, yes, it would've solved the problem to ask for a notarization." He sat back down and leveled his gaze at Jack. "But you never would've gotten Joey in the first place."

They went round and round the situation for half an hour before the attorney looked at his watch. "I'm sorry, Mr. Campbell. I really wish there was something I could do to help you." He sighed. "Try to look at it from the position of the birth father. He gets out of jail and finds out his wife had a baby and gave it up for adoption without anyone telling him." The attorney pursed his lips. "Wouldn't you feel outraged?"

Jack didn't want to consider such a thing. He stood, shook the attorney's hand, and thanked him for his time. Somehow he made it down the elevator, out of the building, and back to his car, though he had no memory of any of it. Now he was on the freeway trying to imagine what he was going to tell Molly.

Traffic was heavy, but it was moving. He'd be home far too soon, and then what? He'd promised her he would take care of the situation, that no one would take their son from him. The idea was ludicrous. Only now, it wasn't so crazy after all. If the top family attorney in the state couldn't think of a single legal reason to fight the Ohio judge's order, then who would help them?

The air in the car was stuffy, and he couldn't grab a full breath. He hit a button and the passenger-side window lowered halfway. Warm air rushed at him, but even so he couldn't fully inhale. Was it really going to happen? In two weeks would they watch Joey leave for a visit to Ohio? And a few months after that, would he really be taken from their lives forever? Their only son?

His throat felt thick, and wetness clouded his eyes. Joey was theirs. He didn't belong with a couple in Ohio, with a father who just got out of prison for domestic violence. Even a single visit could hurt Jocy, right? Jack blew the air from his lungs and tried again for a full breath. He worked the muscles in his jaw. No one was taking Joey from them, no one. The courts might be crazy, the social workers and attorneys might be nuts, but at least he and Molly still had their common sense.

Joey was their son. Period.

He tightened his hold on the steering wheel, and as he did, a billboard on the side of the road caught his attention. "Go International in Less Than an Hour! Roundtrips to Haiti for Under $200!"

It was an American Airlines ad, and for a minute Jack forgot he was even on the freeway. His foot eased up off the gas, and behind him the driver of an eighteen-wheeler laid on the horn. Jack jerked back into motion and pressed hard on the pedal. International in less than an hour?

The wheels in his head began to turn. What if no one would listen to them? What if no attorney took the case? Were they supposed to help Joey pack his bag and then stand by and watch him disappear from their lives? Would they be good parents if they let Joey be placed in a home with a dangerous man?

A fierce determination welled up in Jack like a building tidal wave. He'd try a few more attorneys, of course. But if they couldn't do anything to help him, then he and Molly would have no choice. They could take Joey and leave the country, start a new life somewhere else. Maybe not Haiti, but on some island with miles of empty beach and no social services departments.

They could live off of the equity in their house and rental homes for several years, couldn't they? It would be only a matter of disconnecting from society and finding a way out of the country. What did they have that mattered more than Joey? His job? Their house? The friends they'd made? Family? No, nothing was worth losing their son.

As he got closer to home, the idea seemed more realistic. It could be done, couldn't it? They could get fake passports and make their way out of the country. Find a place to hide for a time, and then take Joey to Europe. They could continue living under their new identities, maybe in Sweden or Germany, send Joey to a private school, and no one would be the wiser. By then people would've stopped looking for them, maybe even assumed they'd died. Fleeing the country could work, couldn't it? He settled back into his seat and focused on the road ahead. If that's what it took to stop the courts from taking Joey, he would gladly move to the moon. Satisfaction welled up inside him. No one was going to paint him and his family into a corner. He would protect Joey with his life, whatever that meant.

Now it was just a matter of convincing Molly.

The kids had grown restless after the movie and naps, and now Molly and Beth were playing with them on Fuller Park's jungle gym. Jack had called, so Molly wasn't surprised when she saw him pull into the parking lot, get out of his car, and walk toward them. His steps were determined. She climbed down the ladder and shaded her eyes. Yes, it was him. And he was certainly upbeat, wasn't he?

"Hey, Beth. . . . Jack's here."

Beth climbed down and stood next to her. "He looks okay."

"That's what I thought." She grabbed onto the metal structure. "It must be good news."

"See?" Beth gave her a quick hug. "That's what happens when you pray. God's will gets accomplished."

"God's will . . ." It was an idea Molly hadn't thought much about. "You think He has a way He wants this to go, is that it? His will?"

"Definitely." The boys were laughing, giggling as they slid down the slide and rounded the corner. Beth leaned back against the ladder. "When you pray, God doesn't always answer with a yes. But you always get His will." She gave Molly a half-smile. "I can't imagine God's will is for Joey to be anywhere else but in your arms."

Molly felt her smile warm all the way to the most terrified places in her heart. "Thanks, Beth."

Joey spotted Jack. "Daddy!" He ran across the field of dandelions, stirring up clouds of seeds. "Daddy, you're here!"

"Mommy?" Jonah tugged on Beth's sleeve. "Where's our daddy?"

"He's at work, honey."

Molly squinted, taking in the sight of her husband and son. Jack swung Joey up into his arms and held him close. Longer than usual. When he eased him back down to the grass, the two held hands and kept walking closer.

Beth was watching. She grinned at Jonah. "Tell you what . . . Let's go get the big kids and get some ice cream."

"But, Mom"—Jonah whined her name—"I like playing with Joey's daddy. He's a good pirate."

"Well, today I think Joey's mommy and daddy need to talk." She pointed to the nearby swings. "Go get your sister and brothers."

Molly flashed Beth a silent thank-you.

"Aw, really, Mom?" Jonah bounced a little.

"That's right." Beth patted Jonah on the shoulder. "No pirates today."

"Aw, okay." Jonah kicked at the dirt. But after a few seconds his face brightened. "Can we have chocolate sprinkles?"

"Of course." Beth took Jonah to the bench and gathered their things. "What's an ice-cream cone without chocolate sprinkles?"

"Can George Brett have some, too?"

"No . . . ice cream isn't good for doggies." Beth watched Jonah run for his siblings. When they were all gathered, Beth waved, and the group started toward the car. She held her hand to her ear. "Call me."

"I will." Molly turned her attention to Jack and Joey. They were twenty feet away, and she could make out Jack's expression better now. Maybe it wasn't exactly upbeat. But it wasn't defeated, either. She braced herself for whatever was about to come.

Beth and the kids waved to Jack and Joey as they passed on their way toward the parking lot. They stopped for a few seconds and then continued in opposite directions. Molly met Jack and Joey in a patch of dandelions. Jack dropped to Joey's level and kissed their son on the cheek. "I have an idea."

"Cops and robbers?"

"No." Jack worked his jaw, his eyes never leaving Joey's. "Not cops and robbers. Not today. Mommy and

I have to talk." He pointed to the swings. "How about you pretend the swings are a great big airplane and you're the pilot?"

"The chief pilot?" Joey's eyes were wide and innocent, all of life as simple as a game of make-believe.

Jack smiled. But Molly could see that his eyes looked serious, almost frightened. "That's right, sport. The chief pilot." He stood up. "Show me how well you can fly that plane."

"Aye-aye, sir." Joey stood straight at attention and gave Jack a crooked salute. He ran toward the swings. "Just watch me fly!"

Jack still hadn't said anything to her, hadn't even acknowledged her. He stood stone-still, watching Joey climb onto the swing and start to pump his legs. Then he jolted into action. "Wait . . . I'll give you a push." Still in his dress shoes and slacks, Jack jogged through the few yards of weeds and grass, onto the sand, and to the place behind Joey's swing. He gave their son a couple strong pushes. "Now you're flying, okay, sport?"

Joey beamed. "Thanks, Dad. The skies are clear up here. You should fly with me."

"Maybe later." Jack looked at Molly, and only then did his smile fade. "Mommy and I will watch from the bench."

Molly realized she hadn't moved since she first saw him kiss Joey's cheek. Now her legs carried her to the bench, but she had the strangest sense that her body wasn't actually attached. That whatever was about to take place wasn't even happening to her, but to someone else. Someone in a movie scene, maybe, or a nightmare.

Jack sat down on the bench first, and she took the

spot beside him. If she didn't ask him, they might never have to talk about it. The awful "it." They could sit here watching Joey fly his imaginary plane and bask in the Florida sunshine without ever giving a thought to something as insane as losing him.

Next to her, she felt Jack shift. He spoke without ever taking his eyes off Joey. "I met with the attorney."

"In Miami?"

"Yes." He narrowed his eyes and turned to face her. "I waited an hour to see him. It was a short meeting."

A short meeting? What did that mean? How was she supposed to read that? She felt sick to her stomach. "Jack, don't do this." Her words were breathy. "What's the bottom line?"

He drew a long breath and released it slowly. He faced Joey again. "There's nothing the guy can do. If the birth father's name was forged, the law is clear-cut. The judge has to assume that the birth father never intended to give his child up for adoption." He slid his hands into his pockets and stretched out his legs. "The birth father, in this case, becomes the victim, and the law works entirely on his behalf."

Molly wanted to scream or cover her ears, but neither action seemed appropriate. They were at a public park, after all. Two moms with strollers were heading toward another bench a dozen yards away. Anyway, it wasn't possible—the words Jack had just spoken couldn't be true. So she did the only thing she could do. She released a single bitter laugh. "I can't believe this."

"Me, neither." Jack took hold of her hand. "I asked him to take the case anyway. We need someone fighting for us."

"What did he say?" The feel of Jack's fingers between hers lent some sense of normalcy to the moment, as if maybe Jack had gotten off work an hour early and here they were, enjoying a late afternoon with their son. Rather than talking about how quickly they might lose him. She looked at Jack. "He'll do it, right?"

Slowly, with some of the shock that she, too, was feeling, he shook his head. "He won't take the case." Jack's chin quivered. "He says it's not winnable."

The air around her suddenly became suffocating. She stood and slid her hand through her hair. Then she moaned and walked in little circles and figure-eights, dazed, unable to think or speak. "No. No—this isn't real." She felt off-balance, dizzy, and the entire park blurred around her. "This isn't happening."

"Molly . . ." He slid to the edge of the bench and patted the spot beside him.

"Daddy! Watch how high I am!" Joey called from the swings. "I'm the best pilot in the world!"

Jack turned to him. "Yes, sport. In the whole world."

"Wanna come fly with me?"

"Not yet . . . Mommy and I still need to talk."

The conversation echoed in her mind. *Wanna come fly with me? . . . Come fly with me. . . .* Yes, that was it, wasn't it? She looked at her son, at his pale blond hair and tanned face, at the blue eyes, so gentle and trusting. That's all she wanted—to run from this horrible conversation and fly with him. High in the sky, hand in hand, and never ever come down. She and her son together forever and—

"Molly."

The sound of Jack's voice snapped her from the moment and she turned to him, startled. "What?"

"Come here." He patted the bench again. "I'm not done."

He wasn't done? Hope surged through her, like oxygen to a dying person. If he had more to tell her, then maybe that's why his step had seemed determined and upbeat. Maybe the attorney hadn't stopped there, and maybe he would take the case after all. *God . . . are You there? Do You see what's going on?*

She took shaky steps back to the bench, sat down, and faced Jack. "What?"

Jack's eyes were serious, more than she'd ever seen them. "I'm going to call a few more attorneys. But the guy I met with today says their answers will be the same. By law, Joey is no longer ours. He belongs to his birth father as long as the man won't give up his right. The attorney was surprised the judge allowed a period of shared custody for transition."

Molly was going to be sick. "I thought you weren't done."

"I'm not."

"Okay." Her heart was slamming against her chest. "How do we make the . . . the birth father give up his right?"

"Look, Mommy, no hands!"

"Joey!" Molly turned to him, frantic. "Don't let go."

The child had his hands straight out, but at her alarmed voice he grabbed hold of the chains again. "Sorry." He looked frightened. "I wanted to be a trick pilot."

"Be a passenger pilot, sport." Jack's voice was

calmer than hers. "If you let go, it isn't safe for the passengers, okay?"

Joey grinned. "Okay."

A flock of birds circled and landed in the nearby maple tree. Molly wanted to shout at them to be quiet. Every breath depended on whatever Jack was trying to say. She pulled one leg up onto the bench and hugged it close to her chest. "Say it, Jack. If we can't get him to give up his rights, then what? What can we do?"

He turned so he was facing her straight on. For a while he only searched her face. The determination in his expression shifted to desperation. She had the feeling that whatever he was about to say, it was their only hope. He brought his hand to her face and with a tenderness that defied the moment, he touched her cheekbone. "We leave." He didn't for a single heartbeat break eye contact. "We take Joey and leave the country."

"Are you kidding?" She eased her foot back to the ground and slid a few feet away from him. She sucked in a fast breath, and then another. Her body had forgotten how to exhale. She shook her head and pulled at her hair. Was he crazy? "Everything was perfect just yesterday morning! This . . . this isn't real." She bent over, lowering her head between her knees. *Breathe out, Molly. . . . You're hyperventilating. . . . You'll pass out here on the sand.*

"Molly . . ." Jack slid close to her again.

"What's wrong with Mommy?" Joey's sing-song voice called out from the swings. He slowed himself and hopped off. "Is she sick? I think she was sick earlier at Aunt Beth's picnic."

"She's fine." Jack's voice was chipper—high-pitched and phony. "Mommy's just a little tired."

Breathe . . . You have to breathe! Molly forced the air from her lungs. There. That was better. She did it again and a third time before she allowed herself to sit up and look at Joey. He was running into the grassy field, into the sea of dandelions.

"I know how to make her feel better!" He stopped and squatted down for a few seconds. When he stood up he had a fistful of dandelions and a lopsided grin. He sheltered them with his other hand and ran, his hair flying in the wind, until he was standing breathless at her feet.

"Here, Mommy . . . watch!" He held out the bouquet of seedy flowers, then he brought them to his lips and blew with all his might. The fluffy white seeds came apart and filled the air.

Then they were gone.

"That's dandelion dust!" He tossed the green stems and held his hands out. "See? It disappears like magic!" He touched her cheek—the same way Jack did so often. "Isn't that fun? Doesn't that make you feel better?"

Molly blinked back the tears. A sound that was more cry than laugh came from her. "Yes, buddy." She wrapped her arms around him and held him close. He had the same summery smell he always had. Grass and little boy sweat and something sweet she couldn't quite identify.

He squirmed from her and looked at Jack. "Did you see the dandelion dust, Daddy?"

"I did." He held up his hands and dropped them. "You're right. It disappeared like magic."

"Yep." He turned and ran back toward the swings. "My plane needs me!"

When he was airborne again, Molly turned to Jack. She felt faint, completely lacking the energy she needed for this conversation, this nightmare. She wrinkled her nose. "Flee the country, Jack? Are you crazy?"

He looked at Joey for a long time. Then he turned back to her. "About my son, yes." His eyes grew wet and for a long moment he shielded his brow with his hand. Then he sniffed and sat up straight. The determination was back. "I won't let them take him away from us, Molly. I promised you that, and I meant it." He leaned closer. "What choice do we have?"

She pressed her palm to her forehead and a desperate stifled cry sounded on her lips. "How can this be happening?"

"You have to stop asking that." It was the first time Jack sounded frustrated with her. Immediately he leaned back and stared at the blue sky. "I'm sorry." He put his hand on her knee. "I guess I've had longer to think about the idea." He hesitated. "It's possible, you know. Like Joey's dandelion dust. Just . . . just disappear from everything."

"Disappear?" She could hardly believe the words were coming from her husband. Jack was the most upstanding citizen she knew. He was on the board of advisors for the YMCA and in charge of the Red Cross chapter at his office. He was the man who paid his taxes early and voted at every election. "You're serious? You'd consider leaving the country?"

He ground his teeth together, his chin trembling more than before. When he had regained his composure, he pointed an angry finger at Joey. "They will *not* take my son from me, Molly." A slight sob shook him, but he swallowed it. "No matter what we have to do."

"And I won't take up a life of crime." She stood and took a few steps in Joey's direction. "There has to be another way."

With that she began jogging toward her son. They were wasting time talking about leaving the country. That wasn't the answer. There had to be another attorney, someone who would take on this fight for them. Joey would be destroyed if someone took him away now. It would be the worst possible thing for him. "Mommy's coming, Joey!"

"Yippee! I'm the best pilot in the world." He grinned at her. "Hop on board!"

Just being near him gave her strength to keep moving, keep breathing. She lifted herself onto the swing next to his and began pumping her legs with all her might. Flee the country? Was Jack losing his mind? There had to be another way . . . had to be. She flashed a smile at Joey. "You're right, buddy. You are the best pilot in the whole world."

He giggled. "Where do you wanna go?"

She said the first thing that came to her mind. "Neverland."

"Neverland?" He hooted his approval. "That's the best place, Mommy."

"I know." Tears slid from her eyes and onto her cheeks, but the breeze dried them almost instantly. "Because in Neverland you never, ever have to grow up."

"That's right. We can stay just like this forever and ever."

For the next half hour, that's just what they did. With Jack watching silently from the bench, she and Joey flew and laughed and dreamed they were in Neverland. Where children never have to grow up, and people could stay just the way they were.

Forever and ever and ever.

Chapter Twelve

Joey didn't want to cry. Babies cry, and he was a big boy. That's what the Cricket Preschool nurse said before summer came, when Joey tripped on Timmy's shoe and skinned his knee. So he didn't want to cry.

But he didn't want to go, either.

Mommy and Daddy told him a few days ago after dinner. He had to go on a trip with a nice lady to visit some people in Ohio. Another mommy and daddy.

"How come?" Joey called Gus and hugged his neck. He looked at them. "How come you're not coming, too?"

"Because we can't this time, sport." His daddy looked sad. Like maybe this wasn't the bestest thing.

"Then I'll stay here with you and Gus." He rubbed his face in the dog's furry neck. Gus turned around and gave him a big lick on the face. "Okay? That's what I'll do."

Only that's when Mommy told him that he didn't have any choices this time. He had to go for the visit and it would only last one single night and two single days. But that was too long, and now the lady would be there in the morning. Which meant he could sleep one more night with Gus and then he'd go far, far away.

Maybe a whole world away. He wasn't sure.

His mommy already helped him pack his bag, and a few times she wiped her eyes. "Are you sad, Mommy?"

"Yes. Very sad." She put her arm around him and held him for a long time. "But you'll be back on Saturday night. So we'll still have all day Sunday to play with Daddy before the next week starts."

Joey lay in bed and stared at the ceiling. He had a poster of Michael Jordan up there, even though Michael Jordan was really old. Still, he was a good player—at least that's what his daddy said. He turned on his side. Gus mostly slept on the floor, but tonight Mommy let him sleep up on the bed. Joey put his arm around Gus's furry middle. "How come, Gus? Why would I take a trip without Mommy and Daddy?"

Gus took a big breath through his nose. His eyes said he wasn't sure of an answer, either, but at least it would be a short trip.

"I know it'll be short, Gus." He gave the dog a kiss near his nose. "But short's still too long."

Gus nodded his head a little.

"Good doggie, Gus. You understand."

Joey looked up at the ceiling again. On his other side were Mr. Monkey and Mr. Growls, his other bestest friends. He picked up Mr. Monkey and talked straight to his face. Mr. Monkey's mouth was falling off, but that didn't matter—he could talk even when his mouth wasn't working. "What do you think this other mommy and daddy look like?"

Mr. Monkey thought for a minute. Maybe he didn't feel like talking, because he only gave Joey a look.

"And whose mommy and daddy are they, anyway?"

Mr. Monkey blinked. *Maybe you should take me with you,* he seemed to say.

"Okay, I'll do that." Joey had another question. "Why would a strange lady take me to see people I don't even know?"

This time Mr. Monkey yawned. *I don't have any answers,* he seemed to say. Joey laid him back down on the other side of his pillow. Mr. Growls said thank you because Mr. Monkey was his friend and he liked to stay next to him.

Joey asked himself the questions all over again. Who were the strange mommy and daddy, and why did he have to go see them? Mommy told him it was something the judge said. That was scary. Judges were on TV, sometimes with big black capes. Only not the kind of capes that Superman and Batman wore. The kind that stayed in close on their shoulders and made them sit higher up than everyone in the room.

If the judge said he had to go, then he had to go.

'Less they throw him in jail with the robbers. He put his face close to Gus again. "If they send me to jail, I'll slide through the bars, okay, Gus?"

Gus made a little whiny sound. He touched his nose to Joey's, and Joey giggled. Even with the scared in his tummy, Gus made him laugh. 'Cause Gus had a very wet nose, that's why.

Joey heard the room get quiet again. He needed to sleep. Mommy and Daddy would check on him pretty soon, and they wouldn't like it that he was still awake. But where was the strange lady taking him tomorrow? Daddy said it was Ohio, but where was that? It sounded like an Indian place, maybe. If it was, then did the mommy and daddy he was gonna see live in a teepee?

Joey's head had a lot going on inside. So much that he saw little circles whenever he closed his eyes. Beside him he could hear Gus making little sleepy sounds. He needed someone else to talk to, but who? He tapped his fingers on his head. *Think, Joey. . . . Think of who to talk to.*

Then his eyes popped open and a big idea hit him right in the head. He could do what Jonah did! Once he spent the night at Jonah's house. He slept in a sleeping bag on Jonah's floor, and they talked and talked, even after lights out and Aunt Beth said no more talking. But when it was very late and they had nothing more to say, Jonah did a little yawn. "Time to say our prayers."

"What?" Joey didn't know about prayers. He'd heard of 'em, o' course. Maybe in the movies or something. He leaned up on his elbows. "Who do you say 'em to?"

Jonah peered over the edge of his bed. "God, silly. You say your prayers to God every night." He smiled. "Sometimes in the day, too."

"Oh." Joey felt a little funny, like maybe he should know about saying prayers to God. So he nodded and lay back down. That way it would seem like he said prayers to God every night just like Jonah.

That's when Jonah started talking out loud, just like there was someone standing right there to talk to. Only there wasn't anyone in the room but themselves.

"Dear God, it's me, Jonah. Thank You for this day and for my house and my mommy and my daddy and my cousin, Joey. But not really Cammie, because she told on me." He thought for a minute. "Okay, thank You for

Cammie, too. But please make her turn into a nice sister tomorrow. Help us be safe, God. Gee this name, amen."

Joey waited a second. "Amen." It seemed like the thing to say. But Joey stayed awake for a long time that night thinking about the prayer. Jonah was lucky that he had someone as big as God to talk to. And every night! Joey was going to go home the next day and ask his mommy to teach him how to talk to God.

But the next day came, and he forgot.

Only now, maybe that's 'zactly what he should do. Jonah didn't use any special words when he talked to God. Joey looked out the window. He felt like crying again, but he didn't. "Dear God . . ." He breathed a few hard breaths. "Hi, this is Joey. I'm a'scared because tomorrow I'm getting on an airplane with a strange lady to see a strange mommy and daddy and I don't even know them." His words were little whispers, and they ran together like a long train. He blinked and waited, in case God wanted to say something back.

He didn't hear anything.

"God, I need someone to talk to 'cause I don't really want to go on the trip with the strange lady." He had an idea. One that made him feel just a little bit of happy inside. "How 'bout You go with me, God? You're invisible so no one would even care if You came, too." He thought some more. "Maybe You could even sit beside me. 'Cause that would make me get back home a little faster I think."

The scared in him seemed a little less. He yawned and remembered. "Oh, yeah. I forgot the last part. Gee this name, amen."

There. That was a real prayer, 'cause it sounded just

like something Jonah would say. He yawned again. Sleep was coming. He still didn't want to go with the strange lady to the place called Ohio and maybe to a teepee. But if God would go with him, then maybe it wouldn't seem so bad.

One more thought came into his head.

"P.S. God . . . thank You for my mommy and daddy and Gus. Because they're the bestest family in the whole wide world." After that he felt a little smile on his face. He put his arm around Gus, and in a little bit of time he was sleepy.

Just like it was any other normal night.

Chapter Thirteen

At five o'clock that morning, Molly sat straight up in bed and gripped the down blanket close to her chest. Her sides heaved as if she were running a marathon. And she was. The marathon of surviving the past week, the race for a way to keep Joey home, to stop him from getting on a plane in just a few hours and leaving for Ohio.

But it was too late. All the running and striving and planning amounted to nothing. Joey was packed, ready to leave, and in five hours he would walk out their door. She relaxed her grip on the sheets and looked at Jack. He was sleeping still, though neither of them had more than a few hours' at a time before reality jolted them awake, forcing them to go through the possibilities one more time.

Molly crept out of bed and walked to the bathroom. She stared at herself in the mirror. Who would she be if she wasn't Joey's mommy? Her chest tightened and she banished the thought. It was one visit—just one night. He'd be home tomorrow. She showered and dressed, and at least six times a minute she wondered if she'd ever be able to draw a full breath again. She needed sleep, needed a good meal.

She needed Joey.

Her heart beat hard against her chest, so loud she wondered if it would wake Jack. She tiptoed down the hall. Joey's door was open. She took a few quiet steps inside and held her breath. Gus was stretched out along the wall, and Joey was curled up, soft little snoring sounds coming from his mouth. Mr. Monkey and Mr. Growls were tucked in close to his chest. Maybe it was her imagination, but in the shadowy early morning it looked like he was smiling. *Poor baby* . . . Chills came over her and she folded her arms. *You don't have any idea why you're leaving today.* How could he possibly understand?

For a moment she considered crawling into bed beside him, but there wasn't room. Besides, she didn't want to wake him. Morning would come soon enough. Instead she stood there, barely able to think, teeth chattering, and watched him. Every memory took a turn playing on the screen of her mind. He was big now, but the face was the same one she used to watch sleep when he was an infant, when he first came home to them.

She would wake up in the middle of the night and think she heard his cry. Then she'd creep into his room and look at him. Just watch him, watch his little chest moving up and down, up and down, up and down. Just in case, sometimes she'd hold her fingers a few inches from his nose. Only when she felt his warm damp breath would she take a step back and smile, relieved. He was a wonder boy, a sunbeam, and as long as he was sleeping down the hall, as long as he was okay, she, too, could sleep.

It was the same way all through his baby time and his toddler days. Some nights she wouldn't feel peace, couldn't find sleep, until she spent a few minutes watching him, listening to him breathe. Tears stung her eyes. It wasn't even possible that tonight he'd be sleeping in another state.

She moved closer, stooped down, and studied him some more. He was beautiful, a piece of stardust with a heart laced firmly to her own. Maybe if morning never came, if she could stop time and keep ten o'clock from ever crashing in on them . . . She leaned down and gave him the softest kiss on his cheek. "Don't wake up, baby. Not yet."

She straightened. What else could she do? Her fingers trembled, her heart pounding harder than before. Then it hit her. The baseboards needed cleaning. She left Joey's room, padded downstairs, flipped on the lights, and looked around. Twice a week a housekeeper put in three hours doing the tougher jobs, so there wasn't much mess to take care of.

But the baseboards . . . They hadn't been cleaned in six months at least.

She poured a bowl of warm soapy water, found a rag, and quietly moved to the far end of the house. She stooped down, dipped the rag into the water, and wrung it out. The house was still, silent. As if all of her existence were holding its breath in anticipation of the terror that lay ahead.

How could it have come to this? Jack had called every attorney in the state—everyone who might handle an adoption case—and all of them had said the same thing. Fraud in the original documents meant that those documents were nullified. As if they'd never been signed at all.

"Think of it this way," one attorney told Jack. "You were lucky to have the boy for four years."

Molly put her shoulders into the task and rubbed at the first section of baseboard. Lucky to have him for four years? Was the world really that insane? Were people really that insensitive? Adoption didn't mean a lesser bond with a child. It was a bond she and Jack had chosen, and it was no different than if she'd birthed Joey herself. He was their son. Nothing could be more clear and obvious.

She scrubbed farther down the baseboard, all her fear and frustration and fury directed at whatever dirt had dared to accumulate there. She and Jack and Gus were all the family Joey had ever known. He was too young to understand about adoption, so when this came up—when it was clear that they had no choice about the impending first visit—they told him the only thing they could. A judge wanted him to take a trip, and so he had to take it.

He was scared to death.

They could both see that. Last night when they tucked him in, he hugged Molly's neck longer than usual. "How 'bout you go with me, Mommy? Would that be okay?" He looked at Jack. "Or you, Daddy. They wouldn't care if I brought you, would they?"

She and Jack were out of answers. How were they supposed to tell him that his birth parents wanted him back, that he had a biological father somewhere who was just released from prison, a guy who liked to hit people— especially his wife?

And now a judge was making him visit those same people.

It made no sense no matter how they looked at it. They could hardly expect Joey to make sense of it, or to find peace in their answers. Instead he tried to be brave. Jack sat on the edge of his bed and stroked his hair. "It'll be a short trip, sport."

Joey nodded. He sucked on his lower lip, probably trying not to cry. "Okay."

But what must he think about the whole thing? She put the rag back in the water, swished it around, and wrung it out again. What sort of parents let a stranger take their little boy to another state? Even if she was a social worker? Joey wouldn't understand that.

Molly scrubbed the next section of baseboard. She replayed the conversation she'd had with Jack in the park that day, the first time they were forced to realize the truth about the situation: that it was more than a slight wrinkle in their plans—it was a machete positioned directly over their family. *We can leave the country, Molly ... disappear ...* With every day that passed, she'd given his idea more thought. At first she'd figured he was delusional, crazy with fear and grief, the way she was. But he'd made it clear since then. He was absolutely serious.

The decision was Molly's. If she gave her okay, Jack would set the plan in motion, and sometime before Joey's fourth visit, the three of them would disappear. Like Joey's dandelion dust. She slid across the floor a few feet and rubbed out a dirt smudge on the shiny white wall. No smudges—not here and not in their life. Everything had been perfect, hadn't it? What happened to the pixie dust?

God ... what about Beth's prayer? Molly barely spoke the words, and once she'd said them she blew at a stray piece of hair on her cheek. What had Beth said? People who prayed could at least be sure of God's will. Sometimes God gave people the answer they wanted and sometimes He didn't. But either way, if you talked to God about it, the outcome would be in line with His will.

At least that was the way Beth saw it.

Jack's take was entirely different. They'd had the conversation three nights ago. "God's will?" He laughed and raked his fingers through his hair. "Are you kidding? You want me to wait around for God's will when my son's future is at stake?"

Molly didn't know what to say. "It's not my idea, it's Beth's."

"Well." Jack rolled his eyes. "I think we both know about Beth and Bill. They're a couple of religious fanatics, Molly. We can't let them sway us now. We have to do something before we run out of time."

"But if God wants us to have Joey, Beth says everything'll work out somehow."

"Look, Beth is not the one about to lose her son." Jack lowered his voice. He took her hands and begged her with his eyes. "Please, Molly. Don't consider such a thing. Besides . . . what if God's will is for the Porters to have him?"

That was something Molly hadn't thought about. She figured that if God could see the big picture—the way Beth believed He could—then He would know implicitly that Joey belonged with them. Certainly the child didn't belong with a convicted felon, a man given to violence. Right?

The conversation about God died there. She and Jack had been on edge, but they'd agreed not to fight. There was no point. They needed each other now more than ever. Molly didn't push the issue, and last night after they tucked Joey in for bed, Jack gently pulled her into his arms. "Help me, Molly." His voice cracked as he spoke into her hair. He held her tighter than usual. "I'm out of options. I don't know what to do."

Neither did she. The tears had been nearly constant, and they came again now as she scrubbed the baseboards. She wiped her eyes with her sleeve since her hands were both wet with soapy water. Allyson Bower would be there in less than four hours, and their precious Joey would walk out the door with her. They could do nothing now to stop the visit from happening.

Molly kept cleaning, working the rag painstakingly over every inch of baseboard until it was cleaner than it had ever been. The project killed two hours. Just as she was finishing, she heard Joey's voice upstairs.

"Mommy! Mommy, where are you?"

Every morning he fell out of bed, and before he rubbed his eyes or took a first look at the world, he stumbled down the hall and crawled in bed between them. Gus was usually not far behind. It was their special way of waking up, with Joey snuggled in the middle, whispering good morning first to his daddy, then to her. She dropped the rag in the soapy water and turned toward the sound of his voice. He must've gone into their room and seen she wasn't there. Now he was wandering the hall looking for her.

She stood and felt a sudden pain in her knees. All that time kneeling without once taking a break—of course they hurt. "Joey . . . I'm down here."

"Mommy!" She heard his feet padding down the stairs. He came into sight, his eyes still only half open. He was wearing his basketball pajamas, one of the few pairs he owned that still had feet sewn into them. He held his arms out and took little running steps to her. "Mommy, there you are!"

She stooped back down and held him close, ignoring her knees. With his little body tight against hers, she rocked him and whispered near his ear, "I'm here, baby. I didn't go anywhere."

"I thought the strange lady came and took you instead." He pulled back and looked at her. Confusion filled his expression, and he blinked a few times, trying to wake up. "But you're still here."

"Aw, Joey . . ." She hated having to hesitate, because the words she was about to say might not be true. But she spoke them anyway. "I'll always be here, buddy. No matter what."

Jack came down then, dressed in jeans and a T-shirt. Their eyes met, and she could see his were swollen. "Good morning." His tone was subdued, the desperation barely hidden.

"Morning." She stood up and found a smile for Joey. "Let's cook your favorite breakfast."

"Blueberry French toast?" He jumped up a few times. But the excitement in his face faded almost as soon as it appeared. "You mean a'cause I'm leaving on a trip?"

Molly picked up her bowl of dirty water. She wanted to throw it out the window, grab Joey's hand and Jack's, and run for their lives. And wasn't that all Jack wanted to do, anyway? Instead she took Joey's hand with her free one and nodded. "Yeah, I guess that's right. A good breakfast makes a trip go by more quickly."

"Okay." Joey followed her to the sink. "Should I get dressed first?"

The idea sent terrified chills down her arms. Get

dressed? To leave the house with a social worker and start a process that would take him from their lives forever? She set the bowl of dirty water down in the sink and held on to keep from losing her balance.

Jack came up behind her and put his arm around both of them. "Yes, sport. Let's get you dressed."

"I'll do it." Molly was quick with her answer. What if something happened to him—a car accident or a plane crash? What if the social worker lost track of him at an airport or this Porter man harmed him in some way? What if the couple ran off with him and they never saw him again? The possibilities were frightening and endless. She gave Jack a look that said she was sorry for snapping. "I'll get him dressed, okay?"

"Okay." He smiled at Joey. "I'll make the French toast."

Molly led him up to his room and picked out the clothes: a pair of blue denim shorts and a white polo shirt. She dressed him and combed his hair, then found the right socks—white with blue basketballs. His favorites.

He steadied himself against her shoulder as she bent down and slipped the socks on his feet. "Thanks, Mommy. You picked good today."

"You're welcome." She smoothed his hair and kissed his forehead. "You have Mr. Monkey, right?"

"Yep. He's in the bag even though he's a'scared of the dark."

"He'll be all right."

"But not Mr. Growls." He shook his head. "He wanted to stay here with Gus."

"That's a good idea." The lump in Molly's throat wouldn't let her say more than that.

"Yeah." Big tears threatened to spill onto his cheeks again. His lip wobbled a little.

Molly took hold of him and held him. No matter how much she hurt, Joey was hurting more. Right now that's all she could think about. Making him feel better. "Listen, buddy. You'll be back tomorrow night, okay?" It was what she needed to hear, anything to keep from going over the list of possibilities again, the car accident or plane crash. The possible kidnapping. She held his shoulders and rubbed gentle circles into his small muscles. "Stay with Mrs. Bower, okay? When you're in the airport, there'll be lots of people. Make sure you hold her hand."

"Mrs. Bower?" Alarm filled his face, and in the corners of his eyes the pool of tears grew.

"The woman who's taking you, Joey." She hated this. How could she be Joey's mother and have no say in what was about to happen? She forced herself to speak calmly. "The woman's name is Mrs. Bower."

"Oh." He blinked, and two teardrops slid down his cheeks. He brushed at them quickly, as if maybe they embarrassed him. "Will she know?"

"About holding your hand?" Molly lifted herself to the edge of his toy chest, her eye contact even with his.

He nodded. "I don't want to get lost." Gus trotted into the room and took his place at Joey's side. "Maybe I should take Gus in case Mrs. Bower forgets about me."

Molly chided herself for making him worry. "No, sweetie. Mrs. Bower won't forget about you." She reached out and scratched Gus under his white floppy ear. He was big for a Lab. Big and friendly. If she could've sent him along with Joey, she would've. "You can't take

Gus this time. Sorry. Just hold the lady's hand and every-thing'll be okay."

"All right."

They heard the sound of Jack coming up the stairs. "French toast is ready."

"Wow!" Again Joey's eyes lit up. "Daddy's fast."

They held hands as they went back down to the kitchen. Something about Joey's enthusiasm for breakfast made Molly even sadder than she'd been before. Kids were resilient. If Joey was taken from their home at this age, he'd struggle and miss them for a season. Maybe even for a year or two. But eventually he'd rebound. He'd get excited about basketball socks and swings and French toast. Same as now.

The thought brought with it a torrent of tears, but Molly stuffed them all. She could cry later. Joey needed her to be positive so he could walk out the door knowing that come tomorrow night everything would be okay. If she were crying, what would he think? Probably that his world was falling apart.

She swallowed back a few sobs and took a piece of French toast from the platter. Jack caught her eye and slipped his arm around her again. "You okay?"

"No." She looked at him. She imagined her eyes looked like those of someone about to die. They were headed straight for a cliff and there was nothing they could do to keep from plunging over the edge.

Joey was already at the table, setting the juice glasses out for the three of them.

"No juice for you, Gus." Joey bent down and kissed the dog on top of his head. "Not today." He framed his pudgy hands around the dog's face. "But maybe a left-over piece of French toast if Mommy says so."

Molly leaned into Jack and watched him. "He has no idea."

"No."

Breakfast flew by with conversation about why dogs snore and how fun it would be to go swimming on Sunday. Molly's stomach hurt more with every passing minute. She managed to eat just three bites of her French toast, and Jack did little better. Joey did most of the talking.

"Guess what?" He had syrup on his cheek and all ten fingers looked sticky. "I talked to God last night. Out loud, just like Jonah."

Jack looked at Molly. She shrugged and turned to Joey. "That's interesting." Her tone was kind, curious. "When did you start doing that?"

"Last night was the first time." Joey frowned a little. "I had Gus, but he fell asleep. I wanted someone to talk to, so I talked to God." He shrugged his shoulders a few times. "It made me feel sleepy."

Jack cleared his throat. He wiped his mouth with his napkin. "What did you talk to God about?"

Under the table Molly gave Jack's leg a quick squeeze. Her eyes told him to be careful. Their son could talk to God if he wanted to, no matter what they might think about it.

Joey took another bite of French toast. With his mouth still full, he began to answer. "I told him I was taking a trip with a strange lady." He finished chewing and swallowed. "I asked God to go with me, since my mommy and daddy and my Gus couldn't go."

Molly felt her eyebrows lift. "That's . . . very nice." She held back another rush of tears. Not once had they ever prayed with Joey or taken him to church or taught him how to talk to God. But now, all on his own, he'd done the very thing Beth would've told him to do. He'd asked God to go with him so he wouldn't be alone.

"Yes." Jack kept his tone light. He pushed back from the table and angled his head, curious. "Did Aunt Beth tell you to do that?"

A strange look crossed Joey's face. "No . . . Aunt Beth never tells me anything about God." He smiled. "I heard Jonah do it when I had a sleepover. If he can do it, I can do it."

Molly wanted to give Jack a look that said she told him so. Of course her sister would never consider going behind their backs and teaching their son to believe in God. Jack shouldn't have even suspected such a thing. But it was nine-thirty and there was no time for bickering or proving who was right.

Joey was about to leave.

They finished eating, brushed teeth, and brought Joey's little overnight roll-aboard suitcase downstairs. Jack went over some of the last-minute things that had been on both their minds. They were standing near the door, and Jack swept Joey into his arms. "Mrs. Bower has our phone number. If you need to call us for any reason, you can ask her."

Joey nodded. The lighthearted look from earlier was gone. Now he had enormous tears at the corners of his eyes, but still he wouldn't cry. "What about at night? When Mrs. Bower isn't there?"

"Then you'll be with the Porters. They have a phone,

too. Any time you want to call us, you just tell them and they'll let you call."

It was a detail they hadn't actually discussed with the social worker, but it made sense. He should be able to call home if he needed to. In preparation for this moment, she and Jack had worked extensively with Joey so he'd have his phone number and area code memorized. That way he would always know how to reach them.

"Okay, one last time." Jack leaned Joey back enough so he could see his face. "What's your phone number, sport?"

With ease, Joey rattled off all ten digits.

"And what do you have to dial first?"

"A one."

Molly stood next to them. She put her arm around Joey's shoulders. "And you'll hold onto her hand at the airport. When you're with Mrs. Bower, right?"

Before he could answer, the doorbell rang. Instantly, Joey wrapped his arms tight around Jack's neck. "No, Daddy. I don't want to go."

This was the worst part. Molly felt herself melting, but she couldn't. She had to stay strong for him, otherwise none of them would make it. She closed her eyes and leaned her head on Jack's shoulder. "I can't do this," she said, her voice meant for only him to hear. "How can we do this?"

Jack coughed twice, and Molly knew why. He, too, was trying not to cry. He clung to Joey and rocked him a few times. "I don't want you to go, either. But maybe it'll be fun. Like an adventure."

The doorbell rang again, and again Joey tightened his

grip on Jack. "I don't want a 'venture. I want you and Mommy."

Molly pushed herself the few feet to the door and opened it. A tall woman was standing on the other side. Molly stood back and ushered her in. "Mrs. Bower."

"Yes." She held out a card identifying her as an employee with the Child Welfare Department of Ohio. Her face was kind and troubled all at the same time. With Jocy still clinging to Jack, she spoke only to Molly. "I'm so sorry." She looked down for a few seconds. When her eyes lifted, they were damp. "I want you to know I'm completely against this decision." She paused as if she were looking for some way around it. "Nevertheless, it's my job to carry it out."

"Is there any way?" Molly clung to the door. Her voice was a strained whisper, pinched with pain. She could feel the blood leaving her face. There had to be other options if even the social worker was against the idea. This was the first she'd heard of that. "We can't let them take him from us. Please, Mrs. Bower . . ."

Allyson closed her eyes and breathed out. When she opened them, she shook her head. "I'm sorry. I wish there was something I could tell you. The law's painfully clear on a case like this." She looked at Jack and Joey, the two of them still lost in their own private conversation. Joey was crying now, sobbing, his little face pressed against Jack's neck. The woman shifted her attention back to Molly. "Your husband tells me he's spoken with a number of attorneys. There's nothing anyone can do."

"What about the governor, or the President of the United States?" Molly had heard of cases like this one where the media helped create a great public outcry and the case gained the attention of top officials. "Should we start making phone calls?"

"I've looked into it." Allyson gave a sad shake of her head. "If I thought it would help I would've already suggested it. But in every case I looked into, where fraud was the reason for restoring parental rights, the child always went back to the birth parents. Even if the adoptive parents contacted the White House." She took another step inside. "Every time."

Molly was shaking. This was the part she couldn't let herself think about, the part where a social worker took hold of Joey's hand and led him out of their house. If it were a movie, she'd take this moment to visit the restroom or slip outside for a breath of fresh air. It terrified her even to imagine such a scene, and now here they were.

The social worker looked at her watch. "I'm afraid we have a plane to catch." She handed a packet of papers to Molly. "This has his itinerary, the airline information, my cell phone number, and the name and phone number of the Porters, where Joey will be staying. Normally this information is not shared, but under the circumstances, the judge authorized my giving it to you. Joey is very young. You need to have a way to reach him in case of an emergency."

"An emergency?" Molly's heart leaped at the thought of having the Porters' information. She could call Joey every hour if she wanted to.

"Yes, Mrs. Campbell." Allyson's face was serious. "If you make unnecessary calls to the Porters, the judge will frown on it. He might decide to have the transfer take place sooner. So that the process will be quicker, easier on everyone."

Jack closed the distance between them. He eased Joey's arms from around his neck. There were tears on his face, but Molly couldn't tell if they were his or Joey's. "Okay, sport. Time to go."

"Please, Daddy, don't make me." Joey clung to Jack for all he was worth.

Molly leaned against the wall so she wouldn't collapse. How was this happening? What were they doing, standing by and letting a stranger take him from his home? The room tilted and nothing made sense. "Joey, baby. Come here."

At the sound of her voice, Joey slid slowly down from Jack's arms and ran to her. He was heavy, but she could still sweep him up and hold him. He wrapped his legs around her waist and buried his head in her shoulder. "Come with me, Mommy. Please!"

She said the first thing that came to mind. "God's going with you, remember? You asked God to go."

For the first time in ten minutes, Joey's sobs let up. He was still sad, still crying. But he seemed more in control. He straightened himself and rubbed his nose against hers. "That's right, huh, Mommy? God'll be with me, 'cause I asked Him."

"Exactly." Molly wondered if God was right there with both of them, even in that very instant. Otherwise how was she standing or talking or doing anything but falling apart? Tears blurred her vision, but again she refused them. She smiled at him. "Eskimo noses, okay?"

In the background, she saw Jack turn and press his forehead against the wall. His shoulders were shaking.

Joey didn't notice. He rubbed Molly's nose with his. Then he blinked his eyelashes against hers. "And butterfly kisses."

"Yes." She pressed her cheek alongside his and held him, memorizing the feel of him in her arms. Then she brushed her eyelashes against his. "Butterfly kisses."

"Joey . . ." The social worker stepped up. "I'm Mrs. Bower."

Joey looked at her. He dragged his hands across his cheeks. "Hi."

"Hi." She smiled. "I'll take very good care of you and I'll bring you back before you know it. I promise."

Jack came to them then. He circled his arms around Molly and Joey, and they stayed that way for a full minute, none of them wanting to let go. Finally, Jack helped Joey to the floor. "Remember what we told you."

"I will." He was still holding Molly's hand. His eyes met hers. "Mommy?"

That was all he needed to say. In that single word he was asking her all the same questions again. Did he have to go? Couldn't she come with him? Why couldn't he stay with her and Jack and Gus?

Molly bent down and brought his hand to her lips. She kissed it and looked straight into his eyes, to his heart. "I love you. I could never love any little boy as much as I love you."

"I love you, too." He gave her one last hug.

When he pulled back, she held her breath. She had no idea how she was going to do this next part, but it had to be done. She pursed her lips and blew out. "Mrs. Bower will take good care of you, buddy." Then, slowly, she tucked his hand into the hand of the social worker. "Don't forget about God." She took a step back. Maybe she would have a heart attack or a stroke. . . . The pain was strong enough to kill her.

Again, peace eased the worry and fear in his precious features. "Yeah. God's going with me. I hafta remember that."

Jack stepped up and kissed him once more on the forehead. "I love you, sport. Call us if you get lonely, okay?"

" 'Kay. Love you, too."

"Bye, Joey." Molly clung to Jack's arm, leaned on him so she wouldn't fall over.

"Everything will be okay. You'll come home tomorrow." Allyson Bower gave them a final look, as if she couldn't bear the words she was saying. Everything would hardly be okay. And though he'd come home this time, in a few short months they'd have to say good-bye forever.

The social worker took Joey's suitcase with one hand, and held onto Joey's fingers with the other. They walked through the entryway and down the sidewalk. Molly and Jack moved to the screen door and watched them go. Joey looked over his shoulder every few steps and waved at them.

He looked frightened still, but he wasn't crying. Mrs. Bower helped him with his suitcase, and then buckled him into a booster seat. Mrs. Bower said something Molly couldn't quite make out—something about getting ice cream at the airport. Joey gave her a weak smile, and a minute later, the social worker climbed into the driver's seat and the two of them drove away.

Molly had expected to collapse on the floor, screaming and wailing, frantic for her son. She'd been holding back the tears all morning, after all. Instead she only stood there, staring at the empty road outside their home, listening as the sound of the woman's car grew more and more distant and eventually faded altogether. When it did, Jack finally led her back inside and shut the door. She found her way to the sofa and sat down.

Neither of them spoke or cried or screamed. There was nothing they could do; Joey was gone. His entire next two days were completely out of their hands. Molly covered her face and wondered about herself. Where were her tears? Where was her heart in all the hurt and terror of the moment? How come she was still breathing?

And suddenly she knew.

Her body was carrying on in an auto-pilot sort of way. But her heart and soul and emotions . . . Everything else inside her was dead. She'd lost all connection with life the moment Joey walked out of their house. Yes, it could take a lifetime before her heart stopped beating, but without Joey she felt completely and wholly lifeless. Only one thing would breathe meaning back into her existence.

The moment Joey ran through the door and into her arms again.

•

Chapter Fourteen

The visit wasn't going all that well.

Wendy and Rip had everything all set when Allyson and Joey walked through the door that afternoon. She'd gotten the day off work, and even though Rip was scheduled to start work at the theater, they were letting him wait until Monday.

Ever since the day of the home study, she and Rip had gotten along fine. He was a little uptight now and then, but who wouldn't be? The changes in their lives were huge. He was out of prison, and now they were getting their son back. Neither of them had ever been a parent before, so sure, they were anxious.

Rip fixed the hole in the wall, like he'd promised, and for the most part he'd been a dream to be around. Even today. They baked chocolate-chip cookies, and Rip stayed with her the whole time.

"So they don't burn," he'd told her. But he wasn't mad; he winked at her and the job was actually fun. Something they could do together.

Joey's room was all made up, too. Rip had come home the day before with a stuffed bear. "Think he'll like it?" Rip arranged it just so, right at the center of Joey's pillow.

"Of course." She loved this side of Rip, the side that wanted to be a good father. "Do you like his new bed?"

"How much did it set us back?" Rip raised a wary eye.

"Not much. It was on sale."

"Three hundred?"

"Three-twenty." She winced. "But I charged it. Twenty dollars a month. We can afford that, right?"

He smiled and took her in his arms. "With my new job, we can." The pride in his face was contagious. "Everything's looking up for us, Wendy. I always knew it would happen this way one day. I just never thought we'd have a son so soon." He chuckled. "It's like all my dreams are coming true."

The trouble started when Joey arrived.

Mrs. Bower almost dragged him through the door. He looked tired and weepy, and Wendy's heart went out to him. This was her little baby, all grown up. The one she'd held in her arms all those years ago in that hospital bed. This was the boy who seemed to whisper to her, *Mommy . . . don't let me go. Don't give me up.* He was beautiful, all golden hair and pale blue eyes. She could see herself in the shape of his face, and Rip in the child's athletic build.

But the joy of seeing him for the first time was short-lived.

"No!" He turned and cried the word into the social worker's leg. "I wanna go home."

Allyson stopped and bent down. She said something they couldn't hear, but Joey shook his head. His tone wasn't rude, just very, very sad. Sad enough to break the hearts of everyone in the room. Allyson whispered something else to him. Joey sniffed a few times. "No . . . I want my mommy and daddy!"

Next to her, Wendy heard Rip chuckle. He sounded nervous, the way he got right before his anger took over. "Uh . . . this is awkward." Another chuckle. "Let's get the boy inside. Maybe that'll calm him down."

The social worker managed to lead Joey into the house and over to the kitchen table a few feet away, where he sat close to her. Wendy took her place at the table, in the chair on Joey's other side. Rip remained standing, leaning against the nearest wall and shifting positions every few seconds. He couldn't have looked more uncomfortable if he'd been standing on a bed of nails.

"Please . . ." Joey folded his arms on the table and buried his tearstained face. His words became muffled. "I wanna go home."

Rip made a face and gave an exaggerated sigh. His lips parted as if he might say something, but then he changed his mind. He worked the muscles in his jaw, his anger bubbling close to the surface. He moved into the kitchen, grabbed a glass from the cupboard, and poured himself some water.

Wendy prayed he'd keep his mouth shut. They'd been warned about this, right? The social worker told them not to say anything argumentative to the boy the first day. They weren't to tell him that they were his real parents, and they weren't to make him think their own house was his home if he talked about wanting to go back to Florida.

Still, staying quiet looked like a struggle for Rip. She gave him a stern look, the hardest look she'd given him since he'd been out of prison. Normally he wouldn't have let her look at him that way, but here—with Allyson Bower in their kitchen—Rip knew better than to say anything.

Wendy put her hand on Joey's shoulder, and the sensation was like magic. This was her son, her baby. It was the first time she'd touched him since she handed him over to the nurse that terrible afternoon. She wasn't prepared for the feelings that stirred in her soul. "Honey . . ." She struggled to find her voice. "I baked you some cookies. Are you hungry?"

From across the room, Rip chimed in. "*We* baked 'em." He raised his water glass in their direction. "It was my idea."

Mrs. Bower shot him a strange look. But she quickly turned her attention back to Joey. "Did you hear what the mommy told you?" The judge had asked that Joey call them "the mommy" and "the daddy" from the beginning. That way it'd be easier on everyone when he came to live with them for good. And the social worker was clear about the wording. She didn't say, "your mommy." She said, "*the* mommy."

Wendy was fine with that. The poor boy. He looked scared to death.

At the mention of cookies, Joey lifted his head. Even though his tears had stopped, he inhaled in sets of three quick breaths, as if the sobs were still cutting at him on the inside. That's when he looked at her, and for the first time since he was a newborn, their eyes met.

In that instant, Wendy knew she could never let him go. He'd found his way home by some strange miracle, because of a lie she'd told. What she'd done was wrong, yes. But now here he was looking straight to her soul, and the feeling was amazing beyond anything she could've imagined.

"Hi, Joey." She reached out and touched his fingers. He didn't pull away. "Can I get you a glass of milk?" She smiled. "Chocolate-chip cookies are really yummy with milk."

He narrowed his eyes, suspicious. Then he looked at Mrs. Bower and back to Wendy. "Yes, please." His words were so quiet she could barely make them out. But at least he wasn't crying. And he was so polite! Her little boy already had wonderful manners. The process would take time but everything would work out. Joey was amazing, so of course he would adjust.

"Okay, honey." She started to stand.

But a few feet away, Rip went after the milk before she could move. "I'll get it." He was acting like a spoiled child, jealous of every attempt she made to break the barriers between herself and Joey. He poured the milk and set it down, a little harder than necessary.

"Rip . . ." She kept her tone soft. "Be careful. You'll scare him."

That was all Rip needed to hear. His eyes grew dark, but before he might say something he'd regret, he seemed to remember the social worker. He smiled at her, but it fell just short of looking mean. "If you'll excuse me, I have some things to take care of out back."

"I think that might be best." Allyson looked at Joey. "Let's have your wife make peace with him first. Maybe he'll feel more comfortable."

Rip cast one more stern look at Wendy. Then he turned and hurried down the hall to their bedroom. He slammed the door behind him, leaving an uncomfortable silence hanging over the kitchen table.

"Sorry . . . Rip's a little nervous about . . ." Wendy looked at Joey. "Well, you know. This is our first time to . . ."

"I understand." Allyson slid her chair farther away, giving Wendy and Joey their own space.

Wendy took the cue and pulled the plate of chocolate-chip cookies closer to Joey. "Here, honey." She handed him one. "You can dip it into your milk."

Joey wiped his eyes again. His breathing was calmer than before. "Thank you." His voice was pitifully small, scared to death. He took the cookie and broke it in half. "It's easier in halfs."

"Yes." Wendy smiled. It was a victory. He'd talked to her! She felt her heart melt a little more. Never had she imagined this day, the chance to sit at the table with her son and share a moment like this.

He held out the other half to her. "Want some?"

She was about to say no thanks, but at the same time she considered something. Maybe he was reaching out, trying to make a connection the only way he knew how. She took the piece and smiled at him. "Thanks, Joey. You're a very nice boy."

He nodded and dipped his cookie. After one bite he cocked his head. "I go home tomorrow, right?"

Reality slapped her in the face. The child wasn't

warming up; he was surviving. This wasn't his home, and she wasn't his mother. He was lonely and afraid, so many states away from everything he knew to be safe and good and true. She swallowed her disappointment. "Yes, tomorrow."

"Okay." He looked at the social worker. "You'll come with me, right?"

"Right." Allyson Bower clutched the file to her chest. She glanced at Wendy. "If you don't need me, I think I'll let you two visit."

A lump of fear settled in Wendy's gut. Could she handle it, being alone with her son? What if he started crying? What if Rip came out and got angry? The boy wasn't reacting the way he wanted, that's for sure. Still . . . they would never know if they didn't try. She gave a quick nod. "Yes." She smiled at Joey again. "We'll be fine."

"I'll be nearby. I need to put in a few hours at the office, but I'll have my cell phone the whole time. Call me for any reason, day or night." She tapped the file. "Everything's in here. Joey knows that he can telephone me or his . . . parents if he needs to."

Wendy caught the way she hesitated on the word parents. Joey had no idea what was happening, that his understanding of "parents" was about to change. Allyson stood and put her hand on Joey's shoulder. "Remember what we talked about? You can call if you need anything."

"Thank you." He took another cookie and broke it in half. "See you tomorrow."

The social worker bid them good-bye, and then they were alone, Wendy and Joey, with Rip in the other room. She folded her arms and rested them on the table. "Did you like your plane ride?"

"Yes." He dipped the cookie and stuffed most of it in his mouth. When he could talk he gave her a crooked smile. "Sometimes I take plane rides with my mommy and daddy. Once we went to Mexico and watched the dolphins."

"Wow . . ." Wendy wasn't sure what to say. This was something else she hadn't thought of. Joey's adoptive parents were obviously rich people—taking Joey on trips to foreign beaches and giving him opportunities she and Rip could never afford. She straightened herself. Never mind all of that. A couple didn't need money to be good parents. They needed love, that's all. And who would love Joey more than his real parents, his biological parents?

"Also I took a plane ride to France once." He finished chewing and swallowed. There were cookie crumbs on his lips and cheeks, and he looked beyond adorable. "I saw the iceberg tower."

"The iceberg . . ." She squinted. "The Eiffel Tower, you mean?"

"Yeah, that one." He gulped the rest of the milk. When he set the cup down, he had a white creamy mustache that only added to his charm. He looked straight at her. "Do you have a dog here?"

"No." She looked around. The cat must've been in the back room with Rip. "We have a kitty named Tigger."

"Oh. I have a doggie named Gus."

The lump in her stomach grew. A doggie named Gus. One more reason it would be hard for Joey to make this transition. Harder than she'd ever thought. "Well . . . we might get a dog someday. I think dogs are nice."

He scrunched up his face. "'Cept dogs eat cats."

"Oh, Joey . . . not always." She heard the alarm in her voice. "Sometimes they just chase cats."

"I guess." He looked around. "So where is he? The kitty?"

Before she could answer, Rip's voice sounded in the hallway. "Is she gone?"

"Yes." Wendy stood and met him halfway across the living room. She lowered her voice. "Joey's doing much better. Probably just needed time to get used to us."

Rip nodded, but he looked suspicious. "He doesn't like me." He peered over Wendy's shoulder to the table, and her eyes followed his. Joey was swirling his glass, playing with the last few drops of milk and cookie crumbs.

"That's ridiculous." She kept her tone hushed. "He doesn't even know you."

"Well, he'd better start." Rip thrust his shoulders back and stuck out his chest. "I'm his daddy, after all."

"Rip . . ." She held up her finger. "Don't go saying anything about that. Mrs. Bower told us, remember?" She peered at Joey. "He doesn't know yet."

"Okay, I get it." He made a mock show of putting his finger to his lips and zipping them closed. "I won't say a word."

Rip led the way back to the kitchen table. Wendy took her chair, and Rip sat on Joey's other side. "Hey, little man." He patted Joey's back, maybe a little too hard. "How'd you like the cookies?"

Joey lowered his chin. His eyes got big and he slid closer to Wendy. "Good, thanks."

"You don't need to be shy, kid." He stood and took Joey's hand. "How 'bout we show you to your room?"

"No, thank you." He leaned into Wendy and pulled his hand free. "I just wanna sit here."

Rip wore a look of disbelief, and Wendy wasn't surprised. People simply didn't tell Rip Porter no. He took Joey's hand again and this time gave him a tug that brought him to his feet. "We have to put your suitcase away, little man." His voice was stern. "Around here if I say we're doing something, well, then that's what we're doing."

Joey had no choice but to be pulled along. Rip grabbed the boy's suitcase on the way, and Joey started to cry. He pointed back at Wendy. "I wanna sit with her."

"You can sit with her later." Rip tugged Joey again and this time the boy fell into step beside him.

Wendy understood what Rip was doing. He wanted to show Joey the bear, the stuffed animal he'd brought and so proudly set up on the child's pillow. But this was no way to do it. He should've waited until Joey was tired. Then they could've taken him back to his room together and the surprise might've been a good thing. She stood and followed them. *God . . . please let this go well.* "Rip . . . wait for me."

It was too late. By the time she reached the bedroom, Joey was sobbing and shaking his head, pointing back to the door. "I wanna be with her."

"Look!" Rip gave his arm a sudden jolt. Not enough to hurt him, but enough to make him stop crying. The fact seemed to please Rip. He relaxed a little and led Joey all the way to the bed. "See there." He nodded to the stuffed bear. "I bought you a gift."

Joey nodded. His shoulders still shook, but he wasn't making any noise now. "Th-th-thank you."

"Well . . ." Rip picked it up and handed it to Joey. "You can hold it if you want."

"I already . . . have Mr. Growls. He's b-b-back home." He pointed to his suitcase. "And Mr. M-m-monkey is in there." The child's words were quiet, but from the doorway Wendy understood them. Obviously he already had his favorite stuffed animals. He pulled free of Rip's hand, unzipped the top of his little suitcase, and brought out a well-worn stuffed monkey. "Th-th-this is Mr. Monkey."

"Fine." Rip's face showed his hurt. He fired the bear back at the bed, and Joey jumped, dropping the monkey to the floor. Rip brought his face close to the boy's. "One day soon I'm gonna teach you some manners, little man."

Rip's tone and mean eyes must've scared Joey even more. He started crying and this time he dropped the monkey, ran around Rip and spread out, face down, on the bed. Wendy met Rip's eyes and Rip gave her a look that said, *What?* He glared at the weeping figure on the bed and then back at her. "I'm doing my best."

She shook her head, walked past him and sat on the edge of the mattress. If Rip was going to make a mess of things, then it would be up to her. She stroked Joey's back. "Honey, I'm sorry you're upset." She reached down to the floor, picked up the child's toy, and tucked it in near his shoulder. "Here, Joey. Here's Mr. Monkey."

He only cried harder. "I wanna go home! Please!" He lifted his tear-streaked face and gave her a look that broke her heart. "I want Mommy and Daddy."

"That's it." Rip slapped the wall and took two threatening steps toward them. He grabbed Joey's arm and jerked him into a sitting position. "Let's get one thing straight." He brought his face inches from Joey's. "As long as you're here, *this* is your home."

"Rip . . . don't!" Wendy tried to pull him from the boy, but he wouldn't budge. She knew better than to get in his way when he was at the start of a rage, but she wouldn't let him hurt Joey. Not even if it meant laying down her life. She snapped at him. "You're going to ruin everything."

"No." He put his arm hard around her shoulders. "I'm just clearing things up." He glared at Joey again. "Like I said, when you're here, this is your home." He jolted Wendy even closer to him. "This is your mommy." He grinned but it was the meanest look he could've given the boy. "And *I'm* your daddy." He shoved Joey back down on the bed. "Understand?"

"Y-y-yes." Joey's face was pale.

Wendy watched Rip's anger fade as quickly as it had come. He looked down for a moment and rubbed the back of his neck. Then he turned and left the room in a hurry, without looking at her or saying another word to the child.

The moment he was gone, Wendy instantly returned to Joey's side, stroking his back, sheltering him. She could've spat at Rip for what he'd just done. If the boy said anything, Allyson Bower would run to the judge, and that would be that. Joey would stay with his adoptive parents for sure.

"Honey, it's okay," she whispered near Joey's ear. "He's just a little uptight. He isn't always like that."

Joey was whimpering. "He . . . he's mean."

She cursed Rip under her breath. She'd told a few of the girls at church to pray for them, but nothing could make Rip behave the way he should all the time. Not when Rip had a will of his own. She smoothed Joey's hair. He rolled onto his side and looked at her. His breathing was uneven, his body still shaking with sobs. "Why is he . . . mad at me?"

"He's not." She sorted through her words, trying to find the right ones. "He just wanted you to like the little bear he bought you."

Joey nodded. He made his hands into fists and rubbed his eyes. "Maybe Mr. Monkey could be friends with t-t-two bears."

A ray of hope shone on Wendy's heart. "Yes, that's it. Maybe so."

"What time is it?"

"Almost dinnertime." She rubbed his back some more. "Think you could come out of your room and have some pizza with us?"

"Yes." He sat up slowly and looked around the bed. He found the bear on the other side of the pillow and he picked it up. "It's a nice bear."

"It is." Wendy held her breath. If only Rip could see the child now . . .

Joey took the bear and placed it carefully on the pillow. Then he took the monkey and set it right next to the bear. Last, he took the bear's paw and the monkey's arm and crossed them so it looked like they were holding hands. "Listen, Mr. Monkey. This is your new friend—Mr. Bear. He's not Mr. Growls, but monkeys can have t-t-two bear friends. Okay?"

Wendy watched, fascinated. Just minutes ago Joey was cowering on the bed, falling apart under Rip's harsh words and hands. But now he was directing his attention to helping his toys get along with each other.

Dinner was less eventful. Joey asked Rip if he could have pineapple on his pizza.

"No." Rip snarled at him. He seemed to be making no effort to recover from the earlier disaster in Joey's room. "Pineapple's terrible on pizza."

"Okay. S-s-sorry." Joey didn't speak to him again the rest of the evening.

Rip spent most of the night watching a baseball game on television. Halfway through the pizza, Joey tugged on Wendy's sleeve. He talked quietly, as if he was too nervous to speak up with Rip around. "Is he watching baseball?"

"Yes. The Indians." Wendy was still mad at Rip. He could've done so much better for Joey's first night. She smiled at the boy and put her arm around him. "The Indians are from around here." She looked at Rip. "He watches all their games."

Joey nodded, but he yawned at the same time. When dinner was over he helped Wendy clean up. Having him work at her side was amazing. All those years without him Wendy had wondered what it would be like to be a mother, to have the incredible privilege of raising the infant boy she'd cradled that day in the hospital. Today, for the first time, she had a chance to know the feeling for real.

As she tucked him in, she could only hope about the future, that this would be the first of countless nights of tucking him in, knowing that her son was asleep down the hall in the same house as herself.

Just as she thought he was falling asleep, he sat up, his eyes wide. "I need to call home. My mommy and daddy told me I could."

Wendy hesitated. She had hoped they could get through this first visit without his making any calls home. Otherwise how was he going to get used to them in just a handful of trips? She eased him back down onto the bed. "Let's call in a little while, okay?"

His eyelids were heavy. "Promise?"

"Promise." She rubbed his back until she heard little snores coming from him. Then, when she was sure he wouldn't hear her, she whispered close to his head, "Good night, Joey. Mama loves you."

As she left his room, a thought hit her. Rip had better figure out how to get along with Joey, how to treat him. Because now that she'd found Joey, one thing was sure.

She wasn't ever going to let him go.

Joey wasn't sure how late it was or how long until morning. His eyes opened and he sat straight up. He looked around. Where was he, and why was his bed different? He could feel his heart bumping inside him.

Hard and fast. His fingers moved around his pillow. "Gus . . . Gus, where are you?"

But there were no little dog noises, no furry tail wagging beside him.

Then he remembered.

He wasn't at home tonight. He was with the other mommy and daddy, sleeping in a strange bed. His hands reached around some more and . . . there he was. "Mr. Monkey!" He held the fuzzy friend close to his face. Then he whispered so only Mr. Monkey would hear him. "I wanna go home."

A light was coming in through his window, so he could see Mr. Monkey's face. *I wanna go home, too,* Mr. Monkey was saying. *But I like my new friend, Mr. Bear.*

"Yes, Mr. Bear is nice. I think Mr. Growls will like him." He patted his pillow and found the other stuffed friend. Then he held them both close and lay back down again.

The daddy at this house was very mean and mad. Not like his own daddy at all. Plus his arm hurt where the man grabbed him. He blinked in the dark. His heart was still bumping loud and fast. Then he thought about the mommy at this place. She was a nice lady. She made good chocolate-chip cookies, plus she had soft hands. Her eyes had nice in them, and that made him not so scared about the mean man.

He wasn't sleepy, but it might be a long time until morning. Mommy's words from a long time ago filled up his head. *Sleeping makes the nighttime go by a lot faster.* That's what she told him. He closed his eyes and tried. *Sleep. Sleep . . . sleep . . . sleep!*

It isn't working, Mr. Monkey told him.

"I know it isn't." He lay very still, but he opened his eyes and looked around. What did the mean man say? That as long as he was here, this was his home and they were his mommy and daddy? A scared feeling happened to him and his heart bumped even faster. Why would he say that? Maybe the nice lady would tell him tomorrow at breakfast.

He closed his eyes again, but still he couldn't sleep. He remembered the Indians. He knew Ohio was an Indian place, but how come no teepees? He shivered a little.

That's when he remembered about God. He smiled, and next to him Mr. Monkey and Mr. Bear smiled, too. This time he kept the words quiet, just in his heart. *Hi, God . . . It's me, Joey. Thanks for being with me on the plane today and at this house. Remember, God? A few times I was scared, only then I could feel You beside me.* He smiled again. *That's why I know You're real. Even though You're 'visible.*

He felt a little tired come over him. *Can You do something, God? . . . Can You please stay with me tomorrow and on the way home, too? 'Cause Mommy and Daddy and Gus aren't here, remember? And also can You tell my family something, 'cause I didn't get to call 'em? Tell them I love them and I can't wait to get home.* He tried to remember the ending, the way Jonah ended his prayer. He wasn't sure what it meant, but he said it in his heart anyway. *Gee this name, amen.*

Mr. Bear was already asleep, but Mr. Monkey tapped Joey's arm. *I like when you talk to God,* he said.

"Me, too." He was much more sleepy now. "I like it 'cause it means I'm not alone."

You're not alone, Mr. Monkey said. *You have me.*

"I know." He smiled a little, but he was almost asleep. He didn't want to tell Mr. Monkey, but he liked having God even better than his fuzzy friend. Because God was the strongest one in the whole universe. And that made him feel very safe. Safe enough to close his eyes and sleep. Because God was stronger than anyone.

Even the mean man who lived at this house.

Chapter Fifteen

Their plans came together at Fuller Park.

The place was quiet and close, and it gave them complete confidence that Joey wasn't listening to their conversation. Molly still couldn't believe it had come to this, but Jack was right. They were out of options. She settled in against the park bench and watched her husband, the man she trusted and loved with her whole life. He was pushing Joey on the swing, saying something about airplanes or pirates or reaching the sky. Molly appreciated the distraction.

Joey had been home just fifteen hours, and already she'd replayed his homecoming a dozen times in her head.

She'd been wearing out a path along the kitchen floor waiting for his return. When he walked through the door with Mrs. Bower, she rushed to him, dropped to her knees and held him close.

"Mommy! I missed you so much!"

"Me, too, buddy."

But even before she could ask questions or tell him

hello, the social worker tapped her on the shoulder. "Can I speak with you . . . alone?"

Jack had been in the workout room upstairs. At the sound of Joey at the door, he hurried down and into the entryway. He, too, stooped down and pulled Joey into a hug. His words were tight with emotion when he could finally speak. "We missed you, sport. I'm so glad you're back."

Molly motioned to him that Allyson Bower wanted to talk to them. Gus was the perfect distraction. The dog trotted up and nearly knocked Joey down in his hurry to say hello. "Gus!" Joey sounded happy, healthy. Normal. Molly could finally draw a complete breath. Her son was out of danger. For now.

They followed the social worker into the kitchen where Joey couldn't hear them. She opened a file and took out a single sheet of paper. "You'll see four finger-print bruises on Joey's left upper arm." Her face was shrouded in concern. "The Porters told me about it. Their story goes that Joey was falling or he needed help up." Her words dripped disgust. "Apparently, Mr. Porter took hold of Joey's arm to help him." She showed them the piece of paper. "It's all here in the report."

Once again, Molly felt the room start to spin. What was happening here? They were talking about documented bruises on their son's body? At the hands of a convicted felon? A domestic-violence offender? Had the whole world gone crazy? Joey would never be safe with a man like that—never! She tried to focus. Jack was talking now.

"What I'm saying is, did anyone ask Joey what happened?"

"The Porters told me the story in front of him." She

shook her head as if to say that wasn't how things were supposed to work out. "I pulled Joey aside and asked him if the story was true, if that's how he got the bruises."

"What did he say?" Molly couldn't sort through her emotions fast enough. One moment she was furious, the next she wanted only to take Joey in her arms and rock him until he felt safe again.

The social worker gave a thoughtful nod. "He said it was true. What I didn't like was how he kept looking over his shoulder while I was talking to him." She hesitated. "I think he's afraid of Rip Porter, but I can't prove it."

"So, isn't that enough?" Jack's voice was a study in controlled fury. "The man's served time for domestic violence. He leaves bruises on my son's arm. Certainly the judge won't give the man custody now."

Mrs. Bower pressed her lips together. "If you and Joey were walking and he tripped, you'd reach out to catch him, too. And you might leave bruises on his arm." She lifted her shoulders. "I have no choice but to believe the story. Without Joey's testimony, no one would ever blame Rip Porter for a few little bruises."

Molly read more into the woman's statement. "Meaning what, exactly?"

"Meaning it'd take a lot more than that for anyone to accuse him of abusing his own biological son." She looked intently at them. "Children rarely testify against adults, Mrs. Campbell."

"But if the Porters are lying"—Jack's mind must've been headed in the same direction as Molly's—"and if we could get Joey to tell us that, then wouldn't the judge throw Porter back in prison and let us keep him?"

"No." Allyson was a strong woman from what they

knew of her, a businesswoman. But in that moment she looked sad, even vulnerable. "The system doesn't work that way. The paperwork was forged, so by the court's standards, Joey's adoption was never completed, never official. If Rip Porter walked into a downtown bank and held it up at gunpoint with a dozen witnesses, they could send him to jail for the rest of his life, and still Joey would not belong to you." She tapped the file in her hand and looked from Molly to Jack. "Joey's adoption never took place. Not legally."

After Allyson left, Molly and Jack cuddled with Joey and Gus on the sofa. They watched Disney's *World's Greatest Athlete* and laughed when the coach's team was so bad, his football players didn't know which direction to run. When Nanu, the jungle boy, came with the coach to the United States to help the team, Joey sat on the edge of his seat. Clearly he was amazed at the way the jungle boy could run and jump and hit and throw. But near the end of the program, Joey cried quiet tears. "Nanu doesn't want to win. He just wants to be home."

"That's right, Joey." Molly kissed his head.

He looked up at her. "'Cause home's the best place."

Jack and Molly exchanged a look. Then Molly said it was time to get Joey's pajamas on. They walked him up to his room and she took his T-shirt off. The bruises were easy to see. They couldn't have been made by anything but an intentional grab at their son's arm.

Molly ran her fingers over them. "Joey . . . what happened here?"

Joey stayed silent.

"It's okay, baby." Molly kissed his cheek. "You can tell us. You're not in trouble."

Joey bit his lip. Gus moved into the room and for a few seconds he was distracted, petting the dog.

Jack tried this time. "Joey, tell us about the bruises, sport. What happened?"

"You can't t-t-tell that other d-d-daddy, okay?"

Molly wanted to cry an ocean of tears. When had he started stuttering? Was he that afraid, that worried that somehow the "other daddy" would hurt him? In just one brief visit? What would a lifetime with a man like that mean for Joey?

"That other daddy is Mr. Porter." Jack's tone flowed with compassion, putting Joey at ease. "He won't find out. I promise."

Joey ran his other hand over the bruise and his eyes grew damp again. "That m-m-man was m-m-mad at me. I was laying d-d-down and he wanted to talk to me." The stuttering was worse with every sentence. "He grabbed me and made me sit up. Then he yelled at me. He t-t-told me pretty s-s-soon he would t-t-teach me a lesson."

Jack groaned and leaned against the wall.

Molly could only imagine the battle her husband was waging inside his head and heart, because the war inside hers was just as fierce. If Rip Porter were standing in front of her, she would punch him square in the face. How dare he lay a hand on her son? It didn't matter that Rip was Joey's biological father. The man was a stranger, and a bad guy at that.

She ran her fingers gently over the row of marks on Joey's arm. "Buddy, why didn't you tell that to Mrs. Bower?"

"'C-c-cause . . . that mean daddy was watching us. If

I t-t-told the t-t-truth he might hurt me again. M-m-mostly I talked to God. He stayed with me the whole trip."

Jack rolled his eyes. Molly understood. What was God doing to help them? Joey had gone to Ohio despite her prayers and Beth's, and he had come home physically and emotionally damaged. Still, Molly refused to be cynical, at least where Joey was concerned. She leaned close to him. "I'm glad God was with you, buddy. I'm glad you weren't alone."

Jack took Joey into his bathroom to help him brush his teeth, and Molly unpacked his bag. Near the top she found the stuffed bear. She held it up. "Joey? What's this?"

"What?" Joey peered out from the bathroom. "Oh, that's Mr. B-b-bear. He's Mr. Monkey's new friend." Even ten minutes after talking about the bruising incident, Joey's stuttering was less than before. "The other daddy gave it to me."

In that moment, Molly knew what Mrs. Bower meant about children and abuse. Of course they didn't testify. Something inside children made them forget about traumatic events, like a safety mechanism in their hearts. One minute Joey had been terrified of Rip Porter. The next, he was happy about having received a stuffed animal from the man.

Half an hour later, when his bag had been unpacked and Mr. Monkey and Mr. Bear and Mr. Growls were tucked in on one side and Gus on the other, and when Joey was asleep, Molly and Jack stepped out into the hall. Molly stopped and faced him. She had just one thing to say.

"Jack . . ."

"I won't have it, Molly." He was fuming, pressing his hands against his temples and dropping them to his sides again. "I'd like to get my hands on him just for one minute! Grab a little boy who's already scared and alone and—"

"Jack . . ."

"No, I'm serious, Molly. This isn't right. There has to be a law in place that'll protect kids, because I'm not standing around and waiting until that man does something drastic to my son before—"

"Jack!"

He stopped. "What?"

She searched his eyes. When she had his full attention she opened her mouth and said the thing she never thought she'd say. "I'm ready for your plan."

That had happened just the previous night. Now here they sat in the park, ready to set the plan into motion— whatever the plan might be. A plan that would force them to cut ties with everything and everyone they knew in the United States and start life over again.

Molly felt as terrified and shocked about the idea as ever. No matter what they did, life was about to take a wild, frightening, uncontrollable turn. Jack's plan was worth pursuing because at least they would take that turn with Joey. Not without him. At the end of this very long, very dark tunnel, that was the only light whatsoever.

Jack walked back to Molly and took his seat on the bench. He turned to her, "I love you." His hands came up and he framed her face, studying her. With all the tenderness in the world, he kissed her lips. "Before we take this any further, I need you to know that. I've been in love with you since the day I met you."

She felt her throat grow thick. How had he known? This—his love for her—was exactly what she needed to hear right now. That whatever they faced, they'd face it as lovers and friends. She returned his kiss. "You're all I need, Jack." She allowed herself to get lost in his eyes. "I trust you. Whatever we have to do, we can do it together."

They settled back against the bench and kept their eyes on Joey. "Okay, Molly." Jack put his arm around her and cradled her head against his shoulder. "What we're about to do, our plans, our conversations, all of it must never— not for a minute—be discussed with anyone else."

Molly was about to say that his warning was unneces- sary. After all, they were making plans to leave the coun- try, to create new identities for themselves.

But then he looked at her, his eyes full of sorrow. "That means Beth, too."

Everything around her faded. The sound of the birds, the subtle breeze, Joey on his swing, even the pounding of her own heartbeat.

Beth.

Why hadn't she thought about her sister? Molly sat back and looked straight ahead again. Her junior year of high school, she had played a pick-up game of basketball at lunch with some of the drama kids. None of them had much experience in sports, and one of the guys winged the ball at her when she wasn't ready. She had taken it right in the gut, and it was half a minute before she could breathe again.

She felt that way now.

Leaving Florida, leaving life as they knew it, leaving everything about Jack and Molly Campbell—she was ready for all of it. But leaving Beth? Forever? Molly bent at her waist and leaned over her knees. She was getting her wind back, but her heart was still spinning out of control. Beth had been her best friend all her life. She shared everything with her sister.

"Molly . . ." Jack put his hand on her lower back. "You hadn't thought about Beth?"

She squeezed her eyes shut for a few seconds, then slowly sat up. She turned to Jack and shook her head. "I guess not."

"You can't tell her any of this."

"No." The right answers were easy. Putting them into play would be another thing. She would be working through the most difficult, most painful time in her life, and she wouldn't be able to tell a word of it to Beth. Then, when all the plans came together, she would have to do the impossible. She would say good-bye to her sister and friend, knowing they would never see each other again.

Once more she faced forward and looked at Joey, at his pale blond hair dancing in the warm breeze as he pushed himself higher, higher. She had no choice about Beth. In a few months, Molly Campbell would be dead, and so would her relationship with her sister. Molly steeled herself against the pain that would come. She would do it all for Joey.

There was no other way.

She nodded. "I understand."

"All right." Jack sounded relieved. He angled himself so he could see her better. "I've been thinking of a plan."

"Okay." Her heart bounced around inside her. She felt like she was standing at the open door of an airplane, about to jump. Only she wasn't even sure she had a parachute. "We have to get out of the country, right?"

"Right." Jack's words picked up speed. "That's the hardest part, because we have to answer to Allyson Bower."

"Not for everything." Molly felt the fight finding its way back to her. The energy felt wonderful, like she was less of a victim. "We share custody of Joey until that last visit. Isn't that what she said?"

"True." Jack thought for a moment. "In that case, it just might work." He tapped his knee a few times, something he only did when he was excited or nervous. "I went online and looked at work trips to Haiti. You know, the sort of trip Beth and Bill are taking with their church."

Molly felt a chill pass over her arms. Were they really doing this? Really having this conversation about how they could find their way out of the country? The temperature was over eighty degrees that afternoon, but she was suddenly cold. "Okay."

"Anyway, I was looking for a humanitarian group, the Red Cross or one of the international groups for humanity. Because it might look funny for two people who've stayed away from church to have a sudden interest in missions."

"True."

"Except here's the problem." He turned his hands over, baffled. "I couldn't find any in our area taking a trip in the next few months." He chuckled. "The only groups I could find were a handful of churches."

"Hmmm." Molly wasn't sure why, but she felt vindicated. At least on Beth's behalf. "Maybe we've been wrong about church." She thought about Joey's recent conversations with God. "About God, too."

"Maybe." Jack waved his hand, clearly anxious to move on. "We can talk about that later. The point is, most of the work trips won't let volunteers bring children younger than twelve."

Molly was confused. "So how is this going to help us?"

"One church in our area is doing a trip over Labor Day—it's an outreach to an orphanage." His eyes danced, and he lowered his voice. "People are encouraged to bring their whole families. That way the American children can play with the Haitian children while work is being done on the building."

Again Molly's heart beat harder than before. Jack had never looked more serious. "What church?"

He looked intently at her. "Bill and Beth's."

She froze for a moment. "You're kidding."

"No." He shook his head. "So first thing when we get home, you need to call Beth and tell her we'd like to come to church with them next Sunday." He covered her hand with his. "I know the two of you are close, but you have to do your part here, Molly. You can't give her a reason to suspect anything."

"Oh, sure." A sarcastic laugh came from her. "Just call her up and tell her we've changed our minds? After a decade of thinking they're weird for going to church and believing in the Bible, all of a sudden we're supposed to want to go to Sunday service?"

Twenty yards away, Joey waved at them. "Hey! Guess what?"

"What, sport?" Jack instantly turned his attention to their son.

"I'm gonna land this plane and go on that rocket ship."

He pointed to the jungle gym, the one with two slides built into it.

"Sounds good!" Jack kept his tone cheerful. If anyone was watching them—even someone who knew them well—no one would have guessed they were making plans to leave the country, to run from the authorities and start life over again.

Joey slowed down, jumped from the swing, and ran to the jungle gym. He would be busy for another fifteen minutes at least.

"Yes, Molly." Jack turned back to her. His voice was quietly urgent. "That's exactly what you do. We're in the middle of the biggest crisis of our lives. People go to church when they're in crisis, right? Isn't that what they do?"

Molly thought about that. He was right. After September 11, record numbers of people filled churches for months. Tragedy, she remembered hearing a newscaster say, is the open door to finding faith. From the first day she'd learned about the fraudulent adoption papers, she'd discussed the matter with Beth. Her sister was praying for her and with her. Maybe she wouldn't think it was so strange that now they wanted to go to church.

"Okay, so I call Beth." She was still confused. "Then we become members and get involved in a work trip all in the same afternoon? We don't have a lot of time."

"I know." Jack didn't look worried. Whatever he had in mind, he'd thought through the details. "You said Beth's family is going, right?"

"Right. Last I heard."

"Okay . . . so let's just ask about it. It would be the last time our families could all be together before we had to give up Joey—barring some change by the judge." He sat back a little. "I don't think that's so strange. We could even say that we're thinking about adopting again—this time internationally. We'll say we want Joey to be part of the process."

"And the judge is going to let us go? Let us leave the country?"

"Work trips to Haiti happen all the time." He pinched his lips together, determined. "We've always been involved in civic groups, Molly. Of course we might want a trip to Haiti to be one of our final memories with Joey."

Molly had her doubts, but she didn't say anything.

"Besides, we won't be telling Allyson Bower." Jack leaned over and dug his elbows into his knees. "The social worker said nothing about leaving the country, no rules or mandates from the judge." He looked at the ground for a minute. "They aren't checking up on us, right? We haven't heard from Mrs. Bower since Joey's visit." He straightened again. "I say we just go. She and the judge won't figure out what happened until we're long gone."

She heard the bitterness in his voice, but his idea made sense. She and Jack were adventurous, and they loved taking on civic projects. They had helped raise funds for the YMCA building in West Palm Beach, and they'd taken part in several 5- and 10-K runs to raise money for a local homeless shelter. Taking a trip to Haiti to help repair an orphanage was something they would have done.

Beth and Bill wouldn't think that was strange, certainly.

It would be only natural that they'd want to get in on the work trip. The adventure would give them something to look forward to while they hammered away every day at the task of finding an attorney to fight for Joey's custody.

"Okay . . ." Molly was still shivering, but she was catching on, understanding what Jack was thinking. "Then what?"

"By the time we'd leave for the trip, we'd have to have all the details in place. Our ultimate destination—at least for the first couple of years—would be the Cayman Islands."

"Cayman?" Molly had to hold onto the edge of the bench. Again she felt like she was in some strange dream or acting out someone else's life. She'd been to Grand Cayman once with Jack. The place was beautiful, surrounded by gorgeous beaches and endless blue-green water. But could she spend two years there? She steadied herself. "Where would we live?"

"I'll take care of that." He was still composed, still anxious to tell her the rest of what he'd been thinking. "We'll need fake passports, but I made a few phone calls. There's a guy in Miami who'll work with me. He thinks we're missionaries."

"Why would missionaries need fake passports?" Molly's head was spinning faster than ever. It was all she could do to keep up with the conversation.

Jack made an effort to slow down. "Some missionaries visit countries that are hostile to the Christian teaching. If missionaries become targeted, they might need to flee the country under a different identity." He shrugged one shoulder. "The guy I talked to says he believes in freedom of speech. If we need fake passports to further freedom of speech, he'll do them half-price."

Molly pressed her hands to the sides of her face. "I can't believe this . . ."

"Hey, look at me!" Joey was standing straight up at the top of the highest slide. "I'm a fireman!" He slammed an invisible helmet onto his head and plopped down hard, sending himself flying down the slide. At the bottom he looked in a dozen different directions, spraying invisible water at what must've been ferocious invisible flames.

"You're a hero, Joey!" Jack paused for a few seconds. "Mommy and I are still talking, okay?"

"Okay!" He raced up the ladder on the opposite side of the structure. "Now I'm going to the moon!"

Another couple strolled by on the sidewalk that wound through the park. Jack waited until they had passed before starting in again. "So we have our fake passports, and the day before the trip, we transfer funds to an account in Cayman. It's the world's second largest off-shore financial center. Then"—his voice grew more tense—"on, say, the third day of the trip, we'll take an excursion into town and we'll disappear. By the time they realize we're missing, we'll be on a plane with our new identities, headed for Europe. We'll stay there for a few weeks—just to make sure no one's onto us—then we'll fly to Cayman." He lifted his hands. "What do you think?"

What did she think? She had a thousand questions, all of them firing at her from different areas of her heart and brain. She opened her mouth and asked the first one that came. "Why *wouldn't* they be onto us?"

"We'll be using new identities. The authorities in Haiti won't have any trouble letting us through, and then we'll become part of the throng of millions of people in

Europe. It's not like our faces will be plastered up in every police station in England. The authorities won't have a clue where to look for us." Jack's expression told her this was obvious. "See, we leave for a day trip, and we're never heard from again." He hesitated. "After a while, they might even assume we were victims of foul play."

"We disappear a week before losing custody of Joey? The story'll make national news!"

"Yes. In time." His words were coming faster, as if he'd thought through even this detail. "By then we'll be in Europe with new identities. Tourists, mixing with other tourists. When the commotion in the press dies down, we'll fly to Grand Cayman."

The plan sounded plausible, but still she had more questions than answers. "Why would we take our four-year-old son into the streets of Haiti? Isn't it dangerous?"

"Yes, I've thought about that, too. These work trips include day excursions, trips to small villages to pass out food—that sort of thing." Jack wouldn't be swayed. "Don't worry, I'll find a reason to get us out on the streets. Then we'll find a ride to the airport. Once we get to Haiti, that'll be the least of our worries."

"All right." She would have to trust him. What else could she do? Another question hit her. Maybe she was wrong about her sister—maybe Beth would be suspicious after all. "What if Beth thinks it's strange, taking a trip out of the country right before Joey goes?"

He raised his brow. "You'll be in charge of that, of making her see things our way." He put his hand on her knee. "You can handle that, right?"

A man and his little boy came up along the sidewalk

from the other direction, carrying a baseball and two gloves between them. Jack waited for them to pass. He dropped his voice another notch. "Of course it'll be suspicious, but Beth will believe what you tell her. Don't you think so?"

"Maybe." Fear built in her again, and the fight took a backseat. "But maybe not. Maybe we'll do something that causes Allyson Bower to suspect what we're up to. Then we could get caught." She nodded in Joey's direction. "Our little boy could be turned over to the Porters and we could go straight to prison. Have you thought about that?"

"Of course." Jack's tone was just short of angry. "Listen, Molly. We won't be traveling under our own names. We'll have new identities, new passports. We'll leave Haiti under those names, arrive in Europe, and buy a few Eurail passes. We'll travel the region like a family on vacation, and at every hotel we'll check the news and the Internet. When the search dies down, we'll get over to the Cayman Islands."

"What about our money?" She was shaking now, trembling from her fingertips to her toes. "Couldn't they trace the money? You said we transfer it to Cayman, so once they find out, they'll put a lock on our funds and that'll be that." She hated that she was making this difficult for Jack, but if she didn't talk about her doubts now, she'd never feel right going through with the plan. "If they find the money, it'll just be a matter of time before they find us."

"I've got that figured out, too." He leaned forward again. His eyes were sharp and intelligent. "We'll move the money through a series of transfers. It's complicated, but when it's all said and done, the money will be in an account in Cayman under our new identities." He gave her a single nod. "Leave that part to me, Molly."

She felt weak, nauseous. Were they really going through with this? It was much more than she could handle or imagine. She looped her arm through his and leaned into his shoulder. "How much money?"

"That'll take some work." He kissed the side of her face. "But I've thought about that, too. We'll pull the equity from our rentals and from our own house. It should be more than a million."

"A million dollars?" The amount raised another list of questions, but she didn't have the strength to ask them.

"Yes." He put his arms around her and stroked her gently. "We'll be fine, Molly. We will. Once we're in Cayman for a few years, when the search for us has grown completely cold, we can travel under our new names. We could go anywhere, really. Just not back to the United States."

"And not back to Jack and Molly Campbell."

He gave a slow nod. "Right."

Molly closed her eyes and took a long breath through her nose. "Jack . . ." She clung to him. "I can't believe we're doing this."

"Me, neither." Jack held her tight, and for a long time they said nothing.

What was left to say? The judge had made his decision, and now they had made theirs. They would set the plan into motion, and they would have to hold discussions like this one often, making sure the details were coming together. They would say good-bye to everything they knew and loved about their lives as Jack and Molly

Campbell, and they would start over again. If the courts wouldn't look out for the best interests of their child, then they'd have to take the matter into their own hands.

Whatever they had to pay in the process, the cost would be worth it.

All for the love of Joey.

Chapter Sixteen

Molly made the phone call that afternoon, when Beth and Bill would be home from church. She had practiced her part in her mind enough times that when Beth answered the phone, Molly kept her voice casual, normal.

The conversation started with talk about Joey and how he had handled his first visit.

"He's fine, but something has to be done." Molly sounded upset, the way she would've felt if they didn't have the plan to leave the country. "Tomorrow morning we're calling a list of politicians."

"That's a great idea." Beth was still ready to fight on their behalf. "I'll make calls, too. Whatever I can do to help." She exhaled hard. "This is ridiculous, Molly. That boy belongs with you."

"I know." She kept her tone sorrowful. At Jack's direction, she left out details of the bruises on Joey's arm. No reason to give Beth cause to suspect they were crazy with fear. She steadied her voice. "Jack's going through a new list of attorneys tomorrow, too. Someone will help us. I have to believe that."

"I'm so sorry, Molly. I can't even imagine going

through this." Beth hesitated. "It may not make you feel better, but everyone in our Sunday school class is praying for you. No one can believe a judge could order a child back to his biological parents almost five years later."

"That means a lot." This was her opening. "Hey, that reminds me. You won't believe this. Jack and I were talking today at the park." She pinched the bridge of her nose. She'd never lied to Beth before. Even now, everything in her wanted to share the details with her sister, but she couldn't. Not a word of them. "Anyway, Joey's been talking to God." She uttered a sad laugh. "I guess Jonah taught him."

"Really?" Beth sounded like her heart was melting. "That's so sweet."

"We thought so." She forced herself to take the next step. "Jack wanted me to tell you . . . we'd like to go to church with you next Sunday."

Beth's gasp was quiet, but it was a gasp all the same. "Are you serious?"

"Yes." Molly made a sound that was part laugh, part cry. "We need all the help we can get."

"Molly . . . I'm so glad." The happiness in Beth's voice was pure and complete. She had no suspicions whatsoever. "God has a plan for Joey, I mean that. No matter how things look now, if you seek God . . . if you really trust Him, I know He'll make those plans clear to you."

Molly hated this, hated lying to her sister. "That's what we're starting to believe."

"Well, let's not wait until Sunday. That's a week away. Bill and I can meet with you a few times this week so we can all pray. There's power in prayer, I tell you, Molly.

I'm just so glad you're seeing it now." Beth's words ran together, her excitement and fervor tangible. "Talk to Jack about that, okay?"

"Okay." The words felt like acid on Molly's tongue. And this was only the beginning. "Hey, Beth, I have to go. But thanks. I'm not sure we would've thought about turning to God without you."

"Oh, Molly." Beth's voice cracked. "I love you so much. It's only because I love you that I've always wanted your family to find faith."

"I know." Molly clenched her fists. She had to get off the phone, had to end the conversation before she burst into a confession about all she was doing. "I love you, too."

Beth went on a little longer about the benefits of having a strong faith. Molly wasn't really listening. Instead she did something Joey would do. She talked to God— just a little. *It's not a complete lie, God. . . . I do want to know more about You, and I do think it's better if people are praying for us.*

Beth was winding up. "Okay . . . so talk to Jack and we'll figure out the details later."

"I will." They said their good-byes, and Molly hung up the phone.

The week played out just as they'd planned. Twice they met with Beth and Bill and talked about God, about His plan for all of them, His salvation. They looked at Bible verses, and Molly couldn't help but find herself really listening, really finding truth in the things Beth and Bill were sharing with them.

"It makes sense," Molly told Jack one night that week.

"It makes our plan work." Jack smiled at her. "That's all."

She didn't push the matter. Sunday came and Beth was sweet and tender. She gave Molly an envelope with her name written across the front. "It's a little card I found." Beth gave her a hug. "Don't open it until later today."

Molly didn't know what to say. With every heartbeat, she could hear a voice shouting at her, *Liar . . . Liar . . . Liar!* She returned her sister's hug. "It feels good to be here."

"It feels wonderful." Beth held onto her shoulders and studied her face. "I think God's about to work a miracle, Molly. I can feel it."

The four of them checked the kids into Sunday school classes and took seats together in a pew halfway back. Jack purposefully opened his bulletin and began reading it. Then, as if on cue, he leaned around Molly and spoke to Bill. "You and Beth and the kids taking this work trip to Haiti?"

"We are." Bill's expression was a mix of genuine friendliness and pure awe. Molly understood. Beth and Bill had probably prayed for this day ever since they became Christians. Bill opened his bulletin and pointed to the blurb about the trip. "There's an informational meeting about it today after service."

Jack gave Molly a pointed look. "Did you tell Beth?"

Beth was sitting between Molly and Bill. She looked curious. "Tell me what?"

It was Molly's turn. She plunged ahead, hoping the entire conversation didn't sound like a poorly acted script. "About the work trip." She looked at Bill and back to Beth. "We're thinking about going, too."

"You're kidding!" Beth said the words a little too loud. "I'm just getting used to the idea myself." She giggled and lowered her voice. She looked around, sheepish about being too noisy in church. Then, just as fast, her smile faded. "What about Joey?"

Jack squeezed Molly's knee. "We're believing that everything will work out. We have to believe that." He shot a sad smile at Bill. "But at this point in our lives, we need a distraction, something positive we can do with our son."

Bill nodded. "I understand."

"I went online a few nights ago and read about the work trip. It seems, well"—he looked at Molly—"like a good idea all the way around."

"It'd be a chance for our two families to be together." Beth sounded helpful. No question she liked the idea. She stopped short of saying that it would be their last time to travel together with Joey, if he were taken away. Instead she nodded. "We'd love it if you came."

"Do you think they'd let us—I mean, since we're new?" Jack kept his tone tentative.

"I think so." Bill looked at Beth, and then back to Jack. "You'd be with us. People bring friends or family on these trips all the time. It'd be different if it were a mission trip. But work trips aren't as regulated by the church staff."

"Right." Beth's eyes sparkled. "This trip's different. They'll run a background check on you, but other than that . . . if you can swing a hammer, you'll be welcome." She looked at Bill and then at Molly again. "Can you come to the meeting after church?"

"I think so." Molly met Jack's eyes. There wasn't a

hint of duplicity there, and she was amazed. Maybe Jack had missed his calling. He was proving to be an amazing actor. "Do we have time?"

"Definitely." He directed his next question to Bill. "We can bring the kids on this trip, right? So we can bring Joey?"

"Yes." Concern slipped into his tone. "You think they'll let you take him? With all this custody stuff going on?"

Jack appeared as innocent as their son. He exchanged a look with Molly. "I don't see why not. We'll tell the social worker about it, of course." He breathed the lie as if he'd been telling lies all his life. "She'll have to give the okay."

Molly gave a look that confirmed their innocence. "We'll still have joint custody of him, no matter what."

Beth reached for Molly's hand and squeezed it. "Maybe by then it'll be permanent custody."

"Yes." They all settled back against the pew. A group of people were playing music up front. The service was about to begin.

"We'll talk more at the meeting after church," Beth whispered.

"Okay." Again Molly convinced herself it wasn't a lie, but still she hated herself for what they were doing. Beth and Bill believed their intentions completely. She smiled at Beth. "Thanks for everything."

Her sister slipped her arm around her and gave her a side hug. "I told you we'd be here. We'll do whatever you need us to do, Molly. I mean it."

During the service, Jack filled out a prayer card. Molly watched as he turned it over and scribbled, "Pray for our family." On the front he filled out their names and address and phone number. The church Bill and Beth attended was a large one—several services, six thousand members. Molly guessed no one was keeping close tabs on the infrequent attendees. At the bottom of the card, Jack had the choice to check "Visitor" or "Member." He checked the Member box, folded the card, and dropped it into the offering plate.

And just like that, the plan was in motion.

Chapter Seventeen

The prop plane was just about to land in Grand Cayman. Jack could hardly wait.

The trip to the Cayman Islands was something Jack had to do every few years. He had a fairly large account there, and most of the time business could be handled by telephone. But every so often the company smiled on his decision to take a trip to the island, further goodwill, meet with the account executives, host some high-end dinners, and strengthen relationships.

Trips like that kept the competition at bay and the accounts loyal.

It had been fourteen months since his last trip to Cayman, so when Jack went to his boss and suggested a trip to the islands, there was no hesitation. The man looked at his calendar. "Great idea." He grinned at Jack. No question his boss saw him as the most-favored officer in the company. "You taking Molly and Joey with you?"

"No, sir. Not this time." He gave the man an easy smile. At least this part was honest. "Maybe next time."

No one at work knew about the custody battle Jack

was facing. From the beginning, he'd thought it better if
he said nothing. Now he was relieved he'd kept quiet.
He didn't need people in every area of his life feeling
sorry for him and wondering about the moves he was
about to make.

The plans for the trip came together in a few days,
and now Jack was minutes from landing in Grand
Cayman. He looked out the window and let the scene
wash over his weary conscience. Every now and then it
occurred to him that what they were about to do was
illegal. If for some reason they got caught, they would
lose everything—their freedom, their reputation. Worst
of all they would lose Joey.

Jack was careful not to let those thoughts come up
often. It wasn't that he and Molly had accepted the idea
of being criminals. In his gut, he believed that what he
and Molly were about to do was wrong—people shouldn't
take the law into their own hands. But if it meant saving
Joey from a life of abuse, if it meant holding onto his
son, Jack could justify it. He would do anything to keep
his son safe. Absolutely anything.

It made him think about fathers who stole money to
feed their families during the Depression. He'd never
given much thought to the idea, never taken sides on the
issue until now. In light of what was happening with
Joey, he knew for certain what he would've done. If his
family needed to eat, he'd find a way to feed them. Even
if it turned him from an upright citizen into a common
thief.

Whatever it took to save his family.

Below the plane, the ocean water grew pale where it
splashed up against the land. The beaches in Cayman

were beautiful, nothing short of paradise. He felt calmer just looking at them. He would buy an old guitar once they got settled and write songs on the beach. Just like he'd always dreamed of doing. Yes, he was taking the law into his own hands, and yes, it went against his nature. But the plan was a good one. It would work. And no one would be hurt in the process.

Joey's birth parents didn't deserve the child. His mother hadn't wanted him in the first place, and his father was a violent criminal. If they could figure out how to live a normal life, let them have more kids down the road.

Joey belonged to Molly and him. Period.

Jack pressed his forehead against the window and shifted in his cramped seat. No one was going to hurt Joey or take him away, not while Jack still had breath left in him. He closed his eyes and let the warmth of the sun calm his heart. His love for Joey was fierce, more intense than anything he'd ever known or experienced. It was proof that the judge was wrong. The Porters weren't the boy's parents.

He and Molly were.

After another few minutes, the plane circled and landed. Once he was off the plane, carrying his single bag across the tarmac, Jack took in his surroundings— the palm trees waving in the mild ocean breeze, the sky so blue it almost hurt to look at it, and the salty smell of the nearby ocean.

He pictured how life would be. Molly helping Joey with his lessons, making sure he was ready for school when it felt safe to move to Europe. Jack would be in charge of venturing into town for food and supplies, and on lazy summery afternoons, he would sit on the beach and play his guitar. They would take long ocean swims and run along the sand. At night there would be a million stars overhead, and endless hours of conversation and time together.

It wouldn't hurt Joey to live that sort of life for a few years. And when the search for them had blown over, they could start again in England or Ireland or Germany—enroll Joey in a private school so he would have the very best education and the chance to meet wonderful children in the process. Two years in the Cayman Islands wouldn't be a burden. If life as they'd known it had to end, there could be worse places to start over.

Jack picked up his pace. He had a busy three days ahead of him. Business meetings with account executives, and high-powered lunches and dinners for the first day and a half. After that he would hop a plane to Little Cayman, where remote rental properties were plentiful. If things went well, he would find a beach house for rent and make a deposit under his new name: Walt Sanders.

The first day went as planned, and over lunch and dinner, Jack resisted the urge to prod the locals for details about which beach was the most remote. He wouldn't do anything that could come back to hurt them. Once the authorities realized that they'd run, certainly his boss would be interviewed, and that could lead investigators to Grand Cayman. It was crucial that he did nothing to give himself away during this trip.

As far as the locals knew, he had business all three days.

The Cayman Islands were under the rule of the

British government, but they lay smack in the middle of the Caribbean. They consisted of just three islands. Most commerce and tourism took place on the big island, Grand Cayman. Jack wanted to stay far from there. Too many people to avoid, too great a chance of being recognized.

He flew to Little Cayman early the next afternoon. There was a small account that operated off that island, which gave him a legitimate reason to be there. He spent half an hour with the client, then took a cab to the closest real estate office. The place was small and dusty, as if the Realtors spent most of their time on the beach—like everyone else on an island that remote.

"I'm looking for a long-term beach rental," he told the elderly woman who sat behind the desk. He and Molly had discussed this. They didn't want to buy a house. In fact, as soon as they arrived in Cayman, they planned to close their bank account and take the money in cash. Yes, it was a lot to be responsible for, but Jack could ask for large bills. With their new passports, they needed to be flexible and mobile. If for some reason people became suspicious of them, or authorities turned their search to the Cayman Islands, they would have a way to escape without leaving money tied up in an account or in real estate.

The woman smiled. "We have many places suitable for you." She had a thick British accent. "Would your schedule permit time to look?"

Jack was beside himself. This was exactly what he'd hoped for. "Yes." He glanced at his watch. "The rest of the afternoon."

They climbed into the woman's open-air Jeep, and

she took him down a road she called Main Street, only it wasn't paved, and the farther they went, the more it felt like a poorly maintained footpath. After a short while, all signs of buildings or villages disappeared. The road wound through thick vegetation and palm trees. Occasionally, without warning, she would hang a sharp right turn and take them down an even narrower road that would put them out into a cluster of homes.

All of the homes were nice, but Jack didn't want other houses around them. Not for a mile. "Do you have something more private?"

"Yes." She gave him a look that said she didn't necessarily think more privacy was a good idea. "Farther out—farther in for food."

"Yes." He smiled. "That's fine."

The woman pulled her Jeep back onto the main road. For the next fifteen minutes, she drove without talking. When she finally made a right turn, Jack figured they were at the clear opposite end of the island. The driveway wasn't like the other ones she'd shown him. This one was two miles long, at least.

When they finally reached a clearing, the ocean spread out like a brilliant carpet in front of him. Up ahead, to the left, was a small white house with a screened-in lanai. It looked almost like something from one of the beaches in South Florida. The building was older and nondescript, so much so that it almost blended in with the white sandy beach.

"This is vacant, and very difficult to rent." The woman gave the house a look of disdain. "Most clients prefer higher-quality amenities. This is not the finest Little Cayman can offer."

No, Jack thought. But it was perfect. He could tell already. They hopped out of the Jeep, and Jack walked toward the water.

"Would you care to see the interior first?" The woman looked confused.

"No . . . I mean, I want to take a look at the beach first."

"I'll never understand." The woman waved her hand at him. "Crazy Americans."

Jack laughed, but he picked up his pace. When he reached the water, the view was breathtaking. Like something from a magazine advertisement or a movie. They might as well have been the only people on earth for all the lack of activity around them. There were no other houses as far as he could see.

Someone had left an old picnic table in the sand a few feet from a small cluster of palm trees. Jack stared at it and he could see them—the way he and Molly and Joey would look there in just a few months. On that very picnic table they would sit and watch the brilliant sunsets. They would play cards and laugh about the things Joey would say and do. He jogged back up the beach to where the woman was waiting. "Yes . . ." He was breathless, his heart pounding, not so much from the run up the sand, but from the thrill of it all. The house was exactly what he was looking for. He pulled his digital camera from his pants pocket and snapped a dozen pictures.

"But your information is incomplete." She lowered her brow. He half expected her to yell at him. "We must take a gander at the house."

Then he remembered what he was doing. He didn't

want to seem strange or out of the ordinary. The odds of anyone ever questioning her about their time that afternoon were infinitesimally small. But still . . .

He chuckled, put his camera back in his pocket, and dusted his hands off on his pants. "Yes. Let's take a gander."

It had three bedrooms and a spacious living room. The lanai screen was ripped in a few places, but nothing he couldn't fix up. The kitchen was plain, simple. But it came with a refrigerator. The laundry room was smaller than Molly was used to, certainly. But again, the machines were part of the deal. He'd just have to pick up a few pieces of furniture now and then, some linens and necessities in the village, and they'd be set.

All the way back to the Realtor's office, Jack said very little. He was too busy taking in the scenery, the lush plants and trees, the tropical smell. It was hard to believe that in less than two months, this would be home. Yes, it would be an adjustment. For Molly, most of all. He wouldn't mind leaving the corporate world. And one day, when they moved to Europe for Joey's schooling, he could find another job. Get reconnected with pharmaceutical sales.

Molly, though—she would have to say good-bye to her friends, her social connections, and everything that made up their way of life. Worst of all, she would lose her relationship with Beth. Jack's throat grew thick at the thought, but he swallowed hard and his emotions eased. They had no choice. By doing this, at least they would have each other. Every time they talked about it, Molly said the same thing.

"You and Joey, baby . . . That's all I need."

By the time Jack boarded the plane for the flight home, he had the deal locked up. Using the name Walt Sanders, he filled out the rental agreement and gave the woman a deposit. He told her they'd be needing the house for at least a year, and that they'd check in with her middle of September sometime, when they landed on the island.

The last thing he did was open a bank account. Things were different on the Cayman Islands. For one, it was the largest offshore banking community in the world. On Grand Cayman alone—in a stretch of land just twenty-two miles long—there were more than five hundred banks or financial institutions. Hiding money would be easier there than just about any place south of Florida. A person could open a checking account and make a deposit with false identification, and as long as they didn't want to borrow money, the bank would never raise a question.

Jack opened an account under the names Walt and Tracy Sanders and deposited three thousand dollars. The bank representative made casual conversation, and Jack mentioned that he and his family would be coming there for a year while he worked on a project.

"Very good." The man was more than happy to take Jack's money. "Your account will be here for you when you come."

Now Jack settled back into his airplane seat and closed his eyes. He'd taken care of every last detail, even getting the names of the local grocer and a few furniture stores on Grand Cayman since Little Cayman Island was too small for more than just a basic food store. He could hardly wait to talk to Molly, hardly wait to show her the photographs of the place on Little Cayman. The few times fear tried to crash in on his satisfied feeling, he dismissed it. They were doing what they had to do.

The plan was coming together beautifully.

Chapter Eighteen

It had been thirty minutes since Joey left with Allyson Bower for his second visit with the Porters, and Molly was in the midst of a full-blown panic attack. She and Jack were in the car with Jack driving, but he wasn't going fast enough. They were still fifteen minutes from the airport.

"Hurry!" She bit her finger, tapping her foot on the floorboard. Faster . . . they had to go faster. "We'll never get there in time."

They had to see Joey before he got on the plane. Yes, he'd been calmer this time when Allyson had picked him up. He had cried, but only a little. Allyson seemed just as frustrated as before. She told them that she'd made several calls to the judge, but still there was no bending. The boy would soon belong to the Porters.

Joey had used the bathroom one last time before he left. When he came out, he was drying his wet hands on his jean shorts. His cheeks were tear stained but he wasn't sobbing, wasn't hysterically clinging to Jack.

Molly held her hands out to him and wondered, was this how change happened? Gradually, what had been horrific and terrifying became sad and uncomfortable, and then one day it became acceptable? A part of life?

Joey's stuttering had been bad for the first week after he'd been home from the Porters the first time. He'd wet the bed a few times that week, too—something he hadn't done in a year. But now he was talking fine and getting up at night to use the toilet, just like before.

She clung to Joey and whispered in his ear, "Call me, okay? Before you go to bed."

He leaned back, his fingers still linked around the back of her neck. "I asked God to go with me again."

"Good." Molly meant it. Her fears were still wild and daunting—that he would die in a plane crash or choke on a hotdog or get deathly sick and no one would notice. When she and Jack met with Beth and Bill the last time, Molly made a decision. Why fake something as simple as prayer? If Joey could talk to God, so could she. She kissed her son's nose. "I'll ask Him, too."

By then, Joey had already hugged and kissed Jack good-bye. Jack stood a few feet away, talking to Mrs. Bower. Joey rubbed his button nose against Molly's. "Eskimo noses."

She did the same. Then she brushed her eyelashes against his. "And butterfly kisses."

He returned the gesture, but he stopped partway through and let his forehead fall against hers. "I'm gonna miss you so much, Mommy."

"Joey . . ." Her heart might as well have spilled out onto the floor. It felt that broken. She tried to picture the little house in the Cayman Islands. This was only temporary, this good-bye business. Very soon they'd be together forever, and no one would ever take Joey from them again. She held him a little longer. "I'll miss you, too."

Gus was sitting nearby, and for some reason he chose that moment to whimper a few times. Joey let go of her and put his arms around his dog. "You don't like when I go away, right, Gus?"

Joey nuzzled his face into the dog's fur. "Did you hear him, Mommy?" He looked up. "Gus says, please, can I stay here?"

"Tell Gus that's what we all want." Molly stood back with Jack. They said another round of good-byes. Then Mrs. Bower was ready, and after they left, Molly did what she'd expected to do the first time he walked out the door, three weeks earlier. She collapsed in Jack's arms and wept. Fifteen minutes later they realized what he'd forgotten.

"We have to get it to him." Molly was antsy, moving from side to side in the passenger seat, checking her watch. "The plane leaves in an hour. They'll be boarding soon."

"I'm doing my best." Jack grimaced.

The whole nightmare was one insane day after another. That Joey was even out of their sight, ready to board a jet to Ohio with a social worker, was still more than either of them could believe. The Porters, the lack of help from attorneys, the stubborn judge, the ridiculous law. Their plan to leave the country. None of it seemed even remotely realistic. Not when life had been beyond idyllic just five weeks ago.

But even with all the insanity, this moment stuck out as being of utmost importance. "We have to reach him before he leaves."

"We will." Jack took the exit for the airport, and after the curve he picked up speed. They were parked and running through the airport doors six minutes later. At the security checkpoint, they explained that their son, a minor, was on Flight 317 to Cleveland, and that he'd forgotten something.

"We have to get it to him."

The agent was happy to help. He wrote a temporary pass and ushered them toward security. The line was short that day, so within five minutes they were racing down the concourse toward the gate. They ran up just as Allyson and Joey stepped in line to board. Joey didn't look like he was crying, but even from twenty yards away his eyes were sadder than she'd ever seen them.

"Joey!" Molly barely recognized her own voice. She sounded like a lunatic, but she didn't care. "Joey, wait!"

He heard his name and turned around. "Mommy!" He broke free from Mrs. Bower and ran to them. "Daddy!"

The social worker stepped out of line. She didn't look altogether angry at them for coming to the airport, but the plane was boarding. She tapped her watch. If they were going to say something last-minute to Joey, they'd better get it said.

Molly pulled the item out of her bag and held it out to her son.

"Mr. Monkey!" Joey's face lit up. "I forgot him on my bed this morning!"

"I know." Molly straightened, her eyes locked on her son's. "I saw it there after you left."

"We hurried here so you'd have him." Jack swept

Joey into his arms and swung him around. "'Cause we love you."

Joey giggled. "And you love Mr. Monkey, too, right, Daddy?"

"Right." It was a moment that shone among days of darkness. The three of them hugging and rocking and Joey holding Mr. Monkey tight against his chest.

In the distance, Allyson Bower shot them a silent apology, then tapped her watch again. Jack picked up on the gesture. He gave Joey one last hug and set him down. "Time for you to go, sport."

"Okay." Joey's eyes grew sad, but not as sad as before. "Know what?" He looked at Jack and then at her. "I always have God with me, 'cause God always comes with you if you ask Him." He held up the stuffed toy. "But it's nice to have Mr. Monkey, too. Because I can cuddle with Mr. Monkey." He made a silly face. "And you can't cuddle with God."

"True." Molly stooped down and kissed him. "Go, buddy. Mrs. Bower's waiting for you."

He waved good-bye, still clutching Mr. Monkey, and in a few short seconds he and the social worker walked through the Jetway and disappeared from sight. Molly felt satisfied. "I'm glad we got it to him."

"Me, too."

Jack took her hand and they walked—like normal people—out of the airport and to their car. Their son would sleep in a strange bed that night, in a house they'd never seen, with two people they'd never met. He was the subject of a custody case that could make national news if they chose to call the papers. He was about to be whisked from his South Florida home to a remote beach house in some island in the middle of nowhere. His name was about to go from Joey to Aaron. Aaron Sanders.

But at least for tonight, if nothing else, he'd have Mr. Monkey.

Wendy stood at the bathroom sink.

Her regular foundation should've been enough to cover the bruise on her cheek, but it wasn't working. The mark still shone through, and Joey and the social worker would be there any minute. Rip had given her orders.

"Cover the thing, or don't show your face. I'll tell the Bower lady you're out."

But that would never do. The agreement was very specific. Both Rip and Wendy had to be at the house to greet Joey, so they could go over any instructions with the social worker. Wendy couldn't be gone—that would raise red flags for sure.

But so would the bruise.

Wendy felt tears in the corners of her eyes, and she blinked them back. She couldn't cry, not now. Her tears would ruin what makeup she already had on her face. She sniffed. *Don't be sad. Joey'll be here any minute. Then everything will be okay.*

She dug through her makeup bag and found a jar of under-eye concealer. It was thick and pasty, but it would cover the bruise. She let out a shaky breath. No matter what she told herself, she wasn't doing well. Having Joey for a visit wouldn't solve the other trouble.

The trouble with Rip.

He had been doing so well until Joey's first visit. But when he didn't immediately connect with their son, something inside him seemed to change. He had grown short with Wendy, snapping all the time and finding reasons to be mad at her. Even that wouldn't be so bad, because his rehabilitation in prison had taught him how to handle his feelings.

But no program could teach an angry man how to drink well.

Some people fell asleep when they drank, and others got silly. Rip, well, as long as Wendy had known him, whenever he drank, Rip had gotten full-blown furious. That's why, when he got out of prison, when he found out they were going to get Joey and have a family, Rip had made her a promise.

He was finished with the bottle.

A few beers now and then, maybe. But no more hard liquor. Not if he was about to be a daddy.

He broke the promise the night Joey left after his first visit. Rip drove out to the liquor store, bought two bottles of Jack Daniel's, and came home. The first one was already opened by the time he walked in the door. Wendy didn't say anything, of course. She knew better than to get in his way when he drank.

Instead, the next morning she brought the bottles to him—one half-empty and the other still unopened—and asked him to make a decision. "They could still change their minds about Joey, you know." She gave the bottles an angry shake. "They're watching us like hawks, making sure we don't take one wrong step to the left or right."

"I'll make my own decisions!" Rip talked big, but he hadn't had any choice really. Later that morning he took the half-empty bottle and dumped what was left down the drain. On Monday afternoon, before he reported in for training at the theater, he took the other bottle back to the store, lied about it being a gift, and got his money back.

She wanted to think that was that.

Since then he'd had a few gentler weeks, working at the theater and feeling good about himself. Most nights he talked nicely to her and told her how important he was at his new job. "They see big things for me, Wendy."

"Good, Rip. I'm so happy." She meant every word. "I believe in you, baby. I always have."

That's when he began drinking beer. Serious beer—a few more bottles every evening. But no more hard liquor, until two nights ago.

It started with questions from him. "What if the kid doesn't like me again this time?"

"He will." She wanted it to work, wanted it with everything inside her. "Just give him time to get used to you, Rip."

After another hour of that sort of conversation, Rip grabbed his keys. "I need fresh air."

When he came back, he didn't have a bottle, but it was obvious he'd been drinking. That's when she did what she never should've done. She confronted him.

"Where is it?" She met him near the front door, her hands on her hips.

"What?" He reeked of more than beer, and his eyes refused to focus. He waved an angry hand at her. "Get outta my way."

"This is all about Joey, isn't it? You're afraid of your own son, Rip. Don't you see that?"

His features tightened, the familiar windup that would release only with a flood of rage. "Don't tell me . . ." He struck at her, but she dodged him.

"This is all your fault!" She was tired of walking on eggshells, tired of hoping he would stay nice, hoping he would stay sober. It was time she told him how she really felt. "What happened the last time Joey was here was because you were mean to him!" She leaned forward, speaking louder than she'd spoken to him since he'd come home from prison. Once more he swung, but his knuckles barely glanced her cheek.

She took a few steps backward. "What are you doing, Rip? It's the same thing you did to Joey. You think you can intimidate people and that'll make you bigger and better, is that right?"

"The brat doesn't have any manners." His words were slurred, and squished between his angry lips.

But she could make them out all the same. Wendy felt her own anger build. "Don't talk about Joey like that! He's a wonderful little boy." She backed up again. "You might try being kind, not grabbing his arm. Treat him like a father treats a son!" She was shouting, out of control. If Rip wanted to unleash on her, then she would have her turn first.

He took another step toward her. Surprise filled his face, and then an anger that scared her. The sort that meant whatever he did next, he would later claim he wasn't responsible for it. An anger that told her he'd slipped into one of his bad spells. He reared back and raised his fist at her.

This time when she tried to back up, she bumped into the wall. When Rip's fist came at her, she had time to turn her face, but not time to get out of the way. The blow hit her square on the cheekbone, and the force knocked her to the floor.

The moment she hit the ground, Rip snapped out of his rage. He looked at her, horrified, and took small steps back. "What . . . what have I done?"

Bruised my face real nice, that's what. Now, struggling before the mirror, Wendy clucked her tongue, still angry at him. She dabbed the concealer over the spot and then worked another layer of foundation over it. There. She stood back and admired her work. It was impossible to see the bruise now. She brushed a light layer of blush over her cheeks.

Good as new.

Rip had been a perfect gentleman since hitting her. Several times he'd apologized, and until a few hours ago, he hadn't even been grouchy with her. Now, though, he wanted the bruise covered. No question about that. He was in the living room watching TV, and he'd made his orders clear.

The doorbell rang, and Wendy's heart danced inside her. Joey was here! The boy had warmed up to her real nice last time. Deep down he must've known that she was his mama, his real mother. She flipped off the light switch, ran lightly down the hall, and opened the door.

The first hour went much better this time. Joey didn't cry, and Rip pretty much kept to himself other than a few polite hellos and one-word answers. The Indians were playing again, and that had his attention. But before she left, Allyson Bower asked Wendy to come out onto the front stoop for a minute.

When they were outside, Allyson squinted suspiciously at her. "How's everything with Rip?"

"Rip?" Wendy laughed in a way that she hoped sounded more surprised than nervous. "He's fine. Anxious for Joey to be ours for good, that's all. This transition time is tough for everyone."

The social worker stared her straight in the face. "Is he hitting you, Wendy?"

"Of course not!" Without thinking, her hand came to her cheek. She dropped it to her side but it was too late.

"You're lying to me." She looked at Wendy's cheek again. "Under all that makeup, I'd bet money there's proof that Rip isn't doing well at all."

Wendy did her best to look outraged. It was none of the social worker's business. "Rip and I are getting along just fine. He took anger-management classes. I thought I told you that."

"Yeah." She frowned. "He took alcohol-recovery classes, too. I read that on his release papers." She nodded toward the house. "But I saw a six-pack of beer in the fridge."

"Now listen . . ." Wendy crossed her arms. "There's no law against having a few beers now and then. Everything's fine with Rip, and everything's great between the two of us." She straightened herself, doing her best to look put out. If the social worker suspected trouble, they might not get to keep Joey. She couldn't let that happen. "I don't appreciate your asking."

"Asking is my job, Wendy." Allyson looked at Wendy's cheek again. "You can take care of yourself. What you do with Rip is your business." She pointed at the door. "But that child is my business. If Rip starts acting out again, you need to tell me right away. Understand?"

"Yes. Fine."

The social worker went back inside and gave Joey the same speech about calling her or calling his parents any time he wanted. This time when she said "parents," she said it strong. So there wouldn't be any confusion about who she thought Joey's parents should be.

When she was gone, Wendy let out a long, heavy breath. That had been close. The social worker was wrong. Rip might hit her once in a while, but he'd never hit Joey. Not a child. Sure, he might grab his arm, but that was normal, right? If a child wasn't cooperating? But he'd never come unglued at Joey the way he did at her.

Would he?

Wendy took her place at the kitchen table next to Joey. Again she had cookies for him, and again he dipped them into a glass of milk. But something inside her refused to settle down. Allyson Bower's words haunted her all that afternoon and into the night.

Rip mostly kept his distance, but that didn't help. Wendy still couldn't find peace, and as she lay down to sleep that night, she finally figured out why. When she had told herself that Rip would never hit a child, never strike his own son, it wasn't a statement; it was a question. And the truth was, no matter what she wanted to believe, when it came to Rip, she didn't have the answer. That left her with another question, one that kept her awake most of the night.

What sort of mother would willingly place her son in danger?

Chapter Nineteen

Beth couldn't quite put her finger on it, but something was wrong with Molly. They were at church, the second time Molly and Jack had come with them, and Beth was thrilled. Yes, the circumstances were dire, but what better place to get help than at church? God certainly did have a plan for Joey, and He would see it through. Beth was praying for that, so was Bill.

They were convinced.

The fact that Molly and Jack had decided to join them in praying for Joey's custody was a miracle, nothing less. But even with all that was going on in her sister's life— with the phone calls she'd been making to senators and congressmen and even to the Florida governor's office— Molly seemed different. Distant, maybe.

Always before, no matter what issue they were facing, Beth and Molly faced it together. That's why they'd stayed so close over the years.

Beth thought back to when she had suffered three miscarriages between Cammie and Blain. She had wondered if she'd survive. All those babies she would never know, never see until heaven. All those children who wouldn't grow up with her loving touch or Bill's kindness.

It would have been more than Beth could handle, except that she had Molly.

Molly had called her every night for a month after each miscarriage. Whatever else was going on for either of them, they would put it aside and make time to talk or laugh or cry together. And over the weeks, Beth found her way to daylight, found her way back to a strong faith and an understanding that God knew the number of their days. Even if the number was painfully short.

But now, in the midst of Molly's greatest trial, the two of them hardly talked at all. Sure they took the kids to the pool a few days each week, and they still visited the park. But Molly was distant and short. The way she'd been even at church that morning.

They were seated in the pew—Bill and Beth, then Molly and Jack. They'd made some small talk when they first sat down, mostly about the Haiti trip. The Campbells were all signed up, excited about taking Joey on his first work trip.

But Beth could sense something wasn't right, the rhythm of their conversation nowhere close to natural.

When Molly first got the news about the possibility of losing Joey, she'd been beside herself. She wept and shook and barely found the strength to breathe. Now, though she was still sad—always sad—she seemed less desperate. There was an emptiness in her voice, and her eyes held something Beth hadn't seen before, something she didn't know how to work with.

Beth sat back as the music started to play. She loved worship, but today she couldn't stop thinking of Molly.

Was there something else going on? Was she missing something? Was there more trouble than Molly would admit? Maybe her relationship with Jack? She glanced at her sister, inches from her on her right side. Molly was singing, keeping up with the words. It was hard to tell if her heart was in it, but at least she was here. In church. Facing what she was facing, there was no better place to be.

Maybe that was it. Maybe the distance was because of Molly's struggle with faith. Beth faced the words on the overhead screen. Then there was the other possibility, the one she hadn't wanted to talk about with anyone—not with Bill, and certainly not with Molly.

Though Molly reported nearly every day that she was making phone calls to officials, and Jack was contacting attorneys, they seemed to be making no progress. If someone were going to take away one of Beth's children, Beth would have the story on the news by now. There would be reporters hounding the judge, asking him why he'd allow such a terrible ruling to stand when it would only hurt the child involved.

Molly and Jack seemed almost passive. Maybe they were in shock, paralyzed from fear and grief and hoping for some last-minute miracle—the miracle Beth and everyone else was praying for. It could happen, of course. It *would* happen somehow. Beth believed that. What she didn't believe was that this was all the effort Molly and Jack were willing to make on Joey's behalf.

Miracle or not, she would've expected Molly to be going crazy by now, pulling out every stop, turning over every stone, willing to fight the judge herself if no attorney would take the case. Instead, her sister's conversations centered mostly on her latest phone calls to various politicians, and on the upcoming work trip.

"What type of clothes are you packing?" was her question last week. And, "Are you getting your kids immunized before you go?"

Beth wanted to scream at her, "Molly! Wake up! They're about to take your son away, and all you can think about is whether Joey should take long pants or shorts to Haiti?"

Beth squirmed in her seat. If her sister was riding out the journey in blind faith, then more power to her. God was almighty, powerful enough to keep Joey at the Campbells' house if that was His will. But that's when the other possibility crept into Beth's conscience.

Maybe Molly and Jack weren't worried because they had a different plan, a more drastic one. Could that be why they were attending church and coming along on the trip to Haiti? Was it possible they were thinking of fleeing the country and taking Joey with them? Beth focused on the words to the song they were singing. No, Molly would never do that. Never. Beth hated when her mind took that path. It was an awful thing to think about her sister. Molly and Jack were law-abiding citizens. They wouldn't consider fleeing the country, living in hiding, and going against the authorities. They were fine, upstanding people, connected to their community and their neighborhood the way most people only hoped to be.

Beth sang another few lines.

Right? There was no way her sister and her brother-in-law would take Joey and leave, would they? Beth chided herself and dismissed the thought. Molly had a right to be distracted. Life probably felt like it was spinning out of control. Of course she wasn't acting like herself. She was in shock.

Still, when the service ended and they finished up with yet another meeting on the Haiti work trip, Beth pulled Molly aside. "You've cleared this trip with Joey's social worker, right? I mean, with the custody thing pending, I'm sure you'll need her okay before you take him out of the country."

For the briefest moment, Molly's expression became one of sheer panic. Maybe it was Beth's imagination, but she could've sworn Molly looked absolutely terrified at the idea of clearing this trip with the social worker. But just as quickly, she rebounded. The corners of her lips lifted in a gentle smile. "Of course, Beth. We've already gotten the okay."

"Good." Beth nodded. Relief filled her heart and soul. "Just wanted to make sure."

All the way home, Beth allowed herself to feel relieved. She must've been loopy to think her sister would take Joey and flee the law, flee the United States. She was probably just distracted with finding an attorney or a politician who could help them. And someone *would* help them. They would get their miracle.

Beth believed that with every breath she took.

Allyson Bower hung up the phone and replayed the conversation in her mind. It was Tuesday afternoon, and she'd just spoken with Molly Campbell, calling with a special request. She and her husband wanted to take Joey on a work trip. They would go to Haiti with their church for five days, work on repairing an orphanage, and spend time with the children who lived there.

That would be okay, wouldn't it?

As a state-certified social worker, Allyson was trained to recognize red flags. Children were her business, and children did a poor job of knowing when they were in trouble. That's why in many cases they needed a state-appointed adult to help decide whether a situation was safe or not. A person working on their behalf.

Now this couple faced the loss of their only son after having him in their lives for nearly five years, and a week before they would lose custody permanently, they wanted permission to take the child out of the country?

Normally the answer would be an easy one.

No way.

Allyson couldn't open herself up to that sort of potential trouble, that sort of scrutiny if things went awry and the Campbells disappeared. Once the adoptive parents were out of the country, even if they bought a house in Port-au-Prince and posted their names on the front door, it would be difficult to get them back to the States.

Still, for some reason, the idea appealed to Allyson. A last vacation, a last time to bond with Joey and show him what was important to them. Besides, maybe Joey would make friends with one of the orphans, and maybe the Campbells would go on to adopt that child. A Haitian child.

It was possible.

The trouble was, Allyson hadn't seen any mention in the Campbells' file about church or faith, about religion being important to them. She had asked Molly Campbell the name of the church, so now it was easy, really. She could do a little checking, and if their story held true—if they really were signed up with their church to go on a work trip—then Allyson would take the situation to the judge and recommend that permission be granted.

She didn't need a judge's order, not for this. At the time of the trip, the Campbells would have joint custody of Joey. Not until the Friday after the trip would they lose custody forever. If they wanted a farewell trip with their son, she wouldn't deny it.

As long as it checked out.

Allyson found the number for the Campbells' church. After being transferred to the secretary, she explained why she was calling, that she was a social worker and needed to verify the attendance of a few of their members.

The secretary was pleasant. "Go ahead."

"Their names are Jack and Molly Campbell. They tell me they've been attending regularly as members."

A series of clicking and tapping sounds filled the lines. "Just a minute, I'm checking the computer." She paused. "Yes, here they are. Jack and Molly Campbell."

"So they *are* members?"

"Let me see. Yes . . . their information chart says they're members."

"Which means they've been attending for how long?"

"Oh, well . . . that varies. We don't have specific requirements for membership." She thought for a few seconds. "But I'd say most people don't become members until they've been going here for at least a year."

Allyson smiled. Things were checking out. "Is there

any record, any way of proving that the Campbells have been members for a year?"

"Well, we don't take attendance. But we do watch the pattern of giving. Our members tend to be regular contributors, as well."

"What about the Campbells? Have they been regular givers?"

"Let me scroll down here." Another pause. "Yes . . . why, it certainly looks like it. The Campbells gave regular donations every month for the past, let's see, thirteen months."

Allyson quickly jotted notes on everything the secretary told her. Then she asked about the work trip.

"It's a special time for our members. This particular trip is for families. It gives them a chance to make a special memory with their children while they're helping out at one of the six orphanages we support in and around Port-au-Prince. We've put together teams of twelve to fifteen people for each orphanage."

"What about supervision, someone from the church?"

"Yes, a church staff member will accompany each group."

Allyson smiled and added that information to the piece of paper in front of her. "Very good. Thank you for your time."

That afternoon she took the issue to the judge.

He read the file, looked over Allyson's notes, and frowned. "A work trip to Haiti?"

"You have to understand, Your Honor"—she was already passionate about getting approval for the Campbells—"work trips to Haiti happen all the time.

They'll be with a group, and someone from the church will supervise."

He gave her a wary look. "So close to the transfer of custody . . ."

"Your Honor, the population of Haiti is almost entirely black. If the Campbells tried to get away on foot in the middle of the night, they'd be picked up at the airport for sure. They'll stand out, believe me." She sighed and waved her hand at the clock. "I'd like to call the Campbells with permission before the end of the day. Your Honor, this is very important to them. I feel good about it."

The judge tapped his finger on the paperwork in front of him. After another twenty seconds he took a slow breath. "Okay." He shot her a stern look. "I know how you feel about this case, Mrs. Bower. But the law is the law."

"Yes, Your Honor."

"I'll grant permission." He narrowed his eyes. "But you'd better be right."

She could hardly wait to call Molly Campbell. "Thank you, Your Honor."

Fifteen minutes later she was back at her office and on the phone. "The judge granted you permission, Mrs. Campbell. Everything checked out." She tried to keep her tone professional, tried to keep the sound of victory from her voice. She was supposed to be a voice of the state, not someone who took sides. "You've been granted permission to take Joey on the work trip, so long as you stick to the dates you've provided this department."

"Thank you." Molly's relief poured from every syllable.

Allyson felt her throat choke up. "I hope you have a good time, Mrs. Campbell."

"Yes. It'll be very precious time for the three of us."

When the conversation was over, Allyson hung up the phone. She was too street-smart not to have at least a little suspicion about the reason for the Campbells' trip. But she'd fought hard for the approval because of one single image: Wendy Porter's heavily made-up cheek. Rip Porter was being abusive again, and if she suspected one of the couples in this situation to be lying, no question she suspected the Porters first. Besides, she'd done her part by checking out Molly Campbell's story.

Anything else was out of her hands.

Chapter Twenty

Jack had promised Molly he'd take care of the finances, and so far he was making good on his promise. The church thing had been nothing short of brilliant.

Their first plan was to keep the trip a secret from the social worker. It wasn't anyone's business if they wanted to take Joey on a work trip. But when Beth brought it up to Molly at church last Sunday, they had to revert to their second plan: calling Allyson Bower and asking permission. Before they could do that, they had to be sure to cover their trail. If they told the social worker they were members at Bethel Bible Church, then they had to be able to prove as much.

Thankfully, the church had virtually no requirements for members, and with thousands attending services every weekend, they had no real way to determine the actual attendance of any one member. Except by tracking whatever money people gave. That Sunday, after Molly's conversation with Beth, Jack went home and wrote a series of checks, each for two hundred dollars, and each dated the first of the month back some thirteen months. He put each check in an envelope, sealed it, and wrote the month on the front. Then he put all the envelopes in a larger manila envelope and hurried the package back to church.

Services were still going on—the last one had just started. He went to the church bookstore and explained that it was rather urgent, that he needed to see the church secretary. She wasn't there, he was told. Then he explained that he had checks to turn over, and in no time the bookstore manager found someone who worked at the church office.

A college intern, as it turned out.

Jack saw how young she was, and he had to work to contain his excitement. "We've made a mistake, and I feel terrible about it," he told the young woman. She didn't look a day over twenty. He poured on the charm. "More than a year ago, my wife and I made a decision to give regularly—a set amount each month." He held up the envelope. "We wrote out the checks and placed them in here. And wouldn't you know it?" He made a silly face. "I thought she was turning them in each month, and she thought I was."

"I see." The girl looked completely baffled. "Why don't you drop them in the collection box at the back of the church? Anyone could make a mistake."

"Well, you see, it isn't that easy." He grimaced and looked over his shoulder. "My wife's mortified about this. She thinks people will see us as heathens for not giving all those months." He pointed to himself. "It's my fault, so I told her I'd make it right."

The girl shook her head and made a face. "Sir, how can I help?"

"If you could promise me you'll take these checks and

enter them into your system by date, I'd be forever grateful." He gave her his famous smile, the one that had earned him sales bonuses every year since he'd been out of college. "What we want is for the record to show our intentions. That we planned to give this set amount every month. You understand, right? Rather than adding up all the checks and putting it in as one big donation in our file."

"For tax purposes, you mean?" She looked nervous. "We can't change records for tax purposes, I know that."

He shook his head and waved his hand. "No, no. Nothing about taxes." He grinned again. "This is July, ma'am. All I want is for my wife to feel good about our giving statement. You know, when it comes in the mail at the end of the year. I actually want it to be *less*, because half that money should've been given last year. See?"

"So you don't want a statement for last year? Even though some of the entries will be dated for last year?"

"That's right. Last year's taxes are over and done with. I'm not looking for a deduction, just a way to keep our heads high here at Bethel Bible."

She still seemed puzzled. "So you mean, just enter them by the date on each check?"

"Exactly."

Her frown deepened. "But if I do that, you won't get tax credit for the ones dated last calendar year."

"I know that." He gave her a lopsided grin. "We're not concerned with the tax break, ma'am. Seriously. This is about making my wife happy."

Those seemed to be the magic words. She smiled and nodded. "I wish more people were like you. We'll show it as one large donation for the church's budget. But on your records I guess we could enter each check by its date. I don't see why not."

"Thanks." He did his best to sound humble. "Do you think you could see that it gets done right away? My wife's worried about setting foot in church until it's taken care of."

"Tell you what." The girl smiled and checked the clock on the wall. "I'll do it right now. I have access to the computer." She gave Jack a knowing look. "But please tell your wife that no one would've looked down on her for not giving. Lots of people don't give. This is a church, not a club. Besides, only a few people ever even see those records." She took the envelope from him. "Just so you know."

"Thank you." Jack celebrated silently as he watched her go. One more step taken care of.

Now the memory of that day faded. Jack wasn't sure if Allyson Bower had asked the church secretary to check their giving record. But he was certain the social worker called to verify their membership. She said as much yesterday when she talked to Molly and passed on the judge's approval for the trip. The decision was based in part, she said, on the fact that her information about the church membership and the details of the trip to Haiti all checked out.

So far so good.

Now Jack was at the office of Paul Kerkar, one of the sharpest, most brilliant Realtors he knew. Paul dealt with high-end homes and commercial property. He had sold Jack and Molly their current home, and every now and then he called with investment opportunities.

This time Jack called him. "Look, I've come into some cash."

Music to Paul's ears. His tone was immediately cheerful. "How much cash?"

"More than a million, maybe a million and a half." He didn't skip a beat. "Molly and I talked about it, and we'd like to buy something commercial, something in old downtown West Palm Beach—the area where the renovation is taking place."

Jack heard the sound of buttons being pressed. Paul always had a calculator with him. "Okay, so you're looking for a property in the four-million to six-million range, is that right?"

"With 25 percent down, yes."

"That's how we'll work it. Twenty-five is minimum for commercial property, but with your excellent credit, that shouldn't be a problem."

Jack smiled. "I didn't think so."

Paul called him back an hour later with three possibilities. Jack took the day off from work, met Paul at his office, and toured all three. By the end of the day he was ready to make an offer on a medical office building, one that had a higher-than-usual vacancy rate, but was a better price per square foot than anything else downtown.

"This property has great potential," Paul kept saying. *Potential* was his favorite word. "The investment potential here is unmatched."

Jack was convinced. He called Molly and asked her to join them at Paul's office, where they spent nearly an hour going over the numbers and signing the offer. Jack wrote a check for ten thousand dollars earnest money.

Before the end of the workday, he placed a call to his mortgage broker.

"How're my loans looking?"

"Great." The man chuckled. "It's not every day I have a client walk in and request an equity loan for more than a million dollars." Another chuckle. "Let me tell you how it's coming together."

The loan officer explained that he was drawing equity from each of the Campbells' three rental houses, still leaving at least 30 percent equity in each. "That's a safe cushion."

"Right." Jack was at his desk, the one in their home office. He tapped a pencil on a pad of paper. *Bottom line, buddy. That's what I need here—the bottom line.* "So what's the total you can get me on the rentals?"

"Just under a million." Pages shuffled in the background. "Here it is, the mid–nine hundreds. That's the best I can do."

"Good." He tapped faster. "What about our existing home?"

"The existing home . . ." More turning pages. "A comfortable amount takes us into the high four hundreds."

"More than four hundred thousand?" A thrill surged through Jack's veins. "That's higher than we thought."

"The appraisal came back high." The broker sounded proud of himself. "Property values are skyrocketing, Jack. It's a good time to be in real estate."

"I guess."

"Uh, Jack . . ." The man's tone changed. "You mind me asking what you need all this cash for?"

"I thought I told you."

"No . . ." The man let out an uncomfortable laugh. "I

mean, it's none of my business. But one-and-a-half million? You and Molly starting a new business or what?"

Casual, Jack . . . Keep it casual. "Commercial real estate. Found the perfect medical office building downtown, the area they're renovating."

"Really?" The man sounded impressed. "It's hard to find anything down there."

"I have connections." Jack chuckled. "It'll be a money-maker right off the bat."

"Great." He hesitated. "And by the looks of it, your income on the rentals will take care of your payment on the equity loan."

"Exactly." Jack leaned back in his chair and set the pencil down on the desk. "It's a win-win for everyone." He didn't want to sound anxious. "When can we expect funds from these loans?"

"We should sign papers in a week. Funds can be issued within a few days after that."

"Perfect."

They chatted for a few minutes more, and then the conversation ended. Jack could hardly believe it had all gone so well. He needed the real estate piece. Because if the social worker or the judge found out there were 1.4 million dollars sitting in the Campbells' savings account, they might be concerned, at least enough to watch them or deny them permission to leave the country.

But with a pending commercial real estate deal, it made perfect sense. That money was exactly what they would need to close the loan on the building. Of course they would have it sitting in their savings account. It was all perfectly explainable with the real estate deal in place.

The work trip was just one month away. Every time

Jack thought about it, he was tempted to panic, to stay awake all night looking for loopholes, details he hadn't worked out. They had one chance to pull this off, just one. Anything short of perfection, and they would all lose.

But with those phone calls, the financial part of the plan was all but solved. There would be the last-minute transfer of the funds to a series of accounts, winding up eventually at their new account in the Cayman Islands. Jack had arranged for the money to arrive in Grand Cayman a few days before they did. Then almost immediately they'd withdraw all the money in cash. By the time the authorities figured out where the money had gone, the account would be closed. Another dead end for the officials.

Yes, everything was coming together. They would have to say good-bye to Joey just one more time, when he left for his next visit the second week of August.

Then, if the plan worked, they'd never have to say good-bye to him again.

Beth hated herself for what she was feeling, but there was no way around it. She was worried about Molly and Jack, worried they might actually be planning something crazy. Molly had remained distant, even when Beth probed and prodded.

It was the first Wednesday in August, and they'd spent the day at the neighborhood pool. Now they were at Molly's house, the kids gathered around Molly's dining-room table with grapes and string cheese.

Molly washed dishes while Beth stood beside her at the sink. "So you've heard nothing?" She kept her voice low. Joey still didn't understand what was happening to him.

"Nothing." Molly scrubbed at some dried egg on a breakfast plate. She flipped her dark hair over her shoulder and out of her face. "Every politician's office I've spoken with is writing a letter to the judge asking that he reconsider. We have to think that's going to make a difference."

Beth was baffled. "Make a difference when?" She leaned her hip into the edge of the counter and studied her sister. "Joey's final visit is next week. Then he's home for three weeks and gone for good."

"I know that." Molly stopped washing. She turned her head and stared at Beth. Her voice was laced with frustration. "That's why I haven't stopped trying." She began scrubbing the plate again.

"Okay." Beth held up her hands. "You don't want to talk about this. I get that." She let her hands fall to her sides. "But it feels like your house is on fire and you're throwing glasses of water at it."

Molly threw her scrub rag into the sink and frowned at Beth. "Are you saying I don't care about losing Joey? That I'm not trying hard enough?" She looked back at the kids in the dining room, and lowered her voice. "We're doing everything we can. We've asked for a hearing the third week of August. That's when the judge will look at the letters from political offices, and hear our reasons why we don't think Joey should be taken from us." She made a harsh grab at the rag again. "I go to bed crying and wake up crying, Beth." She paused. "You have no idea how much I care. I'd lay down my life to keep that child. What else do you want me to do?"

Beth was instantly sorry. She stayed still, silent for a moment, giving Molly a chance to calm down. Then she tentatively touched her sister's shoulder. "Molly . . . forgive me. I can't imagine being you, going through this."

"It's like . . ." Molly's hands went limp. Her eyes met Beth's and the pain there was so strong it was like a physical force. "It's like he's dying." Her lower lip trembled. "Like we're all dying." Her expression took on the bewildered look of a lost child. "I don't know how to act, Beth. I've never done this before."

The phone rang, and Beth held up her hand. "I'll get it." Molly kept her kitchen telephone on a small built-in desk adjacent to the pantry. Beth caught the phone on the third ring. "Hello?"

"Hey . . . I hoped I'd find you there. I got a message you called."

It was Bill. "Yes—" She motioned to Molly that the call was for her. "Hi, honey." She turned her back to Molly and stared absently at the clutter on the small desk. A few greeting cards, invitations to an upcoming wedding, and a baby announcement. Off to the side was a stack of papers from Bank of America. "Hey . . ." Beth looked a little closer. "Could you pick up a can of olives on the way home? I need them for the casserole."

"Sure. How was the pool?"

"Good." Beth tried to make small talk, but she was distracted. She leaned closer and read the first line on the Bank of America papers. *Congratulations! Your equity line of credit for $987,000 has been approved. As per our*

conversation you will sign papers next week, and the loan
will be funded shortly after you . . .

"Guess you have to go?"

"Sorry." Beth caught hold of the back of the desk chair
so she wouldn't lose her balance. Why in the world would
Molly and Jack need nearly a million dollars? "Yeah . . ."
She tried to concentrate. "Can I call you back?"

Bill laughed. "Sure. We can talk later."

She hung up and looked back at Molly. Had she
noticed Beth snooping? Beth didn't think so. Molly was
still washing dishes. Even though Beth was dying to ask
her, she kept her questions about the loan papers to herself. But that night she shared every detail with Bill. By
then she'd created a dozen scenarios in her head, reasons
why Molly and Jack didn't seem to be scrambling to save
Joey.

"Bill"—she put her hands on her hips—"I think
they're going to run."

"Honey, you watch too much television."

They were in their bedroom, the kids asleep down the
hall. Bill was watching ESPN. Beth positioned herself in
front of the screen. "I'm not watching too much television, Bill. I'm serious. They're dragging their feet about
getting someone to help them, and they're running out of
time." She threw her hands up. "Molly hasn't even told
Joey yet! And why would they need a million-dollar
loan? It doesn't make sense."

"Maybe for attorney fees." Bill peered around her,
determined to keep his eyes on the TV. "Maybe Jack's
found a high-powered lawyer who knows how to win the
case." He looked at Beth. "Isn't that possible?"

"A million dollars?" She frowned. "The guy better work a miracle for that kind of legal fee."

"What I'm saying"—he looked exasperated—"is that Molly doesn't have to tell you every last detail."

"She always did before." Beth walked to the window. It was dark outside; only the sliver of a moon hung over the cluster of oak trees that separated their house from the neighbor's. She turned around and groaned. "Don't you see, Bill. I know my sister. Something isn't right. The loan papers are proof."

He held out his arms. "Come here."

She didn't want to. Bill was clearly dismissing her, making light of everything she was feeling. But she needed his hug, so she went. Slowly she crawled into bed and curled up beside him, her head on his shoulder.

"The only one who can work a miracle for Joey is God." He kissed the top of her head. "Remember?"

God. She thought about that for a minute. Bill was right. She drew a long, slow breath. "I'm praying for that." She relaxed and her shoulders dropped a few inches. "I guess I keep forgetting."

"I think Jack and Molly really believe in what God can do here." He looked thoughtful. "Otherwise they wouldn't be coming to church and praying with us."

"True." She looked down, searching for something she couldn't quite get her thoughts around. "I guess I can't make up my mind. On the one hand I'm asking Molly to trust God, to believe that God has a plan for Joey. Then I doubt her because she isn't panicking."

"Exactly." Bill turned off the television.

George Brett loped into the room and wagged her tail.

"Thanks for talking." Beth started for the door but did

a double-take at the dog. "Who let you in here?" She clucked her tongue against the roof of her mouth. "Bad dog. Come on, let's go outside."

As she put George Brett outside, Beth closed her eyes and tried to connect the pieces. Yes, Molly and Jack were trying to be proactive. They were making phone calls, asking for a hearing, begging God for a miracle. When she thought of it that way, her fears were completely unfounded. Molly and Jack weren't going to run; they were going to wait for God's will. Everything Bill had said made sense, except the obvious. And it was the obvious that kept Beth awake most of the night and into the morning.

Why, in the middle of all that was going on with Joey, would Molly and Jack need a million dollars? Even though she shouldn't have snooped, shouldn't have looked, it was a question that needed answering. By noon the next day, Beth made up her mind.

As soon as the moment seemed right—whether Molly got mad at her or not—she was going to ask.

Chapter Twenty-One

The door closed and Molly let herself fall against it. She reached out and took hold of Jack's hands. Gus whimpered a few feet away.

"I hate this. . . . I can't do it again."

"I know."

Joey had just left for his third visit. This time he was less tearful, but more afraid. He had come home without any bruises after his second visit, but he was stuttering again, and he didn't want to talk about Rip Porter.

"He doesn't like me, Mommy," was all he'd say about the man. Then he'd change the subject.

"Does he hurt you, buddy?"

"No!" Joey shook his head fast. "He doesn't hurt me. P-p-promise."

Her son had never lied to her, not as far as she knew. But his quick answer and fearful eyes made her worry. Regardless of their plans, she would not let him go back to the Porters if the man was harming him. It had been hard enough to let him go back a second time after the bruises on his arm.

Now, her stomach knotted and her heart pounded

against her chest. "Every time I say good-bye to him, a piece of me goes dead until he comes home."

Jack rubbed the back of his neck. He looked exhausted. "Can you imagine having to let him go forever? In three weeks?"

"No." She came to him, put her arms around his neck. "I told Beth it was like knowing he was about to die, like we all were."

He studied her. "That's all you've told Beth?"

"Of course."

"And you're sure she didn't see the loan papers on the desk?" His words were slow, weary, as if he couldn't stop running through the possibilities.

"I'm pretty sure." She pressed her fist against her forehead. "That was so stupid of me. The mail came that morning. . . . I opened the stuff from the bank, and Joey needed sunscreen on his back. I set the mail down and made a mental note to put it away before we left." She lifted her hands. "I don't know how I forgot."

"But you don't think she saw it."

"No." She pictured that day. "Beth got a phone call from Bill, but it was quick. Besides, if she'd seen it, I think she would've asked. Beth and I don't keep secrets."

"Well . . ." He pulled her closer, tucked her head against his chest. His tone was sad. "You do now, love."

A pain pierced her heart and she closed her eyes. "Yes." She was counting down the days. They were down to fourteen. Fourteen days until the trip. Fourteen days until they would walk out of their home for the last time. Two weeks until she had to start wearing a blonde wig and going by the name Tracy Sanders. Worst of all, fourteen days until she had to say good-bye to Beth, her sister and best friend.

She survived most days by telling herself that somehow—someday—they might be able to find their way back. The Porters would die off, or the case would be forgotten. They could slip into the United States, spend a week with Beth and Bill and the kids, and be on their way again.

But the reality was something entirely different.

Jack nuzzled her. "You okay?"

"It's more than I can think about." She let herself melt into his arms. At times like these he seemed strong enough for both of them. "I wish I could be like Joey and talk to God whenever I'm scared."

She felt him stiffen. No matter how much time they spent meeting with Beth and Bill, no matter how many church services, Jack was no closer to a genuine faith. It was all simply a necessary part of the plan. "You can talk to God whenever you want." A hint of sarcasm crept into his voice. "Ask Him to make the fake passports good enough to pass inspection."

"Jack . . ." She didn't like when he made light of God, or the idea of God. "It wouldn't hurt if you did a little talking to Him yourself."

He exhaled in a way that betrayed his frustration. "Maybe someday—when we're sitting on the beach in Cayman with too much time on our hands." He kissed her lips, slow and tender. "Right now I'm too busy making this happen to ask God about it."

Molly wanted to add something, remind him that Beth and Bill were praying for God's will, and that maybe she and Jack were going about this all the wrong way, and maybe they really should be calling politicians and lawyers and asking for hearings. But it was too late for any of that.

She leaned back. "How're the plans going?"

"Good. Money's taken care of, and I'm getting the passports next week." His tone sounded heavier than usual, full of sorrow. "But there's something we need to talk about."

"What?" Gus came up to them and sat against their legs. Molly pushed him back a little. "Go lay down, Gus."

Gus did as he was told and Molly looked up at Jack. "What do we need to talk about?"

"Him." Jack looked at Gus. "We can't take him, Molly. You know that."

"What?" She took a step back, horrified. "Why haven't we thought about that before? Jack, we have to take him. Joey would be crushed."

"I *have* thought about it, and there's just no way."

Molly let out an exasperated cry. She went to Gus and dropped to the floor beside him. "We're leaving him at the kennel, right? When we go to Haiti?"

"Right."

"So let's pay someone at the kennel to ship him over to the Cayman Islands at the end of the week."

Jack came to her. He eased himself down onto the floor and rubbed Gus behind the ear. "The whole state will be looking for us by then. Maybe the whole country." He tilted his head, doing everything he could to help her understand. "It'll be big news, Molly."

"But we've kept the story out of the news on purpose."

"Right. But the Porters will be talking to every

reporter who knocks on their door once they figure out we're not coming back."

Gus yawned and pressed his head against Jack's hand. "Good boy, Gus."

Molly looked at the ceiling for a few seconds. "So you're saying the people at the kennel could notify the authorities and tell them we left our dog with instructions that they ship him to the Cayman Islands?"

"Exactly. We can't risk everything for Gus, honey. We can't do it."

"If it makes the news like you think it will . . ." Her eyes found his again. "They'll be looking for Molly and Jack Campbell."

"Right."

"So let's use a new kennel. I'll wear my blonde wig and explain that we're moving to the Cayman Islands and we need someone to ship our dog to us in a week."

"I don't understand. How's that any different?"

Molly took hold of Jack's shoulders. "It's easy." She could feel her whole face glowing. "We'll register with the kennel as Walt and Tracy Sanders."

"Molly . . ." Jack's eyes welled up. He patted Gus and nuzzled his face against the dog's. When he looked at her, it was obvious that he wasn't going to change his mind. "I can't risk our future—our lives—just so we can keep him." He bit his lip. "We'll use the same kennel as always. That way when we don't come back for him, Beth and Bill will bring him home."

Beth and Bill? Gus didn't even know them. Suddenly the reality became clear for her, too. No matter what they did, what name they used, it wouldn't take more than an hour to call every kennel in town and ask if a yellow lab had been shipped out of the country. Jack was right.

They'd have to say good-bye to Gus, too.

Molly looped her arms around the dog's neck as the tears came. Gus was Joey's best friend. Why hadn't she thought about what would happen to him? It was a blow, one that took her breath away. Poor Gus . . . He would never be the same without his family—even if Beth and Bill did take him.

It was another blow, and with Joey gone to the Porters again, it was enough to do Molly in. The losses were so great, she could barely imagine them all happening at once. Sobs racked her body, and her tears spilled onto Gus's furry coat. He made a whimpering sound and looked up at her, his eyes gentle and trusting.

Next to her, Jack rubbed her shoulders. There was nothing either of them could say to fix the situation. They would say good-bye to everything they knew and everyone they loved, and they would do it all willingly for Joey. Then they would do the thing that would hurt Joey most of all, something he would never understand.

They would say good-bye to Gus.

Joey was finally asleep, and Rip had left for the bar—same as nearly every night for a week. Wendy lingered on the edge of Joey's bed, watching his small sleeping body as it finally relaxed.

She was falling head over heels for her little boy, no question about it. This time he smiled when he walked through the door with Allyson Bower. Even though he didn't exactly run and jump into her arms, he wasn't crying, either, so that had to be a good sign.

He still talked about missing his mommy and daddy, and Wendy was puzzled. The Campbells should've explained things to the boy by now. That was part of the deal. By the third visit he was supposed to know that he was going to come and live with the Porters in Ohio. That they were his new family.

It didn't matter. Rip told Joey every chance he had. Tonight was no different. They were eating dinner—chicken nuggets and macaroni and cheese. Rip waved his fork in the air. "You can start calling me Daddy now. That's what the judge says."

Joey blinked. He looked both puzzled and frightened. "My d-d-daddy lives in Florida with me." He poked his fork into another bite of macaroni.

"Doesn't he know yet?" Rip looked at her. For once he wasn't angry, just curious.

"I guess not." Wendy wasn't hungry. She pushed her plate back and smiled at her husband. Anything to keep him calm. "It'll be obvious soon enough, Rip."

He looked back at Joey. "Here's the deal, little man." He waited until Joey's eyes were on him. "I'm your *real* daddy and this"—he gestured to the small living area made up of the kitchen and living room—"this is your *real* home." He leaned over the table so his face was closer to Joey's. "The Campbells adopted you, only there was a mistake." He pointed at Wendy. "Me and her, we're your real parents and the judge says you're gonna come stay with us. Starting in three weeks."

Tears gathered in Joey's eyes and he shook his head.

"My mommy and d-d-daddy and Gus are in Florida." He dropped his fork. "That's my real f-f-family."

Rip was getting madder by the second. Just when it looked like he might throw a glass of milk at the boy, he jerked his chair back, stood, and grabbed his car keys. "I'll be at the bar."

That was that. It took Wendy an hour to calm Joey down, and she did it by agreeing with him. Yes, his real parents were in Florida. Yes, that was his real home. "But we're like your mama and daddy, too," she told him. Because if she didn't say so now, how would she explain the situation when he came to live with them in three weeks?

Joey looked confused. He didn't finish his dinner, and he talked to the Campbells on the phone longer than usual. He didn't really relax until Wendy led him into the TV room and turned on *SpongeBob SquarePants*. Halfway through the program, he even laughed a little. The sound of it made Wendy dream of the days ahead, days when the transition would be over and having Joey could be part of their regular routine.

When the program ended, Joey wanted to watch more cartoons. They found *Bear in the Big Blue House*, and after it got started, Wendy did something she'd been wanting to do since Joey's first visit. She reached out . . . careful not to startle her son . . . and she took hold of his fingers.

He looked at her and smiled. Then without hesitating, he tucked his hand the rest of the way into hers. The feeling of that single touch was so amazing, so right, it stayed with her the rest of the night. Even when he said his bedtime prayers.

"Please, God, bring me home safe and fast 'cause I miss Mommy and Daddy and Gus so so so much. Gee this name, amen."

Now Wendy looked at his sleeping form again and gently patted his back one more time. "Good night, Joey. Mama loves you."

She wandered down the hallway and back to the kitchen. Along the way she picked up her Bible. Actually it was her grandma's Bible, but lately she'd been reading it. Taking it with her to church on Sundays and trying to find meaning in it. Strength or peace or wisdom. Something to help her be the sort of mother Joey needed.

She'd been reading a part called First Kings, because that was where Solomon made a lot of decisions. That's what the pastor had said a few weeks ago. And no Old Testament person was as wise as King Solomon. Of course, Rip didn't like her reading the Bible. Made him nervous, he said. But Rip wouldn't be home until well after midnight.

She looked out the window and sighed. Rip had hit her again the day before, this time on her back. She hadn't looked, but she was pretty sure she had a bruise. He was sorry, he told her so. When she looked at the big picture, he did seem to be doing better with his rage than he'd done before he went to prison.

But things weren't headed in a good direction. He'd quit his job at the theater. Too stressful, he'd told her—working nights when he was trying to learn how to be a father. Wendy wasn't sure how hanging out at the bars was helping, but she didn't ask.

She opened the Bible. She was on the third chapter, the part with the little heading that said, "A Wise Ruling."

The story was about two women who shared a house, and each of them had a newborn baby. It was fascinating and it caught her attention right away.

The story went on that one morning one of the babies was dead, and an argument broke out about which of the women was the mother of the living baby. The women took the baby to King Solomon and asked him to decide, so the king pulled out a long sword. He told the mothers he would cut the living baby in half and give them each a part since they couldn't agree about who the mother was.

The real mother stepped forward right away. "Give the baby to the other woman," she said.

But the other woman was defiant. She had no trouble allowing the king to cut the baby in half. The king then awarded the baby to the first woman. The reason was obvious—only the child's real mother loved him enough to give him up, rather than see him die.

Wendy finished the story and quickly shut the Bible. What had she just read? A story about two mothers, two women with a claim to the same child. Wasn't that just like her and Molly Campbell, Joey's adoptive mother? The two of them both loved Joey, and both of them wanted to have him for their own.

She pushed the Bible away. The story rubbed her the wrong way. What sort of wisdom did it have for her? In this case, she was the real mother, but she wasn't willing to give Joey up, not even if that was the best thing for him. She loved him too much. Especially now.

Enough Bible stories, she told herself. She put the big book away and turned on the television. Reruns of *American Idol* were on. That would help her forget the strange story in the Bible. At least in today's world, judges didn't decide custody issues by threatening to cut a baby in half. They handled it fair and square. Even if the decision seemed hard at the time. Wendy was beyond glad, too. She might've let Joey go once, back when she didn't know him. But now that she knew what it felt like to hold his hand and feed him dinner and sit beside him watching cartoons, one thing was certain.

She would never let him go again.

Never.

Chapter Twenty-Two

The office was as small as it was seedy. Jack sat in one of two available chairs. The other one was near the door, empty. Copier fluid and printer cartridges were stacked on two filing cabinets, and the place smelled of thick cigar smoke and ink. Angelo St. Pierre worked his machine in the back corner by the light of a pair of small, dusty table lamps. Jack guessed the place was maybe a hundred square feet altogether.

Angelo pushed a button on the machine and stood back. "Mr. Sanders?" He turned to Jack. The man was from the Dominican Republic, and his accent was almost too thick to understand. "You need these today, yes?"

"Yes." Jack folded his hands on the man's small desk. The legs were uneven and the desk wobbled hard to the right. "That would be best."

"Tell me your story again."

The man seemed to like stories. For the job Angelo was doing, Jack was willing to indulge him. "My wife and I are missionaries." He smiled, not his standard grin, but the humble smile he'd seen people at Bethel Bible

Church use with each other. "We're taking our little boy to Indonesia." He frowned. "Very dangerous."

"Yes." Angelo St. Pierre punctuated the thought by jabbing his finger in Jack's direction. "I know that place. Very dangerous."

Jack had found Angelo's information in an Internet chat room. He did a search and wound up on a site where people with broken English wrote in what seemed like a code. It took Jack a few nights in the chat room before he realized that nearly everyone was—or claimed to be—an illegal alien. Fake passports were a hot topic, and when it came up, Jack joined in.

"I need documents fast. I live in Florida. Any suggestions?" *Fast* was the code word for "illegal." Jack had picked up that much.

"AAA Copiers is a good place to start," someone wrote back. Two other people in the chat room agreed.

Jack looked it up the next day and had a phone conversation with Angelo St. Pierre. Again the conversation was in code. Jack talked about needing passports quickly, and Angelo said it wouldn't be a problem. He said he was in favor of American freedom. Whatever that meant.

"Just bring in your photos and we can do things very quickly." He paused. "There will be fee for very fast passports."

Jack agreed, and that was exactly how things had gone. When he got there, he filled out a piece of paper for each of the three of them, providing their new names and making up every other answer needed. Angelo didn't ask for identification; he merely looked at the papers, collected the small passport-size photos, and went to work.

Behind Angelo St. Pierre, the machines ground to a

halt. He worked and folded and pressed the documents into another machine on the floor. He used a series of what looked like stamps and then a fine-point pen. After ten minutes he laid three passports on the desk and smiled. "There. You have your passports quickly."

Indeed.

Jack picked them up and looked them over. He'd used his own passport often enough to see that—at least to his eye—there was no difference here whatsoever. Angelo's work was brilliant. Certainly the passports would trick officials in Haiti. And once they did, once there were stamps in the back, it would be even easier to trick officials in Europe and Grand Cayman.

"You do good work, Angelo." Jack had already agreed to the price. Quick passports were expensive. Two hundred dollars each. Cash, nothing else. He paid the man.

Angelo smiled. "Angelo St. Pierre in favor of American freedom." He nodded. "Good day."

No need to wait for a receipt. Jack collected the passports, nodded one last time to the man, and left the building. Just as he stepped out, as he tucked the passports into his suit-coat pocket, a car approached from fifty yards away—one that looked an awful lot like the car belonging to Bill and Beth Petty.

Jack wanted to run or hide, but he didn't have time. It couldn't be them, not here in Miami in the middle of the week. Once in a while Bill did business in Miami, but the corporate offices were blocks away. Jack kept his pace normal, not too hurried. Angelo's shop was on a busy street, but it was smack in the middle of the worst part of town, the part run by drug lords and mafia and friendly swindlers from the Dominican Republic who believed in American freedom.

This section of town was no place the Pettys would come. But as the car approached, all doubt vanished. It was the Pettys' car, and Bill was driving. There were at least three other businessmen in the car with him. Jack kept his eyes straight ahead.

After the car passed, he allowed himself to breathe.

Ten more steps and Jack reached his car. Bill hadn't seen him—he was too busy making conversation with his passengers. But what could he possibly have been doing in that part of Miami? And what if he *had* spotted Jack? Wouldn't he have stopped and made casual conversation? Bill was driving, after all. He could've pulled over. Jack felt the adrenaline work its way through his body and out of his system. If Bill had seen him, he would've stopped. It was that simple. Jack put all thoughts of Bill and Angelo St. Pierre and what he'd just done by purchasing false passports out of his head, and focused instead on what was still left to do. He'd already done the unthinkable—lying and taking part in criminal activity. Every detail from here on out needed to be perfect.

The trip was in ten days; there was no room for error.

Beth and Molly were at the pool when Beth decided she'd had enough. They were leaving for Haiti in eight days. It was time to come straight out and ask the question.

The kids were in the pool, the boys gathered in the

shallow end playing a wild game of water volleyball. Cammie sat with a few of her neighborhood friends at the far side of the deep end. All of them were out of earshot. Beth and Molly sat on the edge of the pool, their feet in the water. Molly had her eyes on Joey, and Beth made little splashes with her toes. So far there hadn't been much conversation between them. Beth decided to start with the easy questions.

"When's your hearing?"

"What?" Molly didn't turn her head. She leaned back on her hands.

"The hearing. The one in Ohio to see if the judge will change his mind about Joey." She tried not to sound short. "That hearing."

"Oh. Right." Molly nodded. "Jack says it'll be Monday or Tuesday."

Beth hesitated. "So when are you leaving?"

"Leaving?" Molly blinked twice and turned to her. "Friday, same as you." She turned her focus back to Joey again.

This was ridiculous. If she didn't know better, she'd think Molly was on drugs. "Not for the work trip. When are you leaving for Ohio? I'm assuming you and Jack are going to be there."

Across the pool, Joey climbed out, dripping water, and waved at Molly. She waved back and then turned to Beth. "Jack found an attorney. He said we don't have to be there. He can get a continuance to buy time." She found Joey again. "I thought I told you."

Beth wasn't sure whether to feel relieved or to call her sister a liar. Bill had told her about seeing Jack in downtown Miami. He said he thought Jack recognized him, but since Jack looked away so quickly, he assumed whatever Jack was doing he didn't want to be caught. Even Bill was suspicious now. But Beth never got the chance to call Molly about it. Blain and Jonah had the stomach flu that day, and it had been all she could do to keep them hydrated between bathroom runs. Now, twenty-four hours later, the boys were well again and Beth was desperate for answers.

She swirled her feet in the water. "A continuance? You mean, you don't have to give Joey up the week after we get back from the trip?"

"Nope." Molly smiled, but something about it was flat. In the background, the sound of kids laughing and splashing water seemed to fade. "You were right, Beth. God worked a miracle for us. The attorney is buying us time— a month, maybe more. He says he can help us keep custody of Joey."

"So where's the hooting and hollering?" Beth laughed just once. "I would think you'd have called me with that news the minute it came in."

Molly looked at her, and her eyes were somehow deeper than before. "I can't call you with everything that happens in regard to Joey."

Beth had the strangest feeling. As if there was something Molly wanted to say, but she couldn't or wouldn't say it. "You always did before."

"I know." Sorrow welled up in Molly's eyes. "We're not out of the woods yet. That's the reason I didn't call."

It was time. If Beth didn't ask now, she would never have the courage. She angled her body and looked straight to her sister's heart, beyond whatever walls she'd put up in the past few months. "Can I ask you something?"

"If it's about Joey, there's not much else to say." Molly picked up the bottle of sunscreen beside her, and poured a small amount into her right hand. She rubbed it slowly onto her knees.

"Look at me, Molly. I have to see your eyes."

Her sister made a face that showed her surprise, but she did as Beth asked. "Okay."

"Why did you and Jack take out a loan for almost a million dollars?"

And there it was. The moment she asked the question, the walls in Molly's eyes fell and what remained was pure, terrifying fear. It was a deer-in-the-headlights sort of look. A look that said Beth had caught her.

But in just half a second it was gone. Molly raised her brow. "Nice. Snooping through our mail now, are you?"

"Of course not." Beth hissed the words. She didn't want to fight, but she couldn't stand by and do nothing. Not if Molly and Jack were really thinking of running. "It was out in the open."

"Right." Molly leaned closer. She was mad, and her tone didn't hide the fact. "Why do you think it was out in the open, Beth? Because Jack and I have nothing to hide, that's why." She straightened, indignant. "And if you must know, we're purchasing a medical office building in downtown West Palm. Okay? Any other questions?"

"In downtown . . ." Beth wanted to cry. The last thing she intended was to make Molly mad, but even with her sister's explanation, she still wasn't convinced. She swallowed and summoned her courage. "Yes. One more."

"Okay, shoot. Wanna know how much the building

costs? Four million. Wanna know how we found it? Jack's real estate connections—Paul Kerkar, to be specific. He's listed. Look him up." She made a tight line with her lips. "Go ahead, Beth. What else do you want to know?"

The air around them grew still, the voices of the children almost silent. Beth never broke eye contact with her sister. "I want to know . . . if you're going to run."

Molly's shock was genuine, or at least it seemed that way. "Beth Petty! Are you asking me if Jack and I are going to run away with Joey?"

"Yes." It was too late to back down now. "Bill told me he saw Jack in downtown Miami, near a place where they make phony passports." Tears blurred her vision. "I had to ask, because, Molly—you can't run. If they catch you, you'll spend the rest of your life in prison."

She didn't mention the other obvious consequence. That the two of them would be finished, their relationship over. It was the heartbreaking part of the possibility that Beth tried not to think about. It was one thing to want to protect Molly from herself, from doing something that might land her in prison. That sort of motivation was okay. But it was entirely different if she was concerned mainly for herself, because she loved Molly too much to lose her.

Molly lifted her legs out of the pool and pushed herself up onto her feet. She stared down at Beth, her face a mask of hurt. "I can't believe you'd think that."

Beth stood, too, so they were eye-to-eye. "What was Jack doing in Miami?"

Then, as if something came over her, Molly's expression eased. "Beth . . ." She sounded kind, almost apologetic. "I'm so sorry. How long have you been thinking about this?"

"Since yesterday, for sure." Beth took a few steps back and sat on one of the pool lounge chairs.

Molly took the one next to her. "Jack was working with a document specialist, something about the deed to the building we're buying. He's done all his paperwork in Miami."

Beth wasn't convinced. Not then, and not later that afternoon when she was home mulling over everything Molly had said. Real estate transactions for property in West Palm Beach would take place here, not in Miami. Certainly whatever documents were needed, they could be picked up in town.

The evidence was still more than Beth could ignore. And she was running out of time to do something about it. The money, the phony passport place, the almost casual way Molly and Jack seemed to be handling what was happening with Joey. They were like pieces of a puzzle, and suddenly the picture seemed too great to ignore.

It was against God, against the law, against everything right and true for Molly and Jack to take Joey and run. They could get killed or arrested. They could lose both Joey and their freedom forever, all at the same time. With everything in her, Beth wanted to believe that her suspicions were outrageous, impossible. That her sister would never do such a thing.

But there was one detail Beth couldn't deny. Something Molly herself had said a few weeks ago. She said she'd lay down her life for Joey if she had to. And wouldn't she be doing exactly that if they ran? Giving up life as she knew it, everything about the old Molly Campbell, all so she could keep being Joey's mother?

There was only one way to make sure it wouldn't happen, to know for certain she'd done everything in her power to stop her sister from making the greatest mistake of her life. Beth knew the social worker's name. Molly had talked about the woman countless times in the past few months.

Allyson Bower.

She worked in Cleveland, Ohio, at the Child Welfare Department—Beth knew that, too. And with those two bits of information, in three quick minutes she was on the phone, being transferred to Allyson Bower's office.

On the fourth ring, a machine picked up. Beth took a deep breath, and when the recording asked the caller to leave a message, she waited for the beep and began to talk.

"Mrs. Bower, you don't know me. This is Beth Petty, Molly Campbell's sister." She paused. "This is a very hard phone call to make, but I think you should know I'm very concerned that my sister and her husband might be thinking of running, disappearing with Joey.

"As you know, we're leaving the country a week from today for a work trip to Haiti. I have a suspicion that the Campbells will take false passports with them on that trip. They also have access to an awful lot of money." Tears choked her throat. Her hands shook. Molly would never speak to her again if she knew about this call. She coughed a little. "Please, Mrs. Bower, if this concerns you, call me as soon as you get this message."

Beth left her number, and then hung up.

There. She'd done everything she could do. The social

worker would get her message, and if Molly was lying to her, it was only a matter of time. Allyson Bower would stop them before they had the chance to do something stupid, something they would regret forever. They didn't have to give up Joey. There was still time for legal intervention, time for God to work a miracle on their behalf. But if Molly and Jack ran, there would be no turning back, not ever.

Beth's head pounded. She took two Tylenol and stretched out on the sofa. The kids were playing in the kiddie pool out back, and dinner was an hour away. Not that she could bear the thought of eating. Her stomach was in knots. Making that call was the hardest thing Beth had ever done.

Now she could only pray that Molly never, ever found out. If she did, there would be no need to worry about whether her friendship with Molly would end because Molly would be in prison or living in some foreign country.

If Molly found out about the call, Beth would've killed the relationship herself.

Chapter Twenty-Three

They were in Joey's room, tucking him in and making sure his suitcase was packed for the morning. Molly's head was spinning so fast she could barely complete a sentence. They were just hours from setting their plan in motion.

"I won't see that other mommy and daddy on this trip, right?" Joey wore his dinosaur pajamas that night, the ones with the shorts and short sleeves. The Florida humidity was in full force, and even with their air-conditioning, the room felt muggy.

"No, buddy." Molly sat on the edge of his bed and smoothed his sweaty bangs off his head. "This is a special trip with just us and Aunt Beth's family."

"What about Gus?" Over the past few months, Gus had made a regular habit of sleeping on Joey's bed. He was sitting on the floor now, patiently waiting for Molly to move so he could take his place.

Molly could feel her heart breaking. "Not Gus." She reached down and patted Gus near his ear. "He's going to a doggie day care."

Joey giggled. "I bet he has fun there, Mommy."

Molly wanted to weep. "Me, too."

Jack had gone down the hall to get something, and now he came back with his guitar. Before life had spun so wildly out of control, Jack had often come into Joey's room at night with his guitar. They'd turn off the lights and Jack would play something soft and melodic, something he'd made up or something retro from the Eagles or Boston.

Now Jack motioned to the suitcase. "All packed?"

"Yes." She leaned down and gave Joey butterfly kisses with her eyelashes. "Want a backrub, buddy?"

"Okay." He smiled at her. "The other mommy does that for me, too." He started to turn over, but he held her look a second longer. "She's nice to me."

Molly gulped. The other mommy was nice? She covered her surprise. "That's good, honey . . . I'm glad."

"But the man . . . he's still really mean."

"I'm sure." She looked at Jack. He'd heard every word, she could tell by his expression.

Jack played three songs, all lullabies he'd written. When Joey was asleep, they tiptoed out of the room. They had a lot to talk about and only a few hours left before they got on the plane.

After Jack put his guitar away, they met on the front porch. Even with the sticky night, it felt better being outside. It made the whirling thoughts in Molly's head somehow manageable.

They sat in the glider, the one that just perfectly fit the two of them. The crickets were louder than usual, and Jack leaned his head back, peering at the starry sky. "It's our last night here."

"Yes." Molly pulled her feet up onto the glider and

hugged her knees. "I have so many questions still. Tell me again what you did today."

Jack looked calm. "Everything's done." He put his arm around her shoulders. "I transferred the money. It went through half a dozen accounts all designed to break up any paper trail."

"And it'll be in our account in the Caymans the day before we get there?"

"Yep." He kicked his feet up on the porch railing. "I double-checked. The instructions I gave the banker in Sweden were very clear. Wait twelve days and send the money on."

"And you're sure the money made it to Sweden?"

"Before noon today."

"You made it look like it was going to an escrow account, right? From our savings?"

"Right. That way when the authorities interview Beth and she tells them we were purchasing a commercial building, everything will line up. At least for a little while."

"What about the Realtor?"

"He'll hear about our disappearance and assume the deal is cancelled." Jack was unruffled by her questions. "He'd have no reason to contact anyone about a broken real estate deal. Happens all the time."

"Okay, what else?" Her heart was going double-time. After all the talking and planning, she was suddenly scared to death. The way she'd felt since Beth asked her point-blank if they were running. "I've got our entire photo library on CDs and jump drives, all packed in the suitcase."

"Good."

The photos had been Molly's idea. She couldn't leave her past life without bringing photographs. At first she'd tried to imagine packing a dozen albums, but then she remembered. Since they'd adopted Joey, all their photos were taken digitally. All they needed were the CDs and a back-up copy of the files on a jump drive. They could make new photos when they got situated in the Caymans.

Late at night when she couldn't sleep, she'd scanned special photos from before Joey's adoption into a file. Then she carefully put each photo back, so that when people went through their belongings, nothing would be out of place, no sign that they'd been planning this.

Molly packed only one photo album—the one Beth had made her when she graduated from high school. Also one small file of Joey's artwork. Otherwise everything was being left behind.

Jack leaned forward, elbows on his knees. "I cancelled our life insurance policies, effective today."

"Good. I like that." It was something they'd discussed a few weeks ago. If they didn't cancel the policies, and if eventually everyone presumed they'd drowned or been kidnapped or killed by a street gang in Port-au-Prince, disbursement on their policies would have to be made. Beth and Bill would wind up with at least half, since Molly's parents were both dead.

"I like it, too. We're not trying to get an illegal life insurance payout. We just want our son; that's all."

"Exactly." She hugged her legs a little tighter. "What else?"

"You'll take Gus to the kennel at seven in the morning. You've already called and set everything up, right?"

"Right. Last week." Molly started to shake. What were

they doing? It still felt like something from a terrible off-Broadway production. People had kids taken away from them; it didn't happen often, but it happened. How many times did a couple run away with their child? And why hadn't she heard of anyone getting away with it? She clenched her teeth to keep them from chattering. "What else?"

"Beth hasn't asked you any weird questions lately, right?"

"Not since the pool." She'd already told Jack about that conversation. "I think she believes my answers."

"Okay. Then we're all set. The getaway is something we have to figure out once we're in Port-au-Prince." He stood and leaned on the railing.

Molly couldn't sit still another moment. She joined him, leaning against his shoulder and staring out at their front yard. The yard they wouldn't see again after tomorrow.

He laced his fingers with hers. "What are you thinking?"

"A lot." She let her head hang for a moment. Strange that she was shaking. It had to be almost ninety degrees out. She looked up and studied the stars. "I remembered something the other day, something Joey and I watched last Christmas."

"Mmm."

"It was a cartoon, a half-hour show on the birth of Jesus. The story of the Nativity."

"You thought of that the other day?" Jack gave her his most charming smile.

His look settled some anxious part of her heart. In her new life, the one that would start tomorrow, she would have Jack and Joey. Despite all the other losses, having them would be enough. Once they got through the next week, they'd find their way together. She nodded. "Yes. After Jesus was born, there was this evil king. He wanted to kill baby Jesus."

"Okay, an evil king . . ."

"Right, and an angel came to Mary and Joseph in a dream and warned them. They got up and left for another country. Then and there, no warning."

"Ah . . ." He looked at her, his eyes dancing in the starlight. "Sort of like us."

"Right."

They were quiet for a minute, listening to the sound of the crickets and croaking frogs in the marsh on the other side of the neighborhood. "I keep thinking about Joey's dandelion." He breathed in slow through his nose. "That day at the park all I knew was I couldn't let him go. I wanted to disappear."

"Like Joey's dandelion dust."

"Yes." They were quiet again.

Molly wondered if he could hear her heart beating. No matter how many times they went over the details, she was still terrified. They weren't the sort of people who did this kind of thing. They were good people, law-abiding people. What if they weren't good at being bad? She pressed her forearms against the railing. "What about God's will?"

Jack smiled at her, the sort of smile he gave Joey when Joey talked about Neverland. "God's will?"

"Beth said she's been praying for God's will. Bill, too. If God's will is for Joey to be with us, won't it happen anyway? Couldn't all of this be for nothing?" She didn't pause long enough for him to say anything. "But what if it's God's will for Joey to go to the Porters?"

"You mean, if it's God's will for him to leave us, then somehow he'll leave us no matter what we do? Is that what you're saying?"

"Yes." Her voice was quiet, sad. Beyond afraid. "What if that?"

Jack took a moment before he answered her. "I'm not sure about God's will, Molly. I told you, we can talk about that later." He put his arms around her and together they straightened and eased their way into each other's arms. "All I know is that my plan is going to work." He held onto her shoulders and looked intently into her eyes. "It is, Molly. Nothing's going to happen to us."

Through that night and as the sun started to come up, it was the only thought that made even breathing possible. Nothing was going to happen to them. Nothing. The plan was going to work.

It had to.

Joey wasn't quite asleep. He lay there petting Gus and staring at the ceiling. There was something he hadn't told his mommy and daddy, and he felt bad inside about it. Last time he was at that Ohio house, where the Indians played baseball, the mean man told him scary things.

He said Joey was really his little boy, and he was the real daddy. Joey told the man no, that his real family was here in Florida. Then there was something else even worse. The man came really close to his ear and he said,

"If you say that again, little man, I'll give you a spanking you'll remember forever."

Then the man pushed Joey's head into the pillow for a long time. It was scary down there. His breaths were tight and small and he hoped the nice lady would come and make the man stop.

When she did come, she yelled at the man.

Joey looked at Gus. His eyes were open 'cause he was a good friend, that's why. "Hi, Gus . . . know what?"

What? Gus said with his eyes.

"I don't ever wanna see that mean man again. And maybe I won't have to. Know why?"

Why? Gus said.

"Because I asked God." Sometimes Gus forgot things even when he'd told him a hundred times. "'Member, Gus? I asked God to go with me on the trips to Ohio and He did. So I asked God if I could please stop taking the trips so I could be home with Mommy and Daddy and you."

Don't forget Mr. Monkey and the bears.

"I know, Gus. I won't." He reached over and picked up Mr. Monkey. "But I can't be with Mr. Bear because I left him at the Ohio house. Under the bed. Know why?"

Why? Gus made a whining sound.

"Because he made me think of that mean man every time I saw him o' course."

Gus yawned and closed his eyes. He didn't like to talk much at night. That was okay. It gave Joey a reason to talk to God again, 'cause God never, ever fell asleep. He asked Jonah at the pool last time, and that's what Jonah said. God stays awake all the time. In case we need to talk to Him about something.

"God . . . it's me, Joey. I asked You before, but I think I'll ask You again. In case You were busy last time." He looked out the window. "God, please, could You tell the judge that I don't want to go back to Ohio? I just want to be here with my family. Mommy and Daddy and Gus and Mr. Monkey and Mr. Growls. And that's all."

He thought for a minute. "Oh, and Aunt Beth and Uncle Bill and the cousins. Especially Jonah." He closed his eyes. Sleep was easy after he talked to God. "Thank You, God.

"Gee this name, amen."

Chapter Twenty-Four

Beth had never felt so sure of anything in all her life. The social worker never called her back, and now it was nine o'clock, the night before the mission trip. She hadn't confronted Molly again about the possibility that they might run, but even so, she felt the strain in her relationship with her sister.

In the past few days she asked Molly about the hearing—the one that was supposed to buy them more time with Joey. Even with the tension between them, Beth expected Molly to get excited about the hearing results. If they were good, anyway. Instead Molly only shook her head. "It was postponed until next week."

"Is that a bad thing?"

"The attorney still thinks he can get us more time. We're believing him, Beth. What else can we do?"

Nothing Molly had told Beth in the past few months could actually be verified. So Bill had snooped around and called Paul Kerkar, the Realtor. He mentioned his brother-in-law's purchase of a medical building and asked whether Paul knew of other similar properties.

"Perhaps." Paul was pleasant, not suspicious about the call.

"Jack tells me he's closing on the deal any time now—is that right?"

"In the next few weeks, for sure. The building inspection showed the need for a roof repair. That has to be done first."

Bill worked his way out of the conversation. Afterward he looked at Beth and held up his hands. "It's legit. Jack and Molly are buying a building in West Palm."

Still, Beth was worried. She hadn't seen one letter from a politician's office, or any reason why she should believe an attorney was really involved. Molly hadn't gone to any meetings, at least none that she'd mentioned. And even Jack never talked about the person he'd found, the guy's name or his law firm or how come he was able to help them when no one else could.

Now, with the plane leaving in twelve hours, Beth was still terrified that her sister was planning to disappear. She couldn't prove it, but she felt it deep in her bones. The way she had always known what Molly was going to do or how she was feeling or whether she was in trouble.

Because of that, earlier in the day she had called information and found the phone number for Wendy Porter in Cleveland, Ohio. Back when the social worker first contacted Molly and Jack, the details of the case were always a part of Molly's conversation. Though she hadn't mentioned the Ohio couple's name in recent weeks, Beth remembered.

Now, with Bill busy packing, she went upstairs and took a small piece of paper from the pocket of her jeans. The kids were asleep, packed and ready for the morning.

She was pretty sure Bill wouldn't want her interfering this way. The conversation with the Realtor was enough to convince him that Molly and Jack weren't planning to run. But what if they were? What choice did she have? If she didn't make the call now, she wouldn't have another chance.

Her heart skipped a beat as she picked up the receiver and punched in the numbers. After a long pause, she heard a ring, and then another. Then the sound of someone answering and a woman's voice saying, "Hello?"

Beth held her breath, willing her heart to settle down so she could focus on what she needed to say. "Yes . . . hello." She shut her eyes. How could she be doing this, and what would it accomplish? She had no answers for herself, but she was out of options. She rushed on. "My name is Beth Petty. I'm the sister of Molly Campbell."

There was a hesitation on the other end. "You mean, Joey's adoptive mother?" The woman sounded baffled. Her words were breathy and laced with shock. "Why are you calling?"

Here goes. . . . Beth exhaled and plunged ahead. After this there would be no turning back. "Well, Mrs. Porter, here's the situation. . . ."

Wendy Porter was by herself when the call came in.

She pressed the receiver to her ear and tried to understand why the sister of Joey's adoptive mother would call. The woman was going on, talking about how much the

Campbells loved Joey, and what sort of life he lived there in Florida.

"I don't understand." Wendy sat at the kitchen table and put her head in her hands. "I already know the Campbells have been wonderful for my son. But my husband and I are doing very well now, Mrs. Petty. We think it's right for us to have this chance at being Joey's parents—especially since my husband never knew about Joey until a few months ago."

"Right, well, that's why I'm calling." The woman on the other end sounded nervous. "See, something's come up and I think you should know about it."

At that moment, the door flung open and Rip walked in. He had a bag in his arms with a few liquor bottles peeking out the top. Wendy motioned at him to be quiet. She pointed at the phone and covered the speaker. "It's about Joey," she whispered.

He rolled his eyes, set the bag down on the kitchen counter, and pulled out a single bottle. A minute later he was pouring his second glass. He dropped a handful of ice into it and came to stand beside her. "Who is it?"

Wendy was trying to hear. Something about a trip to Haiti and this woman's thoughts that maybe the Campbells wouldn't ever come back to the United States.

"I said, who is it?" Rip's voice boomed at her. Wherever he'd been, he was already drunk. He could barely keep his eyes open.

She waved him off once more. With the phone pressed tight to one ear, she covered the other and tried to hear. "So they're leaving the country? How come I don't know about that?"

Rip made a face. He staggered a little and set his drink down on the table. "Who's leavin' the country?"

"Look." Wendy was sure the woman could hear Rip. The last thing she needed was Molly Campbell's sister knowing that things were out of control at the Porter house. "Can I call you back? I need to take care of something here first."

"Don't wait, please. I'm very concerned about this."

"Okay." Wendy got the woman's number. "Five minutes."

The second she hung up, Rip was on her. He grabbed her shoulder and jerked her to her feet. "What was that about?"

"Rip . . . please, give me some space." She tried to push him back, but he only dug his fingers into her arm and held on tighter.

She ignored the pain and lowered her voice, anything to help him be calm. "Look, everything's going to work out." Lying was the answer in this case. "No one's leaving the country. Let me take care of the phone call."

He gave her a shove and another glare. "You *make* me do it, you know that?"

This was the worst part of his drinking. He got sloppy and angry, and he started blaming her. "Don't, Rip."

He brushed her off, waving his hand in the air, almost losing his balance in the process. As he turned back to the kitchen, he grabbed his drink and downed it in seconds. A loud belch came from him as he finished. He chuckled and headed into the kitchen.

She watched him, the way she had to watch him when he was in this mood. In case he came at her swinging.

Rip held the liquor bottle up to the light and grinned.

"Only the good stuff for me, baby." He poured a third glass and slammed the bottle down. That fast the rage was back and he glared at her. "It's all your fault." He was too unsteady to do much more than lean against the kitchen counter. "You deserve everything you get from me."

Wendy waited for the tirade to die down. There was nothing she could say to him, not now while he was drunk. Tomorrow they would have a talk and she'd encourage him to get back to counseling, back to the alcohol meetings. They were going to lose Joey if Rip didn't do something about his drinking—either that, or he was going to do something to wind up back in prison.

After a minute or so, Rip took his drink and staggered into the living room. He plopped into his recliner, flipped on the television, and immediately got lost in some sports show.

This was her chance. Wendy picked up the phone and dialed the woman's number. Whatever she'd been trying to say, something about Haiti and leaving the country, the details sounded serious. Serious enough that the woman would call. Not just to say how much the Campbells loved Joey.

But maybe to warn Wendy of something the Campbells were about to do.

Allyson Bower had enjoyed every minute of her vacation. She and the kids loved taking a week each summer and heading south to Walton Beach in the Florida panhandle for sun and surf and relaxation. There was nowhere Allyson would rather be than sitting on a beach, staring at the water.

Never was the timing of the trip more perfect. The Campbell case had eaten at her all summer, but not for the past week. For most of the past seven days she'd been able to forget about work—at least long enough to enjoy her kids. Now, though, she was back, and her heart was heavy. It was Friday, the first day of Labor Day weekend. In just seven days the Campbells would lose their son forever.

The courts were wrong this time. No matter what the law said, Joey belonged with Molly and Jack Campbell. Allyson had no doubts. She couldn't prove that Rip was back to his violent ways—the little bruises where he'd grabbed Joey were explainable, and not enough to stop the transfer of custody.

But Wendy Porter could cover for her husband for only so long. The man was trouble, and Allyson worried about Joey, about his future once social workers and the system stopped looking in on him.

She surveyed her office. It was perfectly put together, as always. Every paper had its place, every file organized alphabetically. She had a dozen phone calls to make, but first she needed to listen to her messages. After a week away, there were bound to be dozens of them.

Halfway through the messages, a woman's voice rang out from the machine, one Allyson didn't recognize.

"Mrs. Bower, you don't know me. This is Beth Petty, Molly Campbell's sister."

What? Why would Molly Campbell's sister call? Allyson leaned in and turned up the volume.

"This is a very hard phone call to make, but I think you should know I'm concerned that my sister and her husband might be thinking of running, disappearing with Joey. As you know, we're leaving the country a week from today for a work trip to Haiti. I have a suspicion that the Campbells will take false passports with them on that trip. They also have access to an awful lot of money."

Allyson felt the floor beneath her give way. The Campbells' story had checked out; she had convinced the judge. Sure she'd had mild doubts, but never for a minute had she felt convinced that the couple would run. She looked at the calendar on her wall.

By now they would be halfway to Haiti.

The message continued to play. There was a coughing sound, as if maybe Molly's sister was choked up or crying. "Please, Mrs. Bower, if this concerns you, call me as soon as you get this message." The woman left her number, and the message came to an end.

Allyson pushed the Stop button on the answering machine, gripped the armrests of her chair, and hung her head. Had she missed something? And how come this Beth Petty hadn't called someone else at the department if she was so worried her sister would leave the country and never come back? If the woman was right—if the Campbells had a plan to run—it would be all Allyson's fault.

The judge would demand to know why she had recommended in favor of the trip, and the Porters would have grounds to sue the department. Especially since they weren't notified. If Molly Campbell's sister was right, Allyson's career, her livelihood, and her future, were about to be destroyed.

Never mind that. She didn't blame the Campbells. It was her job to see that the law was followed, to make sure that whatever the system deemed best for a child was carried through. She pressed her knuckles to her brow. Who should she call first? The judge, probably. Yes, definitely. He could get things moving the fastest, contact authorities in Haiti and see that the Campbells were apprehended and brought back. Before they had time to commit a crime.

She went to pick up the phone, but just then it rang. She jumped, startled, then grabbed the receiver. Whoever it was, she needed to hurry. She didn't have time for other business until she contacted the judge. A quick tap on the right blinking light and she pressed the phone to her ear. "Hello?"

"Allyson Bower?" The woman on the other end was crying.

"Yes, this is she." Allyson looked at the clock on the wall. Every minute counted. She took a quick breath. "How can I help you?"

"This is Wendy Porter." The woman was definitely crying.

Allyson felt the blood rush from her face. "What's wrong, Wendy?"

For a long while, there was only the sound of the woman's sobs. Then, with a shaky voice she said, "There's something I need to tell you."

Chapter Twenty-Five

The main road out of the airport and through Port-au-Prince was littered with potholes and broken-down cars. Molly and Jack sat in the third row of a rusty old van, Joey tucked safely between them. Molly's mind kept shouting the obvious at her. They were really here. They'd gotten out of the States, and in just a few days they'd be in Europe, pretending they were tourists—and a few weeks after that, they'd be in the Cayman Islands. It was working. The plan was working.

Her heart filled with equal amounts of joy and sorrow at the prospect.

Jesper, their driver, pointed to a building on their right. It was made of white crumbling bricks, and it looked seriously damaged. "This is hospital." He smiled. "Hospital stay open even after hurricane."

Seated in front were Beth, Bill, and Jonah. The backseat was filled with the other Petty kids, most of whom were sleeping. In the van behind them were three college kids who would round out their group, and a leader from the college group at church. He would supervise their work at the orphanage.

Molly did everything she could to listen to Jesper. It took her mind off the details that still had to come together before they could leave Haiti.

Jesper was a gracious man with dark skin and bright eyes. He had a deep faith, that much was clear from the moment he met them.

"God give you a good trip, yes?" His smile lit up his face.

"Yes," Bill answered for them. "God gave us a great trip. Thank you."

Jesper went on about God's favor and God's mercy and God's providence, all while he was gathering their bags and leading the way back out to the van. He hadn't stopped talking since he picked them up.

At the moment he was talking about the faith of the Haitian people. "God is everything to people in my country. The people not committed to darkness." He gestured to the masses teeming on either side of the highway. "You see? You see how people live? God is everything."

Molly could hardly believe how the people lived.

Because of the broken-down cars and the occasional cyclist pulling a cart or the random person herding animals along in one of the lanes, travel was slow. It gave all of them a chance to take in the surroundings. Joey was sleeping between the two of them, but Jack was mesmerized by the sights, same as her.

They passed rows of dwellings that were little more than shanties, small shacks with dirt floors, some of them without even a roof. Very obviously most of them did not have electricity or running water. The people moving on the broken sidewalks carried large containers on their heads, and wove their way around what looked like one continuous flea market.

Jesper came to a grinding halt and slammed his hand on the horn. All the vehicles around him did the same thing. Up ahead, a pick-up truck had stopped in the middle of the road so six or seven guys could jump out the back and dodge through traffic to the side of the road.

The guys waved, friendly-like, but before traffic could pick up again, there was a thud and the van jolted.

"What was—" Bill and Beth spun around.

Molly and Jack did the same thing, and there, clinging to the back of the van, were two young men.

Jesper laughed. "Americans think strange that people take rides from each other." He rolled down his window and gave a thumbs-up sign to the men now hanging from the back of the van. "Bondye reme ou!"

Molly knew that one. *God loves you.* She smiled despite the absurdity of it all. Jesper picked up speed, and somehow the men clinging to the back held on. The next time traffic ground to a stop, they hopped off, waved, and went their way.

The stop gave Molly the chance to notice a village woman sitting in front of a dirty stone table. She looked haggard and weary, dressed in a rag skirt and blouse, her hair tied back. Before traffic eased enough for Jesper to move the van, the woman grabbed a chicken from a cage of squawking birds on the ground next to her.

She pressed the chicken's neck against the big dirty rock and grabbed a butcher knife. In seconds, the deed was done, and deftly the woman skinned and gutted the bird, tossing the meat into a bin behind her. A swarm of flies lifted as the meat fell into the container.

Molly felt a wave of nausea and looked at Jack. His face was pale and he nodded. He'd seen the same thing. Bill turned around and whispered, "Good thing we brought canned tuna."

"Definitely." Molly managed a smile. She tapped Beth on the shoulder. "Did you see that?" Her voice was barely audible, since Jesper was still talking up front.

"What?" Beth looked distracted. She'd been that way ever since they boarded the plane in West Palm Beach.

"The chicken, did you see the woman with the chicken?"

"No." Beth held her gaze for a moment. "I guess I have a lot on my mind."

Molly wanted to ask what, but she was afraid of her sister's answer. They had struggled since the day Beth asked if she and Jack were going to run. Molly guessed her sister was still worried about that fact. But Beth must know there was nothing she could do now.

An ache filled Molly's heart as Beth turned and faced the front of the van again. *My sweet sister . . . if only I could tell you, if only I could say good-bye the way I want to say it. Please . . . don't be mad at me forever.* She sighed and Jack looked at her. He put his arm along the back of the seat and stroked her shoulder. His look said not to worry. Everything would be okay.

She gave him a worried smile. It would have to be okay. They had no choice now.

Jesper was going on about the worship times. "Hours of singing, because the people know that God is everything. All we have, all we need."

Molly had a feeling that someday very soon, if she and

Jack and Joey were going to survive their new life, they just might be saying the same thing.

Beth wanted to focus on the trip, on the experience at hand, especially as they approached the orphanage. But every few minutes she found herself looking at her sister, trying to read her actions, her eyes, her tone. Was she wrong? Was everything really the way Molly had explained it? Could it be that she was only the victim of an overly active imagination—the way Bill suspected?

Jesper directed their attention to the buildings on their left. "The first is the orphanage, and next to it, the mission house."

Both sat behind thick brick walls, easily eight feet high. Along the top row of stone were loops of sharp razor wire. The windows in the van were open now, and they could hear the clamoring of children on the other side of the wall.

"Orphanage and mission house need security," Jesper said.

Beth assumed that most of Port-au-Prince must need security, since all the buildings on that street had similar walls and razor wire.

A guard with a rifle rolled open a heavy iron gate for them. He grinned at Jesper and tipped his worn baseball cap. The van pulled in and parked in the narrow driveway. "This is the mission house. We will walk to orphanage."

The Petty kids and Joey were all awake now, asking

Jesper questions as quickly as he could answer them. They piled out through the side door, grabbing luggage from under the seats and trying to make sense of the chaos. The van with the three college kids and the young pastor pulled in and parked behind them.

"Who lives at the mission house?" Cammie climbed out of the backseat. Blain and Braden followed her.

"Volunteers and visiting Americans." Jesper smiled. "Today . . . you and your family!"

"What do people eat here?" Braden rubbed his eyes. "I'm hungry."

"Faun will have rice feast in one hour." Jesper's voice rang with pride. "We take good care American guests."

The questions continued as they pulled their suitcases into the house. "Were we supposed to bring pillows?" Bill uttered the question quietly as they made their way up the walk.

"I don't think so." Jack looked over his shoulder and smiled. "But I did, anyway. You never know."

Beth watched the men, not sure what to feel. This was something new, the way they got along and made small talk so easily. Was it genuine—something that had come from their prayer meeting? Or was this new camaraderie only Jack's way of getting along with Bill, keeping suspicions at bay until he and Molly and Joey made their break?

The men from the other van trailed them into the house. The leader said something about putting their suitcases away and heading over to the orphanage to meet the children. *Good,* Beth told herself. *Let them go.* It would take longer to get their two families settled at the mission house, and that meant Beth had more time to study her sister. Without the group leader interrupting.

She watched Molly, the easy way her sister smiled at Joey and Jack as one of the volunteers met them and directed them to a room off to the left. If they were planning a getaway, they didn't show it. They seemed surprisingly at ease. Beth was suddenly assaulted by doubt. What if she was wrong? How could she ever expect Molly to forgive her for the questions she'd asked, and the way she'd been acting?

Beth had no answers for herself. They were led to their rooms, and Bill nodded his approval. "Running water and electricity. I'd say they treat their guests very well."

"I hope they treat the orphans this nicely." Cammie grabbed her suitcase and flung it on her bunk bed. "I can't wait to meet them."

Again Beth was pulled back into the moment. They were here to take part in a work trip, after all. It was time to stop worrying about Molly and Jack and Joey. This was a once-in-a-lifetime experience for her own kids. She worked her bag beneath her bunk and sat on the edge of the mattress.

Suddenly tears blurred her vision, and she closed her eyes. For months she'd been preaching to Molly and Jack that the answer lay in praying for God's will. Trust God, she'd told them. He knows what's best for Joey, even if it doesn't seem best to you. But what had she, herself, been doing?

The whole time she'd been trying to teach Molly and Jack about faith, she'd been walking in her own strength entirely. Not once had she prayed about her doubts where Molly and Jack were concerned. Sure, she kept praying for Joey, that her sister would get to keep her son. But every time she felt doubts about what Molly and Jack might be planning, she turned into a detective, firing questions at her sister and snooping for clues.

Even the phone calls to the social worker and to Wendy Porter were done without so much as a single bit of communication with God. No wonder she'd been plagued by doubt and fear. She had no peace, because she hadn't taken her own advice.

Now she bowed her head and covered her face. The kids were distracted, heading out into the main room with Bill. Only Jonah remained, and he must've heard her crying.

"What're you doing, Mommy?" Jonah bounced down next to her. "Are you sad?"

"No, not really." She sniffed and put her arm around him. "Mommy needs a minute to pray."

"Is it okay if I play with Blain and Braden?"

"Yes, sweetie. Go ahead."

Jonah ran off, and Beth covered her face once more. Then she did what her soul had been crying for since she woke up that morning. *God . . . forgive me for my doubts and suspicions. I've tried so hard to be my sister's keeper, when You already know exactly what's going to happen. Help me remember the joy of my salvation and the certainty of Your truth, Father.* She wiped at her tears. They were meeting for the rice feast in just ten minutes. *And, God . . . I beg You that Your will be done for Molly and Jack and Joey. From this minute on I'll trust You—whatever happens.*

She opened her eyes and stood up. Without a doubt

she knew what she was going to do the moment she saw Molly. She would sit beside her at the rice feast, and before another minute passed, she would do what she should've done a long time ago.

She would apologize.

Chapter Twenty-Six

Jack could feel his heart changing.

On the inside where his existence had been all confidence and self-assurance, something was happening, a softening—a knowing that somehow all his life, just maybe he'd been wrong. He hadn't expected this kind of change to happen at this stage of the plan. The trip to Haiti, the work . . . It was all part of the guise to get them out of the country. But after a day of working with the Haitian people and the volunteers at the orphanage, Jack could see that Jesper was right.

God *was* everything to them.

It was their second full day in Haiti, and Jesper suggested a trip into the city. Day excursions were a scheduled part of the work trip, a way to take food and supplies to the people in the streets. For Jack, the day trips had been his guarantee that the plan would work. Once they were on the city streets, anything could happen. And he would make sure it did.

They'd spent that morning working with the children and the volunteers at the orphanage. Bill watched as Joey and the Petty kids mingled with the orphans. The children had only one small play room, a square area with a tile floor and no furniture. There were maybe four or five toys among more than forty boys and girls.

"I thought the church back home sent toys and clothes to these kids," Jack said to Jesper.

He smiled. "Kids get lots of toys and clothes. Much more than children on street." He motioned toward the front gate. "Volunteers box up things Americans send, give to family and friends on street who have nothing."

The answer was humbling.

They set to work repairing a collapsed wall on the south side of the orphanage, and at break time Jack found Joey with six little boys. He had a protein bar for his son, and a few others for the orphans. Hardly enough to go around.

He pulled Joey aside. "Hey, sport, I have a snack for you. Think you could share with the other boys?"

Joey's blue eyes shone with love. "O' course, Daddy." He took the bars and ran back to the circle of boys.

Joey broke the bars into small bits and gave each of the boys a piece. The children were overwhelmed with joy. They marveled and held up their snack, chattering in Creole, obviously excited. What Jack saw next only added to the strange feeling inside him. Each of the Haitian children took their piece and ran to a group of the other children. Still chattering and gesturing in sheer joy, they broke off piece after piece until every child in the orphanage had a small bite.

Jesper found Jack watching. The man put his arm around Jack's shoulders. "They understand God's teaching. Better to give than to receive."

Jack didn't know what to say. He could hardly wait to

tell Molly. What children back home would act that way, would think of others the way these kids did? Here they had nothing to their name, but when given a gift, they couldn't wait to share it. Back on the damaged wall, Jack took up his place with a hammer and a bag of nails alongside. Working next to him was an orphanage volunteer named Franz. Franz spoke broken English, and, like Jesper, he was talkative.

"God saved my family." Franz positioned a nail and sent it through a new piece of wood with a single blow from his hammer. He was built like Mike Tyson, but he had the tenderness of a child. "We have no food, dying on streets. Me and wife beg God for mercy, for help." He motioned to Jesper. "Next day Jesper come to us and ask work at orphanage for food and house." He pointed up to the hazy blue sky overhead. "Good God, our God. Very good."

"Yes." Jack would've had trouble denying the fact.

The day trips took place at three that afternoon, during naptime for the orphans. The college guys—including their group leader—were going to the roughest neighborhood in the area. The Petty family was headed for a busy street of townspeople a few blocks away, and the Campbells to another. They would take food bags and supplies to the people and distribute booklets written in Creole, explaining the message of hope in Christ and the path to salvation.

The pastor back at Bethel Bible Church had encouraged them that they didn't need to do anything more than smile at the people and be kind. "Anyone can do this; theological training isn't necessary. Remember . . . it's a *work* trip. The booklet says it all."

As they set out, Molly turned to Jack. "I'll be watching."

He nodded. They'd talked about it the night before. Being out on the street that afternoon would give them their only chance to make a plan. Then, the next day, they would ask to go to the same place, the same neighborhood. From there they would figure out their escape.

They had packed lightly for the trip, because there was no way to take their suitcases on a day trip into Port-au-Prince. Whatever they could fit in their backpacks and Molly's single roll-aboard would be all they could take. So that they wouldn't raise suspicions the following day, they brought the exact same bags with them for this current day trip.

"Why the suitcase?" Franz was their driver. He gave Molly a funny grin. "You Americans always take bags."

"I have allergies." Molly patted her bag. The lie tasted like rotten eggs on her tongue. "This has my food and medicine. In case we're gone for longer than we expect."

Franz gave an exaggerated shrug, but he never stopped smiling. "Fine with me. Throw in the back."

On the way to the neighborhood, Molly leaned around Joey and spoke low near Jack's ear. "I forgot to tell you. Beth apologized yesterday."

"Really?" He was surprised. "I sort of figured she still doubted us, like she'd be the first one on our trail when we go."

"She will be." Molly angled her head. "But I think she's done worrying about it. Almost like whatever her fears are, she's letting them go."

Jack let the notion settle into his heart. More proof that the faith Beth and Bill lived by was strong enough to change people. He looked out the window and studied the shacks and makeshift tables with wares for sale. There were so many people, all of them existing without any reason for hope.

The people who walked the streets were empty-eyed for the most part. Some sat on street corners, their heads in their hands, waiting for another day to pass. Others were hunched over in front of a table of dusty candy or bottled water, hoping to make a few dollars before evening came.

Only at the orphanage and in the mission house were the Haitian people alive and full of love and joy. Whatever Jack had thought about Christianity in the past, there was no denying its positive impact on their hosts.

Franz drove another ten minutes, then he turned down a narrow alleyway. At the other end, a village of people was gathered in what looked like a small courtyard. "We work here, yes?" Franz glowed at the possibility.

"Yes." Jack glanced around. Every eye was on them. He had thought once or twice about the possibility that this part of the trip could be dangerous for them, for Joey. He gave Molly a look. "Don't let go of his hand."

"I won't." He saw the fear in her eyes and he knew. She was afraid of more than the villagers.

Last night after everyone else was asleep, she had climbed into Jack's bunk and held onto him. "I'm so scared, Jack. What if we get caught?"

"We won't." He smoothed her hair and kissed her. "Have I told you lately how beautiful you are?"

She buried her head in his shoulder. "I'm serious, Jack. What if it doesn't work?"

"It will." The whispered conversation went on for

nearly an hour before she fell asleep, her head still on his chest.

Now, her eyes were wide with the enormity of the task that lay ahead of them. They would have to greet people, pass out food and supplies and the church tracts, and somehow make contact with someone who would help them. That, or figure out a way to get lost, and then catch a ride to the airport before anyone found them.

Franz climbed out first. With his big voice and bigger smile, he announced something in Creole. Then he took the food and supply boxes from the back of the truck and set them on the ground. He said something else, and the people drew closer.

"I hope he told them we're friendly," Jack said, his voice low.

"Me, too." Molly clutched Joey.

"Is this the part where we tell people about God?" Joey was excited, but not the least bit worried. He had no idea of all that lay ahead.

"Yes, buddy." Molly kissed the top of his head. "This is that part."

They were waiting in the car for the signal from Franz, and at that moment he opened their door and motioned for them to climb out. "People are ready for their gifts."

Jack knew it was up to him. With Molly terrified and worried about Joey, the three of them wouldn't be friendly enough to attract the right type of people. His behavior would have to make up for theirs. While Molly and Joey stayed with Franz, Jack would mingle with the people.

The first half hour, they worked so hard filling the people's needs that they didn't have time to think of anything else. But after that the crowd started to break up. Somehow word must've gotten out, because carloads of people arrived, looking for a handout. The weather was much like South Florida, humid and tropical. Cumulus clouds gathered in the distance, and Jack checked his watch. It was four o'clock. They didn't have long.

Now and then he looked over the crowd to Molly and Joey and Franz. Once in a while Franz would see some-one he knew and follow that person. Sometimes he was gone for three, even four minutes. Once he didn't return for fifteen. He had explained that he knew people in this area, and that sometimes he needed to visit someone at their house. "They need pray and visit," he said. "You be fine here."

The situation was working out perfectly. If Franz was given to brief disappearances, then tomorrow they could use a moment like that to run. But none of it would hap-pen if Jack didn't figure out a contact. If not today, then tomorrow, when they were fleeing on foot. Someone who could get them to the airport.

"Bondye reme ou," Jack told each person. "Do you speak English?"

Most of them shook their heads. They took the food and supplies and tracts and didn't linger around the Americans. Jack began surveying the perimeter of the square. In the distance he saw several cars, each of them with a driver.

He made his way back to Franz and Molly and Joey. "What are they doing?" He pointed to the drivers. "Should I take them some gifts?"

"Why not?" Franz grinned. "They are drivers. Like . . .

cabbies in America." His smile faded. "Most have no work, just sit. Some run drugs for drug lords."

Jack had wondered as much. In the distance there was a light rumble, the first bit of thunder. "How much longer, Franz?"

"We stay until gifts gone." He squinted at the sky. It was still sunny where they were. "Or until big storm. Whatever first."

Molly cast him a nervous glance before turning her attention back to the people. The women and children were gathered around her and Joey—there seemed no shortage of them.

Jack scanned the cars again.

He filled his arms with gift bags and tracts and approached the drivers. Two looked uninterested, and a third was in a conversation with someone—a shady-looking older man. But the fourth smiled at him and held out his hand. "Hello, American."

English! The man spoke English! Jack held up the gift bags and made his way to the man. "Hello! Bondye reme ou."

"God loves everyone!" The man chuckled. "I speak English, friend." He leaned out his car window. "What you bring me today?"

Jack gave the man several bags, some with food, some with supplies.

"You keep your book." He pointed up and winked. "I already know God. Good, good God."

"Yes." Jack felt a shiver pass over his spine. Indeed. He looked over his shoulder. Franz was deeply involved in a conversation, and Molly and Joey were still reaching into the supply box, handing out bags. He rested his elbow on the man's car. "You are a driver?"

"Yes." He gripped his steering wheel. "God gives Tancredo enough work." He motioned to the other men. "Others, dirty drivers." He lowered his voice. "Drugs . . . bad." His smile was back and he thumped his chest. "Tancredo drive for God."

Jack would've believed anything at that point. He took a breath and steadied himself. "My wife and son and I need a ride to the airport tomorrow. At this time."

Tancredo clapped his hands. "Yes, I do that. Tomorrow. Same time."

Jack took a few steps back. He didn't want to attract attention. "I will pay you a hundred dollars for the ride, okay?"

The man's mouth hung open. "One hundred?"

"Yes. But you say nothing. God has told us that we must escape tomorrow. For our boy's safety." He pointed down the alley. "You meet us at the end of this street. Okay?"

Tancredo looked slightly confused, but he nodded. "God tells you, I say nothing." He placed his hand over his mouth. "Tancredo drive, nothing more. I meet you in hidden place. End of alley, two streets to the left."

"End of alley, two streets to the left." Jack couldn't believe their luck. A driver who spoke English and understood their need for discretion. From the corner of his eye, he saw Franz walking toward them. Jack took another few steps backward and waved at Tancredo. "Bondye reme ou."

"Oui, Bondye reme ou!" The driver held up his gift

bag and then leaned back against his headrest, resuming his wait for a customer.

"You did good, Jack." Franz fell in step beside Jack. "You make friends with Haitian people. God smiles at you."

Jack wasn't sure what to feel. How could God smile at him? He wasn't making friends, he was making plans to break the law, to run from his own country. He dismissed the thought and pointed at the supply box. "Are the bags gone?"

"All given out!" Franz held up his hands toward heaven. "God glorified this day, this place."

The ride back was quiet except for the occasional Bible reference or exclamation by Franz. Jack couldn't wait to tell Molly what had happened, but he didn't dare do it until they were alone. As they started back, he turned to Franz. "Can we come back here tomorrow— same place? I told one of the men to bring his friends because we'd be back."

"Yes, good plan." Franz grinned and stared at the sky. "Storm will be big tonight."

Halfway back to the orphanage, they stopped for gas. Rain had just started pelting the area. The station was a cacophony of chaos—fifteen or twenty people selling a hundred worn-out, tired-looking things, and large mounds of trash dotting the perimeter, each with a couple of skinny pigs rooting through them.

As soon as Franz left the car to find the attendant, Jack turned to Molly. "It's perfect. I met a driver."

"I saw." Their conversation was hushed, their words fast. Once more Joey was asleep between them, so there was no danger of him hearing. "What's the plan?"

"His name is Tancredo. We meet him there tomorrow. We'll keep your bag with us at all times, our backpacks on. When Franz goes off to meet with one of the villagers, we wander down the alley and run for it. The driver will be waiting."

He gave her arm a tender pat. "I have it all figured out, Molly. You can relax."

"I feel sick." She pulled Joey close and buried her face in his blond hair. Jack wasn't sure, but he thought she was crying. Tears stung his own eyes, too. They were doing what they had to do for their son, the only way they knew to protect him.

Jack would like to have left on the first or second day, but they needed to follow the schedule, needed a day in the village in order to make connections. And now they were just one day from seeing it all work out.

When they got back to the orphanage, they put Joey down for a short rest and made a plan to play cards with Beth and Bill in the common room before dinner. The college guys and the group leader had gathered with them that morning for breakfast and a briefing about the dangers of heading into the village. That night the group would split up so the guys could work with the orphans. Jack was glad for the sense of privacy. Before meeting with Beth and Bill, he led Molly to the corner of their room.

"Listen, I have an idea." He looked over his shoulder—no one was listening in on their conversation. His eyes met Molly's again, and he spoke quickly. "Tomorrow I'll take one of my T-shirts, rip it and get it dirty, and smear it with my blood."

"Jack!" The color drained from her face. "That sounds like a horror film."

"No, I'll just prick my finger. It won't be much blood, just enough that it'll look like something bad happened to us. I'll leave that on the street when we take off with the driver."

Molly still looked shocked. But gradually, as the information sank in, she nodded. "So it might throw them off the trail?"

"Yes, even for a few days." His mind ran ahead of him. "Because of the custody issue, it won't take them long to figure out we staged the shirt thing. But we can use every extra hour to get away."

"Okay. I get it."

"Anyway, by the time people realize what happened, we'll be on our way to Stockholm." They would buy tickets at the airport counter for a flight out to Europe. Jack had the schedule memorized. If there was room on the flight, they'd book one with Sweden as a final destination. Small enough that international police wouldn't yet have word of their disappearance, and with a local population blond enough that they'd fit right in.

"Molly?" It was Beth. She was standing at the doorway holding a deck of cards. "You guys ready?"

"Sure." Molly practically lurched from her spot. She took Jack's hand. "Come on, we can talk about this with Beth and Bill."

Jack was impressed. It was the best cover Molly had done since they'd gotten there. An hour later they were still gathered around the table playing cards and swapping stories of their day in the villages. The rice and bean dinner was almost ready, and like every other day, their hosts wouldn't think of letting them help with preparations.

A sense of euphoria and sorrow mingled and swept over Jack. This was their last night with Bill and Beth. Just when he was beginning to really like them. Their kids were all awake now, playing their own card game on the living-room floor. Molly had mentioned several times that maybe someday—when the heat was off—they could return to the United States and reconnect with Bill and Beth.

Jack doubted it, but in that moment, it was a nice thought.

His eyes met Molly's and he knew. She was feeling the same thing, the nostalgia of the moment, the finality of it. Their last night of any sort of normalcy for what could be a very long time.

Molly laid down the final card in her hand. "Beth . . . how could I forget?" She groaned. "I should've saved you a spade." She pressed her fist against her forehead. "And we were winning, too."

"It's okay." Beth leaned back and grinned. "We're still killing the guys. I can't really be—"

Before she could finish her sentence, the front door of the mission house burst open and five armed officers rushed in. "Police!" Their English pronunciation was better than most. "Everyone freeze!"

Jack's head began to spin. What was this? How could police get past the guard at the gate without at least a warning to the people in the mission house, and why were they there? All nine of them froze, and from the kitchen three volunteers rushed into the room, shouting at the police in Creole.

On the floor, the children didn't know what to do. Cammie and Blain lifted their hands slowly, as if they were under arrest. Braden and Jonah and Joey scampered to their parents. Jonah started to cry.

One of the mission-house workers took the lead. He stormed across the floor right up to the police, gesturing and talking in Creole. His tone was angry, offended. One of the policemen seemed to be in charge. He gestured back, and rattled off several lines of some sort of a response.

Across the table, Molly looked at Jack. She was pale, and he shot her a stern look. *Don't lose control now.* She swallowed and barely moved her head in a single nod. She wouldn't give them away.

"What in the—" Bill whispered to Beth, and she shook her head.

Only then did Jack see it, the look in Beth's eyes. It wasn't fear and shock like the rest of them. It was something unmistakable, a look Jack had never seen in Beth as long as he'd known her.

The look was guilt.

Chapter Twenty-Seven

Molly couldn't breathe or speak or move. She didn't need anyone to tell her why the police had barged in shouting orders. She knew as certainly as she knew her heart was about to beat through her chest.

She looked at Beth. The guilt in her sister's eyes was so strong it might as well have been written on her face, and suddenly Molly could feel their plans unraveling. They were caught! They would be taken in and questioned and sent back to the United States. Law enforcement would be waiting for them, and Joey would be whisked away forever.

Black spots danced before her eyes, and she felt faint. That's when Jack fired another look at her. She couldn't fall apart, not now. Not with Joey clinging to her and the children watching. She turned away from Beth and saw the mission worker approach them. His face was troubled.

"The police have an order." He twisted his expression, confused. "This never happen before." He came closer, his steps slow. His eyes met Jack's. "You and your wife and son—police want all three. They have orders from embassy."

Molly clung tightly to Joey. There it was. She was right; they were caught. Only one person could've done this to them. She turned and looked at Beth. In a rush all the thousands of times she'd looked at her sister came back. . . .

Beth was tugging on her arm, and they were three and five years old. "Wanna play dolls, Molly?"

And Molly was taking her sister's hand and finding a place on the floor beside her. And then they were a little older, and Beth was looking at her from her bicycle seat, Molly the hero for taking time to work with Beth while their dad was in the house. And they were in high school and Beth was holding her up, telling her that Connor Aiken was a jerk. And they were a year older, cheering at a basketball game and grinning at each other because no other two cheerleaders were ever as much in sync as they were. Then it was the middle of the afternoon, Christmas break, and Art Goldberg's mother was on the phone. "I have some bad news for you, Molly. . . ." And Molly was in a heap on the floor, and through her tears, through her swollen eyes, there was Beth, promising her everything would be okay, someday, one day. And they were sitting next to each other at the park a few months ago, and Molly was saying how glad she was that they were neighbors, and Beth was hugging her and saying, "You'll always be my best friend."

Every one of those scenes flashed through her mind in the time it took her to look at her sister and say the only thing she could think to say. The question that would haunt her until the day she died. "How could you?" Her words were barely audible.

Jack and the mission worker were talking, trying to make sense of the police order. But the police had barked something else, filling the moment with urgency.

Beth shook her head, as if she might try to deny her part in what was happening. Her lips parted but no words came.

The kids were crying now, all of them. The older ones hung on to each other, still sitting cross-legged in the middle of the floor. The younger boys still clung to their parents. Joey climbed up in Molly's lap. "Are the police taking us away?"

Molly was furious with herself, and with Beth. With Jack, too. What had they been thinking? Of course they couldn't get away with their crazy plan. Now Joey had to be exposed to more trauma, and worse—their chances at keeping custody of him were over. Forever.

She stared at Beth, unwilling to turn away. "You turned us in. . . . Beth, how could you?"

Beth opened her mouth again, but this time Jack interrupted. He stood and held his hand out to Molly. "Let's go. We need to see what they want. It's an order from the embassy."

Molly felt detached from her body. She shot a last look at Beth and Bill and the kids. Then she took Joey's hand and followed Jack. Halfway across the room, she stopped. "Our things."

Jack said something to the mission worker, and the man spoke Creole to the officer. After a brief exchange, he shook his head at Jack. "Police say you need nothing. Just yourself."

"M-M-Mommy . . . where are we g-g-going?" Joey clung to her. His eyes were wide, and though he had stopped crying, he looked beyond frightened.

"Stay with me, buddy. It'll be okay."

Her last glimpse of Beth was enough to stir a new level of fury inside her. Beth had her head bowed, as if she was praying. Of all things. Molly wanted to scream at her and cry out to her all at the same time. It was too late for prayer now. The damage was done, and it was done by one of the people she loved most in the whole world.

The police led them out to a van, helped them inside, and hurried off through the streets. It was just after six o'clock—still daylight. Molly and Jack and Joey sat in a compartment clearly designated for criminals. A plastic shield separated them from the officers.

Molly reached for Jack, grabbed at his arm. "I . . . I can't breathe."

"Mommy!" Joey jumped up onto his knees and looked her right in the face. "Why can't you breathe?"

"Molly . . . don't!" Jack faced her, his eyes stern. "We haven't done anything wrong."

She closed her eyes. *Come on, Molly, get a grip. Don't panic.* She held her breath. Then she forced air from her lips, once, twice, and a third time. After that a slight bit of air made its way into her lungs. She opened her eyes and somehow smiled at Joey. "Mommy's fine." Her words were breathy, hardly okay. "Don't worry."

"Listen . . ." Jack took hold of her wrist and gave her a light shake. "We've been caught, yes. But we haven't done anything wrong, not yet." He changed places with Joey so he could whisper to her without their son hearing.

Molly's head hurt. What was Jack talking about? Of

course they'd broken rules—they'd made a plan to leave the country illegally under assumed identities. "Jack . . . think of our plan. The false passports, the money. Of course we've done something wrong."

"No, not yet. There's nothing illegal about buying a passport, or moving cash to a foreign account, or taking a work trip. The crime comes in *using* the passport or leaving Haiti under our new names." He was whispering, his words sharp and intense. "Being here doesn't make us criminals. We had permission from the judge, remember?"

Gradually, like the sun breaking a new morning, Jack's words started to make sense. He was right. They hadn't broken any law yet. "So what's this about?" she hissed, still terrified. In all her life she never dreamed she'd be here, in the back of a police van heading to the U.S. Embassy. They were in bigger trouble than they ever imagined.

Jack thought hard. "Ever since the police burst into the place, I've been asking myself the same thing. Was it the driver, Tancredo? Did he talk to Franz, maybe?"

"I didn't see them say anything to each other."

"Maybe it was Franz, maybe he heard something." Jack leaned his forehead against hers. "Baby, I'm so sorry. I can't believe this is happening."

"So you're saying . . ." She forced herself to breathe slower, to catch her breath before she started hyperventilating again. "We haven't done anything illegal, but someone found out about . . . about our plan?"

His eyes welled up with tears. "It looks that way."

"So . . . it had to be Beth." Molly raised one shoulder. "She was the only one who suspected anything . . ."

"Beth?" Jack gritted his teeth. "This better not be her doing." He pressed his fists into his knees. "How could she call herself a Christian if she turned us in for protecting our son? Can you tell me that?"

"Jack . . . please." Molly felt dizzy, unable to process everything that was happening. This was their fault, not Beth's. She had only done what she must've thought was best, maybe thinking somehow that she was helping them. But they were to blame, she and Jack. They had mocked God, using the church as a means of breaking the law. If anything, this was happening as God's way of punishing them. "This isn't about Beth—it's about us. We never should've tried to escape. If we're caught, it's too late for anger."

"I know." His shoulders slumped a little. "It's too late for everything. But we had to try, Molly."

"Meaning they'll take Joey from us?" She felt panicked by the idea. She wasn't ready to say good-bye. "Jack, is that what you're saying?"

"Molly . . . I'm so sorry, baby." Jack put one arm around Joey and the other around her. Joey looked at them, wondering. But he didn't ask questions. Instead he buried his little blond head in Jack's side and the three of them said nothing else the rest of the ride.

The police took them to a two-story red brick building with a small sign that read "U.S. Embassy."

This is it, Molly told herself. *They'll take Joey and we'll never see him again.* Some crazy part of her wanted to turn around and run, grab Joey and Jack by the hand and run until she felt the rip of bullets in her back. Life would be over, anyway. If Joey was taken from them, how would any of them survive?

"This way." One of the officers opened their door. His voice and face were equally stiff.

Dear God . . . No! Was this what Beth meant by God's will? Had God wanted Joey with the Porters all along, the nice lady Joey had talked about? They walked across a bumpy street and the police officers led them up a narrow outdoor staircase. At the top of the stairs, the officer who seemed to be in charge opened the door and ushered them inside.

It was a holding room, a waiting area. The police formed a fortress that blocked the door. The one who spoke English pointed to the sofa. "You sit there."

Jack took her hand and the three of them did as they were told. Joey sat between them. Molly could feel him shaking, and she wasn't sure what to do. If these were their last moments together, then she had things to tell him, things that would take a year at best. But now they had only minutes, and she didn't know where to begin.

She put him on her lap and cradled his head close to her face. "Joey, Mommy loves you." The tears came then. They choked her voice, but she pressed on. If this was her only chance to tell him good-bye, then nothing was going to stop her. "Whatever happens, I want you to remember that, okay?"

He brushed up close to her ear. "I love you, too."

Jack seemed to sense what was going on. They exchanged a look, and the heartache between them was suffocating. Jack put his arm around Joey and leaned closer. "You know what? You're Daddy's special guy, sport. I love you so much." His voice cracked. He dropped it to a whisper. "You keep talking to God, okay?"

Molly hurt all over. When this nightmare came to an

end, when she and Jack were left to pick up the pieces and start over again, maybe they would make the next attempt at living life the way Beth and Bill did. With God in the lead.

She was about to tell Joey that if someone ever took her away from him, she would love him all her life and always she would ask God to bring him back to her, but she didn't get the chance. The door beyond the officers opened, and two uniformed men entered the room.

One of them stayed near the officers, the other—clearly an American—stepped toward them. He had a piece of paper in his hands, and he looked at Jack. "Jack Campbell?"

"Yes, sir." Jack straightened. His voice wasn't afraid, but resigned.

Molly hung her head. They were caught; there was no getting around the fact.

"Molly Campbell?"

She looked at the man and nodded. "Yes, sir." This was the part where he would explain that the authorities knew about their plan. He would tell them they were being immediately deported because of their flight risk, and he would explain that Joey would be traveling with a police escort to Ohio, where his biological parents awaited custody.

Molly held her breath and waited.

The man came a few steps closer. "Mr. and Mrs. Campbell, I work for the U.S. Embassy here in Haiti. I've received urgent word from the United States. I was asked by order of a judge in Ohio to locate you and give you details of a message from"—he looked at the paper—"social worker Allyson Bower."

A message? What was the man talking about? Again Molly's head was spinning. She held on to Joey so she wouldn't topple onto the floor.

Jack leaned forward. "Sir . . ." He looked equally confused. "I'm not sure I understand."

The man held up the paper. "Let me read the message. 'You are hereby notified that by order of Judge Randall Grove, Cleveland District Court, the case regarding custody of Joey Campbell has been dropped. From this point on, full and permanent custody is assigned to you, Jack and Molly Campbell.'"

"What?" Jack was on his feet. He looked at Molly and then at the man standing before them. "The case has been dropped?"

Relief washed over Molly immediately. Sobs tore at her, and she leaned back into the sofa, holding Joey close, rocking him. It wasn't possible. They were here to say good-bye, to be hauled back to the United States and reprimanded for ever thinking they could outsmart the system.

But God had worked a miracle, after all. Even when they had made a mockery of prayer and faith, church attendance and this work trip. Almighty God could've destroyed them for what they had tried to do. But instead He was showing Himself so clearly to them, she could hardly take it in.

Jack eased back down to the edge of the seat. He was crying openly, unable to talk. He motioned for the man to continue.

For the first time, the uniformed man smiled. "I take it this is good news."

"Yes," Jack managed. He wiped his eyes. "Very good. You have no idea."

The man cleared his throat. He looked back at the letter and continued. "'New adoption release papers have been signed by both biological parents, and notarized. You are required under conditions of the release papers to accompany Joey Campbell to one additional meeting at the Child Welfare Department in Cleveland, Ohio, in two weeks, after which time you will no longer be subject to any conditions by this department. Congratulations.'" The man grinned at them. "I have a copy of the paperwork for your records."

But Molly and Jack barely heard him.

They were too busy hugging Joey and each other, weeping and laughing and trying to believe what had happened.

"Mommy, Daddy . . . what is it? Do we have to get arrested?"

"No, baby." Molly kissed him again and again on his cheek, his forehead, his hands. "We get to finish our trip and go home with Aunt Beth and Uncle Bill and the cousins."

"And you never have to go on a trip without us again." Jack stood and swung Joey in a circle. Then he settled him on his hip. "How's that sound?"

Joey raised his fist in the air. "Great!"

The police escorted them back to the mission house, but everything about the ride was a blur. They had come so close to losing him. By now Joey could've been in custody, heading back to the United States never to be seen by them again. Molly was exhausted, drained, too giddy to do anything but try to somehow understand what had happened.

The Porters had changed their minds about Joey, obviously. But why? What had done it? And why the visit to the social services office in two weeks? Molly didn't care. She would've traveled around the world to meet the requirements of the adoption release papers.

And what about Beth? Obviously she'd been wrong about her sister. Beth hadn't turned them in, clearly not. Otherwise the meeting at the embassy would've gone very differently. Beth, her best friend, her closest ally. How could she have thought anything but good of her sister?

They reached the mission house before she had time to sort through her feelings. Somehow—as if they were floating on clouds—they made their way back inside. Beth and Bill and the kids sat around the living room, their faces tearstained.

"Molly!" Beth stood. She looked at Jack and then Joey, and finally back at Molly. "What happened?"

Molly released Joey's hand and closed the gap between her and her sister. "He's ours, Beth. Joey is ours. The Porters changed their minds."

Beth's entire countenance changed. She started to cry and took Molly in her arms. They both apologized at the same time, and then they looked at each other and laughed.

"Beth, I'm sorry. . . . I thought you turned us in." She kept her words quiet. Behind them Jack was explaining to Bill about the trip to the embassy while the Petty kids asked Joey about his adventure. "I figured you'd called the social worker."

"Wait . . ." Beth's smile faded. "I thought you were going to run. I mean, I really thought that."

"We were! I couldn't tell you, but you were right. Of course. I could never fool you, Beth." Molly let her head tip back. She had never felt so good in all her life. The nightmare they'd been living for the past few months was finally over. They had Joey back, and they had their lives back. It was more than she could take in. She looked at her sister again. "Really, I thought you turned us in. I'm so sorry, Beth."

"But . . ." Beth's face froze, confused and afraid all at once. Guilt covered her features once more. "I did, Molly." Her voice was so quiet it was almost soundless.

"You did?" Molly felt her own smile fade. "You called the social worker?"

"Yes." She hung her head for a moment. When she looked up, tears filled her eyes. "And Wendy Porter. I told her Joey belonged to you, that you loved him so much. But I told her I was afraid you were going to run."

Molly held her breath. Her head was spinning again. She wasn't sure what to say or do. Beth had indeed turned them in, but what did it matter? Here they were, and Joey was theirs. Forever and ever more. She found her smile again and hugged her sister. "I love you, Beth. I'm not mad at you."

"You're not?"

"No." She had never felt so good in all her life. "Don't you see? In the end it wasn't up to you or us." Her eyes were dancing, she could feel the glow deep within her. "It was up to God. We have Joey because that was His will—just like you prayed."

There was no other way to explain it.

While the party continued, while the rejoicing led to worship and the worship to rejoicing, a deep and abiding truth settled into the hearts of all of them. That night they had witnessed something very special. For reasons they might not ever understand, they'd been given the gift of their son for a second and final time. More than that, they'd gotten their lives back.

It was a miracle.

And before they turned in for the night, they made plans for an urgent morning call to a bank in Sweden. Jack grinned at her. "What about that medical building? It really is a good deal."

Molly laughed and pulled Joey onto her lap. "I don't care!" She kissed Joey's forehead. "Buy the whole block, as long as we have this little boy."

Before they turned in, Molly and Jack knelt near Joey's bunk bed. This time—for the first time—they talked to God together.

Jack went first. "God"—his voice broke—"I don't know what to say. I'm sorry. . . . I'm so sorry." He bowed his head. Then he motioned for Molly to pray.

Molly's heart went out to him. He was thankful, but he was sorry first. Sorry for going through the motions of faith, and not until now believing there was actual power in the name of God. She found her voice and began. "God . . . thank You. We have no words that can express how grateful we are. When we get home, everything will change. You worked out a miracle for us." She gave Joey a soft squeeze. "Now we'll give You our lives."

"Yes, God." Jack's voice was sure, strong.

It was Joey's turn. "Hi, God . . . it's me, Joey. 'Member I asked You if I could stay with my mommy and daddy and Gus and not have to go back to that other house in Ohio? I asked You two times, 'member?" He took a breath. "I knew You would do it for me, God. Thanks for this happy day. Gee this name, amen."

Her precious son. Molly kissed him and Jack did the same. As they left the room, a thought occurred to her. They wouldn't have far to go to learn how to talk to God, how to find a relationship with Him.

Their son was already showing them the way.

Chapter Twenty-Eight

It was the middle of September, and still Allyson Bower couldn't believe the way the events had played out. She'd been seconds away from contacting the authorities when Wendy Porter called. Now, the meeting between Wendy and Molly Campbell and Joey was only minutes away.

Allyson sat back in her chair and tapped her pencil on the open folder in front of her. The final straw for Wendy Porter had been Rip, of course. The man had been drunk that Thursday night, the night before the Campbells' trip to Haiti. He had been angry that Wendy was on the phone, and when she hung up, he had ordered her to tell him everything.

When he wasn't satisfied with Wendy's answers, he came unglued.

Allyson saw her the next day, after Rip was in custody, after Wendy was released from the hospital. She had a broken arm, stitches near her ear, a bruised liver, and two black eyes. Still she'd found the strength to call the social worker.

"You're pressing charges, Wendy. You have to."

"I called the police." Wendy was crying. With careful

fingers she dabbed at her tears, but still she winced from the pain. "He's going back to prison."

"What about Joey?"

"I told Rip I'd testify that he didn't mean it, that it was just the alcohol making him crazy." She sucked in a few quick breaths. "As long as he'd sign the release papers."

Allyson hadn't known what to say. She wanted Joey to stay with the Campbells, she always had. But Wendy needed to understand the law completely. "You know that you can keep Joey if you want."

Wendy nodded. "His adoption wasn't valid, right? Because Rip never signed the papers?"

"Right." Allyson had held her breath. This was delicate territory. "Rip can go to prison and you can have sole custody of your son. It's up to you."

"I know." More tears slid down her face. Quiet tears, from a deep sorrow that had already counted the cost. "But one day Rip will get out and he'll find me again. He always does." She wiped at her eyes again. "When that happens, I'll take him back." She lifted her hands, helpless. "I always do." She looked at her lap, ashamed. "I gave Joey up once because I couldn't stand the thought of Rip hurting him. The reason's the same today."

The papers were signed and notarized over the next two days, and immediately Allyson set about getting word to the Campbells. They were a flight risk, and she wanted to get word to them before they fled. It had taken two painfully long days of red tape between her and Judge Grove and the embassy before the word finally came. Police were going to the orphanage to bring Jack and Molly and Joey to the embassy, where they would be informed of the change in custody. By some amazing set of circumstances, word reached the Campbells before they could pull off whatever they might've been planning.

Allyson smiled.

How she would've loved to have been in the room when the Campbells got word that the custody case had been dropped. Joey was theirs. It was a miracle—that's what Molly Campbell said. And maybe it was. Allyson had taken her kids to church each of the past two weeks—for the first time in years. If for no other reason than to thank God for pulling off what neither she nor the Campbells could've.

In the weeks since, the Campbells had filed all necessary paperwork. Joey was officially their son without any further question. Wendy Porter hadn't asked for any visitation rights, so none were granted.

Allyson looked at the clock on her wall. The meeting was scheduled to take place in two minutes. Molly Campbell and Joey were already in the child-care room, a private meeting area set up for comfort with sofas and overstuffed chairs and baskets of toys.

The phone on Allyson's desk rang. She pressed the flashing button and brought the receiver to her ear. "Hello?"

"Yes, Mrs. Bower, Wendy Porter is here to see you."

"Thank you. I'll meet her in the waiting room."

Allyson released a heavy sigh as she stood and reached for the door. Wendy Porter's only request had been this: that the Campbells bring Joey to Ohio for one last visit at the Child Welfare Department.

So she could say good-bye.

It felt like the longest drive in Wendy Porter's life.

The whole way to the Child Welfare Department, she replayed every event that had led to this moment. But especially her recent visits with Joey. Tears streamed down her face, and she looked in the rearview mirror. *You've gotta stop, Wendy. Right now. Joey won't know what to think if you're crying.*

She exhaled and straightened her bangs.

Her hours with Joey had been the best in her life. In some ways, she wondered why she didn't take Allyson Bower up on her offer. She could keep Joey if she wanted to. All she'd have to do is find a way to never let Rip Porter back in her life. That was the problem.

Even now she loved him, sick as that was. He needed help; they both did. But she couldn't put Joey through that process—not for a minute. Rip would've beaten the child; she knew it as surely as she knew her name. He wouldn't have meant it, and when he was sober he would've been deeply sorry.

But she loved Joey too much to ever let that happen.

He was such a nice little boy, so handsome and kind. Even though he was scared to death, even though he missed his adoptive parents and his dog and his bedroom back in Florida, he'd still been kind to her. He liked her chocolate-chip cookies.

Wendy climbed out of the car, and with heavy feet, she forced herself up the stairs and into the waiting room. Allyson Bower came for her in just a few minutes.

"Hello, Wendy. You look . . . better." She held out her hand.

Wendy shook it. She had been careful with her makeup that morning. Other than the cast on her arm, it was impossible to tell what she'd been through just two weeks earlier. "Is Joey here?"

"Yes." Allyson studied her. "He came with Mrs. Campbell."

A sad smile tugged at her lips. "His mommy."

"Yes." The social worker gave a gentle nod. "His mommy." She took a step back. "Are you ready to see him?"

"Yes. I'd like to meet Mrs. Campbell, but then . . ." Her voice caught. She wasn't going to cry, not now. A quick breath and she found her voice again. "Then could I have a few minutes to say good-bye to Joey? Alone?"

"I'm sure that'll be fine." Allyson led her down a hall past three doors, and then into a room, and there they were.

A pretty woman with dark hair and a quick smile stood as they walked into the room. Joey was playing with Legos on the floor, but he looked up, confused at the sight of Wendy. He lifted his fingers and gave her a slow little wave. Then he went to Mrs. Campbell's side and pressed himself close to her. Like he was trying to hide.

Allyson took charge of the moment. "Molly, I'd like you to meet Wendy Porter."

The Campbell woman came toward her, and for a moment it looked like she wanted to shake hands. Then she held out her arms and pulled Wendy into a hug, one that lasted longer than she expected.

The social worker left the two women and went to sit with Joey on the sofa. She distracted him with a book from a nearby table.

"I . . . don't know what to say." Molly had tears in her eyes. She bit her lip to stop it from quivering. "Thank you for giving us Joey." She made a sound that was more cry than laugh. "A second time."

Wendy looked past the Campbell woman's shoulder to the place where her son was playing. Then her eyes met Molly's again. "Did you ever read the story of King Solomon, the one in the Bible?"

"No." Molly looked surprised. "But we're reading the Bible a lot these days." Her eyes glowed. "Last week Joey asked Jesus into his heart."

The news was bittersweet: one more step, one more milestone that Wendy had missed. She managed a smile. "Anyway . . . the story is in First Kings, chapter 3. It made me realize something."

Molly waited, never breaking eye contact.

"It made me know that any real mother would sooner walk away from her child than let him come to harm." Tears clouded her eyes again. "For any reason."

The Campbell woman didn't quite look like she understood. But she nodded anyway. "I'll read it later."

Wendy tried to focus. She didn't have long. Anything she might ever want to say to Joey's adoptive mother, she would have to say now. "Take good care of him, okay?" The tears spilled onto her cheeks, but she didn't try to stop them.

"I will." Molly was crying, too. They were both mothers now. Nothing about the moment was easy.

"And if . . . if he ever asks about me, tell him how much I love him. So much that I gave him to you."

"Okay." The Campbell woman brought her fingers to her lips, so she wouldn't cry out loud. "And if he ever wants to find you, I'll help him."

"Really?" The offer was more than Wendy would've asked for.

"Yes. Definitely." Molly pulled a tissue from her purse and handed it to Wendy. Then she took one for herself and pressed it beneath her eyes. "Anything else?"

Wendy looked at Joey again, at his towheaded hair and his earnest face, his precious smile. "That's all." She took a step back. "Can I have a few minutes with him?"

"Of course." Molly signaled to Allyson Bower, and then to Joey. "Mommy will be right outside, honey. Mrs. Porter wants to talk to you for a little bit, okay?"

"Okay." Joey looked less nervous than before. "Then we go home, right? To Gus and Daddy?"

"Right, buddy." Molly waved at him, and then she and the social worker left the room and closed the door behind them.

Wendy drew a slow breath. This was it. She crossed the room and sat on the sofa next to Joey. "Hi, honey."

"Hi." Joey still held the book, the one Allyson Bower had been reading to him. "Where's the other daddy?" Joey peered around her, his eyes suddenly fearful.

"He's not here. You won't see him again." She looked into his eyes, and suddenly she was back nearly five years ago, lying in a hospital bed, looking into those same eyes, her heart breaking. Trying to find a way to say good-bye. *I'm doing this for you, child of mine. Only for you.* She smiled at him. "You won't be coming to Ohio anymore, Joey. Do you know that?"

He nodded. "I asked God for that."

"Oh." She felt the cut in her heart go a little deeper, but she smiled anyway. "I'm glad. You keep talking to God, okay?"

"Okay."

She could still feel the way he felt in her arms that morning, hours after his birth, still smell his newborn smell and hear his little coos as she cradled him close. He was her son, her very own. She would only walk away now because she loved him—just like she'd told Molly Campbell.

Joey cocked his head and studied her. "How come you're sad?"

"Well—" She caught her breath. The tears came, but she kept her happy face. "See . . . today I have to say good-bye." She held up her good hand. "After today I won't see you again."

"You won't?" He was so young, so unaware of the battle that had been raging around him. It hadn't dawned on him that if he wasn't coming back to Ohio, then he wasn't coming back to her, either. He frowned, his eyes locked on hers. "Good-byes are sad."

"Yes." She wanted to hold him, hug him close and memorize the feel of him one last time. But that might scare him, especially with the Campbell woman out of the room. So instead she did what she'd done a few weeks ago when they sat on the couch and watched *Bear in the Big Blue House*.

She reached her hand out and took hold of his fingers.

He grinned and tucked his hand all the way into hers, the way he'd done before. "I like you." His smile fell off a little. "I told my mommy you were nice."

"We had a good time, didn't we?"

"You rubbed my back." He smacked his lips. "You told me, 'Mama loves you, Joey.' "

Wendy opened her eyes wider. "That's right, honey. I

said that." He'd heard her? Those nights when she thought he was asleep, he'd heard her words of love. It was something she could hold onto, a last memory.

With all her heart, she wanted to think that somehow he'd remember her. The chocolate-chip cookies and holding hands on the couch and her voice whispering, "Mama loves you, Joey." But time wouldn't be that kind. A year from now he'd be five, almost six, and the nice lady in Ohio would be only a dim memory. One more year and she'd be forgotten altogether.

She gave Joey's hand a squeeze. *God . . . don't let him forget me. Please.* It would take a miracle, but that was God's territory. "I gotta go."

He seemed to sense the significance of the moment. For a long time he looked at her, then he stood up on his knees and put his arms around her neck. "I'll miss you."

"Aw, sweetie." She gathered his words to the most tender places in her soul. They weren't words of love, exactly, but they were close. And they were the most she would ever get from her precious little boy. "I'll miss you, too."

They stood up, and once more Joey tucked his hand in hers. She led him to the door, opened it, and nodded at Molly and Allyson a few feet away.

Molly hesitated. "Are you . . . are you ready?"

She would never be ready. "Yes." She closed the distance between them, and then she took Joey's hand and slipped it into Molly's. She bent down and kissed his cheek. Then, in a voice too pinched to be heard, she mouthed the word, "Bye."

She gave a final look to Allyson Bower, and through eyes blurred with fresh tears, she found her way to her car. She had lost so much because of Rip. Her youth and her ability to stand on her own, her health and most of all her golden-haired son. She would never see him off to kindergarten, never see him ride a bike or play with his dog, Gus. She would never watch him excel in school or graduate from high school or marry his college sweetheart.

The tears came in torrents now.

Wendy climbed into her car and let her head rest on the steering wheel. Saying good-bye to Joey was the hardest thing she'd ever done. This time more than right after his birth, because now she knew him. And she would never, ever forget him. Yes, she had lost more than she would ever be able to count. But the important thing was this.

Joey had won.

And because of that—in some sad, heartbreaking way—they had all won.

Even her.

Molly spent another fifteen minutes visiting with Allyson and talking about Joey. The last few weeks had been an emotional rollercoaster—signing adoption papers for Joey, knowing he was theirs forever, but then realizing the sacrifice of Wendy Porter, the gut-wrenching sadness of her good-bye.

Allyson had brought all the pieces together, and now the woman looked happier than Molly had ever seen her.

"I need to say one thing before you go." Allyson crossed her legs and leveled her gaze. "I don't blame you for what you were going to do."

This was touchy territory. No question, she and Jack had been planning to break the law. If they'd done it and been caught, they would've gone to prison for many years. Molly didn't want to admit to anything, even now, when the entire plan was nothing more than a bad memory. Instead of responding, she only nodded, the hint of a smile tugging at the corners of her mouth.

"I was prepared to go to the police, because that's my job." Allyson brought her lips together. She tapped the spot above her heart. "But in here I would've been cheering you on." She looked at Joey. "This case, the situation, it worked out like it was supposed to work out. That doesn't always happen."

Joey looked up at her. "That's 'cause God made it happen." He grinned. "I asked Him."

The women exchanged a look, and Allyson laughed. "Well, that settles it."

After a few more minutes, their visit ended. Allyson wished them well, and they set off in their rental car back to the airport. They had done the trip in one day, and Jack would be waiting for them back in West Palm Beach when their plane landed.

Somewhere, headed back to her house in Cleveland, Wendy Porter must still be crying, Molly had no doubt. Knowing Joey, spending time with him, would've made the sacrifice all but impossible. She thanked God every day that the woman had found the courage.

Wendy's broken arm told Molly pieces of the story the social worker wasn't able to tell. Rip must've gotten violent again, and that would've been enough to convince Wendy. She couldn't expose Joey to that sort of abuse. Never. Because she really did love him.

Molly and Joey walked hand in hand, and they were almost to the car when Joey gasped and pointed. Across the street was a field and something Molly hadn't noticed until now.

"Dandelions, Mommy!"

She stopped and looked. The field must've held a million dandelions—just like Fuller Park. How close had they come to making a crazy decision, to doing things that went against the law, and their consciences, and most important—against God Almighty? She shivered and held a little tighter to his hand. "Yes, buddy. Lots of dandelions."

They climbed into the car, and as Molly buckled Joey into his booster seat, she rubbed her nose against his. "Eskimo noses."

He did the same and giggled. Then he batted his eyelashes against hers. "Butterfly kisses."

"I love you, Joey Campbell."

He giggled louder. "Love you, too, Mommy Campbell."

Before she pulled away, she looked at him. "You know something, buddy? I can almost feel God with us right now, making everything work out."

"He is, Mommy." He gave her a silly smile, as if surely she must know this. "He's always with us now. I used to ask Him to go with me on trips 'cause I was scared. Now I ask Him to always go with us."

"Oh." She nodded. "No wonder."

She shut the door and climbed into the driver's seat. But before she started the car, he called to her.

"Mommy, can we talk to God? 'Afore we go?"

"Sure, buddy." She bowed her head and wondered what was on his mind.

"Hi, God . . . it's me, Joey. I'm happy that we're going home. But I'm sad for that nice lady. Jonah says since You're God, You can be with more than one person at a time." He stopped for a second. "I think that's true. So could You please be with that nice lady? 'Cause she was crying, and I think You would make her feel better."

Molly could hardly believe her ears. Here was her son, the one who had prayed without ever giving up—even when the adults around him were going about things their own way. And now—even though he was happy—he was worried about Wendy Porter. Because she'd been crying.

Thank You for this child, God. . . . Teach Jack and me to listen to him, that we might learn to have a faith like his.

In the backseat, Joey finished his prayer the way he always did.

"Gee this name, amen."

Author's Note

Dear Friends,

Always at the end of a book, I stand back amazed. Awed that God would give me another story—one that grew first in the soil of my heart, and then on the pages of this book. But also amazed at the lessons I learned along the way.

I knew, of course, that *Like Dandelion Dust* would be the story of two mothers, and the love that both women had for a single child. But I wasn't prepared for the lessons of faith that would come by way of four-year-old Joey. I don't know why I was surprised. The lessons were there because they are also that vivid in the lives of my own six children.

The image of my eight-year-old Austin sleeping with his snow leopard under one arm and his Bible under the other.

My little EJ telling me that he slept great because, "I just remembered all my Bible verses and God gave me sleep."

My precious Sean coming up to me, all smiles, after

his champion soccer team lost badly in the first round of the state playoffs. "Did you see me, Mom?"

"Yes, Sean," I told him. "You played very hard. I'm proud of you."

"No, not that." He pointed to the empty midfield. "Before the game I got everyone in a circle so we could pray."

The examples in my own life are without limit.

Big, strong Josh, taking half an hour to gather five packs of his own gum and write his sister and brothers each a note with a little cross on it. Josh taping the notes to the packs of gum, and secretly delivering one to the foot of each of his siblings' beds.

"I felt like God wanted me to share."

There's Tyler at thirteen years old, stringing a sign up on his bedroom door that reads "I believe!" and telling me, "I just want everyone who comes here to know where I stand."

And finally Kelsey, who at sixteen is in the middle of strong peer pressure, finding her dad and me and saying, "You know what makes my day absolutely perfect? When I start out by reading my Bible."

Our kids come up with things like this, and my husband and I find ourselves wanting to memorize Scripture and strengthen our faith and wake up early enough to start our day right, too.

Like Dandelion Dust raises interesting questions, questions about what makes someone a mother, and what it means to truly love a child. You'll find more of these questions in the Reading Group Guide at the end of this book.

I realize that there are many true-life stories that start

out like the Campbells'. But sadly, many do not have miracle endings—at least not the endings adoptive parents are praying for. In those cases, my heart and prayers are with you. I can only believe that we—like children—are in the backseat however long the journey lasts. God is driving, and we must trust that in the end, if we stay with Him, He'll get us safely home.

As always, I'd love to hear from you. You can contact me by visiting my Web site at www.KarenKingsbury.com. The site has a new look and many more reader features, including a running blog of my life as a wife, mom, and author, a section for book clubs, and a place where you can connect with other readers.

If you are part of a book club, take a minute and register your group. That way you can connect with another reader group—perhaps in your state or across the country. You can agree to read the same book, and swap e-mails in the process. It's a great way to make new friends!

I pray this finds you filled with joy and peace. May God always be at the center of your families, and may you learn from the children He has placed in your lives. Remember—we have much to gain by watching the faith of our children.

In His light and love. Until next time,

Karen Kingsbury

Reading Group Guide

1. Have you ever known someone who adopted a child and then had that child taken away because the adoption fell through? Describe that situation. How did the adoptive parents handle the loss?

2. What did you think of Molly and Jack's decision to leave the country?

3. Is there any way to justify the decision Molly and Jack made?

4. Read the story of Mary and Joseph's escape to Egypt in Matthew, chapter 2. Did this give moral precedent for Molly and Jack to take Joey and flee the country? Why or why not?

5. What Molly and Jack wanted to do was illegal, no

question about it. If you were Beth, would you have turned them in? Why or why not?

6. Molly and Beth shared a special relationship. What were some of the reasons they were close?

7. Describe a close relationship you have with a sister or a friend. What makes that relationship close?

8. Have there been times when you have had to make a difficult decision—like the one Beth made—for the good of someone you love? Describe that situation. What was the outcome?

9. How might God have blessed Molly and Jack if they hadn't tried to defy the law?

10. Why was Jack so closed to the possibility of God's help while he looked for a way to keep custody of Joey? Explain your answer.

11. What did Beth mean when she said that God's will is always accomplished if you ask Him? Can you give an example of this in your life?

12. Wendy Porter was a woman caught up in abuse. Do you know anyone in a similar situation? Why do people stay in harmful relationships?

13. Read 1 Kings, chapter 3. How does the story of the two mothers relate to the sacrifice Wendy made on behalf of her son? How is the Bible story different?

14. Who was your favorite character in *Like Dandelion Dust*? Why?

15. Which character are you most like? How?

16. Do you think Molly and Jack would've gotten away with their plan? Why or why not?

17. Do you think they would've been happy in their new life in the Cayman Islands? Why or why not?

18. What would you do if a judge ordered that one of your children had to be taken away?
19. If you could make any change to the adoption laws in this country, what change would you make? Do you think the current system protects children most of the time, some of the time, or all of the time?
20. What did you learn from reading this novel?

More Life-Changing Fiction™ and Other Titles by Karen Kingsbury

September 11 Series
One Tuesday Morning
Beyond Tuesday Morning

Women of Faith Series
A Time to Dance
A Time to Embrace

The Redemption Series
Redemption
Remember
Return
Rejoice
Reunion

The Firstborn Series
Fame
Forgiven
Found
Family
Forever

The Forever Faithful Series
Waiting for Morning
Moment of Weakness
Halfway to Forever

Children's Books
Let Me Hold You Longer

The Treasury of Miracles Series
A Treasury of Christmas Miracles
A Treasury of Miracles for Women
A Treasury of Miracles for Teens

Gift Books by Karen Kingsbury
Stay Close, Little Girl: Words of Love for Dads
Be Safe, Little Boy: Words of Love for Moms

Turn the page for an excerpt from
Karen Kingsbury's unforgettable novel

Just Beyond the Clouds . . .

Available now at bookstores near you!

Chapter One

The eighteen adult students at the front of the classroom were a happy, ragtag group, mostly short and squatty, with sturdy necks and squinty eyes. All but two wore thick glasses. Their voices mingled in a loud cacophony of raucous laughter, genuine confusion, and boisterous verbal expression.

"Teacher!" The one named Gus took a step forward, lowered his brow, and pointed to the student beside him. "He wants the bus to the Canadian Rockies." Gus rolled his eyes. He gestured dramatically toward the window. "The buses out there go to the Colorado Rockies." He tossed both his hands in the air. "Could you tell him, Teacher?"

"Gus is right." Twenty-six-year-old Elle Dalton—teacher, mentor, encourager, friend—looked out the window. "Those are the Colorado Rockies. But our trip tomorrow isn't to the mountains." She smiled at the young men. "We're going to the Rocky Mountain Plaza. Rocky Mountain is just the name."

"Right." Daisy stood up and put her hands on her hips. She knew the Mountain Metropolitan Transit system better than anyone at the center. Daisy wagged her thumb at Gus. "I told you that. Shopping tomorrow. Not mountain climbing."

"Yes." Elle stood a few feet back and studied her students. She'd been over this two dozen times today already. But that was typical for a Thursday. "Everyone take out your cheat sheets."

In a slow sort of chain reaction, the students reached into their jeans pockets or in some cases their socks or waistbands for a folded piece of paper. After a minute or so, the entire group had them out and they began reciting the information—all at different times and with different levels of speaking ability.

"Wait"—she held up her hand—"let's listen." Elle knew the routine by heart. She approached the line and waited until she had their attention. "Everyone follow along with me." She walked slowly down the row of students. "Bus Route Number Ten will take us from the center at Cheyenne Boulevard and Nevada Avenue south past Meadows Road, left on Academy Boulevard to the shops."

"Academy Boulevard?" Carl Joseph stepped out of line, his forehead creased with worry. Carl Joseph was new to the center. He'd been coming for three months. His ability to become independent was questionable. "Is that in Colorado Springs or somewhere else?"

"It's here, Carl Joseph." Daisy patted his shoulder. "Right here in the Springs."

"Right." Elle grinned. Daisy could teach the class. "The whole bus trip will take about fifteen minutes."

He nodded, but he didn't look more sure of himself. "Okay. Okay, Teacher. If you say so, okay." He stepped back in line.

And so it went for the next half hour. Elle broke down the directions. The color of the bus—orange—and how much time they'd have to climb aboard and how long it would take to make the drive down to Academy Boulevard, and how many stops would happen between getting on and getting off the bus.

For many of them the lesson was a review. They tackled a different route every week, memorizing it, drawing it out, play-acting it, and finally incorporating it into a field trip on Friday. When they reached the end of the thirty most common bus routes, they'd start again at the beginning. But Elle's students had Down Syndrome, so most of them experienced varying degrees of short-term memory loss. Reviewing the bus routes could never happen often enough.

At the thirty-minute mark attention spans among the group were fading fast. Elle held out her hands. "Break time." She looked out the window again. It was a late April morning, and sunshine streamed in from a bright blue sky. "Fifteen minutes . . . outdoors today."

"Yippee!" Tammy, a student with long brown braids, jumped and did a half spin. "Outdoor break!"

"Ughh! I hate outdoors!" Sid scowled and punched at the air. At thirty, he was the oldest student at the center. "Hate, hate, hate."

"Don't be a hater." Gus shook a finger at the complaining student. "Ping-Pong is good for outdoors."

"Tag, you're it!" Brian tapped Gus on the shoulder and ran out the door laughing. Brian was a redhead who'd been coming to the center since Elle took over two years before. He was the happiest student by far. As he ran he yelled: "We could play tag and everyone could play tag!"

"Yeah!"

"I hate tag." Sid crossed his arms and stuck out his lower lip. "Hate, hate, hate."

The students headed for the door, all of them talking at once. Straggling behind and lost in their own world were Carl Joseph and Daisy. He was pointing outside. "No rain today, Daisy. Just big bright sunshine. That's thanks to God, right?"

"Right." She looked up at him with adoring eyes. "God gets the thanks."

"I thought so." He laughed from deep in his throat and clapped his hands five quick times. "I thought God gets the thanks."

Elle smiled and went to the back room. She poured herself a cup of dark coffee and returned to her desk. Her job at the center had everything to do with Delores Daisy Dalton. Her favorite student, her little sister. Her project. How different life was for Daisy here in the Springs. Two years ago Daisy had spent all her life with their mother an hour east of Denver in Lindon, Colorado—population 120.

The oldest of the Dalton daughters was only nine

when their big strapping father left home one morning for his office job in Denver and never made it back. A patch of black ice on a back country road took his life, and he was dead before the first police officer made it to the scene. There was life insurance money and a settlement against the drunk driver who hit him—enough to allow their mother to stay home, to continue schooling them in their small wood-paneled living room. Enough so, that life wouldn't change in any way other than the most obvious and painful.

Because their daddy had loved his girls with everything he had.

Time flew, and one by one the Dalton girls left home and moved to Denver to attend the University of Colorado. Elle was no exception. She pursued a teaching credential and then her master's. But Daisy was the youngest, and when she turned nineteen one thing was certain.

If she stayed in Lindon, Daisy was out of options. And that wouldn't do, because their mother had never dreamed less for Daisy than for the other Dalton girls. Never mind what the doctors and textbooks of that day said about Down Syndrome. From an early age their mom believed Daisy was capable of great things. She believed in mainstreaming and immersion, which meant if the math lesson was about counting money, Daisy learned to count. If it was time to clean the kitchen, Daisy was taught how to run a dishwasher.

When the short bus for handicapped students drove by, it didn't stop at the Dalton house.

"You girls will show Daisy what to do, how to act and think and behave," their mom said. "How else will she learn?"

As it turned out, their mother's thinking was innovative and cutting-edge. When Elle earned her master's degree in special education, mainstreaming was all the rage. People with learning disabilities could do more than anyone ever expected as long as they were surrounded by role models.

When she was offered the director position at the Independent Learning Center—or ILC as everyone called it—Elle formed an idea and presented it to her mother. They could sell the house in Lindon and the three of them could buy a place in the Springs. Elle would run the center, Daisy would be a student, and their mother could find work outside the home.

Sentimental feelings for the old farmhouse made their mom hesitate, but only for a minute. Life was not a house, and family was not limited to a certain place. The move happened quickly, and from her first day at the center Daisy blossomed. Her friendship with Carl Joseph was further proof.

Elle sipped her coffee, stood, and made her way to the window. She sat on the sill and watched her students. A center like this one would've been unheard of fifteen years ago. Back when most of her students were born, their parents had few options. Half the kids were institutionalized, shipped off to a facility with little or no expectation for achievement. The others were sent to special education classes, with none of the stimulation needed for advancement.

Elle took another sip of coffee. The ILC was good not just for her students—most of whom came five days a week, six hours a day. It gave her a purpose, a place where no one asked about the ring she wasn't wearing anymore. She glanced at her watch, stood, and headed for the door. Some days her work at the center not only gave her a reason to move forward, it gave her a reason to live.

She opened the door. "Break's over. In your seats in two minutes."

"Teacher, one point!" Gus waved his Ping-Pong paddle in the air. With his other hand he grabbed the table. "One more point. Please!"

"Okay." Elle stifled a smile. Gus was adorable, the student who could best articulate his feelings. "Finish the game, and get right in."

The transition took five minutes, but after that everyone was seated and facing her. The center took up a large space, with areas designated for various activities. The bus routes were practiced in a carpeted alcove with a large blackboard on one wall and several benches framing the area. Another corner included a kitchen and three kitchen tables with chairs. Social skills, cooking, and appropriate eating behavior were taught there.

The next session was speech and communication. The learning area was again carpeted, and students sat on sofas and padded chairs—simulating a living room setting. The idea was to get the students comfortable in everyday living situations, learning how to read social cues and interact correctly with others.

Elle looked at her students. "Who would like to share first?"

Daisy's hand was up before Elle finished her question. "Me, Teacher!" Daisy got a kick out of calling Elle "Teacher." Daisy tipped her head back and laughed, then looked at Carl Joseph for approval. "Right? We're ready, right?"

"Uh . . ." Carl Joseph pushed his glasses up the bridge of his nose. He seemed confused, but his eyes lit up as he connected with Daisy. His words came slow and thick and much too loud. "Right, Daisy. Right you are."

"Shhh." Daisy held her finger to her lips. Her eyebrows rose high on her forehead. "We can hear you, CJ." There was no disapproval in her tone. Just a reminder, the way any two friends might encourage each other.

Carl Joseph hunched his shoulders, his expression guilty. He covered his mouth and giggled. "Okay." He dropped his voice to a dramatic whisper. "I'm quiet now, Daisy."

The others were losing interest. Elle motioned to the spot beside her on the carpet. "Daisy and Carl Joseph, come up and show us."

"Yeah." Sid scowled and punched at the air again. He was the most moody of the students, and today he was in classic form. "All right already. Get it over with."

Undaunted, Daisy stood and took Carl Joseph's hand. His cheeks were red, but when he focused on Daisy, he seemed to find the strength to take the spot beside her at the front area of the class. Daisy left him standing there while she went to the nearby CD player and pushed a few buttons. The space filled with the sounds of Glenn Miller's "In the Mood."

Daisy held out her hand and Carl Joseph took it. After only a slight hesitation, the two launched into a simple swing dance routine. Carl Joseph counted the entire time—not always on beat—and Daisy twirled and moved to the rhythm, her smile filling her face.

Elle's eyes grew damp as she watched them. Neither friendship nor love had ever been this easy for her. But this . . . this was how love should look, the simple innocence of caring that shone between these two. The way Carl Joseph tenderly held Daisy's hands, and how he led her through the moves, gently guiding her.

Today's date hadn't escaped her. It would've been her fourth wedding anniversary. She rubbed the bare place on her ring finger and bit her lip. How many years would pass before the date lost significance?

Then, midtwirl, Carl Joseph accidentally tripped Daisy. She fell forward, but before she could hit the ground, Carl Joseph caught her in his arms and helped her find her balance again.

"You okay, Daisy? Okay?" He dusted off her shoulder and her hair, and though she had never hit the ground, he brushed off her cheek.

"I'm fine." Daisy had years of dance experience. It was how their mother made sure Daisy got her exercise. No question the slight trip-step hadn't hurt her. But she balanced against Carl Joseph's arm and allowed him to dote on her all the same. After a long moment, she and Carl Joseph began again, laughing with delight as they circled in front of the class.

The music's effect was contagious. Gus stood and waved his hands over his head, swaying his hips from one side to the other. Even Sid pointed at a few of the other students and managed the slightest grin.

When the song ended, Daisy and Carl Joseph were out of breath. They held hands and did a dramatic bow. Four students rushed to their feet, clapping as if they'd just witnessed something on a Broadway stage. Daisy waved her hands at them. "Wait . . . one more thing!"

Elle stepped back. A situation like this one was good for Daisy. She had spent all her life around able-bodied people, people blessed with social graces. She wasn't skilled at trying to command a group of people with Down Syndrome.

"Hey . . ." She waved her arms again.

The other students danced merrily about, clapping their hands and laughing. Even Sid was on his feet.

"I said . . . wait!" Daisy's happy countenance started to change.

But before she could melt down, Carl Joseph stepped up. "Sit down!" his voice boomed across the room.

Instantly the students shut their mouths. Most of them dropped slowly to their seats. Sid and Gus stayed standing, but neither of them said another word.

"Thanks, CJ." Daisy looked at him, her hero. She turned to the others. "We have one more thing."

"Yeah." Carl Joseph chortled loudly and then caught himself and covered his mouth again.

Daisy nodded at him. "I go first, okay?"

"Okay." The loud whisper was back.

"Here it is." Daisy looked at Elle and grinned. Then she held out both hands toward her classmates. "M-I-C . . ."

Carl Joseph saluted. "See you real soon."

"K-E-Y . . ."

"Why?" He put his hands on his hips and then pointed at Gus. " 'Cause we like you."

Then he linked arms with Daisy and together they finished the chant. "M-O-U-S-E."

Sid tossed his hands in the air. "Yeah, but did you go to Disney World yet or what?"

"Not yet." Daisy grinned at Carl Joseph. "One day very, very soon."

The two of them sat down as Gus jumped to his feet and scrambled to the front.

"Gus . . . you want to go next?" Elle moved in closer.

"Yes." He said it more like a question, and instantly he returned to his seat. "Sorry, Teacher." He raised his hand.

"Gus?"

"Can I go now?"

"Yes."

The training continued for the better part of an hour. Each student was progressing toward some form of independent living—either in a group home or in a supervised setting with daily monitoring. Already twelve graduates had moved on to find independence. They attended twice-weekly night sessions so that they could hold jobs during the daytime.

Elle leaned against the wall and watched Gus begin a dramatic story about playing a game of chess with Brian, a redhead who at sixteen was the youngest student. After Gus had received a standing ovation for his story, they heard a poem by Tammy, the girl with long braids—Sonnet Number 43 by Elizabeth Barrett Browning.

When the girl struggled with one line, Carl Joseph stood and went to her side. He pointed at the paper and put his arm around her shoulders. "You can do it," he whispered to her. "Go on."

Daisy raised an eyebrow but she didn't say anything.

Tammy was shaking when she finally found her place and continued. Her next few sentences were painfully slow, but she didn't give up. Carl Joseph wouldn't let her. When the poem was finished, Carl Joseph led her back to her spot on the sofa, then returned to his own.

Finally Sid told them about a movie his dad had taken him to see, something with dark caves and missing animals and a king whose kingdom had turned against him. The plot was too difficult to follow, but somehow Sid managed a question-and-answer time at the end.

They worked on table manners next, and before Elle had time to look at the clock, it was three and parents were arriving to pick up their students.

Elle spotted Daisy and Carl Joseph near the window waiting for his mother. She went to them and patted her sister on the back. "Nice dance today."

"Thanks." Daisy grinned. "Carl Joseph has good news."

"You do?" Elle looked at the young man. There was an ocean of kindness in his eyes. "What's your good news, Carl Joseph?"

"My brother." He flashed a gap-toothed smile. "Brother's coming home tomorrow."

"Oh." Elle put her hand on Carl Joseph's shoulder. He'd talked about his brother before. The guy was older than Carl Joseph, and he rode bulls. Or maybe he used to ride bulls. Elle wasn't sure. Whatever he did, the way Carl Joseph talked about him he might as well have worn a cape and a big S on his chest. She smiled. "How wonderful."

Carl Joseph nodded. "It is." His voice boomed. He pushed his glasses back into place. "It's so wonderful!"

"CJ . . . shhh." Daisy patted his hand. "We can hear you."

"Right." He covered his mouth with one hand and held up a single finger with the other. "Sorry."

Elle glanced at the circular drive out front. It was empty. She settled into a chair opposite Daisy and Carl Joseph. "Does your brother still ride bulls?"

"No . . . not anymore."

"Did he get tired of it?" Elle could imagine a person might grow weary of being thrown from a bull.

"No." Carl Joseph's eyes were suddenly sad. "He got hurt."

Daisy nodded. "Bad."

"Oh." Elle felt a slice of concern for Carl Joseph's brother. "Is he okay now?"

Carl Joseph squinted and seemed to mull over his answer. "After he got hurt, he rode bulls for another season. But then he didn't want to." He raised one shoulder and cocked his head. "Brother's still hurt; that's what I think."

"What's his name?" Elle spotted Carl Joseph's mother's car coming up the drive.

"Cody Gunner." Carl Joseph's pride was as transparent as his smile. "World-famous bull rider Cody Gunner. My brother."

Elle smiled. She was always struck by her students' imagination. Carl Joseph's brother was probably an accountant or a sales rep at some firm in Denver. Maybe he rode a bull once in his life, but that didn't make him a bull rider. But that didn't matter, of course. All that counted was the way Carl Joseph saw him.

"Your mom's here, CJ." Daisy pointed at the car. She stood and took Carl Joseph's hand. "It's your big day. Your brother's coming home tomorrow."

Carl Joseph's cheeks grew red and he giggled at Daisy. "Thank you, Daisy. For telling me that."

They walked off together, and at the door Daisy gave him a hug. They hadn't crossed lines beyond that, and Elle was glad. Their relationship needed to progress slowly. What they shared today was enough for now. As the last few students left, she and Daisy straightened chairs and tables and closed up for the day.

On the way home, Daisy was quieter than usual. Finally she took a big breath. "We should pray for Carl Joseph's brother. For the world-famous bull rider."

Elle was heading down the two-lane highway that led to their new house. "Because he might still be hurt?"

"Yeah, that." She furrowed her brow. "It's hard when you get hurt."

"Yes, it is." Elle looked at her empty hand, the finger where her ring had been four years earlier. "Very hard."

Daisy pointed at her. "You pray, Elle. Okay?"

"Okay." Elle kept her eyes on the road. "Dear God, please be with Carl Joseph's brother."

"Cody Gunner." Daisy opened one eye and shot a look at Elle.

"Right. Cody Gunner."

"World-famous bull rider." Daisy closed her eyes again and patted Elle's hand. "Say it all."

"Cody Gunner, world-famous bull rider." Elle allowed the hint of a smile. "Please help him get well so he isn't hurt anymore."

"In Jesus' name."

"Amen."

For the rest of the ride Elle thought about the anniversary of a moment that never happened, and the picture of Daisy dancing in Carl Joseph's arms. The world would look at her and Daisy and think that Elle was the gifted one, the blessed one. Elle, who had it all together, the beautiful, intelligent daughter for whom life should've come easily and abundantly. Daisy—she was the one to be pitied. Short and stout with a bad heart and weak vision. A castaway in a world of perfectionism, where the prize went to high achievers and people with talent, star athletes and beauty queens. Daisy was doomed from birth to live a life of painful emptiness, mere existence.

Better to be Elle, that's what the world would say.

But the irony was this: Nothing could've been further from the truth.